BEAST
OF
BURDEN

A BEAUTIFUL DECEIT NOVEL

Jillian D. Wray

Disclaimer

This is a work of fiction. Names, characters, and incidents are a product of the author's imagination or are used fictitiously. Any resemblance to actual persons, living or dead, events, or locales is entirely coincidental.

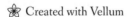 Created with Vellum

For those still figuring out how to not be weighed down by the expectations of others.
This one's for you.

Prologue

Ryan

I *reland*
   Five Months Ago

"Can I talk to you for a second?"

When Emma Donovan curls her slender fingers around my forearm, I can't stop the fireworks that explode in my chest.

"Yeah, sure," I reply calmly. The impassivity of my voice is at direct odds with my level of excitement over being alone with her.

I'm incapable of denying this woman anything even if it means incurring the wrath of her brother ... which I undoubtedly *will* if he catches us sequestered alone.

1

Emma leads me to the home-theater in back of the rented house. Even inside, the scent of the ocean lingers in the air. The house sits atop cliffs iconic of the Irish landscape, the roiling waves below. The theater room has no windows, however, allowing Em and I to have a moment of privacy in this house full of people.

She closes the door behind us and begins to pace, making me instantly concerned.

"Em, what's wrong? Is it school?"

Em sometimes has trouble fitting in thanks to her 177 genius-level I.Q. I've always enjoyed the astute shit that comes out of her mouth but I think it intimidates her peers. She gets a lot of attention because of it, and it causes her to retreat inside herself. Sweet Em would rather fit-in instead of stand-out but neither her brain nor her looks allow her the luxury of doing so.

"No," she starts before amending her statement. "I mean, yes, I'm still nervous about the fall, but that's not what I wanted to talk to you about."

She seems more excited than nervous, however, both emotions are present in the way she's playing with her fingers. Her long auburn hair falls between her shoulder blades and sways gently each time she turns to pace in the other direction. Her emerald eyes are cast to the floor and I wish she'd look at me. I've always felt the phrase "our eyes are the windows to our souls" was *made* a phrase because of Em. But if she won't look at me, I can't tell what's wrong.

"Okay. Do you want to sit down?" I ask cautiously. Her nerves are making me jittery. I'd love nothing more than to hold her still on my lap and ... *for fuck's sake, Battle. Get it together. She's a decade younger than you and the most off-limits woman you know,* I remind myself with a mental punch to the face.

"No, I just need to say it," she says on a breathy exhale, bringing me back to the moment.

Still refusing to look at me, I place a finger under her chin and force her eyes up. *Way up.* Even at 5'8", Emma's still dwarfed by my 6'5" frame ... especially when she's this close to me.

Shit. When did we get this close?

Did I move?

Or did she?

"Did someone hurt you? Threaten you?" I ask, my brow pinching with concern. A low level of fury burns under my skin, making me warm.

"Jesus," she laughs, softly regaining some confidence in her voice. "You're as bad as my brother." I drop my hand from her chin and run it across my own, noticing it's time for a shave. No matter how often the razor touches my skin, it seems to always leave a trail of stubble in its wake.

"Yeah, well ..." My words die on the tip of my tongue because I'm not sure how to finish that statement. The last thing I want to do is remind her of her brother ... or a brother at all, for that matter.

"Look, Ry. I really appreciate you always being there for me." She grips my forearm and I'm pretty sure a platonic touch like this shouldn't be making my dick hard, but it definitely is. "You've always made me feel comfortable in my own skin and not like some freak," she pauses, working up the nerve to continue.

I'm thankful she can't see how fast my heart is beating. *Is she about to tell me she's seeing someone? That we can no longer text or talk like we have been?* Some dormant, feral cave monster rises inside me. For her to tell me she's cutting herself off from me is a big fucking deal, and a move I didn't see coming. The sound of rushing blood enters my ears, momentarily drowning out her voice.

"Ry? Did you even hear me?" she asks impatiently. The

wide neck of her sweater catches my attention as it falls off her left shoulder not helping my focus at all.

"Shit, sorry Em, I was down a rabbit hole. What did you say?"

"Ohmygod, you're going to make me repeat it?" she asks, pursing her lips, color working its way more fully into her cheeks.

I grab her hand and give her my full attention so she can see the exact moment my heart breaks as she delivers this blow.

"I *said* I'm switching to Harvard this fall. Stanford is too far and I want to be closer to home." She drops her voice. "I want to be closer to *you*." As I'm trying to process what she means, she skates a shaky hand up my chest leaving no room for me to misinterpret her words. "Over the past year, I've come to realize my girlhood crush is morphing into something more ... *permanent*."

I still the progress of her hand by placing my own over it, fighting back a groan when she digs her fingers into my shirt.

I can't think when she does that.

I've always been careful to never touch her more than an appropriate hug, maybe a kiss on the top of her head once or twice but never any way sexual. Not like she's touching me now, her fingers impatiently flexing like they're trying to climb through both my shirt and my skin.

Fuck, what I wouldn't give to have her hands on my bare skin.

"*Em*." Her name is a raspy plea on my lips.

This is worse than I thought it would be. I could figure out a way to handle it if it was *me* that got hurt. I hadn't planned on having to hurt *her*.

"I know that tone and I don't want a lecture, Ryan. I don't want to know all the reasons it wouldn't work. I just want to know if you feel the same way I do about this. We can figure the rest out later."

There are multiple problems here.

The biggest of them being her brother. My best friend and bandmate. It might not be so bad if we were a couple of college kids dicking around in a garage band, but we just signed a seven-year/five-album/multi-*million*-dollar deal with our record label. We're preparing a new album and already working on the next tour – and we haven't even finished this one yet.

This is our dream, our livelihood, and the creative process requires that we not only be on good terms, but that we trust each other implicitly. If we don't jive, it sounds disconnected. Our band is so successful because we aren't just business partners. We're friends, roommates, *brothers*.

"Ryan? Can you stop thinking about everyone else for a second and just tell me what *you* want?" Emma asks. She looks up at me as her tongue slips out to slowly wet her lips before she captures her bottom lip in her teeth. Without thinking, I reach my hand forward to free it with my thumb. As a kid, she used to bite her lip until it bled when she was anxious. After that thought, I immediately try to take my thumb away but it seems to have glued itself to her.

While I'm being distracted by her lips, she moves her other hand to my waist. It's too late to stop her by the time I realize what she's doing and she gets her hand under the hem of my t-shirt, teasing me by running her fingers along my skin just above the waistband of my jeans.

I shudder.

So, this is what it feels like to have her touch me here. I like it a lot. Too much.

"Em, stop. We can't do this." *No matter how much I want to.* "I'm sorry."

5

Three years ago today, Emma's twin sister, Penelope, died tragically. It's the reason I flew the entire Donovan family to Ireland and rented this house for us all. It's a tough week for everyone. When Pen died, Brett went off the rails and became even more overprotective of the one little sister he had left, however, he refuses to acknowledge that Emma's an adult now and attempts to keep her locked in a tower.

After the truth Brett revealed today, this would be the worst possible time to start exploring my feelings for his sister because no way in any version of heaven *or* hell would Brett ever be okay with me dating Emma.

"Is your answer based on Brett? Because clearly you feel *something.*"

She's breathing heavily as I watch her look down to see the effect she's having on me. My dick is about to blast through my zipper like a S.W.A.T. team's battering ram.

Fuck.

Her eyes spring back up to meet mine and time stands still as she moves her hand from my waist over my jeans toward my erection. It's only once her small finger grazes the edge of my cock that I finally snap to action and stop her. I now have one of her hands trapped against my chest and one trapped against my thigh, using all of my available willpower to hold them still and not encourage her exploration.

Somehow, I manage to convince myself it's better if Em doesn't know how I feel since it can't go anywhere. If I stop this now, she can hate me, heal, and move on. If I don't, it'll ruin her relationship with Brett, *my* relationship with Brett, jeopardize the band's future, and will ultimately make everyone resent me. Not to mention, it'll thrust Emma in the spotlight she hates so much. I swallow hard, trying to feel good about doing the dirty work once more.

Being the beast of burden has always been my role with

this group. It seems it's destined to stay that way. My guts clench painfully as I deliver the blow that will end our relationship before it even begins.

"Being attracted to you and wanting something romantically, are two different things. I'm sorry, Em."

It's all I can manage to say, coward that I am. And it's a shitty thing to say because it isn't even true. The *truth* is I'm apologizing for not being able to tell her that seeing her on this trip was like a sucker punch to my goddamn balls. That being so close to her, being able to see her and touch her at the same time has me in such a knot I'm surprised I can still move and that my lungs still work.

She finally drops her hands and instantly I feel cold. *Serves you right, you fucking dick.*

Her cheeks abandon their current pink color in favor of fire-engine red, and I know I've just taken Brett's place in the pit of self-loathing.

"Okay, well that settles that," she says calmly, giving me a tight, fake smile and taking a step back. "I'd really appreciate if we could just pretend this never happened ... and if you could lose my number."

"Em, come on. There's no need for that. I'll always be here for you. Call me or text me anytime."

Please, I beg silently.

"I don't think that's a good idea anymore, Ryan. I've thought about this for a while and if you're not interested, I respect that, but there's no option for me but a clean break." She moves to slip past me to the door.

I should let her go because I can see the tears she's fighting, but something grips my heart in a vice and I pull her to me, wrapping my arms around her. She gasps for breath as her sobs cause her body to shake with her face in my chest. I press my cheek to the top of her head knowing this is probably the last time I'll ever get to feel her like this.

Fuck, I hate myself right now.

"Let me go. Please. I can't do this." She gets her hands between us and I feel the pressure on my stomach as she tries to push me away but I don't budge. It takes a helluva lot more than a hundred and thirty pounds to move me. She gives up and sinks into me for the briefest of moments.

"I can't stand for you to be mad at me, Ems."

"Just let me go. You're hurting me," she whimpers into my chest, causing me to immediately drop my arms. I don't know if she meant physically or emotionally, but the last thing I ever wanted to do was hurt Emma Donovan.

She rushes past me to the door, pausing to swipe away her tears and compose herself knowing at least seven other people are in this house. Her only options for escape in this foreign country are either a walk in the blustery winds outside, or the living room.

As she walks out of the home-theater, I swear I glimpse my bleeding heart hanging on to her back for dear life.

I move to the couch as my knees give out, and drop my head into my hands. I know I've fucked up. I can tell because this decision feels awful everywhere: my head, my heart, my stomach. But I don't see a way for it to have had a different outcome.

Knowing someone will likely come looking for me soon, I give myself sixty seconds to pull it together before I face everyone as if nothing happened but when the clock winds down, I feel no more prepared to face the crowd than I did a minute ago. Out of time, I stuff my emotions down deep, and walk out of the room in search of the liquor. I should pump the brakes on that, knowing Brett just admitted to over-indulging as a way to cope with his guilt and shame, but fuck it. I'm in survival mode.

Pouring two small glasses of scotch, I sidle up next to Brett at the bar in the kitchen and pass the glass to him. The sooner I face him, the faster I'll feel better about my decision. The kitchen is open to the living room and I have to work hard to stop my eyes from finding the only person I really want to see.

Brett looks at the glass then back up at me, his brows raised, and I almost gag on the words that leave my lips. "To being man enough to face your fears."

"It was less about being man enough and more about having one woman in particular scare me into submission," he admits, throwing a loving glance at Bri.

"She's good for you," I observe.

"Too good for me is more like it, but I'm gonna try to be worth it."

Some of us just wish for the chance, I think to myself as Bri blows Brett a kiss. "Looks like you already are." My eyes swiftly move to Emma and my chest pinches knowing I caused her frown.

"Where are Noah and Sloan?" Brett asks, steering the conversation somewhere safer.

"Working on a new song. Helluva tour, right?" I raise the scotch to my lips and take a healthy swallow, savoring the burn. Brett narrows his eyes like he's trying to work something out as he glances back and forth between me and the glass in my hand.

"I know the timing is shit for this question, but are you okay? I've never seen you drink during daylight hours."

No, I'm not okay.

"Yeah, I'm fine. Just felt like maybe today called for something a little extra you know?" My smile is weak and my lungs feel as thick and heavy as the tension in the air, making it hard to breathe.

"Hey, I never thanked you for taking care of everything that night with Bri. I knew I could count on you to do whatever needed to be done. I don't know how you manage to take care of all of us but we'd be fucked without you, Ry." Brett clinks his glass to mine but I'm staring past him, failing to keep my eyes to myself. Emma is on the couch with Sienna, her beautiful eyes rimmed in red. Brett catches on to the fact that I'm clearly elsewhere and follows my gaze.

"She isn't giving you more trouble, is she?" he asks, nodding toward his sister. "I don't know when she got so bold but I'll talk to her." I assume he's referring to her blatant moves to be near me on this trip. Which, until ten minutes ago, I was pretty sure was just her trying to piss her brother off.

"No man, it's all good," I reassure him. "She just likes getting under your skin."

Em looks up at us and flashes Brett a small smile before her eyes swing to me and her jaw clenches, a pained expression crossing her face.

"You're sure nothing happened there?" Brett asks, growing wary.

"Yeah." My answer comes too fast, and I know Brett's thinking my *yeah* means *no*.

Perceptive bastard.

He shakes his head. "Jesus. First Noah, now you. I'm sorry if she made you uncomfortable, man." Brett has long since thought Em's in love with our lead singer, Noah "Kinky" Kinkaid. Turns out, he's wrong.

I feel my eyes go wide, and shake my head. "She didn't. It's all good. I think she's just feeling a little left out. Sienna has Noah, Bri has you, hell, even your mom is still hopelessly in love with your dad."

I can't believe I'm lying to Brett's face.

"She'll be back at school soon enough and then you can

help me kick the ass of whoever she sets her sights on next," Brett jokes, making my hand tighten around my glass.

Not finding the relief I thought I would by talking to Brett, I finish my drink and stand. "I'm going to go find Kinky and Sloan." I clap Brett on the back. "It's good to have you back, B."

"Thanks, Ry ... for everything."

Chapter 1

Emma

Present Day

I haven't painted anything in five, agonizing months. Haven't felt the stem of my paintbrush, the softness of the bristles, nor smelled the familiar scent of my acrylic paints. Not since I rode my high-horse straight through the freaking gates of hell as I cut Ryan Battle out of my life over embarrassment and hurt feelings.

After talking to him almost daily under the guise of getting advice on classes for school and asking questions about his father's law career and eventual jump into politics, I had deceived myself into thinking maybe Ryan felt something too. Our conversations flowed easily and seemed to be filled with anticipatory tension.

Turns out that last bit was just on my end.

Deciding a clean break was the only way I would survive, I

asked him to forget my number and give me space. As always, he did as I asked and now, I'm wrecked over it. I'm not eating, not sleeping, and I have no desire to start the process of trying to make friends. It usually all goes to hell once they find out who my brother is anyway.

"Em? You there?"

My best friend Jennifer's voice sounds through the end of the line bringing me back to the present.

"Yeah, Jen. Sorry."

"I'm really worried about you."

I sigh. "I'm fine," I tell her unconvincingly as I look down at the pajamas I'm still wearing even though it's two in the afternoon on the last Wednesday in August and most of my peers are out living their best lives before the semester starts. Meanwhile, I'm wondering if I've even brushed my teeth today. "I'm just in a slump, you know?"

"Usually by now, you've emailed all your professors, gotten all the syllabi, taught yourself half the material, and have started most of the assignments."

"Yeah, I'm just not feeling it. I used to be so excited about law, but it was like once I got accepted to the program, the biggest challenge was over. What awaits me? More tests and papers? Haven't I proven I have the hang of that already?" I ask rhetorically. Not having admitted these feelings to anyone out loud until now, it feels kind of good. It's freeing, and also scary as shit, to realize everything I've been working for isn't nearly as fulfilling as I thought it'd be ... and classes haven't even started.

"So change it up," Jen says casually. "You wouldn't even be behind. Not really, since you're in a graduate program for people three years older than you."

She makes it sound so easy, but I have my parents to consider. And my future. I need to be able to support myself.

To be fair, parents are the best you could ask for, and if I wanted to pursue a career in art, they'd probably be fine with it. But I'd add to their worry. Brett and my twin sister, Penelope, have put them through enough. It's always been up to me to be the "good child". The one that makes the right decisions, follows the traditional path, stays out of trouble, and takes care of herself.

So, I chose law. Challenging, financially stable, and a way to potentially help people.

"Yeah, maybe," I say, noncommittally.

"Classes don't start for another week. Come with me to Virginia Beach this weekend. They're having a Labor Day festival on the boardwalk. It'll be a lot of fun. My boss said I can use his family's beach house. We can stay for the weekend and I'll drop you off at the airport on my way back home on Monday.

I briefly consider the alternative to Jen's request which includes the couch I'm currently sitting on, the pajamas I'm currently wearing, a lot of frozen dinners, and of course no painting. I've lost my muse. All I'm missing is a cat and I'd officially be the most pathetic person I know.

Deciding I need to find myself again, and fast before my situation becomes dire, I agree, knowing I have enough airline miles to snag a cheap flight.

"Sure, Jen. Count me in." I feel the annoying poke of regret as soon as the words leave my mouth.

"Great! I'll pick you up from the airport on Friday afternoon!"

15

By the time Friday rolls around, I'm far more excited than I thought I'd be. I actually put on pants that button and shoved my boobs into a clean bra. My hair is slightly curled and I even bought new mascara.

I almost feel like a new woman.

Jen's parked in the arrival zone allowing me to find her quickly. She's standing on the sidewalk holding a sign that says *Emma's Bitch* and I can't help bursting into laughter. When she wraps me in a hug, I melt into her embrace, finally confident I made the right call in coming. As we're hugging, a truck horn honks and some redneck yells out the window, "Give her some tongue!"

Without missing a beat, my whore of a best friend turns to the truck holds her fingers in a V up to her mouth and wiggles her tongue between her fingers. He hoots, honks, and drives away.

"Bet you don't get treated to gems like that on Harvard's snooty-ass campus, do you?"

"Definitely not," I giggle.

"Where's all your stuff?" Jen asks, popping the trunk on her Toyota Camry.

I hold up my tiny duffle. "Um, this is it."

She narrows her eyes and shuts the trunk. "Bitch, you'd *better* have more than pajamas and a laptop in that bag."

I laugh tossing the bag in the backseat, neither confirming nor denying what's in it. I'm still smiling as I buckle up and Jen merges into the exit lane.

I needed this.

"What's the plan?" I ask, settling in to be the passenger princess.

"We're going to swing by the store, then head to the house so we can shower and change before going to the boardwalk.

The festivities begin at seven, and there's this new bar I want to try."

I groan because I'm not twenty-one yet.

"I'll get you in, don't worry. It's right on the beach. Their grand opening is tonight and it's supposed to have a really cool vibe."

"Whatever you say."

"Oh," she adds, taking the exit for the highway that will lead us to the beach, "And we're going to find you someone to take your mind off of Ryan. A hot-as-fuck guy to fawn all over you and maybe even relieve you of that pesky virginity."

"Jen! Contrary to popular belief, well, *your* belief anyway, I'm not on a mission to lose it and I'm certainly not handing it over to some guy I meet in a bar who's probably looking for a one-night stand."

My only plan had been to give it to Ryan. Since I was thirteen, I've fantasized about him. Just making out at first, but as I got older, the fantasies got dirtier. I can't seem to stop comparing every guy I meet to him and needless to say, it doesn't go well for the new guy. Hence the biggest reason I'm still a virgin but very knowledgeable about how to use a vibrator.

She shrugs and reaches for the volume knob to turn Sia's *Unstoppable* on blast through the speakers. "Suit yourself."

Chapter 2

Ryan

Stupidly, I thought once we got home from tour in June, things would quiet down. It's now the beginning of September and the opposite is true. I'm grateful to be busy though, it keeps my mind occupied. I've accepted every concert request, podcast interview, and magazine photoshoot that comes our way. With Noah in wedding-planning mode, he was happy to hand more of the administrative stuff over to me. Except now, the guys are ready to murder me.

"I know what you're doing," Noah says as we pack the trailer for yet another concert.

"What am I doing?" I ask innocently, guiding my end of the amp into the tight space.

"You're trying to stay busy as fuck so you don't think about her but you're killing us in the process."

I almost drop the piece of equipment on my foot.

"Need I remind you, tonight's concert is a favor to *your* college roommate?" I ask through gritted teeth. I've been on edge for five months. Not hearing Emma's voice or seeing her name come across my phone screen has started to cause permanent damage to my mood cycles, leaving them in the *pissed off* position indefinitely.

"What's the excuse for next week's shitshow?" Noah fires back. "You do remember we're supposed to be finishing an album, right?" His tone is questioning but not accusatory. He's just making a point and damn him for being correct. "It's been like this ever since we got home, Ry, and don't get me wrong, I love this band and I'm happy to do it all, but I also sleep at night. You don't. You're burning the candle at both ends, brother, and one day it's going to catch up to you."

Noah and I walk back into the studio behind our house for the next load of gear. Inside, Brett is on his knees, backwards hat keeping his long hair out of his face as he packs his last snare drum in its travel case.

"How come we're famous enough to have to fly private, yet somehow, I still have to pack my own shit?" he grumbles, not bothering to look up. He definitely has the most gear to break down but he's not responsible for any of the other details, so it evens out.

"Because if someone did it for you, that would mean inviting people into our space, and it means they'd have to touch your set." Noah answers rationally, knowing Brett hates when people touch his stuff.

Brett grunts in response to Noah and pops the clips shut on his drum case before standing up and walking it out the door.

Sloan's amp is already loaded and he's sitting at the computer with headphones on, waiting for the rest of us to get our shit in the trailer before adding his guitar case. Sienna, Noah's fiancée is next to him, bobbing her head, eyes closed. They've been trying to work out the ending to one of our new songs for a couple days. I grimace as Noah moves to Sienna and wraps his arms around her waist. Memories of holding Emma during our last embrace flit through my mind, and I have to turn away.

Once everything is loaded, we all pile into the blacked out Suburban: Sloan, Noah, Brett, Bri, and Sienna. I drive. I always drive. Brett drives like he's still drunk, Sloan blows at directions, and Noah would turn the hour and a half drive into three hours. Security trails behind us in Romeo's matching Yukon since we're unable to travel without them anymore.

From the driver's seat, I hear Bri giggle in the back, and smack some part of Brett. I easily guess it's his wandering hand and I'm struck with a pang of loss that hurts so much I feel another crack splinter through the foundation of Brett and I's friendship. Don't get me wrong, Brett's been through hell, and I'm glad he's got Bri and seems to be doing better mentally, but damn it hurts to watch him be happy with the love of his life when he's the reason I can't even admit my feelings to the love of mine.

"Okay, so tell me again why we're doing this," Sloan says from the seat beside me.

"Because Noah's college roommate just opened a bar on the boardwalk and its grand opening is tonight. It coincides with the Saltwater and Sweaters Festival so it'll give us more exposure."

"And we need more exposure *because*?" he asks. "Hell, just yesterday I went through the McDonald's drive-thru line and had to abandon my Big Mac when the cashier tried to throw himself through my fucking window."

I cut my eyes at him. "Isn't exposure what led to you banging that Icelandic runway model last week?"

He shoots me a wink. "I don't need exposure for the ladies to flock to me, Ry."

I roll my eyes as Noah pipes up, getting me off the hook.

"We're doing it as a favor to Jason, and because this is our community."

"You two are the most boring, responsible rockstars I know," Sloan says. "Ryan, you need to get fucking laid. It's been like a year man. And Kink—"

"You'd better choose your next words carefully Sloan. Don't forget we're still sharing a bedroom wall with you for six more weeks," Sienna laughs through her threat. She and Noah are closing on a house at the end of the month, right before they get married, and we all feel some kind of way about him moving out.

"Kinky, you're perfect and Sienna makes you even more perfect." Sloan makes a kissy face at our lead singer and his fiancée, whom we all adore.

Her quiet laughter fills my ears once more. "Good save," I mutter under my breath.

When we pull up behind the venue an hour and a half later, there are people milling around on the boardwalk but technically, the festival doesn't start until seven. We're able to unload in relative peace because our presence tonight wasn't advertised. Fearing it would incite a riot and a fire hazard with too many bodies inside the building, Jason agreed to not advertise other than saying "live music".

It's not until Noah's doing the sound check that shit hits the fan and our security team sets up a perimeter around the stage. Noah's voice is unmistakable and people start pouring in from the street immediately.

"Hey everyone, thanks for being here tonight," Noah says to the rapidly growing crowd. "This bar is owned by a good friend of mine and we're honored to be here for him at his grand opening. If you could refrain from livestreaming this and wait to post about it until *after* the show, that would really help us out. We're trying to keep a low profile for the festival. Our fans are awesome and really fucking diligent, but this board-walk can't support two million people."

The crowd cheers in response even though we know half of them are going to completely disregard what Noah just said.

"Grab a drink and be sure to give the bartenders some love. We'll start at seven."

The crowd cheers again. I'm pretty sure Noah could tell them all to drink a vat of rat poison and they'd cheer as they slurped it down, happily dying to the sound of his perfect voice.

"*Shit!* Ry! Incoming!" Brett's voice yells from behind me.

I turn just in time to see the cart laden with several of his drum cases rolling toward me. He must've forgotten to lock the wheels again. I plant my feet and brace for impact, needing to stop the cart before it rolls off the stage and potentially fucks his stuff up or hits someone.

Dropping a shoulder and holding up my hands, I grunt as the cart slams into me. A second later, Brett's by my side.

"Fuck, sorry man. Thanks for stopping that." Laughing he adds, "It really helps to have a concrete wall as a best friend sometimes."

I just give him a tight smile. "No problem."

Once he has his cart where he needs it, I turn my attention back to my amp and bass guitar going through the motions. While I'm tuning my G string, I crank too hard, causing it to pop. I toe my case open and bend down to dig in the pocket that holds my spares.

Rifling through the envelopes of strings, my eyes land on a blue package. It's empty but it will live in my case forever.

"I got these for you." Nineteen-year-old Emma holds out the familiar package. Even without seeing the front, I know what it is.

"How'd you get these?" I ask, dumbfounded. Ever since the pandemic, my favorite guitar string manufacturer has been behind. I haven't been able to get my hands on their stuff for months.

She shrugs like it's no big deal.

"I've been searching ever since you told me using a, and I quote, 'cheap, dirty G-string' made you feel like less of a performer," she laughs. It's a sound I haven't heard for a while, and it steals my fucking breath, before she grows serious and adds, "You deserve the best, Ry."

Perhaps I should have known then that she felt something. There've been several moments like that over the past couple of years, but I turn thirty-one next week, making me *eleven* years older than her. I've convinced myself she needs to be with someone closer to her own age, even though that's ridiculous. No twenty-year-old *boy* knows how to treat Em.

Hell, even Emma isn't close to her own age.

I shake my head to clear those thoughts and change out the string. It's almost go-time and the bar is fucking packed.

Chapter 3

Emma

"Oh, there's a spot!" I point through the windshield, directing Jen to the only available parking space for three miles. We've been circling the boardwalk for half an hour, and I was beginning to lose hope of finding a space at all.

"*Finally!*"

She pulls the car in, doing a fantastic job at parallel parking – a skill I don't have.

I hop out of the car in my jeans and flats while Jen takes her time in her heels.

"Okay, makeup check," she says, coming to stand next to me on the sidewalk.

"Flawless," I reply, scanning her face.

"Yours too. Outfit check."

I eye her from head to toe and make her twirl. Jen went with a ruffled, ankle-length skirt and a skin-tight tank top with a plunging neck line.

"Beautiful and perfectly *bohemian beach bitch*." I smile. "Shall I twirl too?"

She purses her lips and gives me an annoyed look. "No need. Your jeans are as boring as ever, even though your butt *does* look good in them." She glances at my crop top mostly hidden by my baggy "boyfriend" shirt.

"You'd attract more attention if you lost the overshirt. Besides," she adds, "it's still like a hundred degrees out.

Maybe. But showing that much skin makes me feel vulnerable.

I loop my arm through hers as we slowly make our way to the boardwalk. "We've been over this. I'm not the one looking for attention, you are. And I will happily be your wingman."

Suddenly, she stops walking. "Just promise me you'll *try* to have fun?"

Never mind the fact that my idea of fun is noise cancelling headphones with Beautiful Deceit blaring as I go to town on a blank canvas. Crowds, people, *cameras?* Not my kind of party. But I came to hang out with Jen and I'd never forgive myself if I rained on her parade.

So, reluctantly, I nod my head, vaguely remembering that I'm supposed to be working on loosening my heart's hold on Ryan anyway.

"I'll make an honest effort," I confirm. Who knows? Maybe she's right and a good make-out session is exactly what I need to remind me there are more fish in the sea.

"Good. Maybe by your fifth glass of wine you'll relax enough to actually have a conversation with someone," she says, nudging me in the side where our arms are linked.

Turning onto the boardwalk a few minutes later, we pull up short.

"Holy shit. Is that the bar you wanted to try?" I ask. "It looks like an ant hill."

There are people spilling out everywhere. The line to get in is half a mile down the boardwalk, and it looks like officers are breaking up a fight out front.

"God, I didn't think it would be *this* popular. It's just a beach bar for fuck's sake," Jen mutters angrily.

"Maybe we can skip the bar and just do the food vendors and stuff," I suggest as she leads me closer to the crowd.

"Don't you want to see what all the hype is about?" she asks excitedly. Jen is blissfully unaware of the night my disdain for large crowds, and the media, was born. Averse to pity, I swore Brett to secrecy, so Jen isn't to blame when she guilts me into these situations. She just thinks I'm an introvert and tries to "break me out of my shell".

Suddenly, the notes from the band playing inside register in my brain. The bass line strikes deep and reverberates in my soul. I know what comes next.

Proving me right, Noah's voice comes crashing through the music, erasing any possibility that this is a cover band.

Well, fuck. That explains the crowd.

Jen hears Noah at the same time and she turns to me with wide eyes. "I swear, Emmie, I didn't know they were playing here. They weren't advertised anywhere, it just said there was going to be a band. Beautiful Deceit sold out a world tour, why would they be playing this local spot?" she asks, panicking.

"It's fine," I say, trying to calm her down. If she's hysterical, that'll only add to my anxiety. Besides, it's not like I was going to be able to avoid Ryan forever, although now I wish I'd taken Jen's advice and worn something cuter.

Steeling my resolve to get this over with, I start walking toward the door of the bar. Perks of being the drummer's sister include never getting turned away, and I never have to wait in line. The downside is that I have to point out that I'm the drummer's sister, which usually earns me more attention than I want.

"We really don't have to do this. I can check the bar out another time," Jen says, trying to stop my forward progress. She doesn't fully understand my anxiety over crowds but she *does* understand how hard seeing Ryan will be for me.

I know if I wanted to, Jen would leave with me right now, but as fucked up as it is, I no longer want to go. I haven't laid eyes on Ryan Ashley Battle in almost six months. I know nothing good can come from it, but I can't deny my desire to see him. My palms are already clammy with anticipation and my stomach feels like I'm repeatedly riding The Drop Zone.

"No, let's go in. It'll be fun to surprise Brett," I say, keeping my tone light.

The look she gives me tells me she sees right through that lie, and sure enough she calls me on it like any good bestie would.

"Do not lie to me, Emma Rose. I know the last few months have been brutal, but remember, he didn't come after you. Nothing's changed. Just protect yourself, okay?" Jen's brown eyes bore into me, and all I can think about is the way Ryan's eyes remind me of milk chocolate with flecks of gold in them as if Hershey™ and Goldschlager™ hooked up and had a baby.

Knowing my words will betray me if I open my mouth, I nod because it's all I can manage.

We make our way to the door, walking outside of the line that's formed, pissing a bunch of people off, where we're stopped by the bouncer, as expected.

"I'm sorry ladies, but the restaurant's at capacity. You should still be able to hear down on the beach, although there's quite a crowd out back too. Your best bet is to wait in line."

Familiar with how this goes, I stand on my tiptoes to see through the open door, before swinging my attention back to the bouncer. "Could you please grab the tall, bald, black man standing right there? He's a friend." Romeo is stage right, just inside the door. Romeo and his wife Tasha moved to the east coast when the guys got done with their tour and began working privately for Beautiful Deceit, as did the rest of the security team. They're honest, loyal and clicked with the guys – and the dancers – right away. Romeo mostly guards Noah, but he's my favorite.

The bar employee eyes me warily like he's heard this story a hundred times.

"Please?" I try again.

"Fine. But if he says he doesn't know you, you and your friend here are going on the do-not-return-list." He points to the camera above the doorway letting us know he's got a record of our faces.

"Noted." I smile as he disappears inside. The crowd is so thick, I can't even see the stage which triggers my fight-or-flight response. Every cell in my body begging for me to start the *flight* part.

Keep it together, Emma. Do not have a panic attack now. You're fine.

A second later, the bouncer comes out with Romeo in tow.

"Emma!" Romeo's face lights up in a smile as I throw my arms around his neck. When he leans down to return my hug, I give a smug smile to the man at the door over Romeo's shoulder. "Does your brother know you're out here? Why didn't you girls come in the back?"

When Romeo releases me, I shrug. "I didn't actually know they were playing here tonight. Weird coincidence."

"Come on, let's get you backstage."

His words do nothing to settle the panic in my heart. "Actually, we're good at the bar, we just needed to get inside. I'd like to surprise Brett, so do me a favor and don't tell him I'm here, okay?"

He narrows his eyes at me, clearly unhappy with my request. If Brett finds out Romeo kept this from him, he'll be pissed.

"I promise I'll find him after the show. I don't want to distract him," I argue sweetly.

While Romeo is mulling it over, a girl in the front of the line leans in closer. "Did you say you're Brett's sister?"

I ignore the girl and give a pleading look at Romeo who finally nods begrudgingly and turns to the man at the door. "They're with me."

No further comment is needed as Jen and I sail through the doorway into the sweltering heat that can only be produced by five hundred bodies and stage lights. Romeo deposits us safely at the bar and instructs the bartender to keep an eye on us.

"You flag me down if anyone gives them trouble. I'll lose my job if anyone so much as breathes in her direction."

"Yes, sir," the guy behind the bar says. He can't be much older than me. There's also only two people behind the bar and they're struggling to keep up with orders from the crowd, so I doubt very seriously he'll notice if someone gets too close.

It isn't until I'm seated and Jen thrusts a cold glass of white wine into my hand that I finally allow myself to glance at the stage.

Big mistake.

Big. Fucking. Mistake.

The veins in Ryan's arms are visible as he caresses the strings of his bass guitar. The instrument is so appropriate for him. It's not flashy like Sloan's guitar or Brett's drums, but it's deep, powerful sound reverberates through your chest, telling you who owns you in that moment.

Ry's eyes are closed, his stance is wide, and his lips are parted. Sweat trails down his neck and glistens under the lights, making my mouth go dry as my own sweat rolls between my breasts. I promptly remove my over shirt, no longer caring about the minuscule top I have on underneath, and throw back my wine shot-style, panting like a dog in heat.

"Easy, girl. You sure you want to stay?" Jen yells in my ear.

I had forgotten she was here. I'd forgotten all these people were here. I only see Ryan. It's like the last five months of pain and separation never even happened. My desire for him slams into me full force and my rapid heart rate now has nothing to do with the cameras or the guy from the newspaper wearing a lanyard.

I don't want to stay but I can't leave either. Not when Ryan's presence is feeding my starved addiction, tethering me to him like an obedient ox to a plow.

"Yeah, I'm sure," I nod.

When the first chords of *Victorious* are struck, liquid heat pools between my legs. Apparently, it's also a favorite of the patrons in this bar because the noise level increases and security has to pull a woman off the stage as she attempts to throw herself at Noah. Similarly, Ryan has to take a couple steps backwards because even though he's elevated above the crowd, fans are still reaching for his shoes.

They want him so badly but it's nothing compared to what I feel.

The crowd is mostly pressing against the stage so the bar offers a little bit of breathing room. This, I can manage. Jen gets another drink for me and we clink our glasses together.

"You think Sloan would be down for a quickie?" she asks, causing my eyes to swing to Beautiful Deceit's guitarist.

"Honestly, I'm surprised it hasn't happened yet," I laugh. "Breathing and willing are usually his only requirements, but that tight ass and a handful of firm, perky tits probably bumps you to the top of the list."

"I'll drink to that," Jen takes a sip of her Cosmo. "I haven't seen them in a while. Swear to God they all got hotter."

"Yeah. You're not wrong," I sigh.

She rubs my back as the song comes to an end and Ryan finally looks out into the crowd. His eyes land on mine for the briefest of seconds before moving on. As my stomach threatens to empty its contents on the floor over his dismissal, his eyes snap back to mine and go wide as he mouths my name.

I give him a smile and wave as if he didn't rip my heart out and stomp on it back in April.

His own smile elicits another excited roar from the crowd. Ryan's stage persona is quiet and serious. He might grin at the end of a concert, but he never reveals much else. However, right now, he's wearing a full-wattage smile and looks like a cover model with his pearly whites on display.

Jen leans in to me, echoing my thoughts. "I don't think I've ever seen Ryan smile that big."

When the song comes to an end, Noah addresses the crowd as Ryan squats down and taps Tim, his body guard, on the shoulder. I see him nod in my direction and suddenly, Tim is pushing away from the stage, headed straight for me and Jen.

"Oh, shit," I whisper too softly for Jen to hear. Despite the mass of bodies, Tim's at my side in a split second.

"Mr. Battle would like for you to watch from the side of the stage. He said this crowd is getting unruly and he'd feel better if you and Ms. Hayes were somewhere protected."

Perhaps I shouldn't give in so easily, but even in my confused state of hurt and desire, I don't want to be responsible for making Ryan uncomfortable or worried.

Jen hops off her barstool, fully ready to embrace being a VIP while I slide to the floor much slower, trying to ensure my knees don't give out.

"Um, yeah, okay."

Tim uses his body to shield us from the crowd as he navigates us toward an alcove off to the side of the stage.

When I glance back up at Ryan, he nods and mouths *thank you* before diving back into the next song.

Shortly afterward, the guys take a fifteen-minute intermission and head somewhere down a hallway on the other side of the stage. Tim quickly walks to Jen and I and ushers us down a matching hallway on our side. We arrive outside a door labeled *Owner* and Tim knocks twice before opening the door to let us in.

I scan the room, my eyes immediately landing on Ryan before finding my shirtless brother who's chugging a bottle of water with Bri draped across his lap. As soon as Brett sees me, he gently moves out from under Bri's legs and rushes to scoop me up at the door.

"Emmie! What the fuck are you doing here?"

"Um, we're here for the Labor Day festival before classes start."

Brett pulls back and searches my face. "Em, you look pale. You okay?" Lowering his voice, he adds, "That's a lot of people in a small space out there."

I know what he's remembering but he's in the middle of a show. Now isn't the time to rehash shit.

"Yeah, I'm fine."

"You guys can sit behind Ryan's amp with Bri and Sienna. I've got extra ear plugs. Don't go back out into that crowd," he instructs. "They've already had to kick about twenty people out."

At the mention of Ryan's name, my traitorous eyes swing back to him. This close I can see the small birthmark in the shape of a seven on the strong column of his neck. The one I've dreamt about licking for years. His long eyelashes frame his light brown eyes, and his straight, white teeth peek out as he wets the most suckable lips the world has ever seen.

"Hey, Em."

God, his voice. I know people prefer the perfection of Noah's, but the deepness of Ryan's just strikes a chord inside me.

"Hi." I have to clear my throat and try again because it comes out as a strangled whisper. "Um, hey everyone."

Bri gets off the couch and pulls me away from Brett to give me a hug. Sienna's next and she passes me to Noah who wraps me in a bear hug and plants a kiss on the top of my head. Sloan's up next. He never misses an opportunity to mess with my brother so he grabs my bare waist, made available thanks to my crop top, and holds me there while openly checking me out.

"You get hotter every time I see you, little Emmie."

Despite what happened to me, I thankfully don't get triggered when it's someone I know. Sloan wouldn't hurt me in a million years. I'm also glad I made Brett swear not to tell. People would be guarded around me and I couldn't handle that. I couldn't handle the pussy-footing, the babying, the tiptoeing and I find relief in Sloan's good-natured teasing.

Brett, on the other hand, does not.

"Sloan, don't make me knock your teeth out. Get your hands off my sister."

Laughing Sloan slides his arms around my back for a hug. "He's so much fun to fuck with," he whispers in my ear, causing me to force out a laugh.

Before I make contact with Ryan, some guy comes in the office and asks if the band is ready to get back on stage because the crowd is starting to get restless.

"Yeah, we're good to go," Noah answers.

Brett turns to me. "Em, grab the ear plugs from my snare case for you and Jen. Stay with Bri, she'll get you squared away." He kisses Bri on the mouth, squeezes Jen's shoulder in hello and follows Noah and Sloan out the door.

Ryan hasn't moved.

I had opened up about my feelings for Ryan to Bri and Sienna when we were in Ireland but unless Ryan has told them the rest of the story, they don't know he crushed my hopes of us ever dating. When Sienna grabs Jen's hand and leads her out of the makeshift dressing room, Bri quickly follows, trying to give Ryan and I a moment alone.

After a minute of silence, I tell Ryan, "We should probably go too."

The proximity is too much for my battered heart to handle.

"It's good to see you, Em," he says, taking a tentative step forward. "I can't believe you're here."

I want to move away but my shoes are glued to the floor.

"I didn't know you'd be here." I've already said this, but I feel the need to reiterate the point. *I'm not here for you. I may not be able to leave because of you, but I didn't come here for you.* I remind myself I'm trying to loosen my grip on this man and tighten it on reality.

He takes another step forward.

Come on shoes! Fucking move!

"Are you coming out with us after the show?"

"I don't—"

"Please say yes," he cuts me off.

Before I can answer, Brett barrels through the door. "Kinda hard to start *Virtuous* without our bassist since the first three measures are your solo, dude. Get the fuck out here. You guys can catch up later."

When Brett's gone, Ryan turns back to me.

"Come. For me?"

I think I'm having an out of body experience when he says those words to me. Never mind he's talking about some stupid afterparty or something, my vagina thinks he just gave her a direct order and she's letting me know she's here for it.

As if one set of lips can speak for the other, I hear myself agree.

"Okay."

Chapter 4

Ryan

Holy shit, I can't believe she's here.

It's a good fucking thing I can play these songs half dead because Emma sitting behind my amp is the most distracting thing I've ever experienced while playing – and I've been flashed, fondled, and fought with while on stage.

With her here, the crowd seems louder, the lights seem brighter, and these songs sound the best they ever have.

I'm probably being obvious as all fuck but I find myself turning around every two minutes just to make sure she's still there. Every time I catch her eyes, I try to read her expression but the woman who is usually such an open book to me is clearly shutting me out.

As she should.

She's just as off-limits to me now as she was five months ago.

At the end of the show, the crowd is still screaming for an encore even though we've played every song we've ever written and I'm fucking exhausted. The thought of hearing Em's voice and seeing her face are the only things keeping me going. As I start breaking down my equipment, a sparkly purple thong lands on the stage in front of me. The immediate reaction, whether I want it to be or not, is to look up and see where it came from. I spot its owner immediately because she's staring right at me, using her hand to mimic sucking dick.

Sloan drops to the floor next to me and pulls his own amp cord from the socket.

"Looks like you've got that one in the bag."

"We both know I'm not touching that with a ten-foot pole, Sloany."

He looks defeated. "I know that. What I don't know is *why*." He grips my shoulder making me look him in the eye, which, considering his next words, is a little uncomfortable. "I never pegged you as being into guys but I know some people that would *love* to ease you into that lifestyle."

I push him off of me using his own arm, laughing when he lands on his ass. I give a dismissive nod to the owner of the panties, knowing she'll get the hint when I make no move to pick them up. Yawning, I glance at the giant clock in the shape of a ship wheel hanging over the bar before my gaze lands on what is directly under it.

Rather, *who* is under it.

How did she get off this stage without me noticing? And who the fuck is sitting next to her, with his hand on her perfect fucking skin. Even from here I can see her tight smile and the way she's leaning away from the guy. The knowledge that she's uncomfortable has me moving before I think it through. Although there are fewer patrons in the bar now, it's still packed, and I'm still me.

But I don't think about any of that as I abandon my shit on stage, walk to the edge and plant a hand to brace myself before swinging my legs to hop onto the floor. The crowd immediately descends on me and I hear Romeo and Tim both yell, "What the fuck, Ryan?"

Thankfully, I'm way bigger than most everyone in here and I easily carve my own path to the bar, stopping directly behind Em's barstool, I possessively plant my hands on her shoulders even as a hundred other hands possessively land on me. Em flinches at my touch and it fucking guts me.

"You mind removing your hand?" I ask the guy seated next Em.

He looks up, his eyes going wide.

"Oh shit! Ryan Battle. Can we get a selfie?" he asks.

"Take your hand off her waist and then we'll talk."

He looks back at Em and yanks his hand away, smiling sheepishly at me.

"My bad, bro. I didn't know she was with you."

"You think we let just anyone sit on stage with us during a concert?" I bark.

I need to cool it. I'm showing my ass in a big way right now but as soon as I saw this stranger's hand connect with her skin, all rational thought abandoned my brain.

"Oh, uh, right. So, that selfie?" he says again, holding up his hands to show me he isn't touching Em anymore.

Keeping my face stern, I lean in and let him have his stupid fucking picture.

And then shit gets crazy.

Someone's pressing into my back, pushing me forward into Em so hard I have to throw my hand on the bar so I don't crush her. Someone else's hands are groping my pecs, another pair of hands are on my thighs. Camera flashes are going off everywhere. People are tugging at me and I know I need to get Emma and Jennifer out of here now before they get trampled. Tim appears to my left, and pulls Jennifer with him, leaving Em for me.

When I spin her to face me, I see the panic in her eyes and her shoulders are trembling. The final straw is when she squeezes her eyes shut and covers them with shaking hands.

What the fuck is going on?

"Em? Emma, look at me."

She doesn't move, doesn't open her eyes, doesn't take her hands away.

I lean to speak in her ear. "Breathe for me, Em. I'm going to get you out of here, okay?"

Finally, she nods.

I slide my right arm under her knees and my left arm around her back. As soon as I lift her off the chair, she folds into me, her arms tight around my sweat-slicked neck, her face buried where my neck meets my shoulder. I feel her shaking in my arms.

People are still taking pictures, but thankfully they make a path for us instead of blocking my way to the back.

When we reach the dressing room, Noah roars. "What the *fuck* was that, Ryan? Why do we even bother employing a security team if you're just going to jump right into a rowdy crowd, offering selfies? You'd better be damn glad Sienna didn't get hurt." It takes him a minute to realize something's not right with Em and that I wasn't just carrying her around for a victory lap.

"Oh shit. She okay?" he asks.

I hand Emma off to Brett who has appeared by my side and is helping his sister over to the couch.

"Excuse me for not checking in," I snap back at Noah once Em sits down. "I looked up to find some asshole touching Emma and figured she could use a little back up since our security team was busy with each of you."

When I finish arguing with Noah - which rarely happens - I notice, Brett's got his arms wrapped around his sister. I can't hear what he's whispering in her ear but she's nodding and squeezing him tightly while Bri hands her a cup of water.

I know Em hates crowds, but I didn't realize it was *that* bad. Brett wipes her tears and kisses her head before moving out of the way for Jennifer and Sienna to surround her.

"Thanks for getting to her, Ry. I swear you always come through."

"She okay?" I ask, repeating Noah's question, hating that I have to ask Brett instead of just asking her myself.

He hesitates for a second, his eyes darting worriedly to his sister. Eventually, he answers *yes* but doesn't offer any more information though it's pretty damn clear I'm missing something big because she's far from okay.

"Well," Sloan's voice cuts in. "I think we can all agree that the last fifteen minutes make going out extremely undesirable. Anyone opposed to just going home? I'm beat."

I feel my heart sink as everyone starts to answer in agreement with Sloan.

No, no, no, I think.

Time.

I need more time but I don't know how to get it.

By the time the security team comes back in telling us the bar has been shut down for the night, the decision is unanimous. They want to go home.

I watch everyone hug each other goodbye, my heart galloping in my chest when Em gets to me. She finally has a little more color in her cheeks and she's stopped shaking but it looks like whatever that was drained all her energy, leaving her eyelids heavy with fatigue.

"It was great to see you, Em. I'm sorry about the guy at the bar," I say, my lips brushing the top of her head so lightly she doesn't notice. I want to comfort her but I don't know how.

She's trying hard not to press in to me, so I drop my arms. She's endured enough discomfort for one night and I'll be damned if I add to it.

"Yeah. You, too," she murmurs. "And, uh, thanks for..." Her words trail off as she waves a hand toward the door.

Jennifer comes over and drapes an arm across Emma's shoulders. "Why don't we head back to the house too?"

I watch Em nod and give her best friend a sad smile.

By the time we get home, it's late. I should let Em be after the night she had, but I can't stop myself from texting her.

RYAN 1:14 AM

So happy to see you tonight. It's been too long.

EMMA 1:15 AM

It was a good show.

A good show? That's all I get? Fuck, I want so much more from her.

RYAN 1:15 AM

Can I call you tomorrow? We didn't really have a chance to catch up.

EMMA 1:15 AM

...

...

The disappearing bubbles are agonizing.

EMMA 1:18 AM

I don't think that's a good idea.

Goodnight Ryan.

Chapter 5

Emma

Unsurprisingly, I slept like shit but I'm perpetually an early riser so I climb out of bed and go in search of coffee, planning to catch the last of the sunrise. I unplug my phone from the charger and open my messages out of habit. One came in after I'd told Ryan goodnight but my phone was on silent so I never heard it.

RYAN 1:22 AM

When you're ready, call me. Please. I miss talking to you.

I throw the phone on the bed. It's too early to be tempted since this man is determined to break me.

Seeing him elicited all the emotions I've tried to keep at bay for months. One thing is clear though, despite the silence and the distance, I'm no closer to being over him.

43

My foot hits the landing on the stairs, and I turn to go into the kitchen of the most beautiful beach house I've ever seen, startled to see the lights are already on.

"Jen?" My best friend is a night owl compared to my early bird and I'm shocked she's awake. Especially considering we only went to bed a few hours ago.

"Hey babe, out here," she calls from the porch where the door to the kitchen is open.

I pour my coffee and join her on the wooden bench swing.

"How'd you sleep?" she asks.

"Same as always."

"Em, I'm seriously so sorry about last night. I had no idea seeing him would affect you that badly."

I grip the handle of my mug in my right hand and pat her thigh with my left. "You didn't know they were going to be there. Besides, it wasn't seeing Ryan that made me freak out. You know I hate crowds and stuff. It just got to be too much."

"You're telling me none of that was due to Ryan?"

I sigh, relenting. "Okay, it was both the crowd and Ryan. That's the thing with addictions. You're never cured. Even after abstaining for years, one hit and you're right back where you started."

I laugh when she gets a mortified look on her face but quickly grow serious when she starts talking.

"That sounds really dark, Em. Like, I want things between you and him to work out somehow, but not if you need him that desperately, you know?"

I know she's concerned and looking out for me, and I'm thankful for it, but her words put yet another expectation on me. *Make good decisions. Be the strong one.*

I haven't felt as safe as I did in Ryan's arms since the last time I was in them. Actually, I want nothing more than to crawl right back there. I'm only keeping the distance now because I can't handle the heartbreak that accompanies being in his vicinity.

I nudge Jen's shoulder with mine. "What I *mean* is I couldn't avoid him forever. I tried to cut him out. I tried to move on. But ultimately, it didn't matter if I saw him last night or at Noah and Sienna's wedding, he's like a hit of pure heroine. You know it's going to fuck you up. You know you should avoid it at all costs but the cravings get worse the longer it's absent from your life."

"Okay, well, that's enough drug analogies for one lifetime, thank you very much," Jen says, taking another sip of her coffee, gently rocking the swing with one foot planted on the porch.

"I'm still not saying it right," I sigh.

"I get it," she finally relents. "I mean I *think* I do at least. I don't want any dick that bad, but even I have to admit, Ryan Battle might tempt me to lose my mind too, if my best friend wasn't so fucked up over him." Jen grins at me. "Honestly, he's so fucking hot, but I hate him for hurting you."

I tell Jen about the text he sent me and watch her eyes bug out of her head.

"Are you going to call him?"

"I can't. You were right. Nothing's changed. He's still my brother's best friend. Brett still won't be okay with it. And I still can't be the reason the world's biggest band breaks up. Besides, he's not asking me to call him so we can start dating. He's always looked out for me and I think he just wants to hear I'm okay after last night."

"What a fucking mess. Let's dump the coffee and switch to mimosas and lay on the beach," Jen says laughing and holding out her hand.

"Sounds like a plan to me."

Make good decisions, Emma.

Chapter 6

Ryan

The name on my caller ID has me bolting up in bed, instantly awake.

The night sounds of this house and the smell of my room are more familiar to me than my own body sometimes so there's no disorientation despite being woken up from a dead sleep. I used to find comfort in the familiarity, but now it's beginning to feel claustrophobic.

"Em?"

She and I haven't spoken a single word since the concert in Virginia Beach a month ago. She never reached out like I'd asked and I couldn't force myself onto her. Back in Ireland, she made it clear she wasn't interested in just being friends and I made it clear we couldn't be anything more. So I'm panicked as to why she's calling me at two in the morning on a random Sunday.

When she doesn't answer right away, I raise my voice as much as I dare, knowing her brother is asleep next door. Now that he's completely stopped drinking, Brett's an annoyingly light sleeper.

"Emma, what's wrong?" my voice is demanding but I'm too anxious to care.

"I need you," her scared whisper has my ass in gear immediately.

Those three words guarantee I'll stop whatever I'm currently doing and start doing whatever she needs me to. Granted, it's always been that way, whether she uttered those words or not, but now it's go-time.

"Where are you?" I ask, already pulling on my jeans from last night, not caring that they have blood on the thigh. Ever since that fucking concert, I've found my way to the jiu jitsu mats more and more in an effort to get the woman on the other end of this line out of my head. I took an elbow to the nose yesterday while I was lost in a daydream and it was still dripping blood when I changed back into my regular clothes.

"Baltimore," she says.

What the fuck? She's supposed to be at school just outside of Boston. I assumed I was about to be en route to the airport.

"Share your location, Em."

A text alert and a pin on a map tell me exactly where I'm headed as I haul ass out of the house I share with my best friends and bandmates. We've lived in this house going on six years, and thankfully, I can navigate its hallways and corners with my eyes closed.

I briefly stop outside her brother's door and like she knows what I'm about to do, I hear Em's voice, small and embarrassed in my ear.

"Please don't involve Brett. I'm not in the mood for a lecture about my safety."

Knowing I'll pay dearly for this at some point in the future, I move on from Brett's bedroom door and continue down the stairs, honoring her request.

I slip into the garage and face the one thing I'm afraid may wake someone: the start of my engine. It sounds like a rocket's launching when I turn her on.

"I'm on my way."

I need to keep her talking to know she's okay.

"What are you doing in Baltimore?" I ask, before clearing my throat and working on taking long inhales and even longer exhales. Emma being scared enough to call me after all this time means something's really wrong and my body is coiling tightly, ready to spring as soon as I reach her.

She keeps her answer vague which pisses me off. She's always been honest with me. I've been a safe place for Em to land since she was five years old. She used to get so frustrated when people would want to talk to her about "kid things", as she used to say. She wasn't into "kid things". She wanted "grown up things". So I'd let her do my math homework. To this day, I swear she's the reason I passed geometry.

"I was invited on a fall break trip."

"And the trip isn't what you were hoping it would be?" I ask, merging onto the highway that will deliver me to my destination.

"You could say that." When I stay silent in an effort to not yell, she fills the space, finally giving me more detail. "I mean it was fine, but I realized I was in over my head when a couple of guys started doing lines of cocaine off the coffee table."

Jesus.

"You're there with a bunch of guys?" I ask, unable to keep my voice even despite trying my damnedest.

"And girls," she says defensively.

I grip the steering wheel harder to focus on keeping my anger in check and work on redirecting the conversation. "I'm glad you called me, Em. Are there any sober girls that can wait with you until I get there?"

It's usually close to three hours from our house outside of

the Fredericksburg area to Baltimore with all the traffic. At this hour, I'm hoping to make it in less time. Mile signs tick by, posted along the highway, but they aren't passing fast enough.

"Um, maybe a couple, but I don't want to go find any of them. I just closed myself in my room."

It doesn't take long to deduce that Em probably thought she was going on a graduate school getaway with people whose intelligence and maturity match her own. What she ended up on was a fall break nightmare with immature brainiacs who have access to their trust funds and all the bad decisions money can buy.

"Good. Stay there." My voice is firm and low giving away my displeasure at her being in this situation. When she doesn't answer, I take a different route. "What happened at the show in Virginia Beach? What had you so freaked out?" I've been dying to ask since the night it happened and right now, she's a captive audience.

"It was nothing."

"So, we're lying to each other now?" I regret the words as soon as they're out of my mouth. I lied to her first when I made her think I didn't have feelings for her.

"Okay, it wasn't nothing. It was something but I don't want to talk about it," she amends.

"We used to talk about everything." I feel my teeth grind as I talk into the empty space of the car.

"That was before," she says quietly.

"Is there anything I can do to make sure that doesn't happen to you again?" I ask, pulling the knife out of my chest at her mention of Ireland.

"You're doing it now."

"By being on the phone? You can call me anytime, Em. You know that."

"By coming to get me, I mean."

"I'll always be here for you. Tell me you know that."

"I know."

With nothing left to say about it, we switch to small talk until the longest two hours and fifteen minutes of my life passes, and I pull up outside the party house.

"Are you comfortable walking out by yourself?"

"I think so. I don't have much to carry so it should be easy to slip out."

"Okay. I'm out front."

"Okay," she whispers on a shaky exhale. I know she's gearing herself up to face me, and I hate it.

She hangs up the phone and I wait, my heart hammering in my chest thinking about her trying to get out of the house unde-tected with a party full of high, inebriated assholes. When five minutes have ticked by and she still hasn't come out, I call her but she doesn't answer.

I send a text, but barely wait twenty seconds for a response that never comes before I'm throwing on a ball cap and pulling my hood up. I'm not sure if anyone would recognize me in their drunken state, but I just want to get Emma and get the hell out of here. The last thing I need are a million cell phones snapping pictures to sell to the tabloids. Especially since there are drugs - and God knows what else – in this house.

My father, Senator Andrew Battle, would *not* be thrilled. It's an election year and things are already tense with the opposing party working hard to discredit my father and prevent him from serving another term.

I open the front door and the scent of weed smacks me square in the face. I'm taken aback at how much trash is every-where. These are Harvard grad students for God's sake. I expected them to have more class when they partied. There are a couple of people passed out on the couch in the living room right when I walk in, but the majority of the party seems like it's coming from the basement. A door down a narrow hallway stands ajar and I hear shouts and music wafting up from the bowels of the house.

I can't believe the police haven't been called yet. This neighborhood is posh and right on the water. I doubt the permanent residents take too kindly to wild parties on a Saturday night . . . well, Sunday morning.

I quietly make my way to the stairs off to the right of the living room and take them two at a time, assuming the room she's staying in is away from the party scene.

"Em?"

Nothing.

"*Emma?*" I try again.

"I said let me *go*, Aiden."

Aiden? Who in the holy fuck is *Aiden?* And he'd better hope his hands are nowhere near Em.

"Emma Donovan!" I shout, not giving a single fuck if someone recognizes me now.

"I need to go," I hear her say behind closed door number three.

Without waiting for her to open the door on her own, I crash through it to find *Aiden*, caging her in against a dresser, entirely too close for my liking. His only saving grace is that he isn't touching her.

Even in her current state of anger, she's fucking breathtaking, and I'm trying like hell to ignore the reaction I'm having to seeing another man in her space.

When Aiden swings his wild, drug-addled eyes to me, I offer him one chance.

"Let her leave *now* and I'll leave your face intact."

The problem with cocaine is that it makes you feel invincible. Larger, faster, and smarter than you actually are. For example, Aiden here, is about six inches shorter than me, on a thin frame that suggests he partakes in the powder often, and yet, he's still squaring up to me.

By the time he's planted his feet and perfected his smirk, I already have my hand lightly around his throat, holding him at arm's length to ensure he doesn't get any closer. I'm only squeezing hard enough to keep him rooted to his spot, but he's acting like I'm cutting off his air supply, causing me to have to squeeze harder to maintain control.

"Stop fucking moving," I growl at the wiggling squirrel in my grasp before turning my attention to Emma. "Em, grab your shit. Car's the last one in the driveway." I hand her my keys and squeeze a little harder as I watch Aiden's eyes follow her as she picks up her bag and heads out the door. Once she's cleared the room, I drop him to the floor and plant my boot in his stomach. "Talk to her again and I'll make you wish you hadn't. Are we clear?"

He dips his head slightly from his position on the floor, his eyes narrowed in rage. *Good enough for me.*

Less is more in these situations and it's a harmless interaction . . . until I get to the driveway and see the mob of people around my car.

"*Shit.*"

Emma's trying to elbow her way through the twenty-or-so people surrounding my Aston Martin. *Where did they all come from?*

"I've gotta go guys, um, family emergency," she lies, walking wide to avoid the crowd to get to the car.

"*Ohmygod, isyourbrotherokay?*" I hear one girl slur in a squeaky voice.

"What? Oh. Yeah, he's fine," Emma answers. I can make out the exasperated look on her face over *her* supposed friends showing more concern for her famous brother than for her.

"Hell yeah, he is," another drunk girl giggles. "I'd let him rail me in the back door and the front door at the *same* time."

"Okay first of all, that's disgusting. Second of all, it's also physically impossible."

I can tell Emma is losing her patience with this crowd. Poor girl just needs to befriend married women in their thirties. Even though she can't legally drink yet, Em would prefer a glass of wine while discussing art techniques or court cases over this bullshit.

The girl making the lewd comments is leaning with her back against my passenger door, preventing Emma from getting inside. The girl rolls her eyes and huffs. *"Fine, Ms. Literal.* Then I'd take your brother in the back door and their bassist in the front. His dick's probably the size of my thigh."

Time to go.

Before I can get to Emma and put her in the car myself, I hear her screech. *"What the fuck did you just say?* They aren't sex dolls! They're musicians. And get Ryan's dick the *fuck* out of your head!"

Whoa.

Em doesn't ever lose her cool, and she's *pissed.* She also just referenced my cock, which he seems to like a lot, and that isn't great for me. People sexualize the guys and I all the time. It comes with the territory. It used to really bother Noah when people would say shit, but honestly, I'd rather have people impressed by my physique than repulsed by it. It's not like any of them are getting close enough to make it personal anyway.

"Em, get in the fucking car," I order from the other side of the SUV.

The drunk girl turns her attention toward me and I angle my head down, hoping my hat shields the top half of my face. Quickly, I hop in the driver's seat after a hard yank to open my own door against the crowd.

Thankfully, Emma climbs in the passenger side at the same time, chucks her bag into the backseat, and slams her door shut. Raising my face to the rearview mirror to make sure I don't run over anyone, I hear, "That's gotta be him. Dude's *huge*," through my cracked window.

Then the cameras come out.

Sometimes fame is a bigger pain in the ass than people realize.

Once I'm clear of partygoers, I floor it out of the driveway and reality hits. I can't make the six-and-a-half-hour drive back to Boston for Emma because I have to do a podcast with Noah later this morning. I head for the highway back toward home planning to drop Em at the Donovan's. If this was a fall break trip, she won't have classes this week.

"Is it okay if I take you to your parents'?" I ask, adrenaline still coursing through my system. "You can tell them one of the girls dropped you off. I'm sure they'll be happy to see you. Or I can take you to Jennifer's, but I don't have enough time to get you back to Boston tonight."

"Yeah, that's fine," she answers, staring straight ahead, her voice almost robotic now that we're alone.

"Em, you alright?" I ask, as a sickening thought races through my brain. "That guy, Aiden, he didn't touch you at any point, did he?" Gritting my teeth, I add, "Did anyone else? I swear to God, I'll turn this car ar—"

"No," she says quietly, cutting me off.

"Are you cold?" I ask, desperately trying to get her to tell me what's wrong.

"No."

"Come on, Em, talk to me."

She takes a deep breath and speaks calmly as she exhales. "I'm grateful you came, but seeing you is still hard," she admits, her voice wobbly like she might cry.

I want to console her but I can't, and it kills me. I can't touch her because I know I won't be able to stop.

Her auburn hair is in a knot on top of her head, poking out in all directions and somehow, she makes it look like the most stylish thing in the world. She has delicate features and, thank God, doesn't really look like Brett at all. The only characteristic they share is color of their eyes.

"I'm glad you called me," I tell her again, desperately wanting to add *I've missed your voice, our conversations...you.*

"Sorry about Lauren's comments. I hate people sometimes," she says, staring out the passenger window, pulling the sleeves of her sweatshirt over her hands. I smile when I realize she's wearing a Beautiful Deceit hoodie.

"I'm getting used to it."

Five months of silence with only one brief, very public interaction and still, my attraction to this woman hasn't waned at all.

Chapter 7

Emma

I can't believe I broke down and called his number.

At least he doesn't know the number of texts I've typed out and erased over the last month. Considering that number is easily in the hundreds, I guess one phone call is a victory.

As soon as his deep, sleepy voice picked up, I didn't care how much it would hurt later, I needed him to get me out of that stupid house.

What was I thinking, agreeing to go on a fall break "retreat" with those assholes? As soon as school started, I realized it would be no different than it's been in the past.

When my peers brought the drugs out on this trip, I was officially over trying to fit in, and I just wanted to get the hell out. Even though I didn't do any of them, my parents would be so disappointed if they knew I was hanging out with people who did.

Needing to think about something else, I try to calm my heart rate, reminding myself I'm in a safe place. Aiden freaked me out because he was unpredictable but he never touched me.

High and horny, he still understood my no meant *no*, even if he was trying hard to persuade me to make it a *yes*.

"Nice car." I blame the lack of a stellar conversation topic on the fact that it's approaching three-thirty in the morning and I'm back in Ryan's orbit after a painful hiatus.

"Thanks," he says, not elaborating.

"I mean, is it new?" I try again as I rub my hand over the soft leather console between us still processing that he came when I needed him and that we're alone now ... in the dark ... and no one knows we're together.

I wish I could turn my brain off or at least turn down a different mental road, but his scent is everywhere, enveloping me, wrapping me in an embrace I should fight to get out of but find myself crawling deeper inside of instead. After the incident with the reporter – the same one that made me hate crowds - I was afraid I was damaged. Maybe part of me is. It's impossible to know because I'm unsure if my previous boyfriends were just inexperienced themselves, or if I made them gun-shy because I was so hesitant.

Either way, I feel none of that hesitancy now. Not while I'm alone with Ryan. I feel nothing but warm, safe, and extremely turned on. It's terrifying to know that he might be the only person that does it for me and he's not interested.

"Uh, yeah," he rasps before clearing his throat. The roughness of his voice makes my breath hitch. "A gift to myself after the success of the tours."

It's painful to look at him so I try to focus my attention on the interior features of the car, but as it turns out, it's even more painful *not* to look at him. I try distracting myself with the soft glow of dashboard lights, the thousand buttons and knobs below the touch screen panel ... anything other than his sharp jawline and the five o'clock shadow that I'd swear was tattooed on his face if I didn't know better.

"A little conspicuous, don't you think?" I ask casually, making an attempt at teasing him to lighten the tension, both in the car and in my chest.

The lopsided smile I'm rewarded with threatens to melt the ice around my heart. His eyes briefly cut to mine before returning to the road, causing my muscles to grow warm and heavy. I reach forward to adjust the temperature settings on my side of the SUV.

"Maybe," he admits. "But Noah drives the most mundane car in the world and he still gets spotted and tailed."

This makes me laugh. "God, he's *still* driving the Toyota?"

"Says it's a classic."

"Classic my ass. It's just *old.*"

"I'll let *you* convince him of that," Ryan says, knowing it's a lost cause.

This banter feels almost in the realm of normal. Is it possible Ryan and I could find our way back to neutral ground? It would be better than where we are now, but still not where I want to end up with him.

The thought sends a torrent of images into my brain and my fingers itch with the desire to paint them: a bird with its wings spread, a flower with its petals unfurling after winter, a heart beating for the first time.

I swallow hard, forcing the images – and their meaning - away. When I start painting again, it can't be because of Ryan. Otherwise, I'll have to burn every canvas I touch. Besides, I have a thousand papers to write, a debate to prepare, and a PowerPoint presentation on our judicial system to put together. I don't have time to think about painting.

"How's the new album coming along?" I try my hand at more small talk.

He sighs. "Like shit." His honesty catches me off guard.

"It's proving to be a bitch to write. The expectation surrounding it is choking us."

This isn't small talk. He's stressed.

Immediately, my concern kicks into overdrive.

"When's your deadline?" I ask, curiosity getting the best of me as his car's headlights continue swallowing up the darkness on the highway, a soft hum of something playing through the speakers in the background.

"We still have a few months, but honestly, we only have three songs done to our satisfaction. Three more are started but we're struggling to clean them up, and we need another two or three that we haven't even written yet. I don't know what the label's going to do if we don't have them done on time."

It's dangerous, allowing myself to feel his emotions like this, but I really don't know any other way to be with him.

"It'll come. I know it's hard, but try not to force it. Maybe take some time to get re-inspired, you know? Take a walk, visit a museum, listen to a new band," I suggest.

He turns his head to look at me in the darkness. Although the glance is brief, I always feel that when Ryan looks at me, he *sees* me instead of just noticing I'm present.

"Yeah, I will. That's sound advice, Em. Thanks."

If only I could follow it myself.

The deep baritone of Ryan's voice cranks up my internal temperature another few degrees so I shed my hoodie and smile a little when I see Ryan following my movements in his peripheral vision.

"So, uh, how's Harvard?" he asks, changing the subject and clearing his throat again alerting me to the fact he knows I caught him perusing my body. "Besides the shitstorm I just picked you up from, I mean."

I debate giving him my standard answer but knowing he

was honest about the album, I change my mind, and divulge the truth.

"Well, my classmates hate me because I understand the material and they don't but instead of asking me for help, they just ostracize me. So basically, it's school as usual."

I hear his teeth snap together before he pushes out another question. "Still glad you chose law?" he asks, keeping his eyes on the road this time.

"Do you really want to hear all this? Because I don't mind the silence."

"*Talk.*"

I roll my eyes. "I'd forgotten how bossy you can be."

"You have no idea."

I let out a sigh and burrow deeper in my seat as I absent-mindedly play with my fingers. "I don't know how I feel about law anymore."

Once I'd gotten to graduate school – and cut myself off from Ryan – everything seemed a little duller. I lost the enthusiasm I'd once had for my chosen career and began to examine the *why* behind the choice in the first place. Notoriety, the ability to make a difference, and good compensation were all on the *obvious* list, however, a different list contained the harsher truth.

It was just another expectation. Albeit, one I put on myself, but an expectation nonetheless.

"What's going on, Em?"

I shove down the desire to unload my baggage. Undoubtedly, he'd know exactly what to say, and what advice to give, but that would mean opening myself back up to him and I'm already walking a fine line after hearing about his own stressors.

I shake my head and change the subject.

"It's nothing. You uh, didn't tell me what kind of car this

is." I absolutely hate the awkwardness pooling between us right now.

Shifting in my seat, I allow myself a minute to take him in. What's the saying? *In for a penny, in for a pound.* I'm already in the damn car. I might as well soak it up. Besides, Ryan has the most glorious profile. A perfectly straight nose – that currently has a cut across the bridge. A jawline so sharp it's like he keeps his teeth clenched all day. And his lips ... sensuous, smooth lips that make it impossible not to think about how they'd feel trailing across my skin.

"You didn't ask," he says, pulling me back to the present. "And don't think I didn't notice the subject change."

His voice is as tight as his knuckles on the steering wheel, but he allows the subject change to stand without any further harassment.

"What kind of car is this, *Ryan?*" I ask, sure to clearly annunciate every word in the sentence including his name, ignoring his last sentence.

"It's an Aston Martin, *Emma*," he answers with another panty-melting chuckle.

"*Whoa.*" I didn't see the emblem back at the house because it was dark out, but still, I wasn't expecting *that.* His breathy laugh damn near undoes me, and I open my stupid, horny mouth again. "This is the kind of car I could lose my virginity in."

He swerves over the line slightly as he enters into a coughing fit.

"Jesus, Em."

Sometimes I'm oblivious as to why the stuff that leaves my mouth, shouldn't. Even a genius-level I.Q. doesn't protect me from saying stupid shit.

"My bad," I shrug, getting high off the new car smell mixed

with scent of a storm on the horizon, which is so perfectly Ryan. "It just came out."

Do I wish I had some kind of sexy super power of seduction that would make Ryan give in to me? Of course. But alas, I do not. Brett got all the swagger in our family, leaving me awkward and prone to stumble over my words.

Not knowing what else to say, we go back to driving and riding in silence. Ryan's left hand is on the steering wheel, his right is resting on the center console. The veins in the back of his hands connect to the map in his forearms, causing my eyes to following the raised flesh until I lose the trail at the sleeve of his shirt. I might've tried not to stare but as soon as he shed his own hoodie after backing out of the driveway, all bets were off. It'd be like trying to stay oblivious to a tank steamrolling across the front yard in a suburban neighborhood.

Im-fucking-possible.

I'd give anything to know what he's thinking. He looks so calm right now, reclined slightly in his seat, his fingers finally having loosened their grip on the wheel. Still in control like always. My presence affecting him far less than his is affecting me.

Of course, I had to fall in love with a man who never lets go.

Then again, we're both so rigid with our lives, drowning in the expectations put on us, perhaps we wouldn't stand a chance anyway.

When we pull up to my parent's house, Ryan cuts the engine and the lights, and moves to grab my stuff out of the back like a gentleman as I quietly close my door.

"I'm really sorry about this," I tell him again. I know his days are busy. Well, I *assume* his days are busy since he has the same days as Brett.

"You can always call me, Em. I mean it. Day or night." I

can't help but notice he's staring at my mouth as he speaks, the timbre of his voice sending a flutter to my stomach.

I give a small head nod and hesitantly step forward into his space, not sure how to say goodbye.

Mostly because I don't want to.

"I'm just going to give you a hug for coming to my rescue." I warn him awkwardly, feeling stupid. I don't want him to get the wrong idea. He's told me *no* and I feel the need to confirm that I heard him even though my traitorous thoughts sent me spiraling on the intimate ride here.

I raise my arms to put them around his neck and inhale as deeply and quietly as I can, savoring the few seconds I get to hold on to him before I have to let go. I work hard to banish the thoughts of some other woman getting to hold him like this someday, and my lungs threaten to collapse, as a tortured exhale rips through me.

Until *his* arms wrap around *me*, pulling me against him, and he buries his nose in my hair.

He feels incredible. Just like he always has. Solid. Steady. Anchoring. Instead of another quiet exhale, a very audible whimper chokes its way out of me before I can stop it as my body presses closer involuntarily. Standing on my toes, like I am now, our groins are flush against each other and it's a sensation I'll never forget.

"Emma," Ryan growls low in warning, causing my flesh to erupt with goosebumps.

"I know," I grumble, starting to let go. I've made him uncomfortable again, damn it.

"No. I don't think you do," he says gruffly, letting me take a step back, but not removing his hands from my waist. His fingers are splayed across my sides but his thumbs are on my stomach like he's about to lift me up.

Taking advantage of his proximity and the fact that he's still touching me, I mirror his hand placement and grab the sides of his t-shirt. The muscles underneath contract at my touch, making me lose my breath all over again. I'm still in just my tank top but despite the cool, early October temps, I'm sweating.

I swallow hard. "Then help me understand." My voice is a plea and I'm dangerously close to begging.

"Just because I can't act on it, doesn't mean I don't find you attractive, Emma."

Based on that statement, it's clear *he's* the one who doesn't understand.

"Trust me, I'm flattered, *but being attracted to me and wanting something romantically, are two different things,* remember?" I throw his harsh words from Ireland back in his face, letting my hands fall from his sides. He may not remember what he said verbatim, but I sure as hell do. "Now, if you'll excuse me, I'm going inside. I think I've embarrassed myself enough for this lifetime."

"*Goddamn* it, Emma," he mutters angrily in the dark.

Before I can process why he's so angry, he pulls me back to him, cups my face with one of his massive, perfect hands, and hovers his lips just above mine. I can barely hear him over the heartbeat in my ears.

"Just this once. And if you value my life at all, never breathe a word of this to your brother," he whispers right before his lips crash into mine.

The light of a thousand stars erupts behind my eyelids.

My strangled moans rush out against his mouth. He's a shot of pure adrenaline and I start climbing him like a tree, desperate to get closer, wanting to imprint this moment on every cell in my body.

My beautiful, selfless, control freak has finally snapped. For *me.* I think I've died and gone to heaven.

His hand slides from my cheek to the back of my head, holding me to him. His tongue moves slowly as if he plans to tease my soul out through my lips. I open hungrily for him. His kiss is dominant, powerful, demanding, and *so fucking hot.* I lower my hand to his belt, desperate for more. For everything. For all of him. I don't recognize my own boldness but I can't stop myself.

The stubble on his face scratches my skin in the most delicious way, reminding me that he is indeed a *man.* The desire to feel it on the insides of my thighs is strong and immediately pulls another groan from me.

He pushes his hips forward at the same time he grabs my wrist to still my hand. God, he can wrap his fingers all the way around every part of my body so easily. I bet he could hold both wrists in one palm and stretch them over my head as he moves inside me.

"*Fuck*," he growls, pulling away, his eyes searching mine. Shaking his head and breathing hard, he says, "That's enough." Disappointment knocks on my heart, but it quickly flees when Ryan brings his lips back to mine before dipping his head and dragging his tongue along my neck. I reach under his shirt needing to feel his skin when he pulls back, his eyes still closed. "Shit. I've got to get it together. I shouldn't have done that."

"Will you shut up? I've wanted you to do that for as long as I can remember," I tell him, begging him to not ruin what has just become the best night of my life, but already, I feel him retreating.

"Em," he starts, and I can tell by the tone of his voice he regrets kissing me.

I sigh heavily. "Just go, Ryan. Thanks for the ride." I bend down to pick my bag up from where he dropped it on the driveway while swiping at the tears beginning to fall.

"Emma, stop."

I should keep moving, but there's something in my DNA that prevents me from doing anything other than what Ryan tells me to do.

I stand up straight but keep my back to him because I can't stop the tears, and I'm pretty sure if I see the pity in his eyes, I'm going to die from embarrassment right here on my parents' driveway.

Calling me out like always, Ryan says, "Em, look at me."

Fuck my goddamn inability to disobey this man.

I bite my tongue as I turn around and look up, blinking rapidly in an attempt to keep the unshed tears at bay even though their siblings are already trailing down my cheeks. He wipes the tears away and smooths the hair back from my face.

"This can't happen, Em. Your brother's still fighting for sobriety and if you think this won't send him back over the edge, you're wrong. If he finds out I have feelings for you, he'll kill me, and everything the guys and I have worked so hard for goes up in smoke. I hate that he's so overprotective, but losing your sister really fucked him up. Not to mention, you hate the spotlight, bab--" he clears his throat before continuing, "Em, and dating me would put you right in the middle of it."

His words warm my heart and chill my blood at the same time because he's right. About all of it. But I choose to focus on the most important part.

"What do you mean you have *feelings* for me?"

"Christ, Em. You need me to say it in a different language?"

"Since *when?*" I demand, starting to get upset that he's kept this from me. "You let me think this was one sided even after I put myself out there, Ryan. I thought I'd gone crazy, wanting you so badly that I'd started making things up when I thought you were flirting back."

"I know. And I'm so fucking sorry." He scrubs a hand across his cheek as his eyes bounce back and forth between my own. "Em, you had barely turned eighteen. I was twenty-eight fucking years old. A grown ass man. What was I supposed to do? Tell my best friend I wanted to take his barely legal sister out for dinner even though I was old enough to have a wife and three kids by then? Fuck, he'd sever my balls from by body if he knew half the shit I've thought about you."

I jerk back like he pushed me. "You've felt this way for two *years?*" The astonishment in my voice is loud and clear. I know I just keep repeating his words but I'm in shock and seem to have lost the ability to create new thoughts of my own.

"You're killing me, Em. The point is, we can't do this," he says, avoiding my question. "There's too much at stake. For both of us."

I want to scream. I want to rail at him with my fists. I want to breakdown and hide or eat two pints of ice cream curled up on Jennifer's couch while having a good cry. Instead, I heave a sigh and slowly acknowledge the position he's in. As much as it hurts, I don't push him further. I think of it as a way for me to give back to Ryan. To help shoulder the burden of self-sacrifice he always seems to bear.

"I understand."

I *do* understand Ryan's loyalty to my brother. I also understand the band is his job, his livelihood, his passion, and I can't ask him to choose between me and his dreams. I also appreciate him wanting to keep me away from the media, even if he doesn't know exactly why I keep my distance. But I wish the sacrifice didn't make him look so miserable.

I just got the best news of my life and it feels like I've been smacked in the gut by a wrecking ball.

Chapter 8

Ryan

"**W**hat the fuck have I done?"

I chastise myself out loud the whole ride home. Brett's parents only live half an hour from us so I don't have that long to process the morning's events before I'm pulling back in our garage, exhausted from the adrenaline finally ebbing out of my system, leaving my nerves frazzled and raw.

Guilt has consumed what little energy remained.

I can't *believe* I let myself get out of control with her. I just ripped that band-aid right off and pulled her against me like I have no fucking sense.

I suppose I've just proven that I don't, but damn she felt so good. All the tension that had settled in my stomach from the drive melted away the second she was pressed against me.

It's only five fifteen in the morning, but Noah's up already. I saw the kitchen light as I turned in, surprised he got out of bed with Sienna still in it. They're having renovations done to the house they bought so they're staying in Noah's old bedroom for now. Weirdly, they both seem perfectly content living with the rest of us asshats, and I'll miss them when they're gone.

I give my head a shake and go in the house from the garage. At least if someone's going to catch me creeping back in, I'm glad it's Kinky.

"Where are you coming from? It's five in the morning." He doesn't bother looking up from the screen where I recognize several bars of scrolling music. When I don't answer right away, he turns to look at me, the tattoos snaking up his neck become distorted with the motion.

"Uh, yeah, just had to run out really quick." I leave my answer short because it won't take him long to figure out the reason I left in the wee hours of the night. Sinking into the chair next to him at the kitchen table, I drop my head into my hands.

Fuck it. Part of me needs to talk about it anyway.

Noah's known about my attraction to Ems for a while. He and I spend a lot of time together and overall, our personalities are more similar to each other than they are to Brett's or Sloan's, allowing us to quietly discuss the things that trouble us without fear of it slipping out when Brett's had too much to drink or resurfacing as a joke Sloan tells, because everything is a joke to Sloan.

Noah lays his pen down on the pad of paper sitting between him and the laptop, giving me his undivided attention. "At this hour? Based on the look on your face, I'm going out on a limb here and assuming this has something to do with a certain young, off-limits, sister of our drummer?"

"Yep." I pop the "p" for emphasis.

"You gonna make me ask a hundred questions or are you just going to start talking?" he asks, crossing his arms in front of his chest as he leans back in his chair. There are a couple pairs of headphones on the table which means Sienna must have recorded something for us on Noah's violin and he's writing down the notes for Sloan and I to play off of later.

"It's bad, man." I pause and take a deep breath before revealing how shitty I am. "I lost it, and I fucking kissed her." I'm whispering even though no one else will be awake for hours. It seems dangerous to even say the words with Brett in the house.

I appreciate that Noah's first question is, "How?" And not *what the fuck were you thinking you goddamn moron?* "Isn't she in Massachusetts?"

I launch into the story of her fall break trip that turned dangerous. Noah's known her almost as long as I have so he's familiar with her constantly being pulled between the overly responsible intellectual and the lonely young woman who wants to fit in.

"I got there and some coked-out, frat-boy-wannabe had her trapped against a dresser. I was about three seconds from breaking his fucking teeth. Then it was just me and her on the ride back and she took her sweatshirt off and I almost veered off the damn road. I *did* veer off the road when she told me she's still a virgin. I swear it took everything in me not to threaten her that it better fucking stay that way." I feel the weight lift from my shoulders talking to Noah like this, so I keep going. "She hugged me to thank me for picking her up and then she was pressed against me and before I knew what I was doing, I was licking her goddamned tonsils. When she got her hands under my shirt, I almost fucked her like an animal in the backseat. It's a miracle I didn't when she reached for my belt."

Noah's snorted laugh pisses me off. "Doesn't sound like she'd mind."

"This isn't funny, Kink. What the fuck am I gonna do?"

He uncrosses his arms and leans forward, planing his elbows on the table. "You're going to keep working us to the bone. Focus on making music and help me fulfill all these requests for livestreams, interviews, new merchandise, and somewhere in there, find time to work on the new album."

"Yeah." Somehow none of that seems to matter as much knowing I just broke the seal on my non-relationship with a girl I've desperately been trying *not* to think of for far too long.

"Was it good?" Noah asks with a smirk on his boyishly handsome face.

"Best fucking kiss I've ever had in my life, man. I'll still be thinking about it fifty years from now."

Noah scratches the back of his head. "Maybe if you talked to him—"

I interrupt before the thought can take hold. Talking to Brett about this isn't an option and I don't want the false hope.

"We both know he'd never be cool with it. He'd feel betrayed by both her *and* me. Things would be tense. The music would suffer. We fucking live together, Kink. How am I supposed to bring *that* woman back to my place when her brother has his ear pressed to my door?"

"So, get your own place," Noah suggests rationally.

In reality, I'm long overdue for a place of my own, but living with the guys has just been what we've always done. Until Noah found Sienna, and Brett basically made Bri move in so she'd never be out of his sight, us living together just made sense. Especially since we just had two back-to-back tours and were gone for months at a time. Leaving four separate properties vacant that long just seems wasteful.

Now, everything's moving so fast and I'm reeling from that kiss too much to process possibilities and major life changes, so instead, I grab one of the pairs of headphones from the table and begin listening to the new song, trying to get lost in the music I live for.

Three hours later, Brett comes downstairs and my guts

clench so fucking hard I think I might lose the eight cups of coffee I've consumed since I got home. I was sorely tempted to throw some scotch in it, but we cleaned the house out in an effort to not tempt Brett.

It would appear he's inadvertently, and unknowingly, screwing me over twice this morning.

"What are you guys working on?" he asks, rubbing a hand down his tatted chest as he pours a cup from the recently refilled, still-warm coffee pot.

"Sienna got a new track down yesterday. I want everyone to listen to it today and tell me what you think. Ry and I have an interview we need to leave for in about thirty minutes, but I think he's gotten a decent bass line down already." Noah answers, nodding in my direction which causes Brett to turn his attention to me.

"Whoa, you look like shit, Ry."

"Yeah, just didn't get much sleep." I avoid his eyes.

"You know what helps with that? Getting laid. You should try it sometime. Hell, as much as you avoid women, you'd think it was *you* that got blackmailed last year." I feel the color drain from my face as my stomach flips again. It only gets worse when he continues, casually coming to take a seat at the table next to me. "I woke up to a text from my mom. She said my sister came home for fall break and was thinking we could all go over there for dinner tonight. You guys in?"

"Yeah, sounds good," Noah answers as if our conversation never happened. "Is Sienna invited?"

"Of course, dipshit. What kind of monster do you think my mother is?" he teases our lead singer. "Bri's coming too. Just take it easy on the PDA in front of Ems. You know she has the hots for you," Brett says, picking up Noah's discarded headphones.

Once he puts them on and is bobbing his head to the music

being piped through them, Noah says loudly enough for me to hear, "No, Brett, I'm certain she does not."

I muddle my way through the podcast as best I can. Usually, I field the more personal questions for Noah since he's completely averse to sharing his personal life with the public and while I don't love it, I'm fairly used to it since my brothers and I have endured countless interviews during my father's campaigning seasons. However, I have last night's kiss on repeat in my head and Noah has to draw me back in multiple times.

"It seems our roles are reversing," he says, mocking me, as we exit the studio. "Have you talked to her since you dropped her off?"

"No. What would I even say? I tried to text Brett and tell him I wasn't feeling great and needed to bail tonight but the little fucker gave me a guilt trip about how I'm his mom's favorite and she'll be so disappointed if I don't show up."

I've been a staple in the Donovan house since I was fifteen.

Turning even more serious, Noah says, "You should just talk to him. You haven't done anything wrong, Ry. You came to her rescue last night. I think he'd appreciate that. You've been there for her a lot over the past couple of years."

"But that's just it. I thought it would only be once or twice that she'd call, needing help with poli sci class, or maybe needing me for my connections for internships or something, but up until a few months ago, we talked almost *every day,* sometimes multiple times in the same day, for over a year, Kink. How do I explain that without him seeing it for exactly what it is?" My anguish runs so deep it rivals the Grand Canyon.

"It's only going to get harder the longer you wait."

"You say that like she and I could ever be a thing and I'll eventually have to tell him," I argue.

"Your only other option is to move on and shut this down completely. Based on the kiss you shared this morning how long do you think that'll last?"

His words follow me all the way to dinner.

At a quarter 'til six, everyone piles in my car because it's the only one that will fit the four of us comfortably. Bri and Sienna are planning to meet us at Brett's parents' because they're coming from the aerial studio where they train.

My button down is straining against my chest, making me a little self-conscious. It seems the increased workouts at the gym and more consistent training have added an inch to my upper body. Without a better option to change into and no time to get something new, I left it in place even though I already stand out like a sore thumb when we dress up. I'm the only one with no tattoos peppering my skin, making me feel a little out of place with my bandmates who give off more "hipster rockstar" vibes, to my "GQ" ones – Sloan's words, not mine, even if they do ring true.

The guys joke that perhaps I'm still destined to become a politician like my father.

I'm so consumed with my own thoughts of what the hell I'm supposed to say to Emma that I miss the fact the guys are giving me their usual shit until I hear Brett's voice at the same time Noah lightly punches my shoulder from the seat behind me.

"Earth to Senator Battle."

"*Fuck off.*" I bite back. My dad is as good as they come. Especially for a politician. He somehow still has a heart for the people of Maryland, but nonetheless, the joke is old. I already give enough of myself to those around me, I couldn't stomach being a politician, a pastor, or a police officer. Always on call. Always needed when shit hits the fan. I already play that role and I don't love it.

"What crawled up your ass?" Brett says in a tone telling me I actually pissed him off a little.

"Nothing. Sorry, man. I told you, I'm exhausted. I guess it's making my fuse shorter than usual," I lie.

Thankfully he buys it, making me feel like a total bastard. I can't believe I'm keeping this from him. I need to come clean before the guilt eats a hole through my stomach or he finds out some other way and then lights me on fire. I need to do it before there's more to tell and it becomes an even bigger deal than it already is.

For the rest of the ride, I try to engage but it feels forced so I let myself fade into the background again.

When I pull into the Donovan's driveway, I'm so nauseated I'm pretty sure I'm going to throw up in the bushes. A part of me is terrified the universe captured an image of Em and I in the driveway and our imprint will still be here in dust particles for everyone to see.

Thankfully, there's no such image as I park, but the anxiety over getting caught triples as I stare at the house.

Once Brett and Sloan hop out of the car, leaving Noah and I alone, Noah says, "Look man. I know you don't want to hurt either of them, but one of them is going to be pissed no matter what, so if you're really into Em and she feels the same, you need to think about being honest with Brett."

Those words are so easy for him to say. His nuts aren't on the line.

"I appreciate that, Kink. But I have to think about the band. There's a major chance we would never recover from this once. And once it's out, I can't take it back."

"All you do is think about others, Ry. Maybe it's time to think about yourself for once. Sienna and I are moving out soon. Brett and Bri probably aren't that far behind. You can't spend your thirties babysitting Sloan between tours. Just think about it."

Before I can tell him *all I do is think about it,* a fist beats on my window, stealing our attention.

"Could you two put your dicks away and get out already?" Sloan yells through my closed window, his curly hair bouncing across one eye as he shakes his head. "I'm starving."

"Someone's gonna have to look after him," I tell Noah.

Sloan is a bit of a wild card and even after living with him for almost six years, making music with him, and touring the world with him, I still don't feel like I really know him that well. He does a brilliant job of hiding behind a mask of jokes and nonchalance but his music is deep, giving away the fact there's more to him than he lets us see.

Opening my car door, I hear her before I see her and I look up immediately, my eyes following the sound.

Emma flings herself out of the front door and into Brett's arms before letting go and making her way to Noah. I'm trying not to follow her every move, but it's pointless. I'm hyperaware of where she is, of the short hunter green sweater dress and brown boots she's wearing, and of the way her dark red hair hangs in waves halfway down her back. Sienna's hair is also red, but far more copper to Emma's russet locks. Everything about the darkness of the color is sultry and enticing. Between that, and her green eyes, her Irish heritage shines through pretty strongly.

She's a fucking vision.

When she gets to Noah, she hams it up for Brett's benefit, jumping in Noah's arms, kissing him on the cheek and cupping his face in her hands as he twirls her around.

She's never once looked at Noah with hearts in her eyes ... never once looked at him the way she looks at me.

"Missed you, Ems," he says, returning her kiss with a loud one of his own on her cheek. Immediately, I'm jealous of how easy it is for him to be around her.

"Watch it," Brett grumbles.

Laughing, Noah sets Emma on the ground and says, "Will you relax, Brett? Would it really be so bad if one of us swept Emmie off her feet?" Noah tousles her hair in a brotherly way before moving to the side so she can continue greeting the rest of us.

I know what he's doing.

He's testing the waters, trying to give me an opening, but instead, he's just making it even more likely that I'll start dry-heaving any second.

Two years ago, when Emma turned eighteen, every thought I'd tucked away, pretended not to have, and did my best to ignore, floated right to the surface. Emma's been a knockout her whole life. Even as a kid, people would constantly comment on her skin, her hair, her eyes, her smile. When she turned eighteen though, it was like she finally started to believe the hype about herself. Her self-confidence finally began to blossom and she entered into adulthood as the most radiant woman I've ever laid eyes on.

"I'm only going to allow you to live because I know you're a fool for Sienna, but do not *ever* suggest that one of you date my sister again," Brett says. His tone would indicate that he's about to have an aneurysm. "I know what dating couples do and I don't want your slimy cocks anywhere near my sister."

"Oh my God, *Brett!*" Emma shrieks. "You don't get to make that call and stop thinking about my sex life!"

"I've told you before ... you'd better not *have* a sex life," he growls, plucking the words straight from my thoughts.

"Ugh. Just go inside and see Mom already, will you, you perv?" Emma moves to Sloan, giving him a hug and says hello.

Knowing I'm up next, Noah, pats Brett on the shoulder and leads him in the house, motioning for Sloan to follow, trying to give Em and I a minute alone.

Chapter 9

Emma

W ell, this is awkward.

I figured I'd be able to get away with giving Ryan a quick hug like I did with Sloan, but now it's just Ryan and I and I don't know what he expects .... or wants.

Trying not to notice the way his black button-down is straining across his chest ensures my attention is repeatedly brought back to him. The t-shirt he was wearing when he picked me up couldn't hide it all, but this shirt hides *nothing*. I know he can feel my stare because he tugs at his collar trying to loosen the fabric like it's strangling him.

I ran out of the house and threw myself at my brother as soon as they'd arrived. It's what I've always done and if I don't want to raise questions, then I must play the role I always have.

Doting little sister and forever Beautiful Deceit's number one fan, specifically *Noah's* number one fan.

Standing a safe distance apart, I take a deep breath, plaster on the king of tight, fake smiles and offer the best greeting I can muster. If I could paint my feelings right now, it would show a dam just before a cliff. A small amount of water trickling through but just upstream, a raging current is barreling toward the dam, ready to overpower it and plummet to the dried ground below, destroying everything in its path. The water obviously representing my emotions and the dam, my pathetic attempt to hold them back.

"Hey. Glad you guys could make it. Mom's been cooking all day." Self-consciously, I pull at the hem of my dress, willing it to magically grow another two inches. I don't know what I was thinking when I put this on.

Ryan just nods.

Okay then.

Not knowing what else to say, I decide the interaction has run its course and I turn to go inside but I don't make it far before I hear another car pull up.

I never thought I'd be a huge fan of the guys' girlfriends – because maybe my brother isn't the only protective one - but so far, Noah and Brett have found women I genuinely like. Sienna is quiet and polite but she's easy to hang around and has a good sense of humor. She and Noah are a lot alike and I couldn't picture anyone better for him.

Bri is an absolute trip and her loud personality is growing on my parents. After she saved my brother's life - and he, hers - it's hard not to love her. It takes a strong partner to handle Brett's bullshit and she's proven she's not only up for the task, she seems to revel in it. If they ever decide to get married one day, she'll make a great sister-in-law. Plus, I'll have a lot of fun watching my Irish Catholic father parade around his Protestant daughter-in-law. I'll start a pool on how many times he makes the sign of the cross when Bri opens her mouth.

I doubt I'll be as welcoming to whoever Ryan brings around. When he starts seeing someone, my time fawning over Beautiful Deceit will officially be over.

"Excuse me." I step around Ryan and head for the girls.

Sienna's out of the car first, wrapping me in a sincere hug, the belt of her camel-colored wool trench coat digging into my stomach.

"Emma, it's so good to see you! I want to hear all about Harvard," she gushes before looking behind me. Her smile instantly widens, telling me Noah must have just sensed her presence and come back outside. The pull between those two is on a whole different level. "Let's catch up during dinner, okay?" She gives me a final squeeze and rushes to her fiancé's side as Bri swings around the car and engulfs me with both arms even though my heels are three inches to her two and I tower over her petite frame.

"Ems! Girl, that dress is *killer!* What's it like to have legs for days? God, you get prettier every time I see you," she laughs, fluffing my waves, and finally pulling back. She swats me on the butt and grabs my hand. "You *have* to come out with us while you're home!"

I can't suppress my laugh at her enthusiasm. Bri makes me feel included, like part of their gang and not like some tag-along they're required to entertain. But then I remind her, "I'm not twenty-one yet, Bri. I still can't get into a lot of places."

She leans her shoulder into me. "Remember Ireland? When you're with the band, no one will check your I.D., babe."

I guess in an effort to protect myself, my brain blocked out the memory of dancing with Ryan at the Irish club. It was the night everything changed for Brett and the whole evening is stressful to recall. Besides, except that once, I've never really used my brother's fame for any gain of my own.

Suddenly, I hear Ryan's voice directly behind me. I'd tried to forget he was back there despite my tachycardic heart rate.

"There's no way Brett's going to let you take her clubbing again, Bri. Hell, he probably won't even let *you* go."

It's true. After Bri's health scare, Brett's gone almost as overboard with trying to protect her as he did with me after losing Penelope.

Bri stops us dead in our tracks, the small buckles on her black leather jacket jingling in the cold air, as she gives him a smile dripping with sarcasm. "Aw, that's cute, Ry, but Brett doesn't *let* me do anything. Besides, we'll all be there. What better way to break her into adulthood than with us? And I wasn't talking about a club. I meant she should come to the preseason hockey game the label got you guys tickets to. The girl's allowed out of the house, right?"

Turning her attention back to me, she leans in and whispers, "My clubbing days are over anyway. I try to keep Brett out of those places as much as I can."

I appreciate that more than she knows.

I wasn't surprised to learn my brother had an issue with alcohol. Our genes sort of set us up for failure there if we aren't careful ... and Brett certainly wasn't careful.

Turning back to the house, Bri pulls me up the sidewalk and through the front door after her. Brett snags her by the waist as we come into the kitchen, pulling her down onto his lap. I watch as my brother curls protectively around her even though they're in our parent's home and she's in absolutely no danger. He breathes in her blonde hair which is up in a stylish ponytail like usual. Underneath her jacket, she's wearing a cute, pale pink, V-neck sweater, and a black pencil skirt, and she looks absolutely adorable. If she ever wants to stop dancing, Bri could make a serious go in the world of fashion.

"Oh, would you just look at you two," my mother coos over Brett and Bri quickly before moving on to her favorite child. Not seeing him anywhere, she frowns. "Where's Ryan?"

"In here, Mrs. Donovan," Ryan's deep voice calls from the living room where he presumably got stopped by my father to discuss the Tornadoes hockey team. Despite having three children of their own, my parents have never kept their fondness for Ryan a secret.

"Mom, what are the rest of us? Chopped liver?" Brett asks, feigning offense, as we settle into the outdated kitchen. The walls are still adorned with wallpaper reminiscent of an earlier time but I hope my parents never change it. The pale-yellow daisies are nostalgic for me and remind me of when our family was whole. "I never could compete with *Saint Ryan*," Brett teases, reaching around Bri for the water my mom placed on the table in front of him.

"Of course you're not chopped liver, honey. We love all our kids equally," Mom teases as if they've adopted everyone in this house.

"Mrs. D!" Sloan yells happily, coming into the kitchen, wrapping my mom in a tight hug. "You're looking mighty fine in that paisley apron. I don't know how Mr. D. isn't in here trying to butter you up right now."

"Sloan, stay the hell away from my wife." My dad laughs from the living room, fully knowing that my mom eats this shit up and that Sloan poses no threat – from what I've read, he's been banging a different model or actress every night for the past three months.

Sloan knocks a knuckle lightly to my chin and takes a seat at the table. "How's it going, kid?"

I bristle at the nickname.

"I'm twenty, Sloan. Hardly a kid anymore." I try to keep my voice even, but I'm not sure it works.

Sloan looks me up and down, pausing at my exposed thigh, and licks his lips. "Yeah, I guess you're right."

He's fucking with Brett again and it works so easily.

"Alexander, if you enjoy the gift of sight, I'd pull those eyeballs off my sister's legs real fast."

"Ooo, the last name. He must be serious," Sloan guffaws, wagging his eyebrows at me and popping a handful of nuts from the bowl on the table into his mouth.

Thankfully, at that moment, Noah and Sienna walk in, having finally gotten away from my father and greet my mother.

"Can I help you set the table?" Sienna asks immediately.

"That would be lovely."

Bri tries to hop off Brett's lap. "I'll help too!"

I can tell she's flustered because she didn't think to offer first and wants to keep making a good impression.

"I don't think so, Bri, darling," my brother coos, his voice much too low to be considered appropriate for present company. "I like you just fine right here." He tightens his arms around her and my mom blushes.

The guys fall into an easy conversation and I can't help but notice Ryan's still in the living room with my father. If I didn't know better, I'd think he was avoiding me.

Once the table is set, he finally ambles in, not looking at me at all. It's a table for six, but we've added three extra chairs so there are now three seats along each side, plus one on each end, and one thrown awkwardly at the corner. My dad takes his place at the head, my mom, to his right. Brett takes his place on our dad's left, like usual. Of course, Bri is next to him and Sienna next to her, leaving Noah to grab the chair in the corner.

I'm about to sit next to my mom and pray Sloan grabs the open seat next to me, just as my mom says, "Ryan, take the seat next to me, honey. We haven't gotten to say hello yet."

The falter in his step is so slight, I doubt anyone notices.

Anyone other than me, at least.

I've noticed everything. The way his slacks fit like they were perfectly tailored for his long, powerful legs – which they probably were. The way his black button down is tucked into said slacks, showcasing his flat stomach and muscular pecs. The buttons open at the top. He still has his black, fleece jacket on, but it's unzipped and I've caught every detail. Especially, the way the whole outfit would look even better on the floor.

Shit. I'm staring. And quite possibly drooling.

While I'm taking my time scouring Ryan's outfit, Sloan grabs the old, wooden chair next to Noah, at the other head of the table, leaving the chair next to Ryan as my only option.

Great.

I deliberately keep to the far right of my chair, lest my leg brush up against Ryan's, but the thought of his hand sliding up my thigh, unnoticed by anyone here, sends a heatwave violently coursing through me. The resulting shudder finally causes his attention to swing in my direction.

"Are you cold?" he asks immediately. His words remind me of early this morning when he asked me the same thing. *Is he transported back to that moment as well?*

"Um," I stutter, "No, I'm fine."

Noah's voice filters through my ears from the corner of the table. "She isn't fine, she has goosebumps on her arms. Ryan, give her your jacket," he throws out nonchalantly as he pushes his water glass out of the way to make more room for his plate as my mother serves him.

I want to say *I'm good, really.* I'm actually burning up. The goosebumps have nothing to do with being cold, but Ryan's already shrugging out of his fleece.

Oh, fuck me.

The movements pull his dress shirt even tighter across his pecs and I'm concerned the material's limits are really being tested. I halfway expect to hear the rip of a seam any moment. The sleeves strain in protest over his biceps as he pulls the jacket from his arms. The strong column of his neck is now more exposed and a tingle sits low in my stomach.

Ryan stands up to help me get my arms in the sleeves and it feels like everyone is watching even though normal conversation has resumed.

When he sits back down, his chair shifts and he allows his thigh to rest against mine. The scent of him is all around me, making my brain fuzzy. Ryan smells like an expensive, masculine cologne but underneath that, he smells like fresh rain on a summer night.

"Now that everyone is seated, we'll say our prayer," my father instructs. No one else at this table is Catholic, but everyone bows their heads out of respect for my family's religion.

And then my father holds his hands out to his sides, palms up, waiting for Brett and my mother to place their hands in his.

What the hell? We never hold hands during prayer.

Guess I'm the only one that questions it because slowly, everyone follows suit, grabbing ahold of the hand next to them.

When I slip my hand into Ryan's, he squeezes. All the breath leaves my lungs when he drops our hands out of view and rubs his thumb across my skin. *Why is he torturing me?*

When my father finishes, my family makes the sign of the cross and I realize I have absolutely no appetite as I stare at my hand where the ghost of Ryan's fingers continues to burn.

My mom and Ryan talk for a few minutes while everyone digs in and smaller conversations float around the table. Eventually, the topic turns to Noah and Sienna's upcoming wedding, which is good because I can just sit back and work on keeping my breathing even.

"How are the plans coming along?" My mom asks Sienna, who dives into the details of their upcoming nuptials excitedly.

"So great! Everything is pretty much all set. The aquarium is gorgeous and they've been so great to work with, *and* I finally heard back from Joslyn, one of the dancers from the U.S. tour, and she and Kara can both make it." Sienna says with a huge smile on her face.

Keeping quiet most of the conversation, I work on getting my food down without it revisiting us in the near future until Brett turns the conversation to me.

"Are you bringing a date, Ems?" he asks, sounding genuine and not all *touch her and die* for once.

Ryan sputters a cough into his water glass but recovers quickly.

"Uh, I hadn't really thought about it," I answer honestly. "Not sure who I would bring," I add as an afterthought.

As if the guys don't know me well enough, my mother has to embarrass me further. "She has trouble connecting with her peers, you know that, Brett."

Note to self: Never share anything with my mother ever again.

Brett throws me a meaningful glance as Ryan shifts in his seat, the discomfort pouring off him in waves.

"And right now," my mother continues, much to my chagrin, "everyone is intimidated by her and the grad students have been less than welcoming. Hence the reason she's home."

"Is someone giving you shit, Em?" Brett says, now getting riled up.

"*No.* It's fine. Can we just move on, please?" I widen my eyes at my mother who just gives me a slight shrug.

And then, because my parents are working *really hard* to get me killed, my father throws out, "Ryan, I forgot to thank you for picking Emmie up and bringing her home this morning. We saw your car in the driveway on our new security camera and Em explained the trip got a little out of control."

Brett's head snaps up so fast I think he might have cracked a vertebra ... or twelve.

"The *fuck*?" my brother asks, narrowing his eyes at Ryan.

"Brett, watch your mouth at your mother's table," our dad says, but his accented words fall on deaf ears.

I've always respected Brett. Even more so these days after he was open about his struggle with alcohol and is trying to make some changes while still living in the environment bestowed on a rockstar, but to say he can be overbearing is the understatement of the century. I understand the reason behind it, but I wish he would start letting it go. It feels like the opposite has happened recently. He's started to hover again like he did right after it happened.

He pins his icy glare on Ryan. "We're going to talk about this," he says through gritted teeth.

I've had enough.

"For God's sake, Brett. Will you stop? This is why I didn't call you. This response doesn't need to happen for every interaction in my life."

"The question is why *you*," he takes his eyes off of me and looks across the table, pointing his fork at his best friend, "didn't tell me about it this morning."

Before Ryan can answer, I lose the rest of what little patience I have left.

"Because I asked him not to! Because I was trying to avoid *this*. I need to be able to take care of myself Brett, and when I can't, I know enough to call the people who can." A look of hurt flashes across my brother's face. "Look, you've been there a lot for me, but you're dealing with enough sh-*stuff* right now," I correct my foul language mid-sentence in an effort to not anger our father even more.

"Don't you dare throw that in my face as a reason why I can't be there for you, Em. You know I would drop everything if you needed me."

I soften my voice, aware that I've hurt his feelings, and

reach for his hand across the table. "I know you would. And I love you for it. I just don't want you to have to do it."

I want to say more, but I stop myself because really, what would I say? *I didn't want you to go ape shit on the guy pinning me against the dresser?* Ryan did that anyway. *You're too easily recognizable?* Ryan got recognized too. *I need to foster my own independence?* I still had to call for help. *I can't depend on you because you're gone so much?* Ryan's gone just as much as he is.

The truth is, I just wanted it to be Ryan.

That's whose comfort I needed. So that's who I called.

"Okay, that's enough. The point is, Emma felt uncomfortable and she reached out to someone she trusts, someone we *all* trust, who got her home safely," my diplomatic mother says, trying to save dinner.

Brett gives me a meaningful look across the table and I know what he's remembering. I know why he's hurt that I didn't call him.

No matter who enters our lives, Em, no matter what's going on, I'll show up for you every time. I couldn't be there for Pen, and I haven't been there for you. But that changes now. Anytime you're in trouble, you call me. Promise me. Brett's words from that night linger in my mind.

I still crave that sense of protection and belonging, but not from my brother. No, at twenty, I crave it from a partner, a boyfriend, a lover. I've tried my best to move on from that night, and Brett clearly hasn't. He still sees me as the frightened girl I was two years ago.

Brett goes back to glaring at Ryan which is infuriating. The look on his face says he thinks Ryan has somehow taken advantage of me. Like Ryan is the enemy.

Suddenly a light bulb goes off. Brett feels like he's being replaced as my protector... by his best friend. *How could I have been so insensitive?*

I push my chair back from the table and stand. "Brett, can I have a word with you?" I push myself away from the table and walk through the doorway to the living room.

His chair scrapes along the linoleum floor as he stands, following me. I only have a few seconds to figure out what to say and I wish like hell I could just tell him how I feel about Ryan but I can't force Ryan to cross that bridge. He has to be ready. So, for now, I'll keep more secrets. Us Donovan kids really excel at that.

"Look, Em—" Brett starts but I catch him off guard when I throw my arms around his waist in a hug.

"I wasn't trying to hurt your feelings, Brett. And just so you know, you're not being replaced. I'll always need you, just, maybe in a different way than I have in the past."

"How did you—"

"I remember wha you said to me that night." I don't elaborate because I know he knows which night I'm referring to.

Brett wraps his arms around my shoulders, returning my embrace. "Fuck, Em. I hate the thought of you being in trouble and not reaching out to me."

"I know, but I've grown up, Brett. I need some distance, some slack in my leash. All my problems can't be your problems."

"Of course they can. We're family."

I roll my eyes getting frustrated that he's not hearing me. "I'm not shutting you out, I just need you to move further into the brother-*friend* camp and not so much in the brother-*parent* camp."

Brett drops his arms and takes a step back. "Why Ryan?"

"What?" I ask, stalling to buy time.

"Why did you call Ryan?"

My heart is pounding and sweat breaks out on the back of my neck. *Do I tell him? Can he handle it? Can Ryan?* Ultimately, I decide what's the point in upsetting Brett when Ryan's already said no. *Twice.*

"There are so few people I trust in my life, Brett. I knew he'd come get me without giving me a guilt trip." I look at my brother pointedly. "And that he wouldn't expect anything in return for driving me home." Not only is that truth, I feel like I've sold my pitch well ... until Brett opens his mouth.

His brows pinch together and he looks uncomfortable. "I'm just going to throw this out there." Before I can vehemently protest, he holds up his hands. "Just listen to me." He sighs. "If you have feelings for Ryan, you need to let them go, Em. I work with him. Hell, I *live* with him. Yeah, I'm glad you felt comfortable enough to call him and he's a solid dude. But what would happen if it didn't work out? I can't have that kind of tension between my sister and my best friend. What if he fucks up on our next tour and I catch him doing shady shit? Then it's *me* that has to break your heart when I tell you. I can't handle that. Not to mention, Ryan has particular..." he coughs into his hand and lowers his voice, "*tastes* and I don't think, given your past, you'd feel comfortable with the shit he likes."

He winces and I realize I've never seen my brother so uncomfortable. It makes me wonder what exactly Ryan's into.

"First of all, we both know Ryan would never cheat on his girlfriend if that's what you're insinuating. Second of all—"

"So, you do like him?" Brett says accusatorily.

"It's *Ryan*, Brett! Of course, I like him!" I practically shout, realizing my voice has gotten louder and I'm sure the entire kitchen can hear this argument.

"Are you in *love* with him?" he asks, down right angry now.

"I'm not talking to you about this. The point is, I love *you*, but you need to back off and let me live my life regardless of who I'm interested in."

"You've got to be *fucking* kidding me!" he bellows. "He's

thirty-one, Em. He's lived a whole life by now and you're supposed to be a sophomore in college." Those words sting. *Supposed to be.* His real meaning clear: you would be, if you were *normal*. But I'm not, am I? I never have been and that's part of the reason for both the rift between Brett and I, and the closeness I feel to Ryan. Ryan's never made me feel uncomfortable or abnormal. He's always encouraged me to be myself.

"Did you even stop to think that not only is he famous because of the band, he's the son of a fucking senator, Emma." Brett continues his rant, pacing back and forth in front of the couch, running a hand over his long hair. "All the goddamn people in the world and you gotta pick my best fucking friend. You think the media will leave you alone once they catch wind of whatever the fuck is going on between you two?"

"There's nothing going on between us, Brett! And thanks to this bullshit, there never will be!"

"Emma." I hear the exasperation in Brett's voice as I turn my back on my brother and take the stairs two at a time, feeling no relief whatsoever when I slam my bedroom door so hard it rattles the walls.

What hurts the most is that Brett's reaction completely validates Ryan's reasons why he and I don't stand a chance.

Chapter 10

Ryan

"Oh dear. I'll go after her," Holly Donovan says as she starts to stand. We all heard the argument that just ensued. While it's not an open floor plan, there are no doors separating the two rooms, allowing most of Brett and Em's heated words to easily drift to our ears.

The rest of the table is looking at me, waiting for me to either confirm or deny that something is going on, but I say nothing. As Brett sulks back into the kitchen, Noah stands.

"Actually, do you mind if I go, Holly?" Noah asks, causing Brett to stop in his tracks at the head of the table.

"You too?" he asks, swinging his gaze to our lead singer.

Noah levels Brett with a tone that puts himself, undeniably, in charge. Not angry, just strong. In his perfect, unwavering voice, with his hands flat on the table, Noah leans forward to make eye contact with him and asks, "Me too, *what*, Brett? Do I care about your sister? Of course. We all do. And I also care about my best friends, so you two need to clear the air and not put Emma in the middle of this. Go kiss and makeup with

Ryan before you make this anymore awkward than you already have."

I'm feeling a mix of things at this very minute. I'm so damn thankful and proud of Kinky for calling Brett out on his bullshit. I'm embarrassed that Emma's parents know it was me she called and I'm certain if they saw my car, they also saw me shove my tongue down her throat – which, mercifully, they didn't mention. I'm ashamed that Brett found out about her calling me this way, and I'm pissed that he thinks he calls all the shots where Emma is concerned. If I'm brutally honest with myself, I'm also a little hurt that Brett clearly doesn't think I'm good enough for his sister despite me being the one he calls when he needs help, too.

However, being older - and in Brett's opinion, the one who committed the crime - I feel like I should extend the olive branch first.

"Brett, Noah's right. Come talk to me on the back porch." I nod my head toward the back door needing more privacy than what the living room just demonstrated it offers.

When Brett looks like he'd rather not, Bri pulls him down and whispers something in his ear. Reluctantly, he nods once waving his hand in a *you first* gesture.

The porch isn't heated despite it being closed in, and the chill makes the air have that distinct, crisp, October scent to it. For some reason the overhead fan is on and the light breeze penetrates my dress shirt, making me realize Em still has my jacket. I suppress my smile at the thought of her wrapped up in it, hopefully finding comfort from it.

Keeping his voice low, Brett dives right in.

"I'm just going to come right out and ask. Is something going on between you and my sister?"

Now's my chance.

I should tell him the truth. Get it out in the open.

I should spill every sordid detail of our communication over the last two years and the kiss early this morning. But based on his reaction to me riding to her rescue, I'm willing to bet finding out about our kiss would have much more catastrophic results. Besides, it can't, and won't, happen again, so I might as well start getting used to it.

"No. She's called a couple of times wanting help with class stuff and we've talked occasionally, but that's it." The lie rolls off my tongue far too easily but I feel a small amount of relief knowing it's the last one I'll tell.

He rubs his eyes and turns his back to me. "Did you know she has a thing for you?"

Carefully, I reply, "Not until recently." No point in lying about that part.

He huffs out a humorless laugh. "And all this time I thought she had the hots for Noah. I figured it'd be him or our parents she called if she couldn't get a hold of me. But she didn't even try me. She went straight to you." I can hear the hurt in his voice, but it doesn't lessen my ire.

"Would that have somehow been better? It would've been okay if Em had called *Noah* at two in the morning but not me? Is there something about me, personally, you don't like, Brett? I'm not perfect but I sure as shit beat a lot of other options." I should stop and give him a chance to answer because I'm so damn curious, but I'm also on a roll, so I keep going. "And she's *twenty*. Would you have called your mommy and daddy to come get you from a party at twenty? No. You wouldn't even call them to come pick your ass up from senior beach week. If I remember correctly, it was *me* that drove down from college to pick you up from Hilton Head when you were black-out drunk. It's always me." I huff out a laugh and finish my tirade. "I never do anything for myself and I *still* somehow get fucked over." Not entirely true. That kiss was one-hundred-percent for me but the point is, he doesn't even know about it and here I am, still getting fucked.

Brett finally turns around to face me again.

"Yeah, Ry. I know. I just . . . she's so *good*, you know? Wears her heart on her fucking sleeve and I just keep waiting for someone to break her heart. When she got stood up at senior prom, I was ready to burn the world down looking for that bastard. I don't ever want to see her hurt like that again."

I remember that night well.

Holly called Brett. Em called me. She was upset and needed to process her emotions without a lecture. She was attending senior prom at fifteen, not eighteen like most everyone else. We were all excited for her when one of the football players asked her to prom, making her feel like she finally fit in. Unfortunately, he only did it to make his ex-girlfriend jealous. When it worked and the girl took him back, he bailed on Emma, but instead of telling her, he just showed up with his newly re-instated girlfriend on his arm, leaving Em all dolled up and dateless to a prom that wasn't her own.

I found the kid at an afterparty and jumped him, giving him a black eye, a bloody nose, and a dislocated elbow that ruined his prospects for a football scholarship. It wasn't jealousy then, it was anger. I wanted him to suffer for making her cry.

Brett's not the only one invested in protecting Emma.

I never told him the reason he couldn't find the kid was because I'd taken care of him first. Perhaps even then I knew what my feelings for Em would turn into and I didn't want them put under a microscope. She may not be a little girl now, but she was back then.

"And you think *I'd* hurt her?" I shouldn't have asked it. I should have just let it go, but the fact that he thinks I could or would hurt Em, has me ready to choke him out.

He looks taken aback and it's then I realize I've shown too much emotion for him to dismiss the statement. Eyeing me with far too much curiosity, he chooses his words carefully.

"I've never really thought about it, but I guess not. Then again, I never thought you'd go on some hero mission to pick her up at two a.m. and not say a word to me about it either."

"Come on, man. You're making a mountain out of a mole hill. Yes, she called me. Yes, she asked me to come pick her up. Yes, I went. And then I brought her back to your parent's house and I came home. You're fucking welcome for answering my goddamn phone when she called and for driving to Baltimore and back to get her away from the cokehead who had her cornered in her room, by the way."

He jolts a little bit with the details of the story laid out like that. He scrubs a hand down his face and folds his arms across his chest. I know he's working through sobriety and he's been on edge a little more than usual, but this seems like overkill, even for his hothead.

"I, uh, didn't know about that last part. I would have fucking killed the guy. Em's been through enough shit like that," he says.

"What do you mean?"

He finally makes eye contact before looking away like he realizes he said something he shouldn't have.

"Nothing. Never mind."

I grab him by the upper arm, startling us both before letting go almost immediately. "What the fuck did you mean, Brett? What else has she been through?" *And why do I not know about it?*

He shakes his head as he stares at the floor. When he finally looks back up, I notice how tired he looks. "I'm sorry, man. It's not my story to tell. Sorry I flipped my shit. I do trust you and I know you'd never mess with Ems. I mean the eleven-year age difference is pretty weird already, but I know she's like a sister to you too. Thanks for keeping her safe."

My mind is racing. I need to know what happened like I need my next breath. I'm also having trouble with him thinking I see Em as a sister because I most certainly do not.

At a loss for the right words, I don't respond.

"So what do we do about her crush?" he asks.

"Nothing. I plan to treat her like I always have. Like the intelligent, kind woman she is. She's going to be in my life because *you* are in my life. Don't make it weird by making it a thing. You embarrassed the shit out of her tonight."

The look on his face tells me he doesn't like what I'm saying, but he isn't arguing either.

"Ugghh," he groans. "I hate this shit. How do I make it up to her? I feel like all I do is fuck things up between us."

"I don't know, man. Offer to spend some time with her before she goes back to school? Listen to her. Just let her be *her*." I suggest.

"When the fuck am I going to find time? *Someone* has my schedule so fucking packed I barely have time to take a shit without having to multi-task," he says, pursing his lips at me.

"Bri mentioned bringing her to the hockey game." I shrug, trying to offer a solution nonchalantly while also ensuring I have a chance to see Emma again before she goes back to school. Even if I can't touch her, being in her presence is like skinny dipping in the Mediterranean with the sun beating down on lust-heated skin.

"Shit. I forgot all about that. That's five days away though and Emmie's only home for a week. I'll keep thinking about it." Finally, he reaches his hand out to clasp mine and pull me in for a bro-hug as I swallow the urge puke on his shoes.

I wasted my chance to tell him the truth but worse, I failed

Em by pretending my feelings for her are strictly platonic, *again*.

When we head inside, Noah's back at the table and the rest of my shepherd's pie is cold.

"I hope you boys got everything worked out. Family has quarrels, but you boys are better than that," Brett's dad, Bill, says.

I barely register the words.

Keeping my communication with Em a secret was fine for the past couple of years. Talking to her is what kept me going on tour. I was always careful not to steer it into the topics of sex or dating, and she never ventured there herself. Which is why I was so shocked when she said she'd wanted more.

Just to try and prevent any sexual feelings for Em from forming, I slept with a few women on the road. I even attempted dating one but it's next to impossible to date when you're trying to get to know someone you're not in the same city with for eight or nine months at a time. I knew I was bullshitting myself when I didn't get off the phone with Emma in order to answer Caroline's call. Then when Brett got blackmailed by that fan, it was the best excuse I had to not sleep with anyone else while on the road. Em and I continued to talk and by the second week of the European tour, she was the more adult one, finally admitting her feelings out loud while I continued to pretend mine were non-existent.

My world both ended and came alive with her admission.

"Yeah, Dad, we're all good," Brett says.

"Let me heat you boys' dinner up and we'll try this again, shall we?" Brett's mom asks.

"Are you done being an overbearing asshole?" We all look up and see Emma come around the corner. My heart pulls a little when I realize she's no longer wearing my jacket.

"Uh, yeah. I just worry about you, you know?"

"I know, Brett. But you can't protect me forever."

"Doesn't mean I won't try."

Thankfully, no more is said about what is or is not going on between Em and I. Sienna talks more about the wedding while Sloan harasses Noah, and things return to normal.

Once we finish the most brutal dinner of my life, we say our goodbyes. I'm not sure how to handle Emma, so I reach in for the side hug as she wraps an arm around my waist, placing her hand flat on my back like she knows this is a permanent goodbye in that brutal way where we'll see each other again but never share another moment like this morning.

Sloan is his usual self and goads Brett by yelling, "Breeeeeett! Ryan's hugging your sister! Should we get the baseball bat?"

It would be funny if it didn't hurt so fucking much.

Chapter 11

Emma

fter my jog Monday morning, I'm trying to get a bagel down when my phone dings twice.

By the time I woke up yesterday, my mom had already invited the guys to dinner so I spent the afternoon trying to knock out a couple of assignments instead of calling Jen to update her on both the kiss and the horrors of the fall break trip. I just need a little more alone time with the whole kissing/*I have feelings for you* situation, but I'll tell her the rest.

Before I call her though, I check the second message.

BRETT 9:08 AM

Sorry about last night Ems. I want to make it up to you. We're going over some new music tonight. Want to hear?

I choose to answer Brett first since I recognize the peace-offering for what it is. Listening to the guys play live in their private studio is one of my favorite pastimes. Hanging out in the studio was always a safe place for me, not just physically – because that was never a concern until two years ago – but mentally and emotionally. I've never had to guard my words or worry about sounding cool in front of them. Not to mention watching the guys in their element – all of them, not just Ryan – is like a religious experience. I haven't gotten to do it much over the last two years because they've been on the road but even with the current tension between Ryan and I, I can't pass this opportunity up.

EMMA 9:12 AM

Just heard from Jennifer. She wants to see me too. Can she come? We'll put our phones in the lockbox.

BRETT 9:12 AM

Sure.

The guys have to keep their new music under lock and key, literally. Anyone in the studio – family included – has to deposit their phones in a lockbox so they can't record or take pictures, and the key stays on a necklace one of them wears the whole time they're practicing.

> See you at seven.

I text Jennifer back and ask her if she's up for it.

> JENNIFER 9:18 AM
>
> Am I up for spending the evening with my best friend, openly gawking at the sexiest men this earth has ever produced?
>
> Is that an actual question?? Because yeah, hoe. I'm down for that.
>
> Are you? I thought we were still avoiding Mr. Tall, Broody, and Fuckable.

I'm still laughing when she picks up on the second ring.

"First of all, you're such a slut, and I love you for it. Secondly, let me fill you in on how this invitation came to be."

I proceed to tell her *almost* everything that's happened since I arrived at the rental house on Friday. As any good best friend does, she laughs, gasps, and *ohmygods* in all the right places.

Never one for competition or cattiness, she's a true ride or die. I know eventually I'll tell her about the kisses between Ryan and I but she's literally going to blow a gasket, and I'm just not sure I'm ready to hash it out yet.

"Behave yourself," I tease my best friend as we pull up to the guys' house. My palms are sweaty and a swarm of butterflies is flapping their wings so violently, I feel it the flutter from my heart to toes.

I had convinced myself coming over would be good for me. A chance to get used to seeing Ryan and interacting without expectations. At some point between last night and this morning - *probably during my post run high* - I became determined that if things can't move forward with Ryan, then I'll work hard to get them back to the way they were.

It's just Brett and the guys. No big deal.

Meanwhile, beside me, Jennifer is vibrating with excitement reminding me that this is actually a very big deal.

"Jen, you're making me jittery," I laugh as she bounces on the balls of her feet outside the studio door. Yes, I'm unashamedly blaming Jennifer for the response Ryan provokes in me.

"Sorry. I'm having trouble switching from *fangirl* mode to *chill, badass bitch* mode."

She glances down at my chest wistfully. "God, I wish I had boobs like yours. Sloan would definitely do me then."

I snort a laugh, glad she's here with me.

"You have great boobs!" I say, patting one of them through the cowl-neck shirt she's wearing for emphasis.

"They're small," she laments.

"They're perfect. Your waist is like non-existent. You'd look weird if your boobs were any bigger. Besides, when mine are down around my knees, yours will still be on your chest, lucky bitch," I remind her, earning a smile.

I take a deep breath and push the door open to find the guys already in full swing. Brett's banging away on the drums with his hat on backwards like usual. A surge of pride jolts through me. He may annoy the shit out of me sometimes, but I'm so damn proud of him.

He looks up, gives me a quick smile, and tips his chin in

acknowledgement before going back into the zone, his arms flying wildly with each strike of his stick, his feet tapping double time on the floor pedals.

"Holy shit. I think I just came," Jennifer yells into my ear.

"Jen! Brother! Remember?"

"Em, he's half naked and sweaty and everything is flexing and *oh my God*. He could be your grandpa and I'd still want to bang him. I would give my left tit to see the half of the tattoo that sits below his waistband."

"Something is seriously wrong with you," I giggle in her ear.

I pull Jennifer toward the couch that's set up in the corner of the spacious studio, trying to train my eyes on my destination and not on the man right in front of it.

No dice.

Ryan's shirt is damp, causing it to stick to him in all the right places. He's so tall and broad shouldered, he holds his bass with ease as his fingers move around the fretboard, knowing exactly where to find the notes he wants. As I survey the guys in front of me, I notice for the first time, they each personify their instruments well.

Jennifer sits down, plants her elbows on her spread knees, and starts bobbing her head to the music. It's easy to guess that sex fantasies are on blast in her head based on the look in her eyes and the way the brunette is biting her lip. She's honed her gaze in on Sloan and honestly? I'm cheering for her. Sloan could most likely give her exactly what she's looking for - blisteringly hot sex with no labels - and vice versa. Although, who really knows what Sloan's looking for?

I flop down, getting settled into the opposite corner of the couch but quickly realize I forgot to lock our phones up. I tap Jen on the shoulder and motion like I'm talking on the phone and hold out my hand. Even though it's been a while, she knows the drill and hands her phone over without question. I pause when I realize Ryan's the one wearing the key.

Of course he is.

For the first time since arriving, I swing my eyes to his but he's already looking right at me. I swallow hard and hold up the phones in my right hand and motion like I'm twisting a key with my left.

My mime game is strong today.

He nods his head in a "come here" gesture and leans forward.

Oh God, he wants me to take the necklace off of him. I only have on a thin, long-sleeved t-shirt but it feels like too much right now as my skin blazes underneath. I set the phones on the couch and my eyes dart to the other band members, but am relieved when all of their eyes are closed, lost to the music.

The chain won't fit over Ryan's head, so I move behind him to get to the clasp and he straightens back up, dwarfing me. My fingers brush the slick skin of his neck and I feel him take a shuddering breath. He finally closes his eyes, trying to lose himself in the music being played around him.

Normal, Emma. Act normal.

As if my emotions weren't enough to get the best of me, my sweaty fingers have a hard time getting the clasp open and I fumble it, grazing his neck repeatedly. Standing on my tip toes to access it easier, I wobble, causing my chest to press against his back. I right myself quickly, but not quickly enough, and I feel the hardness of his muscles against me. I exhale, my breath floating across his neck as I place my hand on his waist to steady myself before I knock him over. Finally, he stops playing and undoes the clasp himself.

"Sorry. Thanks," I mutter and scurry off to the lockbox next to the door while he resumes making music.

Forty-five minutes later, the guys take a break to dissect and discuss what they liked, what they want to try next, and just have a minute to decompress. Bri and Sienna come in during the break as well and the newcomers go to Brett and Noah, respectively. Sloan asks if Jennifer wants to play around on his guitar - to which she asks if that's a euphemism as she catapults herself off the couch, practically running to him - leaving Ryan and I alone, *again*.

I'm starting to think the universe is orchestrating these moments on purpose.

Ryan props his bass up on the stand and comes to sit next to me on the couch. His posture is casual but his facial features are strained. He's to my right, slouched down in the couch, his left arm thrown over the back, his right hand relaxed between his thighs.

"You doing okay?" he asks, the gravel in his voice causing my nipples to peak violently.

I give him a small smile and shrug. "I'm not really sure where to go from here." I drop my voice to a whisper. "I want to be close like we were but I don't know how to get there while still feeling like this," I admit.

"Em, I'm sorry," he says for what feels like the hundredth time since kissing me.

"I don't want your apology, Ryan." And then, because the proximity is really messing with my head, I add, "I want a chance." *So much for moving on and keeping it normal.*

His eyebrows pinch together and I can clearly see the pained expression on his face but he quickly schools his features before anyone else notices. Except his jaw, that's still clenched. He looks at war with himself but finally blows out a harsh exhale.

"You know I can't agree to that," he says and I feel my face fall. Turning to face me more fully, he catches me completely off-guard when he asks. "What happened that makes your brother feel like he needs to shed the blood of anyone that looks in your direction?"

"Wh...what do you mean?" I stutter, feeling my face go pale.

"He alluded to something that happened but said it wasn't his story to tell. Something tells me it's part of the reason he's so pissed you called me and not him."

"I, uh, nothing. It's in the past. Which is where it needs to stay."

"Emma, what happened?" He's beginning to get angry.

"I'm fine."

"That's not what I asked."

"Actually, it is. You literally said, 'You doing okay?'"

His nostrils flare and he pinches the bridge of his nose. "Quit being a smartass, Em. What the fuck happened and why don't I know about it?"

"Can you just drop it, please? I don't need you *and* Brett on my case," I snap. Not only do I not talk about it in general but having Ryan find out would be devastating to me. What if he treats me differently or it somehow taints me in his eyes? Worse, what if he *pities* me? I wouldn't be able to stand it. I really couldn't handle that reaction from anyone, which is why I made Brett swear he wouldn't tell, but it would be especially horrible coming from Ryan.

"As long as you promise me that whatever *was* going on, isn't still happening." he demands.

"It's not."

He nods his head. I know he wants to say more, press me until I spill the story, but that's not Ry's style. Instead, he switches gears entirely.

"Look, there's this charity event my dad has to attend right after Kinky's wedding. He needs the whole family there and having a famous son comes in handy on occasion." I turn toward him, hope blooming in my chest. "I'd need to talk to your brother this time, and I can't be your date, but maybe you could come along as my brother, Trevor's, guest. It would be a great place to network. You're going to need an internship at some point. This could help you lay the groundwork."

As a law student, accompanying a senator's son – even if it's not the son I'd choose - is a freaking opportunity of a lifetime. The spark that should be igniting at such a privilege is noticeably absent. Not only am I not interested in going with someone else, I still haven't found the desire to propel my career forward and get ahead like normal.

Disappointment settles over the bloom of hope like a dreaded frost, causing it to wither and die.

"No, thank you." Unable to tolerate the proximity anymore, I uncurl my legs from the couch and stand up. I need a minute in the cold to get the heat from my lust and disappointment under control.

Ryan reaches out and grabs my hand. "What do you mean, *no?*"

I glance around the room, thankful the other guys – mostly Brett – are occupied. Following my gaze, Ryan drops his hand immediately.

"I mean I'm not interested in accompanying your brother to a charity event where I will have to watch you get groped and fondled a hundred times over while trying to mingle and schmooze. No. N. O. I've done just fine making connections and progressing my career on my own. Now, if you'll excuse me, I'm going to grab some water."

He stands abruptly and snatches his hoodie off the floor.

"I need to take a leak," he announces to the room. "Anybody want anything?"

"Water," Noah says.

"Make it two," Brett replies, fully invested in the woman in front of him.

"Grab me a soda, will ya? And those chip things I like," Sloan says before going back to Jennifer's lesson.

Looking at me and somehow keeping his voice even, but loud enough for everyone to hear, Ryan says, "Em, come help me carry it all."

Bastard.

Outside the studio, I trail behind Ryan and wish I could summon the will to be pissed at the stunt he just pulled, but I can't. A glutton for punishment, I enjoy the pain almost as much as the pleasure.

Stepping into the house, I turn left to go to the kitchen in search of my water when Ryan yanks me into the living room and backs me up against the wall so hard the breath is pushed from my lungs. It takes me a second to realize the back of my head is against his palm which is protecting me so I wouldn't crack my skull open from the force.

"Goddamn it, Emma," he growls angrily. "Let me help you. You won't get this kind of access or opportunity from anyone else."

When he's this close to me, I can't think straight but I'm upset enough to keep *most* of my lust at bay.

"I don't use people like that, Ryan. Besides, you don't get to be angry at me for trying to protect myself!" My shout surprises us both. I'm usually not a yeller. His wince causes me to soften my tone. "Look, it's hard being around you and I'm frustrated with myself because I can't seem to stay away. I'm trying to get to a point where I can handle just being friends but my feelings for you aren't going to change any time soon, and I'm not interested in watching other women get what I can't have." The admission, while painful, works to clear my head a small amount.

He's still leaning down into my space, the wall at my back, giving me no room to retreat. I'm breathing hard because the man of all my dreams, desires, and fantasies is two inches from my face, his chest hitting my own when our lungs expand for breath. Finally, he speaks, letting free an admission of his own.

"I can't stop thinking about that kiss, Em. The way you felt against me. The way you taste. I'm fucking dying over here." His words erase my anger which is rapidly being replaced by an uncontrollable amount of lust, causing my nipples to push painfully against my thin bra. "I thought if you were mad at me —"

I guess the next part.

"That I'd get over my 'crush' and we would both move on?" I lightly run my knuckles over the t-shirt covering his abs and swallow hard. "You have to know this is more than a crush, Ry. You also have to know by now that I don't care about your fame, your money, or your family's connections."

He smirks and licks his lips. "You seem to care an awful lot about what's under this t-shirt though."

I feel my own grin widen, holding my hand still and shaking my head. "I care about *you*. I care if you're happy. I care about the band and the music. I care about all the moments we've shared and all the moments we're going to miss out on because of the impossible situation we're in. And yeah, maybe I care a little about what's under this shirt."

The interesting thing about having hard conversations is they're like anything else that's challenging. They require practice and the more you do it, the easier it gets. My emotions are still running haywire, but it's getting easier to be honest with Ryan and find the words I need despite the gallons of lust coursing through me.

"*Christ*, woman."

He scrubs a hand down his face and blows out a breath. I

stand motionless in front of him, not wanting to spook him as he clearly wages war with himself.

The situation gets more complicated with each passing second but he feels so good leaning his weight into me. When my last boyfriend did it, it made me feel claustrophobic. The need for escape was overwhelming. With Ryan, I lean into it as if he's the light that chases the darkness away. Towering over me with his raw masculinity, he flexes his fingers in my hair and a moan escapes my throat.

I guess it was all the encouragement he needed because he sucks the breathy sound into his mouth and grinds against me, *hard*. I've never been so turned on in my life and it makes me smile, like maybe there's a chance I'm not broken. In fact, I'd love nothing more than to give this man my virginity right here on his living room floor.

"I'm so fucked," he whispers against my mouth. He angles his head and his tongue teases mine. The kiss is rough but not filled with awkward teeth clashing. It feels like he's baring his soul through this kiss, and the need behind it catches me off guard.

"We only have a second," he pants. When he reaches the hem of my shirt, he pulls his head back, searching my eyes. "Can I touch you?" he pants.

"Yes, please."

His hand dives under my shirt, his calloused fingers causing my soul to sing as they land on my ribcage. *Fuck, I wish they'd go higher...or lower.*

"I don't know what I'm going to do, Em. I don't see this ending well, but selfishly, I can't let it go either. I need some time to figure this out but more than anything, I need to know we'll have a minute to ourselves at some point. Give me something to look forward to. Come to the event."

"Come to Boston," I counter.

"I don't know how I'll explain the absence to the band. We have so much going on right now, and whether or not you go to the thing for my dad, I still have to be there. My free time is limited. Just *show up* with Trevor," he pleads in frustration. "I can't have you on my arm or the media will have a field day and we aren't ready for that. You aren't ready for that. Brett isn't ready for that. Hell, I'm probably committing suicide by even suggesting it. We'll get out of there as fast as we can and have the night to figure out what we're doing." He's rubbing his nose along my neck as he talks and when his thumb brushes the underside of my breast, I cave faster than a bat flying out of hell.

I've never seen Ryan this desperate. I've never seen him beg. It breaks my resolve as easily as if it were a toothpick. "Fine, I'll go," I agree, my heart beating wildly against the same ribs Ryan's hand is splayed against.

My hands hastily return the favor and find his bare skin, my nails scraping down his abdomen, eager to feel it tense beneath my touch before I lay my palms flat against him. I've never touched him here, not like this. The brief fingertip I trailed along the top of his jeans under the cover of darkness yesterday morning was heavenly, but having two handfuls of his muscled core is almost enough to drive me insane with need.

"*Shit*," he says, bracing his forearm on the wall over my head and placing his own forehead on it.

"What? And I swear to God, Ryan, if you apologize again —"

Before I can finish my threat, he places his open palm on the back of my head and angles it down so I have a perfect view of the raging hard on he's sporting.

Feeling awfully satisfied with myself, and bolder than

usual, I place my palm against his straining erection and whisper, "Please?"

He closes his eyes and groans the most delicious sound, pushing his hips into my hand seeking friction.

"I wish, angel, but we're out of time. Someone's going to come looking for us soon and knowing my luck, it's going to be your brother. Do me a favor and grab the blue bag next to the fridge and a Coke for Sloan. I'll bring out the waters."

He turns away from the kitchen, heading for the stairs, his nickname for me ringing in my ears.

"Where are you going?"

"To take care of this." He adjusts his dick as he walks up the stairs and the view of him touching himself has me groaning out loud, my own sex clenching with need, as I sag against the wall trying to process this turn of events.

What the fuck just happened?

Chapter 12

Ryan

"**W**hat the actual fuck am I doing?" I mutter to myself out loud, closing the door to my bathroom behind me. The repeated question seems to be my mantra these days. If only I had an answer.

Not wanting to risk someone hearing me, I came upstairs to the bathroom connected to my room before shoving my jeans down and gripping my aching cock angrily in my own hand.

Not only did I just invite her to political event with my entire family - *before* asking my father, I might add – but I fucking kissed her ... again.

And damn if she doesn't still taste like strawberries thanks to her favorite lip gloss.

The way she feels under my hands and against my body is new to me. Her body curves in all the right places and I know if we were to lay skin-to-skin we'd mold together better than any partner I've had in the past.

I want to invade her tight body so badly I'm surprised I'm still conscious. And when she put her hand to me, I swear I almost came on the spot despite the layers between us.

The visual of her nipples trying to stab me through her thin bra and long-sleeved t-shirt ensures that it doesn't take more than three pulls before I'm making a mess of my hand and the sink I'm bracing my body weight against in an effort to stay upright.

As long as there was physical distance between Emma and I, and no knowledge of her desire for me, I was able to keep this under control. But now that it's been given a chance to breathe and stretch its muscles with not just one, but *two* kisses?

No way in hell is this need going back in its secret little box. No, I fear this is here to stay until I sink my throbbing cock in her warm, tight pussy and relieve us both of the ever-growing desire flowing between us. And even now, I know once won't be enough.

I clean up as fast as I can, aware that my absence is most likely becoming suspicious. Thankfully, I have an idea to both buy time, and work on a plan. Since my phone is in the lockbox in the studio, I use our old landline to place a call to my dad's office. Terri, his secretary answers on the first ring.

"Senator Battle's office. Thank you for calling. How may I direct your call?"

"Hey, Terri. It's Ryan. Is my dad around?"

"Ryan! How are you? Congratulations on the success of the tour and thank you again for the tickets. My grandson and his friends had the absolute best time. It's all he's talked about ever since."

"You're welcome. We enjoyed meeting them. I'm glad to hear they had a good time."

"Your dad just got back from a meeting and isn't in a great mood, but I bet a call from you will cheer him right up. Hold on a second, I'll transfer you over."

"Thanks."

A few rings later my dad's familiar voice comes over the

line.

"Hi, son. What can I do for you?" I guess it's the politician in him, but that's always his opening line. *What can I do for you?* Like even in a simple conversation, he's looking for a way to improve your day and ease your troubles. Our last name might be Battle, but my dad ultimately seeks peace.

"Hey Dad. You know the charity fundraiser we're going to right before the election?"

"I should hope so," he says drily and it takes me a couple of seconds to realize he's joking.

"Ha-ha. Anyway, could I bring a guest? It's Brett's sister, Emma, actually."

"Is this a date, son?" he asks warily. "I remember her being significantly younger than you." His hidden meaning is clear. *Do not choose now to start a scandal.*

"No, it's not a date. I was actually thinking she could go with Trevor to keep her out of the spotlight that will accompany me. As you know, she's one of the youngest law students ever admitted to Harvard. It would be a great place for her to network, pick some brains, and get her name out there. She'd be a great asset to any team."

"It sounds like you've given this a lot of thought," he says, still sounding skeptical of the reason behind my request – as he should be.

"Just occurred to me actually. She's at practice with a friend of hers today and it came up." Great. Now I'm lying to my father.

"Of course, son. Why doesn't she go with Carey? He's closer to her age."

"You and I both know I'd never trust Carey with a friend of mine."

"You're too hard on him."

"He has a lot of growing up to do and Emma is too..." I trail off because I almost say *precious* but that word is far too telling so I switch gears. "...fragile for his shit." It may be the better word anyway considering her reaction at the bar a while back.

"Whatever you think is best. Just run it by Trevor first. I'm sorry to keep it short, but I've got to go over a speech I have to deliver tomorrow."

"Great. Thanks, Dad. I will. And good luck."

"You know luck has nothing to do with it, son," he tells me before adding the familiar words he's spoken to my brothers and I over the years. "Hard work and honesty are life's greatest satisfactions." *Well, at least I got the hard work part down.* "Your mother and I will see you soon at Noah's wedding. Oh, and please make sure Ms. Donovan is up to speed on etiquette and expectations while representing our family."

"Of course, Dad. Thanks."

I grab the waters and hustle back to the studio where I receive a couple of raised-brows.

"My dad called," I say in answer to their burning questions as I pass out the waters. Nosy bastards. "What did you guys decide you want to go back over?"

It's hard not to immediately look at Em. Satisfied that I at least still taste her on my lips, I stroll to my bass and slip the strap over my head, ready to pick up where we left off. Inside, I'm a fucking mess but outwardly, I feel the smile on my face.

"I vote we run through the setlist for tomorrow night's concert in Knoxville and call it a night," Noah suggests.

"Aw, fuck. Is that tomorrow already?" I ask, suddenly weary from this overpacked schedule I've created.

"Yep. *Someone* decided to work us to death in an effort to —"

"I get it. Concert tomorrow. It's going to be great," I sneer at Noah as he snickers. I don't mind playing another show, but I *do* mind leaving when Em's only home for a week.

Chapter 13

Emma

I was sorely tempted to drag Jen to Knoxville to see the Beautiful Deceit show tonight but I can't neglect the rest of my assignments any longer. In my childhood bedroom, staring at a blank PowerPoint slide, lost in daydreams about a certain bassist, a knock on my door pulls me out of my head.

"Come in," I yell through the door as it swings open to reveal my mom standing on the threshold with lunch.

"Hey Mom."

"Hey sweetie," my mom says as she puts a plate of food on my desk and sits down on the bed next to me. I'm lying on my stomach doing homework like I'm in the eighth grade. "How are things going?" she asks.

"They're good. Just swamped with assignments. So much for this week being a break, huh?" I joke.

"Are you enjoying your classes?"

"Yeah, Mom. All good."

She pats my back. "Your dad and I are so proud of you, honey. We probably don't say it enough but we're so excited for your future. We always knew you'd do something amazing with that brilliant brain of yours."

"Thanks, Mom."

She leans down and kisses my head. "Well, I'll leave you to it. I don't want to interrupt, just wanted to drop off some nourishment. We're glad you're here, Emmie. It's good to have you home."

Oh, fuck me. Guilt rolls through me until it settles in my heart and makes me pull my mom in for a hug. When things went south between Ryan and I six months ago, I avoided everything, including my parents, choosing instead to retreat inside my own cocoon of despair.

"Sorry I was so adamant about moving into my apartment early. I guess I was just ready to move on to the next phase, you know?"

Lies.

I wanted to get into my apartment before the guys got home from tour because I couldn't stomach the thought of seeing Ryan. Not to mention there's been a low level of guilt residing in my system ever since my sister died. As her identical twin, it's impossible for my parents not to see her face every time they look at me.

"We know. Your dad and I don't take it personally. As long as you know we're always happy to see you. We love having you here."

I look at my mom and nod as she continues. "Of course we miss your sister, Em, but you girls are very different and your father and I love the individuals you are," she drops her voice. "*Were.* Don't feel like you have to stay away because she's gone."

I thought I'd hid those thoughts better over the last three years but maybe I've been wrong about that.

"Thanks, Mom."

She smiles and closes my bedroom door softly.

By the time Jen texts me at three, I'm no further along on my presentation than I was four hours ago and I'm in desperate need of a break which prompts my agreement to go shopping with her. It's time to spill the beans about Ryan and I anyway.

As I'm swiping blush over my cheeks in an effort to bring life into my skin after staring at my computer screen for so long, my phone dings and my heart skips a beat before I realize it's from Bri.

BRI 12:15 PM

So I was able to snag another ticket for the hockey game on Friday. You in?

EMMA 12:16 PM

Hell yes!

BRI 12:16 PM

Great! I'll come by and we can get ready together.

EMMA 12:17 PM

I'm already looking forward to it! <3

I was afraid she'd forgotten.

I make a note to pick up something new to wear while I'm out with Jennifer who comes to pick me up half an hour later.

Once she and I are fully caffeinated and have our plan in place, we start to make the rounds at the mall.

School keeps me so busy I hardly ever go out for anything I need anymore. Why would I when Amazon, UPS, or FedEx can deliver practically anything I want right to my door? But being out and about with Jennifer now, I remember there's something totally fun about trying on obnoxious outfits I'd never wear in public with my best friend and laughing until my face hurts.

"What's got you all giggly today?" Jen asks. "Usually by the time we hit this side of the mall, you're dragging and I have to bribe you with cookies and cheesecake to finish the loop with me," she observes as we walk along, arm in arm.

Jen loves physical contact. The more the better. Sexual or not, she just craves closeness. I'm pretty sure doing multiple guys at once would be her ideal Friday night.

I start small, with the charity event. I don't know why I'm so skittish to tell her about kissing Ryan. Maybe because if I say it out loud, it will somehow jinx what we've started and he and I have enough stacked against us as it is.

"I'm going to a charity event with Senator Battle and his family in a few weeks and I'm hoping to meet someone who can help me secure an internship when the time comes."

Jen stops instantly, yanking me to a halt with her. Whipping her head toward me, her eyes wide.

"Ohmygod, is Ryan going? *Holy crickets on a cracker,* that man is fine."

"Yes, he's going, but I'm accompanying his brother, Trevor."

"All I hear is there's going to be an opportunity to win multiple *Battles,* and hopefully the bedroom is going to be the *Battle*field." She nudges my elbow with her side. "Eh-eh, see what I did there."

I playfully roll my eyes as we resume walking. "I'll be going as a guest of the senator. There will be no *battles* won, lost or fought at all." There is such a difference in the words leaving my mouth and the thoughts in my head. Secretly, I hope to look so amazing Ryan can't keep his eyes off of me which will result in him not being able to keep his *hands* off of me. But I don't say any of that out loud. Instead, my hands fidget nervously with the ends of my hair.

"Well, you're still going to want to feel your best and you know what that means," Jennifer says tugging me in the direction of a large pink and red sign. "New underwear!"

I can't help my laugh. New underwear is how Jen solves all her problems. Today, it might be exactly what I need too.

"I'm thinking virginal white lace," she says, leading me through the opening of the store. The mood is set in here with dim lights, a feminine floral scent throughout, and sultry music being piped through the speakers, sparking quite an image in my mind as I wonder what a night with Ryan would be like.

What *he* would be like.

Slow and gentle or rough and out of control? Does he like to tease or is he straight to the point? I can't imagine him being shy after the kisses we've shared – there was power in them, and possession, but no shyness or insecurity. Riding on the coattails of those thoughts is a fresh wave of anxiety. *What if I'm not good at it? Do I even know how to be sexy? What if he goes to put his hands there and I have a panic attack?*

I take a second to focus on my breathing and bring myself back to the moment.

The panty-topped tables are slightly overwhelming. I usually just order my panties from Amazon. Cheap and practical. Here, there are rows upon rows laid out on the tables. Everything from briefs, to boy-shorts, to thongs, to the full-assed variety are vying for my attention. With such a choice in front of me, it makes me realize that the possibility of being alone with Ryan for a night is *there* in a way it never was before.

"Where should we start?" I ask Jennifer who's making a beeline for the back of the store.

"All the sexy stuff is in the back, so that's where we're heading," Jennifer announces.

Just to make sure she doesn't get any ideas, I add, "Okay, but you know we're just shopping for *me*, right? No one else is going to see these."

"Uh-huh. I know." She flashes me a wink and I know it's a lost cause. "Oh this!" Jennifer gushes as she holds up a white lacy thong.

"Jen, I really don't want *virginal white*, as you so indelicately put it. Even if no one sees it but me, it doesn't exactly build confidence."

"Don't want him freaking out at the last minute about being the one to pop that cherry, huh? Okay, I guess that's a good call."

I roll my eyes. "No one's popping any cherries!"

Thanks to one asshole, that's already been done. Granted, it wasn't with his dick, but nonetheless, that part of me is no longer intact.

"Babe, you're going to be out of eyesight of your brother, *alone,* with one of *the* hottest bachelors on the planet who you happen to have been in love with since you were in diapers. You're going to be in your element, and looking sexy as hell. Not to mention you haven't stopped grinning since I picked you up this morning. *And* you keep checking your phone which tells me there's a high probability that you and Mr. Battle have been texting because that's the only thing that would make you clutch the device like it's your lifeline instead of just putting it in your purse.

"I can't hide anything from you, can I?" I say, only half joking.

Putting the underwear down, she rounds the table and stands next to me. "The question is why do you feel like you have to hide this from me?" she asks.

"I don't. I've just needed time to sort it out ... because the charity event's not even the biggest news."

When I pause, Jen damn near makes the walls shake.

"Well out with it, woman!" she yells, making me glance around to see how much attention she's drawing.

"Shhh!" I whisper, grabbing her hand and pulling her to a corner. "He kissed me. Twice."

If her eyeballs get any bigger, I swear they're going to pop out of her head so I start talking faster.

"The first time was early Sunday morning when he dropped me off. The other was at band practice yesterday when we went in for drinks. After the first one, he said he still couldn't risk ruining things with my brother. But then he kissed me again and told me to come to this thing for his dad. He said he just needed time to figure things out. I'm stressed he's going to change his mind and I'm stressed that Brett is going to find out and fly off the handle. If this gets out then a *lot* of stuff gets really complicated."

"How could you keep this from me, you hussy?" she shrieks, her face breaking out into a smile. "How the fuck was it? God, what does he taste like? Was it sloppy? Where were your hands? Where were his? Please tell me he knows how to kiss. He's too hot to be a bad kisser."

Her enthusiasm makes me smile even though this is exactly the reason I didn't tell her as soon as it happened.

As I answer her questions, I'm not sure she breathes the entire time. Finally, when I finish, she sighs. "I'm so turned on right now."

"You're always turned on," I tease her.

"True."

"This is a big deal, Jen." So much can go so wrong.

"The biggest," she agrees, finally lowering her voice.

"It could just be an off-limits, *best friend's little sister* kink he's acting on. I'm trying really hard not to get my hopes up. Besides, Brett's a pretty big hurdle to get over."

"Oh, I bet you'll get over it. I bet Ryan will pick you up and carry you right over that hurdle. And I want to hear every sordid detail when it happens. Do *not* hold out on me. Our entire friendship is hanging in the balance, Emmie," she says seriously.

"Yes, ma'am," I respond with a salute.

"Oh, that's good. Call him *sir*. I can see him liking that."

"You're ridiculous, you know that? I'm not calling him *sir*. Our age difference freaks him out enough as it is."

"Okay, how about Big Daddy?"

"I hate you."

"You don't."

"Just help me pick out some underwear, will you?"

She rubs her hands together and licks her lips like she's on a mission. I see the evil glint in her eyes and feel bad for keeping this from her.

"Black," she decides, scooping up a pair of cheeky panties with little ribbons laced up the sides. "And pink." She grabs another pair and places it in her fist with the first. "Not red. That's too *seductress*. I think you should play on the young, innocent lamb vibe."

"I don't want to *play* any vibe. I just want to be me," I argue.

"Fine. Granny panties are over there." She waves her hand toward a table several feet away. "Pick some so I can vehemently protest them and then go try these on." She thrusts her choices at me and grabs a matching bra to the black panties and holds it out. "And this. And send him a selfie while you're in there."

I laugh the whole way to the dressing room and start to strip down. As I'm getting the first set in place, a pink bra comes sailing over the top of the door and I hear Jennifer muttering to herself. "I can't *believe* my bitch of a best friend is about to live out all of our fantasies and she tried to keep it from me! I'm petitioning for a new bestie. My next bestie won't treat me like this. My next bestie is going to be a horndog just like me and she's going to spill all the details about the dick she's getting."

"I'm not getting any dick!" I laugh. "And I can hear you."

"I hope you can," Jennifer sings from the other side as another piece of lingerie comes flying over the top of the door, making me laugh.

I pull my phone out, debating on whether or not to take a couple photos. It's certainly not my usual M.O. but maybe it's time for a new one of those anyway. Thinking about our recent interactions, the way his pupils dilate when he sees me, and the way he touches me, I decide to hell with it. I open up my messages and start typing.

EMMA 3:43 PM

I need your opinion on something.

There's a good chance Ryan can't respond. He's most likely already in the arena where they're playing tonight. Usually, for a seven o'clock show, they have to be inside by four or five, but I take a few pictures anyway. I can always send them later.

Considering my extreme dislike of being photographed, *especially* any way like this, I'm surprised when I look in the floor-length mirror and find myself grinning. Ryan would never use these against me and he'll never know how grateful I am that he gives me back my flirty side without even knowing I'd lost it.

As I'm slipping out of the black set to pull the pink one on, my phone dings as some sort of silk nightgown thing smacks me in the face. I quickly snap a picture of the pink set when it's in place, and begin to change again.

"I'm assuming you'll have to stay overnight after the event before going back to your apartment. You'll probably sleep naked, but why not have a little fun with him?" Jennifer says, explaining the nightie she just assaulted me with.

I grab my phone and my heart skips a beat as Ryan's name pops up in my messages. It takes me a second to find my breath so I can answer Jennifer first. "First of all, I can't afford all of this, second of all, you're making a lot of assumptions and I'm supposed to *not* be getting my hopes up, remember?"

RYAN 3:54 PM

Shoot.

It's now or never. I feel like I'm hurtling down the runway and it's too late to hit the brakes so I push the throttle harder, preparing to be airborne.

EMMA 3:56 PM

Black or pink?

Depends on what we're talking about. Car?
Black. Toenail polish? Pink.

I bite the bullet, knowing I'm escalating this thing between us quickly. We're like one of those snowballs that starts small but gets rolled down a hill, gaining size and speed as it goes.

EMMA 3:57 PM

picture image

My hands begin to sweat as I wait for his response. I fight the urge to immediately ask if that was too much and I distract myself by slipping into the next contraption Jennifer throws over the door.

"How does this even go on?" I ask, pulling up the garment made entirely of straps.

"Look at the tag, there's a picture. I can do the hooks for you on the back once your kitty's covered. We're close, but I don't need to see your grooming preferences," she teases.

"Just get your ass in here." I unlock the door and push it open. Jennifer's face breaks out into a smile.

"This is going to blow his mind."

Maybe.

Maybe not.

He still hasn't responded to the picture I sent and I'm starting to feel uneasy. Finally, as Jennifer gets the last hook in place, my phone starts to ring. Jennifer wags her eyebrows at me and gives me some privacy as she exits the small space.

"Are you trying to get me killed?" Ryan growls into the phone, the strain in his voice loud and clear. He sounds pissed. *Why do I like it so much?*

"Is that your way of telling me you like it?" I ask playfully, trying to push aside the feeling of insecurity creeping up my spine.

"That's my way of telling you I need some kind of warning before those pictures come through. Your brother was standing right next to me."

"Oh." I say because I don't know what else to add. I'd hoped for a better reaction.

He softens his voice. "Besides, *like it* is an understatement, sweetheart. That's the hottest fucking thing I've ever seen and now I'm rock hard and hiding in a bathroom *again*. I'm pretty sure the blood vessels in my dick are gonna demand overtime pay or go on strike."

"Send me a picture," I beg. "Please?" What I wouldn't give for a peek at what he's working with, his hand wrapped around himself, knowing I made him that way. I'm so wet I just committed to buying this contraption I have on because the strip between my legs is soaked despite my own underwear still being in place.

"Slow down, Em. We have a few other bridges to cross before we get there," he says.

"But we *will* get there?" The desperation in my voice bleeds into the phone.

"I won't make promises I can't keep, but I know the lid keeping all my feelings for you locked up has blown off, and all I can think about is getting you under my hands again. I'm distracted and wound tighter than my bass strings, and it's only a matter of time before the guys start to notice."

"Ryan, I want to be alone with you," I admit awkwardly even though I'm sure this isn't news to him. "I *need* it. I'm going crazy and I have to go back to school soon. I'll never be able to concentrate until I know what it's like."

"Once I get ahold of you, your concentration won't get any better, Em. And that's a promise I *can* keep."

"Oh hell…" I groan breathlessly at his words.

"I've got to get back to work. Buy that. And everything else. I'll pay for it."

"Okay," I breathe.

"Bye, Emma," he rasps.

"See you Friday."

"Friday?"

"Yeah, I'm coming to the hockey game."

"*Fuck*. Wear those panties under your outfit. I feel like being tortured."

And then, because the moment feels right, and I know Jennifer is listening on the other side of the dressing room door, I cock a half smile at myself in the mirror and say, "Yes, sir."

"*Emma*," he growls into the phone using that voice I love so much. "Text me tomorrow. All day. I have a photoshoot at eleven with the guys and then I'm working on a collab remotely at three. I don't know how long it will take, but we have six months to catch up on so text me everything."

I blow out a breath and whisper into the phone, needing to know where this is going.

"What are we doing, Ryan? All the reasons we couldn't do this in the first place are still there. I won't survive if you walk away from me again."

"Fuck if I know but we'll figure it out. I can't stop now that we've started."

"Me either."

"I've got to run. My sound check is up."

"Have a good show."

"Buy all that stuff, Em."

"I will."

"Say it again."

"I will," I repeat.

"Not that," he says, his voice strangled.

Smiling, I whisper, "Yes, sir."

As I hang up the phone, and sit down on the small stool in the dressing room, fanning myself, Jen comes back in clapping her hands. My volume was low, but still on speaker. She heard the whole thing.

"Oh, he's fucking smitten with you. I knew he'd like that *sir* shit."

"How did we get here?" I ask, dazed and confused, wearing the biggest smile I've sported in years.

Chapter 14

Ryan

Emma's words make my cock twitch in my hand as I feel my true nature slide into place, clicking like the last piece of a Rubix cube, making everything line up exactly as it should. Dancing around Brett has made me feel soft. The guilt causing me to shrink inside myself. With those two words, Emma just reinstated the man I know myself to be.

In control.

Dominant.

A leader.

Confident.

Self-Assured.

Being selfless doesn't make me weak. It makes me the man in charge. The one with all the information. The one on alert. The one who calls the shots. The one with all the power.

Yes, this is complicated. And yes, Brett will have some issues. But I'm a man who knows what I want and I've wanted it for a while. The resolve to finally admit this to myself and stop pussyfooting around the issue does wonders for my mental state, as does settling into the knowledge that I'm going to tell Brett.

Replaying Em and I's conversation in my head, I latch on to her words.

Yes, sir.

Does she somehow know? The guys give me shit all the time about the stuff I like in the bedroom – as if their own tastes are somehow tamer. Except Kinky, I imagine his favorite position is missionary which makes his nickname all the funnier. But how would Emma know? I've never once mentioned my preferences in front of her.

The smug tone of her voice tells me she's *trying* to get punished. She's pushing me dangerously close to the edge, and she'd better be ready for retaliation when she delivers the final blow that knocks me off the precipice.

Emma disconnects the call before I can respond, allowing me to turn my full attention back to the aching cock in my hand. I'm finding myself in this position a lot recently thanks to her smart mouth and irresistible light. I pull on my shaft with punishing force, smiling at her smug tone of voice. *She has no idea the monster she's just unleashed.*

I pause my movements briefly and search one last time, diving deep in my mind, my heart, and my soul, looking for any hint or sign of inappropriate feelings for the young girl I knew, relieved when I find none.

No, I didn't get the first twist of physical desire for Emma until after she was eighteen. Not that that's some magic number that makes this okay, but it *does* make me feel less creepy about moving forward.

I remember the day I first took notice of her sexually. She was home from undergrad and had come over to listen to one of our recording sessions and came bouncing through the door on a late July afternoon in a white tank top, the swell of her breasts poking out from the low-cut neckline, black shorts that showed off her long legs, and neon green flipflops. I remember her toenails were painted the same color as the cheap footwear. Her sunglasses were pushed up on her head and the summer sun had made her freckles stand out on her cheeks. She was swinging her car keys around her index and middle fingers casually, and was sucking something through a straw in a Styrofoam cup she held with her other hand.

That was the first time I noticed Emma Donovan had become a woman.

The memory makes me warm and I pick up my speed trying to find relief. I open my messages to the picture she sent me and immediately feel my balls begin to tighten. She left her face in the picture and her smile is bright. Emma doesn't really know how to mask her emotions – which could become problematic – and the desire on her face is on full display. The black bra and matching panties stand out in stark contrast to her pale Irish skin and fifteen seconds later, I grunt through my orgasm.

"Took you long enough. We wrote thirty-six more songs while you were gone," Sloan says when I get back to the stage.

I shoot him the middle finger.

"I'm surprised your dick has any fire power left. You've been disappearing an awful lot lately," Brett joins in on the let's-fuck-with-Ryan party.

"I didn't realize you guys needed a play-by-play of my bathroom schedule," I respond dryly. "But if you'd like to lend a hand next time, just let me know."

"Hell, if you're going to spend thirty minutes rubbing yourself raw, I'll do it in half the time. I could've ordered Chinese take-out, picked it up, eaten it, and gone back out for a milkshake while you were up there." Sloan whines.

"I'll be sure to tell your mom to be faster next time," I quip.

"Wait, I'm confused. Were you with my mom or Brett's sister?" Sloan laughs.

"Shut your fucking mouth, Alexander," Brett barks back.

"Too soon?" Sloan smirks, his mouth turned up in wicked half-smile that drives our female fan base crazy.

I risk a glance at Noah, who's working hard to keep his face passive.

I sigh dramatically. "Are we going to get these instruments tuned and the feedback out of Noah's mic, or would everyone rather continue speculating about who's family members I'm banging? If it's the latter, I'd like to go ahead and give Noah's grandmother a call while the conversation continues."

Noah's smile tells me he's not upset that I just drug him into this.

After a few snorts of laughter, everyone gets back on track but I catch Brett's eyes on me far more than usual. He finally relaxes when I stop playing and spread the love by giving *him* the middle finger this time.

He's a little more wound up today because Bri and Sienna stayed behind instead of coming to the concert. I can tell he's already itching to get back to his girlfriend.

After the sound check, we have the meet and greet. I usually really enjoy meeting our fans, but tonight, all I can think about is the picture on my phone and the woman I want to lay awake texting all night.

I'm staring into space when Brett nudges my shoulder, bringing my attention to the woman in front of me.

"Hi," I say, stiffly. Quickly realizing how sterile I sound, I try again. "I mean, hey, I'm Ryan. It's nice to meet you." The blonde in front of me gives me a coy look and lets her hand linger in mine too long.

"Brittany," the girl purrs, pushing her chest toward me.

"Do you have something you want signed?" I ask, looking at her empty hands before quickly adding, "I don't sign skin."

Brett whips his head toward me. "Since when is that a rule of yours?" he snorts under his breath.

I shoot him a *shut the fuck up look* and turn back to Brittany who's openly eye fucking me. *I* used to like this kind of appreciation, but now, all I feel is my skin crawling.

"How about you sign my shirt?" she asks, sticking pouty lips out and pointing right at her tits.

Agreeing, just to get her farther down the line, I uncap a sharpie and start a quick signature on the peak of the woman's breast. At the last second, Brittany throws her arms around my neck and presses her lips to mine.

I'm so shocked I don't move for several seconds. By the time my brain kicks back in, Tim, my body guard has pulled her off me.

"Damn, I think she got some tongue in the game," Brett says laughing while I wipe my mouth.

My phone keeps buzzing in my pocket through the rest of the meet and greet but it isn't until our last ten minutes before we go on stage that I'm able to check it again.

More pictures from Em's shopping trip.

Oh, fuck me. Why have I stayed away from her this long? *How* have I stayed away?

"Ry, you're blushing, what're you looking at that could have more potential than *Brittany?*" Brett says, goading me.

I snap my head up and see Brett standing in front of me, craning his neck to get a look at my phone screen.

Shit.

"I'm not into groupies any more than you are," I tell Brett, trying to get him off my back about the blonde assailant as my need to bathe in Clorox grows stronger. Fans aren't usually quite that aggressive. Have I been kissed by fans before? Sure, but all the other times, I egged it on. I wanted the interaction and needed the distraction. But Brittany? That was totally unwarranted and not encouraged at all.

Brett shrugs. "That's fair, but something has you off your game ... or some*one*. Care to share?" he asks.

"Not even a little."

"Afraid she'll be more into drummers with tattoos than your inkless skin and five o'clock shadow?" he laughs.

"Definitely *not*." God, if he only knew what he'd just insinuated.

He narrows his eyes at me. "You're one cagey bastard, you know that?"

I scoff, trying to reroute the conversation. "More than Sloan? We've lived with the fucker for six years and I still don't even know where he was born."

"Germany. On base. His dad was military too."

"How the fuck do I not know that?"

"Stop deflecting."

"Stop being so goddamned nosy."

"Are you ladies about ready?" Noah says, coming over to where Brett and I are arguing in the hallway backstage.

We can tell when they dim the lights in the arena because the crowd erupts and begins chanting our name. It's only been a few months since I heard it on a scale this big, but somehow, I'd forgotten the adrenaline rush that accompanies it. Suddenly, my fingers itch to play our songs and I'm overcome with desire for Em to be here and for Brett to be on board with she and I dating. I can't lose my best friend and this feeling of making music together but I also can't lose my chance with her either.

"Yes." *Please, let's get on with it already.*

Brett claps me on the back. Before he walks to the stairs leading to the stage, he turns serious and says, "Hey, I've found a way to say thank you you for bringing my family to Ireland, and before you protest, it doesn't involve a groupie, but I think you'll like it."

"There really isn't a need to do that, B."

"I know, but I want to."

"What is it?"

He winks and I absolutely hate the smile he's wearing as he throws my words from that train car six months ago back in my face. "It's a surprise."

I can't shake the terrible feeling that he's on to me.

Chapter 15

Emma

By lunchtime on Wednesday, I've completed all my required assignments, Jen's in class all day, and I love my mom but she's been hovering a lot since I got home. With nothing left to do, I reach in my bedroom closet and pull out one of the many blank canvases tucked in the back.

Next, I find the small basket with my acrylic paints in them and open the drawer containing my brushes. Painting in this room feels a little like talking to ghosts.

The act of setting everything up feels so foreign but also right, at the same time. My mind has been a swirl of colors and images since coming home and interacting with Ryan. The highs and the lows all want to be painted. The guilt, the anger, the lust, the desire, they're each a color fighting for center stage.

Choosing orange, I drag my brush through the paint and make an upward stroke. Immediately, I know where this is going. The image is as clear to me as if I were looking at a photograph.

I'm halfway done with the flames when my cell phone

starts ringing. It's a number I don't recognize, so I automatically send it to voicemail. Of course they don't leave one. Just as I find my groove again, my phone goes off once more. Another number I don't recognize. After the incident two years ago, Brett helped me bury my phone number so deeply, it should be impossible to spam call me.

When it happens a third time, I finally answer.

"Hello?"

"Hello, Ms. Donovan."

That voice.

Taking a deep breath, I walk over to my window, throwing it wide. I need open spaces and fresh air when my chest constricts like this.

"How'd you get this number?" I snap.

"I'm sorry but my sources—"

"Go to hell and don't contact me again."

I hang the phone up and slide to my floor. *You're okay. You're home. You're safe.* I repeat those sentences in an attempt to finally believe it.

When my text message alert pings, I almost throw my phone in the toilet until I see it's from Jennifer.

JENNIFER 12:37 PM

> Looks like pictures from the night at the beach bar finally surfaced. Honestly, I'm surprised it took this long. Media assholes got my number so I'm assuming they're blowing you up too?

I don't even have to put anything in the search bar. There, on my Google homepage is a picture of me, Jen, and Ryan. When I click on it, there are more. There's one with Ryan standing behind me. I can't see my face, but I can see Ryan's profile as well as the guy that was touching me. The next one shows Ryan taking a selfie with the same guy. Then there's one of Ryan leaning in, talking to Jen and I, and finally there's one of my face buried in Ryan's neck, my arms thrown around him as he carries me through the throng of people.

The title of the article is **_Another Drunk Donovan?_** There is no name associated with the article, although credit is given to the man who took the pictures. A quick Google search tells me it's not my assailant but I _know_. I know he's behind the article.

The captions are full of innuendos and make it seem like I'm shitfaced and Ryan had to carry me because I couldn't stand up. Not to mention, he uses my name which leads to questions and speculation in the comments about why Ryan came to my rescue and not Brett.

My breathing finally begins to slow down after having a couple minutes with no new phone calls. I quickly place my phone on Do Not Disturb to prevent another wave from coming through.

Okay, that wasn't so bad.

Certainly not as bad as it's been before. I attempt to stand up and discover the mild panic attack has tanked my energy. Attempting to paint now would be useless because my hands are shaking and my strokes would be shit.

Nonetheless, I feel proud of myself for staying in control through the triggering moment, but I celebrate too soon. Standing on wobbly legs, I make it to the edge of my bed and am overcome with exhaustion. A sign that my body is retreating inside itself.

Sleep comes so fast I don't even know it's happened until I wake up several hours later.

Tapping my phone screen to check the time, face ID automatically opens the phone, alerting me to twenty-seven missed calls and fourteen missed texts. Brett is at the top of the list followed by several numbers I don't know or are blocked.

I roll off the bed and take note of my rumpled shirt and wild hair. In an effort to cover my wrinkled clothes, I grab Ryan's fleece jacket that I never gave back and zip it up, inhaling deeply, the scent instantly working to calm me, before heading downstairs. As I slowly take the stairs one step at a time, making sure my knees don't give out as I go, I pull my mass of hair into a pile on my head.

I'll call Brett back, but first I need water and some food on my stomach. Based on how dark it is outside, I slept through dinner.

When I hit the landing, I hear my brother's voice.

"*Damn.* It's another one."

"Maybe you should answer one of them?" I hear my mom say. "Maybe you and Ryan should do it together."

"I'll handle it," Brett says matter-of-factly as I turn the corner.

"Emma, you're awake," he says, a look of relief washing across his features. "When you wouldn't answer your phone, I called Mom. She said you were sleeping, but I wanted to see for myself."

"Hey. Yeah, I was trying to paint and must've dozed off."

"The media have been blowing the guys and I up for comments over that fucking," Brett glances at our mother and corrects himself. "Freaking concert. I was afraid they were hounding you too."

Maybe I'm a coward for not telling anyone except Brett the details of that night. It isn't until right now I understand that it wasn't only his secret about Penelope that was eating him alive, but perhaps my secret is hurting him too and contributed to his excessive drinking and aversion to relationships.

I give my brother a tight smile. "Yeah, I've had a few missed calls."

"How many?" he demands.

"Twenty-seven."

Clenching his jaw, he says, "I only called four times." Turning his back to my mother and I, he types something on his phone and then holds it up to his ear.

"Parker, this is Brett Donovan." Pause. "Yeah, man. You too. The media's bothering my family again. I assume you've seen the pictures and the headlines?" Pause. "No, man. It isn't like that." Pause. "Yes, I'm sure. Besides, I already talked to him about it. He told me no." At this point, I can guess what they're talking about and the room spins. *Why is Ryan destined to always remain just out of reach?* "I want to go on the record and shut this bullshit down before it becomes a thing. If they want to talk shit about him fucking an NHL player's wife, I don't give two fucks, Ry can defend himself, but when they drag my kid sister into this mess? Fuck them. She's been through enough."

He agrees to something one last time and disconnects.

"I've been given the green light to issue a statement but the label wants me to do it through their correspondent which is fine with me. Do you want to say anything, Em?"

I shake my head. The only statement I want to make is to tell the world Ryan belongs to me, dammit.

Brett gets back on the phone while my mom disappears into the kitchen. The fact that she isn't standing over Brett's shoulder means she isn't worried. It's a small consolation, but it makes me feel like I did the right thing by not divulging the dirty details two years ago. She and my dad have dealt with enough.

Curious about how this statement is going to go, I curl up on the end of the couch opposite my brother. I pull the sleeves of Ryan's jacket down over my hands and ignore my brother's furrowed brows at the article of clothing which is obviously huge on me.

The look he's shooting at me tells me he knows exactly who the owner of this jacket is and he doesn't like it one bit. I'll admit it wasn't the best choice, but I needed comfort and when I threw it on, I had no idea Brett was here. Too late to hide it now.

Brett puts the phone on speaker.

"Jake, I need your help in setting the record straight. I don't like what they're insinuating."

"I'm all ears, Brett. Give it to me exactly as you want it printed and I can have it out within the hour with another push in the morning to reach more viewers."

"My sister wasn't drunk. Some guy was invading her space and making her uncomfortable. Ryan saw it first. By the time he got to her, the crowd couldn't be contained and fans were pressing in on them so in an effort to get my sister to safety faster, he carried her."

"I've got it, but you know people are going to ask. Are they together?"

Brett looks at me again, teeth clenched, one brow raised, almost in challenge. I feel trapped, but this time it isn't even the media making me feel this way, it's my own brother.

I shake my head.

No.

Because we aren't. Are we? Maybe we could be, but we haven't defined anything yet. Hell, we've barely had a whole conversation, so we definitely aren't together so I'm not lying. *Ah, justification at its finest.*

My stomach heaves, as Brett continues.

"It's no secret that I struggle with trust, especially when it comes to my sister. Ryan is one of the few people I *do* trust. With no regard for his own safety, he went after Emma, getting mauled in the process. He's a hero. Besides, if we were fucking everyone the media thinks we are, there'd be no time left for music."

The man on the phone chuckles.

"You're probably right. I'll get this out across all the Beautiful Deceit socials and posted in the comments everywhere the pictures show up." I like this guy, right up until he opens his mouth again "It would be quite a scandal, wouldn't it? Your best friend and your little sister, eleven years his junior. I'm sure Daddy Battle would have something to say about that."

Crazier things have happened, I think to myself.

Brett just laughs. "No one in the band would think about laying a hand on Em. Now if we're done here?"

"We're done."

With the statement Brett just issued, Ryan and I are most likely done as well. Done before we even got started.

Chapter 16

Ryan

I don't spend much time on social media but it's hard not to check in when I get notifications that I've been tagged in over forty thousand posts. I see the pictures, I've read the comments, and I can honestly say the only thing that surprises me is how long the photos took to surface. These days, anything regarding the band usually has traction immediately. Especially if one of us is carrying a woman in our arms.

Though, it's not until I read the statement from Brett and the label that I get pissed.

Stalking out of the studio Thursday afternoon, where I'm finishing the collaboration project I've been working on, I throw the kitchen door open to find Brett eating lunch.

"What the fuck is this?" I ask, holding up my phone with Brett's words on display. "You didn't think maybe I'd want to comment on my own actions?"

"Chill, Ry. I issued the statement because the media was starting to harass Em about the pictures and she can't..." he trails off not finishing his sentence.

"She can't what? Talk for herself?"

"She doesn't like to talk to them."

"I know she hates talking to them, but why? She wasn't always like that."

"You know why. My family got hounded when our last record took off."

"Yeah, all of ours did," I point out.

"But not because of your tragic past. Besides, your family is used to the media."

"Brett, what aren't you telling me?" I ask, dying of curiosity.

"I already told you, it's not my story to tell," he says calmly. "And don't ask her about it."

"Somebody needs to tell me what the fuck is going on!" I roar, at the end of my rope.

Brett gets in my face. "You need to calm the fuck down. I gave that statement to protect my sister and clear your name. Speculation was already starting that something was going on and you were bound to be raked over the coals for the age gap because you've known her so long. You think people would believe it just started?" He gives me a pointed look. "Besides, if nothing's going on, all I did was tell the truth and called you a fucking hero. *You're welcome.* Not to mention, those pictures make it look like Em's tanked and she's underage. As Jake pointed out, I don't think your dad would have been too thrilled with that kind of press."

I wish emotions and thoughts only made linear, upward progress.

I wish every time you had a breakthrough, you were guaranteed to never revert to a former version of yourself. Just two days ago, I felt like Emma had made me whole again and reminded me of the man I want to be, of the man I *am*.

Now, forty-eight hours later, her brother has destroyed that victory, reminding me that as long as I'm a public figure known for being my father's son and a member of this band, I'm never actually in control. I'll never have the luxury of just being myself without worrying about how my image affects those around me. I've gone backwards, losing myself once more to the expectations put on me.

Fucking fame.

"I just wish someone would tell me what happened so I could help."

He claps a hand on my shoulder. "You do help. But you need to let this go."

I would if I could but if someone hurt her, I won't let it go until they've paid.

Before I can answer, our phones ding at the same time.

NOAH 4:36 PM

Sienna and I are having a bonfire at our place tonight. 7pm. BYOB.

SLOAN 4:37 PM

Sorry, I'm busy.

NOAH 4:37 PM

I don't care if you're scheduled for a heart transplant, your ass better be here. This is important to Si. Bring your date. We don't mind.

BRETT 4:39 PM

Count me and Bri in.

NOAH 4:39 PM

I already did because Bri's already over here.

BRETT 4:40 PM

So why the text then?

NOAH 4:40 PM

Because you needed to know what time to show up, dumbass.

RYAN 4:42 PM

So what you're saying is even though our album isn't even half done and we're on a deadline, we're having band bonding tonight?

NOAH 4:42 PM

Basically. Since Sienna is the only one who's produced anything new lately, she's the one we're listening to. and she wants a housewarming party.

So she's getting one. See you fuckers at 7.

Turning away from Brett, I immediately reach out to Em.

RYAN 4:45 PM

You coming to Noah's new place tonight?

EMMA 4:45 PM

Yeah, Bri & Sienna both texted me.

Did you see Brett's statement?

RYAN 4:46 PM

Yes.

EMMA 4:46 PM

I had no idea that was his plan. He thinks he's helping.

RYAN 4:47 PM

I know.

I hate that my answers are so short but I don't know what else to say. It feels like every time she and I take a step forward, something knocks us back three. When I stay silent, so does she, and the ever-shifting chasm between us opens wider once again.

Pulling up to Noah and Sienna's new place, the first thing I admire is the privacy. A long, tree-lined driveway winds across a couple acres before ending in a circle in front of the white farmhouse. It screams rural Virginia and honestly, it's gorgeous.

I can definitely see Kink raising a family here.

Sienna comes out the front door and down the porch steps in fashionable, black joggers with a gold belt tied around her waist and a black sweater with gold rhinestones on it.

"Ry! Welcome! I'm so glad you could come!"

I'm about to laugh and tell her I didn't really have a choice, when I see Noah step onto the porch behind her, arms folded across his chest, shaking his head. His expression clearly reads *keep your fucking mouth shut.*

I may be bigger, but Noah can be intimidating as hell.

"I wouldn't have missed it for the world, Si."

I smile when Noah flashes me a thumbs up as I lean down to hug his fiancée.

"Come on, I'll give you a tour." She's so cute when she's excited, it's impossible not to follow her and gush over all the things I don't care about – like crown molding and bay windows.

I do have to admit though, the house is nice. Older, large, and reminiscent of a different time period, it's impossible to not feel like the world slows down here. It makes me think of my parent's cabin in Shenandoah. Man, I miss that place.

Out back is the real show stopper. A huge in-ground pool sits in the middle of a stone and concrete pool deck. Off to the left side is a hot tub that spills into the artificial lagoon. There's an outdoor kitchen, and a very modern, propane fire pit with those multi-colored glass rocks in it.

Assuming this is where we're gathering, I set my cooler on the lounger.

Sienna turns and gives me a coy smile. "I do love this area, but I think you'll like where we're going even better."

Okay, so this isn't it.

I throw the strap over my shoulder and continue to follow my hostess. Sienna is so short, I can see over her head, so I see the trail leading into the woods before we get to it. About two hundred yards into the darkening forest, I stop and whistle.

Surrounded by trees so completely you can't see the house or hear the pool fountain from here, there's a huge pit with a blazing fire in the middle. Eight blue and red Adirondack chairs sit around the fire ring. Lights are strung above us in the trees. It's so peaceful.

"I'm going to run back and wait for the rest of the guests," Sienna says. "I assume you'll be fine out here by yourself?"

I nod. I'd actually enjoy the whole evening out here alone. Perhaps some time soon, I can get back to my parents' cabin. "I'll be fine."

I sit down in one of the chairs and pour a small amount of scotch into the Yeti I brought. When Brett's around, we don't drink often, but I'd like something tonight, so I brought a cup with a lid in hopes the smell wouldn't tempt him.

Sitting in the solitude of the night, no screaming fans, no lights, no cameras, no people, no pressure, I feel the tension in my shoulders loosen despite things with Em being a mess.

I need to find out what she's hiding.

We certainly can't move forward if she's harboring secrets.

Being together is going to make a lot of people unhappy so if we do this, I need her to trust me fully.

"Nice place, huh?" Sloan says, coming into the clearing, a beer in hand. He clinks his beer against my Yeti and takes the chair next to me.

"Yeah, man. This spot is supreme. No date?" I ask, remembering his earlier text.

"Nah. My dick needs a minute to recover." Something about the way he says it makes me think maybe there wasn't actually a date at all.

Silence surrounds us for a minute but I take the opportunity to get to know my friend and bandmate a little better. "Think you'll ever settle down?" I ask seriously, staring into the fire. It must be the lack of eye contact that makes Sloan offer an answer.

"No. I had my chance and I lost it."

The raw pain in his words shocks me to my core and I have to work hard to keep my voice even.

"When?"

"A different lifetime, man."

He must be talking about the Army. I knew him before he went in, and I've been with him almost every day after, and he never mentions either time period, choosing to always live in the moment. Always has his dog tags on, but never mentions the places he went, the people he met, or the deployment he experienced.

"Well, I'm sure you'll get another chance."

He just nods and takes a swing of his beer. He must be remembering her now though, because he's playing with the metal tags around his neck when we're interrupted by more footfalls.

"Oh guys, this is so beautiful!" the sound of Emma's voice has me swinging my head to my left. She's clutching a glass of champagne, matching Sienna. Bri's drinking a Sprite, always staying sober in solidarity with Brett. The girls come in directly behind Em, and Noah and Brett are deep in conversation as they bring up the rear.

Sienna opens the top to a large wooden box I hadn't noticed until now and I realize it has a cooler inside along with shit for s'mores. I smile at the thoughtful decor that has Sienna's name written all over it. Kinky would never buy monogrammed shit ... or make s'mores for that matter.

The girls giggle happily as they get all the s'mores stuff out. Emma's hair is in a side-braid over her left shoulder and she has a Tornadoes Hockey ball cap on. Once she has her roasting stick all set, she walks around the edge of the fire until she's across from me. At first, I'm angry that she isn't right next to me but I can see her better from here and it'll be less obvious when I can't take my eyes off her.

Bri and Sienna move to the other side with Em and they all pull their chairs closer to the fire so they can roast their marsh-mallows while seated. I can't hear them over the crackling flames between us but when Em throws her head back in laughter, my balls tighten in response. She flashes me a quick smile before turning back to Sienna. The light from the fire dances in her radiant eyes.

I *need* her. And I need to know what she's keeping from me.

Next to me, the guys are talking about the album. Some-thing we should probably do more of honestly.

"I have track names down," Noah says. "And the album name."

"Shouldn't we vote on that?" Sloan asks, taking another sip of beer.

"We did vote on it," Brett reminds him.

"Oh, right," Sloan says, making it obvious he doesn't remember. "What did we pick again?"

"Transformation," I answer.

I was particularly fond of both the song and the idea to use it as our album name. I feel like it's time for a transformation of my own so I resonated deeply with the suggested title.

Standing, I grab the bottle of champagne from the ice bucket and make my way around the fire to offer Sienna and Emma a refill, and see if Bri wants another Sprite.

When I get closer to the girls, I look back across the fire at my bandmates and see a snake climbing up the leg of Noah's chair. Noah Kinkaid does not do wildlife.

"Hey, Kink, can you come here a second?" I ask, keeping my voice nonchalant.

"What's up?" he asks, still seated.

"I need help really quick, can you just come here."

"This sounds like a trap," he mumbles.

"For the love of God, man, I'm not Sloan, get your fucking ass over here." The snake is about to begin coiling itself around Kinky's calf so I need him to move *now*. It's too dark for me to see if the snake bears a pattern or not, and that has the potential to be extremely problematic.

Begrudgingly, Noah stands up and I relax as soon as he's out of the slithery guest's reach.

"What has your dick in a wad?" he asks, placing a kiss on Sienna's cheek since he's over here anyway.

I ignore Noah and address Sloan. For all his joking, at least Sloan's not a pussy. Occasionally working with Spec. Ops, he spent a lot of time in the woods and other outdoor areas, and I know he's my best bet to identify and remove the snake. *I'm glad the* one *thing I know about Sloan is coming in handy.*

"Sloan, you mind taking a look at the leg of Noah's chair and telling me if that's a friend or foe?"

Curious, everyone drives their attention to the chair leg. Brett hauls ass out of his own chair, Bri giggles and keeps eating her s'more, Sienna yells "Don't hurt it!" Noah clutches my arm like he's my date at the movies, and Emma catapults out of her chair, runs behind me, and jumps on my back.

"I'm not saying I'm scared, but I also see no need to stay on ground level where that thing's friends and family members are. Sorry, Battle, you're stuck with me as a backpack."

I put my hands under her knees and hitch her higher on my waist.

"It's just here to get warm," I tell her over my shoulder.

"Me too," she whispers in my ear so only I can hear as she squeezes my sides with her thighs.

Sloan reaches down and grabs the snake behind its head. Everyone gasps, making me chuckle silently.

Sloan unwinds the snake from the chair leg and holds it out, revealing a bright orange belly. "Mud snake. She's just cold."

"Throw it in the fire then. She's sure to stay warm there," Brett suggests.

"Ohmygod *no!*" Emma yells from my back. "It's just trying to survive!" she tells them, practically using my own words, immediately making me think of hers. *Me too, baby. Me too.*

Sloan walks further into the woods behind our group and lets the creature go.

Chapter 17

Emma

Once the snake is gone, and people resume their seats, I reluctantly slide off Ryan's back. It's amazing how easy it is to be around him even with everything going on. I get drawn back into a conversation with the girls but my eyes roam across the fire during every story they tell.

Ryan's leaning back in his chair. Sipping slowly on what I'm guessing is scotch. He catches my eyes several times and through the champagne haze, I'm more confident than ever this thing between us is growing. Despite Brett's very public announcement that nothing is going on between Ryan and I, something most certainly is. And I need it to move faster.

The one good thing that came from his statement was it caused the harassment to die down. Because Brett used the label's PR outlet, the label followed up with another statement saying all additional questions should be directed to them. Sleazy, low-grade reporters are more hesitant to go toe-to-toe with a recording giant with deep pockets than they are a twenty-year-old girl, and I've enjoyed the peace.

The evening is so pleasant, and my champagne glass never runs out as the girls and I take turns sharing stories. Sometimes we draw the guys in or listen to their conversations. Everything about this group's dynamics flows so easily.

At one point, Noah looks at Ryan, his eyes alight. "Oh man, I've got the sickest lines running through my head for *Abdication*. Listen to this." Everyone's either tipsy or totally buzzing – except for Brett and Bri – and I think somehow it makes Noah's voice even more incredible. The alcohol he's consumed gives his otherwise flawless voice a slight rasp, mesmerizing us all as he sings around the campfire.

So many threats.
So many rules.
So many eyes.
So many fools.
You put me on a throne I didn't need.
Opened up your veins, and let me feed.
This monster you've created, you now run from.
You've left me no choice,
Abdication.

"Damn, Noah, that's awesome," Bri says while the rest of just look at him with our mouths hanging open in awe.

"Ry, I *hear* it," Noah says, excited. "This one needs your bass line first because that's what I'm going to follow with the vocals. Come lay this down with me." Noah gets up from his chair and tosses his beer bottle in the trash bin next to the wooden cooler.

My heart sinks as Ryan gets up and follows behind Noah as they chat excitedly about finally making some progress for the album.

Sloan, Brett, Sienna, Bri, and I continue hanging out but

time passes quickly and before long, it's midnight. By the time Bri says she's ready to call it a night because it's still about forty-five minutes back to their house, Noah and Ryan haven't returned.

"Em, you want us to drop you off on our way home?" Brett asks, knowing I've had too much to drink to drive myself.

Before I can answer, Sienna pipes up, "She's welcome to spend the night here. It's too big of a pain in the ass to have to drive her back to get her car in the morning. Besides, I've already made the guest bedroom up and the renovation crew isn't due back until Saturday."

Brett looks at me with raised brows. "Em? That good with you?"

"Yeah."

"Well, now I feel like I'm missing out on girls' night," Bri pouts as Sienna pulls her into a hug. "You can stay too, babe. Anytime you want."

"Except tonight," Brett says. "I need more advanced notice. I've got plans for her tonight," my brother says wickedly.

Bri chuckles. "I'm not climbing over the console to give you road-head."

"Oh gross," I reply, covering my ears. I hear Bri's laughter even through my hands.

"I'm the one that missed dinner, so I'll be the one feasting tonight," my brother responds like I'm not even here.

"Okay, shoo," I say waving them away. "It's time for you two to go before I lose my champagne. And it was really good champagne so I'd rather not."

I give them both kisses on the cheek and tell them goodbye before helping Sloan and Sienna douse the fire, collect the trash, and lock up the wooden cooler with bungee cords to keep any curious critters out of it. Sloan says his goodbyes next and Sienna offers for him to stay as well but he says he stopped drinking at 10pm and has an early appointment at a guitar store in the morning that he needs to get back for. He kisses Sienna and I on our cheeks and heads for the driveway around the side of the house.

No one interrupts Noah and Ryan to say goodbye because we know better. They'll emerge when they're done.

Once we're back in the house, Sienna offers me a pair of pajama pants and a t-shirt. "I'm going to have one more glass of champagne while I wait for Noah and Ryan to wrap up. You want one?"

"That would be great." I'd hate for Sienna to drink alone.

We curl up on the couch with our glasses in hand.

"This house is really beautiful, Sienna. I'm so excited for you." I'm gushing because it's the truth although the champagne helps me be more vocal about it.

"Thank you. I never imagined in my wildest dreams that I'd ever be here. You know, my family life wasn't the greatest and I lived with Bri most of high school."

"I didn't know that," I admit.

Giving me a sad smile, she says, "Yeah, my mom was pretty shitty and my dad just never got the hang of being an adult."

I squeeze her hand. "I'm so sorry. I can't imagine how hard that must've been. My parents are incredible." *Which is why I work so hard to not let them down.*

"Yeah, I enjoy your parents a lot." She takes a sip of her champagne and tucks her foot under her on the couch and faces me. "So, what's going on with you?" For a second, I think she's about to ask me about school, like everyone does but she goes right for my heart instead. "How are things between you and Ryan?"

I feel my eyes go wide and she chuckles quietly. "I remember Ireland, Em. You don't have to be embarrassed.

Ryan's such an incredible guy. It's easy to see why you'd fall for him."

Sienna is so sincere and kind, it becomes impossible to keep my mouth shut. I divulge all the dirty details, completely purging my soul over another two glasses of champagne.

"And now, with Brett having issued that statement, if Ryan and I *do* start dating it'll either make Brett look like a liar or it'll be clear we went behind his back. Basically, I'm so in love with him it hurts to breathe sometimes but I just don't know if we'll ever be able to make it work." I end the admission right as the door to the basement opens and the object of my desire appears, a huge smile on his face.

"Maybe we should stay tanked while we write the rest of the album. Seems to work in our favor," he jokes with Noah, giving him a fist bump.

"Agreed. I can't wait to send everything to Brett and Sloan. This shit is awesome."

"Fuck, it got late," Ryan says, glancing at his silver, Omega watch. He pats his pockets, presumably looking for his keys.

"Ry, you're too fucked up to drive. Stay here, we have plenty of room," Noah says.

I can tell Ryan's about to argue, but his gaze swings to me and he takes in my pajamas, and the fact that I'm still here. Noah must see the same conflict raging in his eyes that I do.

"Look, I'll text Brett and tell him I'm forcing you to stay here. Who you're fucking will pale in comparison to you getting a DUI...or worse." He cuts his eyes to me and I know he's thinking of Penelope.

Ryan nods. "For the record, we aren't—"

Noah holds up his hands. "That's your business. You two are adults, as far as Sienna and I are concerned, we hear nothing, we see nothing, we say nothing. We're Switzerland. Right, baby?" He pulls Sienna into his side and kisses the side of her head.

"Right. We'll never forget how you were there for Noah and I when the tour company tried to keep us apart, Ry. Stay." Sienna reaches up high to squeeze Ryan's shoulder and I see the moment he gives in.

"Yeah, okay."

"Good," Sienna smiles. "Master bedroom is down here. Please help yourselves to anything. There isn't much in the kitchen since we don't stay here that often yet. I've set Em up in the yellow guest bedroom. The one across the hall is available, you know, if you want it. Bathroom is at the end. Goodnight."

She and Noah disappear around a corner and we hear a door shut softly.

Okay, Universe. I'm listening.

Ryan gives me a smile somewhere between *shy* and *wolf in sheep's clothing*. "I get the feeling we've just been set up. After you," he says, his low voice hitting my ears and sprinting south.

I swipe the rest of the champagne off the sideboard behind the couch. We'd just opened it and I'd hate for it to go to waste. *Because saving it for another day is absurd.*

Ryan smirks. "That's going to be one helluva hangover in the morning."

"You're one to talk."

"I can hold my alcohol a lot better than you."

"How do you know?" I argue, making my way up the stairs.

"Have you forgotten it was me that held your hair back at your sixteenth birthday party when Penelope challenged you to shots after your parents went to bed?"

I groan. "Ugh, God. I'd forgotten all about that...on purpose, I might add. Thanks for reminding me." My stomach churns at the thought. To this day I still don't really like liquor.

I also puked my ass off after only two shots. My sister made it through five because by sixteen, she'd already developed a tolerance.

Ryan huffs out a laugh as we reach the top of the staircase. Not knowing what to do next, I nod toward the bathroom at the end of the hallway. "You can have it first."

"I have a better idea." He takes the champagne glass from my hand and throws it back in one gulp. Then he takes the bottle, refills the glass, hands it back to me, and grabs my hand, pulling me down the hallway.

"Where are we going?"

"If you think I'm wasting this opportunity to be near you, you're wrong."

I swallow hard. I wasn't prepared for anything. Shit. I need to shave. I smell like campfire. I need a toothbrush. And those concerns pale in comparison to the other thoughts that flit through my mind.

What if I'm broken? What if I can't do it, even with Ry?

Stopping and turning me to face him, he runs a finger along my jaw. "Em. It's just me."

I wish I knew if that was the problem or the solution.

Chapter 18

Ryan

This is the first time Emma and I have been given actual privacy and longer than five minutes to talk face-to-face in quite a while. There's a lot to cover, but first I need her to open up to me. As soon as I push the door to the guest bedroom open, I see the bed and realize maybe this was a mistake.

No, you can do this. Just keep your fucking hands to yourself.

Easier said than done.

I shut the door behind her even though I'm fully confident Noah and Sienna will be true to their word and stay downstairs to give us privacy. The room is sparsely decorated with a king-sized bed, a chest of drawers, a chair in the corner, and a small mirror on the wall by the door, but it's clear they're making this house a home.

"Get comfortable, Em. Do you want the chair or the bed?" I ask.

"Depends on what we're doing, I guess," she says nervously.

"Talking, angel. We're talking."

"Um, chair, I guess. I'm afraid if I get on the bed, I'll fall asleep." She yawns as if her body required that she prove her point.

Deciding avoiding the bed is probably in both of our best interests, I sit on the floor with my back against the wall next to the door.

"So, um, what are we talking about?" she asks.

"I want to know what you're keeping from me. Your brother's always been protective but over the last couple years or so it's almost become an obsession for him, and when I confronted him about that statement he issued, he said he was protecting you but he wouldn't say from what."

She pinches her eyes closed and I want to go to her, but I know I'm pushing her somewhere uncomfortable so I need to give her space.

When she stays quiet, I keep talking.

"I want whatever this is between us to work, Em. The feelings I have for you, like yours for me, aren't going anywhere. This week has changed my entire life. And while it hasn't been easy, it also hasn't even begun to get hard. In order for us to stand any chance at all, we have to be completely honest with each other."

She stands up and begins to pace. I smile at the predictability of the habit.

"You mean you still want to try this? Even after Brett talked to the media and the label?"

"Like I said, it hasn't really begun to get hard yet, but yeah, I can't let this go. I can't stomach the thought of you going back to school this weekend and being cut off from me again. I hate not knowing where you are, who you're with, what you're doing. And now that I know there's some concrete reason for Brett's overprotectiveness, I need to know what it is, Em, because my mind is going down some really dark roads here, and I can't stand being helpless."

She stays quiet for a long time but finally whispers, "No one except Brett knows," as she stares at the cream-colored rug on the hardwood floor.

"I don't want to make you do something you're not ready to do. I don't want to cause you pain or make you uncomfortable, but aside from needing to know there are no secrets between us, I'm scared I'll accidentally trigger a reaction because I don't know what happened. My tastes are..." I have to clear my throat because my mouth is suddenly dry. I can't believe I'm *here*, with *her*, talking about *this*. "Not always gentle. I could really fuck up, Em, and have no idea that I've done it, and that terrifies me."

Her breathing hitches. "I know you wouldn't hurt me."

"Not physically, but I've hurt you before, remember?" It's only the second time either of us has mentioned Ireland since it happened. "It'll never be intentional, but I can't guarantee it won't happen, if I don't know what you're battling." I'm pleading with her to trust me with this. Without it, I don't see how we can move forward, but I don't say that out loud because I'll be damned if I guilt her into sharing something so obviously personal.

Finally, she takes a ragged inhale and sits on the floor opposite me, pulls her knees to her chest, and wraps her arms around them, hugging herself.

I brace myself for the story she's about to tell.

"When you guys rose to fame, seemingly overnight, our family was suddenly interesting. Specifically, *I* was interesting. The identical twin to a dead girl and the younger sister of a newly, but incredibly, famous rockstar, the media sought me out day and night. I didn't mind talking about Brett. I was proud of him. I *am* proud of him. But that wasn't good enough.

They wanted drama. Grief. Heartache, Trauma. That's what sells."

I hate the zoned-out stare in her eyes. She doesn't even see me right now. Her affect is as flat as her voice as she continues opening herself to me.

"Do you think your parents think of her every time they look at you? Do you think your sister was jealous of your intelligence and your brother's musical talent? With such a high IQ, you must be planning on doing great things. How will you live up to your brother's reputation? What do you think your sister would think of your brother's success were she still alive? These were the questions I got peppered with all day every day, and Penelope had only been dead for a year. I was raw.

"Finally, one day, I refused to answer. Keeping my head down and ignoring the large, greasy reporter walking next to me, he decided I should be punished for not dishing the dirt he wanted. When he proceeded to follow me onto campus, I turned back toward main street where the Christmas parade was happening, thinking I'd be safer in an area full of people but all it did was make him press in closer."

My teeth are going to crumble and my jaw is going to fucking snap for as hard as I'm clenching right now. My hands are balling into fists at my sides. I need to hit something. *Hard.* Every muscle in my body is tense. I want to stop her. I don't want to hear this and I don't want to make her say it, but I have to. And she has to. I have to know so I never, *ever* do something that causes her to have to relive this again. And she has to tell me so she knows nothing could ever make her less perfect in my eyes.

"The noise from the firetrucks and the kids' happy shouts drowned out my scream as he wrapped an arm around my waist, his stale breath in my ear. 'Someone's been naughty this year,' he said as Santa rolled by in the back of a Chevy Pick-up truck, waving, totally unaware that twenty-feet away, I was in trouble. The reporter said, 'All I wanted was some information and this whole situation could've been avoided,' but somehow, I doubted that. It wasn't the first time he'd stalked me."

She looks at me, a blank expression still on her face as she reads the not-so-blank one on mine. "Are you sure you want me to keep going?" she asks.

"If you can." It's all I manage to say as I try to prevent my emotions from taking over and smashing everything in Noah's new house.

Turning her gaze to floor, she admits, "I'm afraid you won't want me anymore."

"Emma, look at me, please." I wait for her to lift her head. "Nothing can change how much I want you."

"Okay, well, in the middle of the crowded sidewalk, he shoved his stubby fingers down my leggings, using that same hand to hold me against him. I was too busy trying to remove his hand to notice he'd managed to pull his camera phone out and was now snapping pictures of his hand against my pubic bone right before his finger plunged inside me. Something tore and burned like fire. Someone from the crowd knocked into us and I clutched her arm trying to get her attention for help, but the woman didn't even turn around. Instead, she yanked her arm away from me and moved down the row of people as if I was the offender. When the guy finally pulled his hand out of my leggings, he snapped a photo of my tear-stained face and said if I breathed a word, he'd publish the pictures. After all, *his* face wasn't in them. He left me there, being pressed in from all sides by the hoard of parade watchers and ever since, I've hated crowds and hated the media. That night, I called Brett and he found me curled in a ball on my dorm room floor after standing in the shower fully clothed until the water ran cold."

"What's this motherfucker's name?" My pent-up rage is about to be let loose like the heat of a thousand suns.

"I don't know. He never said. But he called me again after those pictures from Virginia Beach got out. I never told Brett that part because now I'm scared he'll relapse or do something crazy. You guys are so much more famous now than you were when that happened. If he goes off the rails, it'll incite the media all over again and send me right back where I started."

"Christ, Em. Surely we can bust this guy? Who does he work for?"

"I don't know that either. Brett went ballistic and spent months scouring the internet for reporters' photos after it happened, but I begged him to stop. I just wanted to move on, not spend my afternoons scrolling hundreds of faces for my attacker. Besides, I had no proof, no witnesses, and he possessed the images. I was eighteen and I could already see headlines claiming I was seeking attention of my own or some shit. If I had to guess, I think he bought the photos from the Virginia Beach show and he's the one who wrote that stupid article."

She shrugs like it's no longer a big deal. Like this guy's obsession with her is just going to go away even though he's still obviously fixated on her after two years.

I see red.

I've heard the expression, but I've never actually seen the color of fury before but it's clouding my vision now like someone put red lenses over my eyes. I can't breathe. I can't speak. I'm off the floor and out the door before I realize I just walked out in the middle of Em's story which is an asshole thing to do, but I'm about to wake Noah and Sienna and cause a scene if I don't get out of here.

I tear out of the house and make my way back toward the fire pit just needing space, fresh air, and the ability to yell. I don't even think before I sink my fist into the closest tree, the bark cutting my knuckles all to hell. When the tree doesn't give, it pisses me off even more so I pick up one of the Adirondack chairs and smash it against the trunk, just wanting to cause damage. The chair splinters as I roar into the darkness. I bash the chair into the tree over and over until it's in pieces and the tree is bleeding sap.

My arms are covered in blood as it pours from the cuts on my knuckles and forearms from the jagged edges of the chair.

This is why I never lose control. This is why I remain in charge. This is what lurks beneath the surface. I want to kill that motherfucker.

I *will* kill that motherfucker.

I'm doubled over, panting, when Em comes into the clearing.

"Ry?" she asks, tentatively.

"Em, I'm so fucking sorry."

I'm sorry I ran out like that. I'm sorry that sick sonofabitch touched you. I'm sorry you've been living in fear.

"It wasn't your fault, Ryan. Just like it wasn't Brett's. Or mine."

I get it together enough to ask, "Have you seen him since then?"

"No."

"I want to tear that guy's fucking head off. *Jesus,* and to think I basically threw you against the wall at my house and groped you. My God, Emma, I'm so fucking sorry."

She walks over to me and wraps her arms around my waist. I stiffen, hesitant to touch her back for fear of crossing some line.

She looks up at me, arching her neck back, causing me to lace my fingers through her hair and cradle her head.

"This is why I didn't want to say anything to you. I don't

want you to tiptoe around me. The more you let it influence your actions around me, the more power it has. Not everyone heals by talking about it. Some need silence. I refuse to be a victim." She pulls away from me, but I reach for her, catching her wrist.

I sit down on an un-mutilated chair and pull her down in my lap.

"I'll do whatever you want as long as you understand that talking about it doesn't make you a victim, Em. It makes you a survivor. It doesn't change who you are. I don't mean to tiptoe around you, but if we move forward with this relationship, I need to have some awareness so I don't ever make you uncomfortable with my words or actions."

"But that's just it, isn't it? I don't want to become another responsibility for you. Someone you have to constantly watch out for and be on guard around," she says, getting upset.

"It's too late for that, Em. I've been watching out for you for years, and it's been my absolute honor. I'm just sorry I wasn't there the day you needed me at that parade."

"Shit happens. That time it happened to me. At least I'm alive," she says, her strength and resilience coming through in full force.

"Tell me what not to do. I don't ever want to do something that causes you to recall that day, especially when we're having ... being... intimate." I see her pupils dilate in the moonlight.

"Does that mean you plan on being *intimate* with me soon, then?" she asks, the corner of her mouth quirking into a smile.

"Em, be serious."

"I am being serious. Ryan, I've wanted you a long time but I can't help but feel every time we get close, something else threatens to tear us apart."

"Then we should stop wasting time. You take the lead, I'll follow."

She shakes her head. "I don't know enough to take the lead."

Suddenly, I have an idea. "We'll use the stoplight system. Green means *good,* yellow means *this is okay, but slow down,* red means *stop.* If I start moving in a direction you don't like, give me yellow or red."

"Like a safe word?" she asks and I feel myself grin.

"Kind of like a safe word, yeah." She may never be ready for all the things I enjoy, but I'll find other ways to keep us both satisfied.

When she brings her mouth to mine and mumbles *green* against my lips, I know it'll be easy to do.

She pulls back slightly. "Just don't think of me as fragile," she pleads before placing her lips back to mine.

Instantly, I recall my conversation with my father and how the word was such a terrible descriptor for the strongest woman I know.

Chapter 19

Emma

"It's really cold out here without the fire," I tell Ryan as I nuzzle my face against his chest. The heat of desire would keep me warm, but the story I told was too emotional to be able to jump right into full-blown making out. Ry's kisses are tentative, gentle, and slow. I've struggled with the incident for two years. Ry's only had ten minutes to process it. His hands haven't moved from my knee and I know he's thinking about everything I just told him.

"Let's go in and get you to bed," he says.

"Will you stay with me tonight?"

"You're sure you want that?"

"Green," I say, giving him a coy smile.

"Okay, but if I get hard in the middle of the night, it's not intentional, I swear."

"Ry, if you get hard in the middle of the night, it's likely to push me right out of the bed." I can't keep my giggles quiet as we head up the path to the house for the second time tonight.

Sharing the story with Ryan, lightened my burden far more

than I expected. It erased certain expectations I hadn't even realized I'd put on myself.

When I flip on the bedroom light, I shriek. "Ryan! Your hands!"

He slowly bends and straightens his fingers, wincing as he does so. "Yeah, I should probably wash those."

"Come on, I'll help you."

I lead him to the bathroom at the end of the hallway. All I find are towels, washcloths, and a lime-verbena hand soap.

"I think we should just stick with water," I tell him, turning the faucet on warm. I get the corner of the washcloth wet and begin to clean up the dried blood, hoping the cuts underneath aren't as bad as they look.

"I'm surprised you can still hold an instrument for the beating your hands take."

He shrugs. "Something's gotta keep me sane." He puts a finger under my chin and makes me look at him. "Come to the gym with me tomorrow. Let me teach you some basics in self-defense."

"Okay." I swallow hard, savoring the closeness.

"Okay," he whispers, before kissing me lightly on my lips. When he pulls back, my eyes are still closed and I'm panting. "My hands are fine, Em. Let's go to bed."

I shut off the water and follow him to the bedroom, where he goes to slide under the covers still in his jeans and t-shirt.

"You aren't going to take those off?" I ask.

"Not tonight."

"But you smell like campfire. And what if you have ticks on you?" I point out.

"Em, as I demonstrated earlier, I have great control ... until I don't. I'm not ready to trust myself quite yet, so my clothes are staying on."

"Boxers?" I press. Clearing the air about my past seems to

have given my desire for Ryan more room to grow. Unfortunately, it's caused him to proceed with even more caution than before.

"Emma," he growls, just the way I like. "Don't push it."

"I don't want to waste the opportunity. I'll keep my pajamas on. They don't smell smoky," I negotiate, desperate for him to give me this one night.

"Fine," he relents. "But please spare me. Keep your hands above my waist, Ems. Earlier, I needed you to trust me. Now, I need you to show me I can trust you."

"Yes, sir," I chuckle, knowing I'm testing his limits unfairly.

I crawl into bed beside him, mentally and emotionally exhausted. I'd love to keep talking to him but as soon as my head hits his warm, bare chest, his beating heart falling into rhythm with my own, I fall into a sleep so deep I might as well be in a coma.

The next morning, a knock on my door pulls me from my slumber. I'm completely disoriented and I jump when I feel the large body next to me before memories of last night flood my mind.

"Hey guys," Noah says through door. "Are you awake?"

"Yeah, I'm up," I answer, sleep making my voice thick.

"Sorry to wake you, Sienna's got to be at the aerial studio in an hour and I'm meeting Brett and Sloan at the house soon. They want live vocals while they work with Ry's bass line, so I've gotta leave in half an hour.

"Okay, we'll be down in a...I mean *I'll* be down in a second."

Noah laughs. "Em, Ry's bed is empty and his car's out front. Your secret's safe with me and Si. Don't feel like you have to hide here, okay?"

"Thanks, Noah," I reply through the still-closed door.

When I look up at Ryan's face, his eyes are open and he's grinning down at me. "Am I dreaming?"

"Nope," I reply, grinning just as wide. I lace my fingers on his chest and rest my chin on them. "Does that scare you?"

"I'm fucking terrified."

"Me too, but in a good way," I giggle.

"I want to stay here just like this all day but since Kinky is so rudely kicking us out, I'll swing by your parents' house to take you to the gym around one."

My parents.

"That reminds me, Ry, my parents don't know about ... anything. They were dealing with enough wounds being reopened and Brett's drinking problem that I never mentioned anything. I swore Brett to secrecy."

He brushes my hair back from my face. "I understand, Em. And I don't think I said it last night, but thank you for telling me."

Begrudgingly, we climb out of bed and I change back into my clothes from last night before descending the stairs to Noah and Sienna for a cup of coffee on their back porch.

"This house makes me want a place of my own even more," Ryan says wistfully.

Sienna smiles at me over her coffee cup. "You sure it's this house that makes you want that, Ry?"

"Touché, Sienna." He leans over and kisses my cheek. "What a clusterfuck," he chuckles. The sound of his laughter fills my heart. "Thank you, guys, for everything. Em and I have a long road ahead of us, but it helps knowing we have people in our corner."

Ryan and I drove separately, so we say goodbye with a lot of tongue in the privacy of Noah's driveway before going our separate ways, my heart threatening to soar right out of my chest.

Once I get home and shower, I check in with Jen to see if she's free for lunch.

"I wish! They freaking called me in to work another double this morning." Jen's in school to become a nurse but right now, she works as a CNA – certified nursing assistant. It's a hard job. She's underpaid, overworked, and people treat her like the shit she often has to clean up.

With time to kill before Ryan shows up, and Jen busy, I try my hand at picking up where I left off on the last canvas, the original image I saw so clearly, has morphed into something new.

Still, the fire in the middle is needed as it represents the refining process, but now, a series of images develop through the fire. A person lying prone on the bottom of the canvas. A mirror in the middle of the fire with the reflection of a knife, and finally, black wings at the top arching over it all.

The meaning for me is both dark and light. The transformation that happens when you face your fears. The old you that dies and the new you that rises above it all. The painting happens quickly and before I know it, Ryan's texting me that he's outside. I change into workout clothes and rush out the door.

"You have paint in your hair," he says, smiling as he backs the Aston Martin out of my parent's driveway.

"I've finally started again." The excitement in my voice is hard to mistake.

"Why did you stop?"

"The truth?"

"Preferably," he deadpans.

"I haven't painted since Ireland. I just...lost the desire, I guess."

"I'll never stop telling you how sorry I am for that. For what it's worth, it killed me just as much." He leans over to squeeze my knee.

"Just don't ever do that shit again," I tell him, wrapping myself around his arm simply because I can.

When we arrive at the gym, I'm ready to kick some ass. I've never thrown a punch in my life but today, I'm ready. The smell of ball sweat and mildew hits me square in the nose as I follow Ryan into the gym. He greets a few guys with fists bumps and head nods. It's not overly crowded and security is noticeably absent.

"Do these guys know who you are?" I ask, shocked at the lack of fangirling amongst the men.

"Yep, and they don't give a shit because on the mat it doesn't matter how famous you are, if you aren't good, they'll still kick your ass."

"Do you get your ass kicked a lot?"

He throws his head back in laughter.

"No, sweetheart, I *give* the ass-kicking."

Good to know.

"Hey, Ry. Who you got with you?" a large, older man, appearing to be in his late fifties, asks. The man stands a couple inches shorter than Ryan and looks like he spends more time coaching and less time on the mats these days. As he approaches, he leans heavily on a cane.

"Solomon, hey. This is Emma. We're going over some self-defense techniques this afternoon."

"Emma, nice to meet you." He shakes my hand and turns back to Ryan. "Mat three is all yours."

"Thanks, Sol." Ryan grabs my hand and leads me to what I'm assuming is mat three. There's no ring, just two huge mats that when taped together have a full circle painted on them. "Drop your stuff on the bench and meet me in the middle."

I set my water bottle and the towel he told me to bring on the bench and unzip my jacket, leaving it behind too. When I face him in the circle in my workout tank top his eyes are locked on my chest.

"Well, this should be easy. Your balls are wide open," I tease as I drive my knee toward his nuts to bring him out of his trance.

He catches my thigh and uses it to pull me closer, which knocks me off-balance. He's ready for it though, and sweeps one arm under me, lowering us both to the mat gently, landing with his knees on either side of me, pinning me easily.

"Never underestimate your opponent. That's rule number one."

I skate my hands up his abs over his t-shirt. "What's rule number two?"

"Don't molest your instructor." He immediately winces at the joke. "Fuck. That wasn't funny. I'm sorry."

I prop myself up on my elbows. "Hey. None of that. I don't even think about it when I'm with you. Don't stop making jokes. Don't change who you are in an effort to make me comfortable. I can't have you on eggshells, Ry. I need you to just be yourself. Got it?"

He gives me a crooked grin. "Got it." Rolling off of me, he hops up and offers me his hand. "Okay, let's be serious. The first thing I want to teach you are grip breaks. If someone grabs you, the first thing I want you to do is break their hold and run like hell."

"What if—"

"This is just where we're starting. We're going to play to your strengths. You're light and fast. There won't be many grown men you can outfight without training regularly, but I know you can outrun most of them."

I nod. "Makes sense."

"For obvious reasons, we're going to start with how to get out of someone's hold if they've got their arm around your waist. You're at an extreme disadvantage here because of our height difference but most people aren't as tall as me."

Ryan moves to stand behind me and wraps his massive forearm across my stomach as he speaks instructions in my ear. My inner slut is backing into him, wiggling from side to side, reveling in the feel of him behind me. I smile. *Not broken.*

"Emma." Ryan's sharp tone snags my attention as his hand stills my hips. "I'm going to need you to stop doing that."

My turn to apologize. "Sorry."

"As I was saying, the best place to break a grip is the weakest part of it. If someone has their arm around your waist, their fingers most likely are not in a fist. Therefore, their fingers are the weakest point of that grip. Specifically, their *individual* fingers are the weakest. I want you to grab my index finger and start pulling it back."

I do as he tells me to, careful to not dislocate his finger.

"Try to hurt me, Em. I need to know you can hold your own."

I crank harder.

"Good girl." While I'm lost in a daydream brought on by those two words, Ryan starts instructing me on what to do next. "Em, you with me?"

"Uh, yeah, sorry, what was that?

"The instinct is to turn away from the person holding you, but you'll just end up dancing in circles. As you crank my finger back, I want you to turn into me. Slowly at first, so you can get the hang of it."

I do as he says but grow confused. "Now I'm even closer to you and you can just wrap your other hand around my back to trap me," I point out.

"True." He does exactly what I just explained and brings his other arm around my back. "But if you bring your knee up, since you demonstrated a fondness for that maneuver, you'll connect, and now I don't have a free hand to grab your leg or protect myself. But maybe let's not practice that part at full strength. I do want to go over it again though, faster."

So we do. Over and over and over again until he's satisfied.

"Now let's go over wrist grabs. Same principle. Find the weakest spot, which is the space between the thumb and index finger. I want you to exploit it by yanking hard. If your other hand is free, grab your fist and use both hands to pull yourself out of the grip."

After we cover three moves, I'm so turned on I can barely see straight. I've spent the last two hours brushing up against Ryan's body and feeling his arms around me.

"Hey Ryan, if you've got a second, I need a partner to work something out with," a young guy with brown hair says, approaching our mat.

I could use a quick break for some water anyway. Although the moves aren't challenging, it's still a lot to process and I've worked up a sweat and if I don't get my lust under control, I'm going to rip Ryan's shorts right off his hips.

At least he still has his shirt on.

"Em, you good hanging out for a few minutes? There's one more move I want to show you and then we'll call it a day."

"No problem. Take your time." Happy to be a spectator, I

sit on the bench but choke on my water as Ryan tears his shirt over his head, laughing. *So much for that.*

"No way am I giving you the opportunity to choke me with my own shirt, Dillon. It's either skin or gi and I don't have my gi so take it off, man."

Dillon's shoulders are narrower than Ryan's – *aren't eveyone's* – and he doesn't have as much muscle mass covering his torso, but he's still plenty muscular. Watching these two bent low and going full bore on this mat, does something to me. Ryan flips Dillon over and the man grunts when he lands on his back. He quickly throws his knees up and wedges his arm in between he and Ryan's bodies and latches on to Ryan's left wrist and tugs him down while simultaneously trying to lock his ankles behind Ryan's back.

"I see what you're trying to do here," Ryan says through panted breaths. "But you've left yourself vulnerable because I'm bigger than you." All at once, Ryan throws his chest down and pops his hips up breaking Dillon's ankle lock. "You're so focused on controlling my arm, you haven't noticed that I've passed the guard and am about to mount you."

Dillon's face turns red as he tries to fight Ryan off of him but it's clearly no use. Once Ryan's straddling poor Dillon's frame, Dillon taps the underside of Ryan's thigh since it's the only spot he can reach.

When the guys stand, Ryan shakes Dillon's hand. "You've got something good there and it'll be useful for an opponent closer to your size. Just don't get too focused on controlling the arms when the power and control is in the legs. Let's go again."

Dillon ends up on his back again, but this time, he throws his hip out to the side, and draws his bottom leg into his chest. He still has Ryan's left arm in his grasp and when he pulls hard, it knocks Ryan off balance onto his back. Dillon quickly sits on Ryan's thighs and grabs his left wrist with both hands, pulling his arm straight. He wraps his right leg over Ryan's upper arm, forcing Ryan to tap *his* thigh this time.

"Much better, man. Get that control early. You get anyone's elbow in that position and they either tap or they're headed to the emergency room."

"Yeah, thanks, Ryan," he pats Ry on the back and then dips his head to me. "Sorry to interrupt your training, ma'am." Dillon says to me, respectfully.

"Everyone here is so nice," I point out once Dillon's out of ear shot.

"Respect is a large part of this sport. The mat is a great equalizer. In here, no one cares what you do for work, how much you make, what you drive, or how big your dick is." He rakes his eyes down my body and leans in close. "But just so we're clear, I have the coolest job, make the most money, drive the hottest car, and I definitely have the biggest dick."

I laugh the hardest I've laughed in a long time.

"As if there was any doubt, Ry."

He grabs my hips and pushes me out onto the mat. "Okay, last one and then we'll call it a day."

He's still shirtless and sweating. With my back to whoever is left in this gym, I step closer and lick a line from his nipple to his collarbone.

"I have a better idea," I smile using the words he told me last night.

"Em, I can't hide a boner in these shorts."

God, his shorts. Fight shorts are *short* and his powerful quads are on full display. It's a miracle I even found his chest because everything else looks so fucking hot too.

"I think it's time to go," I rasp.

"Soon, Em. Let's go over that last move. I'm trying to figure out a way to spend more time together, but right now, if we leave, our time is up. You can't come back to my place and I can't go back to yours because I can't ask your parents to keep this secret from Brett. Speaking of, we're going to have to talk about your brother at some point."

"Yeah, I know. I just wanted the easy part to last a little longer."

"I'm not sure you and I have ever had an easy part."

Truer words have never been spoken.

Chapter 20

Ryan

Friday morning the guys and I powered through two more songs bringing our total of finished songs to six. I've been able to lay down new lines for a couple more and I know it's because my emotions are running wild with all that's going on between Em and I.

By the time Friday evening rolls around, I'm in a weird state of elation at the progress on the album, kissing Em, and finally getting her to open up to me, extreme anger over someone touching her, *assaulting her,* and finally, ungodly stress over having to talk to Brett. It can't be avoided any longer.

Figuring it's going to suck no matter what, I prepare for another fight, off the mats this time, and go in search of my bandmate. My knuckles still protesting from the round with the tree, but they'll deal. It'll mostly be Brett doing the punching and me defending as best I can. I'd love to have this resolved before the game tonight.

As I'm walking through the living room to find Brett and get this over with, the doorbell rings.

On my doorstep is a very attractive blonde with her hair in

a severe knot on the back of her head, not a single hair out of place. She's in a fitted black dress that hits just below her knee, and plain black pumps. She kind of looks like a hot principal.

Her ruby red lips spread into a smile when she sees me.

"Your size tells me you must be Ryan." Her hand darts forward quickly for me to shake. "Nina Cosgrove."

"Neen! Is that you?" Sloan yells, barreling down the steps half dressed.

Opening the door wider, I usher her in, letting my guard down a little. "You must be Sloan's date, although let me be the first to say, you're way more attractive than he is." I say it loud enough to fuck with Sloan more than pay this lady a compliment. She's attractive but she's not my type.

At that moment, Brett comes around the corner in a black band shirt with a gray blazer and black jeans.

"I'm glad you feel that way Ry, because Nina is *your* date."

"Come again?"

He grins, obviously feeling proud of himself. "You didn't want a groupie, you make no time to find someone, and Sloan mentioned she's a huge fan of the Tornadoes. I figured if she's good enough for Sloany to keep around, she's got to be pretty solid so I reached out to see if Nina was interested in accompanying you tonight." He holds his fist up for me to tap with my own. "You're welcome."

That's when it hits me. "This is the surprise you set up for me?"

"Yep." Brett finally sticks his hand out to Nina. "Brett. Nice to finally meet you. Thanks for coming tonight."

Nina's eyes flick to my chest. "The pleasure is all mine."

"Brett, can I talk to you privately for a second, there's something we need to discuss."

"It'll have to wait until after the game. I'm about to hop on a conference call," Brett says, walking into the kitchen, headed for the fridge.

"This is really important," I call after him, annoyed.

"So is this call," he says over his shoulder, dismissing me.

"Neen, I'll catch up with you tonight, I need to finish getting ready." Sloan kisses Nina's cheek and heads back upstairs leaving Nina and I mostly alone.

Fuck. I need to text Em.

As I pull my phone out, Brett jumps on me. "You're not going to be the douche that ignores his date and plays on his phone all night, are you?" He asks, passing back through the living room before following Sloan up the stairs.

This house isn't big enough anymore.

"Fuck off, Brett. I still have business to attend to just like you. Go get on your damn call." He knows I'm pissed. He knows I didn't want this. My reaction now isn't doing anything to lessen his suspicion and Nina doesn't deserve my attitude.

I pocket my phone.

I'll explain to Emma when we're face to face. She'll understand. She has to.

I try my best to smile at Nina.

"It was really nice of you to come tonight but contrary to Brett's belief, I'm not looking for a relationship."

"Not a problem, but we could all use more friends, right?" I can't quite figure out if she's being serious and genuine, or if she's offering to be fuck buddies with no strings. The way she's playing with the silver necklace at her throat suggests the latter.

"So, how long have you known Sloan?" If we're forced together, I might as well attempt small talk.

"Alexander and I go way back. We met in basic training. Ran into each other again on deployment."

"And you've kept in touch all this time?"

"We have," she shrugs. "It's only been six years."

"That's a lifetime for Sloany." *Plus, he's never mentioned you,* I think to myself. "You guys ever date?" I ask, just making conversation, not thinking about how it probably makes me sound jealous.

"*God, no.* Sloan was more interested...you know what? Never mind."

I'm intrigued. My level of respect for Nina just went up for keeping Sloan's secrets but what kind of secrets does he have?

"Has he always been so closed off, deflecting with jokes?"

"Ryan, if you want to know so much about Sloan, maybe you should take *him* as your date," she says, not unkindly.

I huff out a laugh at being called out. "Sorry. You're right. He just doesn't open up much, even to us."

"Sloan went through some shit. Knowing he had the band to come home to kept him going. You guys are his family."

What the fuck happened? I wonder, not for the first time.

"Can I get you a drink?" I offer her, realizing we're still standing in the living room and I'm a terrible host. "We don't keep alcohol in the house, but I've got soda and water."

"Water would be fine, thank you."

I lead her into our kitchen and look around. We're pretty clean for four guys, mostly because Bri and Sienna have been living with us, but I'm slightly embarrassed as we walk into the small room. It's dark and the small counters are cluttered with dishes, someone's hat, and opened mail. I think of Noah and Sienna's big, open kitchen. Especially the light from the bay windows – that I didn't care about at the time, but now oddly wish for.

My hands ache to touch Em.

I try to discreetly pull my phone out of my pocket again to text her but as soon as I do, Noah bursts through the back door.

"Hey, Ry, I need your phone."

"Why?"

"Because I moved my professional recording system to the studio at the new house and I can't play your bassline off the computer and record at the same time on the one I have here. Plus, I deleted the file off my phone after I sent it to you because it was so big."

I don't get my phone back until it's time to leave.

Chapter 21

Emma

My nerves and excitement grow in equal measure as the evening draws near. I love hockey and have no time to go during the semester but I do try to catch a game when I can. Halfway between ripping every item out of my closet and rationally piecing together potential outfits, my phone pings.

BRI 5:09 PM

> I've got something for you. Is now a good time to come get ready?

EMMA 5:09 PM

> Yes, please!

I hop in the shower to make sure I have enough time to do my hair before Bri gets here and am in a towel, drying said hair, when I see my bathroom door open behind me in the mirror.

Bri looks absolutely stunning. Like *holy-crap-girls-aren't-my-thing-but-she's-making-me-think-they-could-be* kind of stunning.

Dressed to kill in a red, sequined Tornadoes jersey, black leggings, and red thigh high boots, if the players catch sight of her, their concentration is going to be screwed. Her eyes are dark and her lips are pale, creating quite an alluring effect.

"You're way too hot for my brother," I laugh, the sound coming far easier since opening up to Ryan.

"I know, but I love the grouchy fucker anyway," she teases, winking at me. "Okay, let's get you dressed, shall we?" She sashays out of the bathroom and heads back into my bedroom, laying out the garment bag on my bed and puts a shoebox next to it, as well as a small black bag I'm hoping contains makeup.

She's a godsend because after foundation and mascara, I'm pretty much clueless.

She leans forward to unzip the garment bag and reveals a custom Tornadoes jersey just for me. This one is black with a red funnel cloud on the front. The right winger's last name has been embroidered down both sleeves, as well as across the back ... in white sequins.

I may be in love with Ryan Battle, but the Tornadoes right wing has been a longstanding source of lust for me. At 6'4" and 220lbs, I'm starting to think I have a type.

"How'd you know he's my favorite?" I ask Bri, running my fingers along the sparkling dots.

"I asked your brother," she says simply, catching me off guard.

"I'm surprised he knows that."

"Brett's more observant than he gets credit for." It feels like a warning even though there's nothing in her tone that makes me feel like my secret is in danger.

The women's jerseys are long, so it will hit mid-thigh, even on me, but it has a slit in the side that I can already tell will land high enough to piss Brett off. This particular version has ties at the neckline like a regular jersey, but instead of only going down an inch or two, it plunges a good six inches.

Bri winks at me and I know she did this with extreme purpose.

"I had our costume designer at the aerial studio start the alterations on this beauty on Wednesday," she says shyly – which so isn't like Bri. "It's time to live a little, Ems. You work so hard in the classroom, fuck those nerds for being jealous and insecure."

I can't help the laugh that follows. I like this woman a lot.

As she lifts the lid of the shoe box, my excitement kicks up another notch. She's given me matching thigh-high boots like hers, in black. I've never worn anything like them in my life. I spend so much time in practical clothes. There's an expectation of conservative dress on campus and I don't really have time to go out, so getting to be a little wild with my wardrobe tonight adds to my excitement. Coupled with my new panty purchase, I'm really feeling good about it.

"You like?" she asks nervously.

"Very much. Thank you, Bri."

She beams and I wrap her in a hug, grateful she's found her way into my life.

"Come on, let's do your hair and makeup." The devilish glint in her eyes tells me I'm in for a treat.

The hired car service pulls into the parking lot, and I can already see there's a pretty massive crowd gathered around the players' entrance at the back of the arena. Feeling sexy and ready to play with fire, I sit up straighter to take in the masses who would give almost anything to be in my shoes right now. I've never been envious of Brett for his fame, but I'm sure going to eat the perks of it up tonight.

"Wow, that's a lot of people," I mutter as the crowd seems to go on forever around the back of the arena. The signs held aloft don't bear the names of the Tornadoes players ... these people are here for Beautiful Deceit. To be honest, I'm not sure who has more fans here tonight: the hockey team or the band.

"Yeah, it can be overwhelming." She bats my hand away from my eyes where the fake eyelashes tickle my eyelid. "Dab. Don't rub."

"Do you ever get used to it? The crowds and attention, I mean." I clarify, unable to shift my focus from the masses.

"Eventually. Your perception of what's normal just shifts to accommodate the weird reality of fame," she says reasonably, catching my hand and walking me toward the door being propped open by security.

A giant sign with my brother's name catches my eye. Taped to the corner is a red thong. Looking closer, I realize our last name has been crossed out and under ~~Donovan~~ is the phrase DiveRightIn. I fight the urge to throw up in my mouth as my heart rate kicks up a notch, and the question is out before I can think about it too much.

"What's it like knowing all those women want to sleep with your boyfriend?"

Bri doesn't grill me about why I'm asking. She just begins to explain. "When I first started seeing your brother, before it was 'official', it drove me crazy. I'm a terribly jealous and territorial person," she admits. "But, once the world knew we were together, it got a little better. They can scream and cry and hold up signs all they want, but I know Brett only has eyes for me

193

and whether they like it or not, they all know he's taken." And then she shimmies her shoulders and adds, "And I make sure he knows he'll never have it better anywhere else."

I throw my head back in laughter. Bri has a way about her and I hope my brother realizes he'd be a total dumbass to let her go.

But my brain won't release her words: *once the world knew we were together*. If I could only be with Ryan in secret would that be enough? I don't think so. I don't want to hide. Not from the world, and certainly not from my brother.

"Come on, let's face the masses and gorge ourselves on someone else's dime while watching these sexy fuckers fight for the puck."

We're led by security through the checkpoint where our bags are searched and then escorted to an escalator that takes us up to the club-level box where we're greeted by more security, someone who checks our tickets, and a hostess.

The pencil-thin, three-inch heels on my boots took a couple of tries to master but I've finally figured out how to distribute my weight to keep my balance. I feel undeniably sexy as the jersey swishes across the nude tights covering my thighs. I would have preferred black leggings like Bri's but she'd argued, *your thighs are too sexy to cover with leggings.*

I tried to point out that her legs were nicer than mine and *she's* in leggings, to which she responded, *my legs are nice, but my boyfriend is not, and if he catches someone checking me out, he'll cause a scene. You, on the other hand, are trying to draw the attention of a quiet, stubborn man and we need to hit him hard if we want to see progress.*

I smile at the exchange.

I step into the suite and look around in wonder. Instead of the cheap plastic arena seats, there are leather chairs facing a low bar top. There is no glass obstructing our view because we're too high for the puck to reach us even if it were to clear the plexiglass down below. Three levels of leather seats are in the portion of the box that juts out over the crowd below. No one is in them yet because the game doesn't start for another hour.

In the back, the suite opens up to a full bar and food stations.

"This is unbelievable. I could live my whole life in this box," I laugh, still clutching Bri's hand as she leads me around like she owns this place even though I'm pretty sure this is her first time here as well. Rounding the corner of one of the stone columns, we enter the lounge-style portion of the suite and I bristle immediately.

A beautiful woman with a tight, tidy bun and a tailored black cocktail dress outlining her fit figure is standing next to Ryan. Her hand is on his back and she's clearly making seductive googley eyes at him as he talks to her. I clutch Bri's hand tightly as a wave of hurt rolls through me.

Bri turns to me, but I can't pull my eyes away from Ryan and the woman next to him, and damn it, they're stinging with unshed tears.

"Ems, are you . . . oh . . . *oh*," she whispers as realization dawns. She spins me back around the corner of the column, out of view, and whispers, "That *asshole*."

I shake my head. "It's fine. Really. I don't want to jump to conclusions."

She pins me with her gaze. "Something *is* going on between you two, isn't it?"

Lying is pointless now, my emotions are written all over the tight features of my face. "Yes, but we aren't exactly sure what," I admit. "Brett doesn't know anything about it yet. *Please,* Bri. You can't tell him. Everything's kind of a mess at the moment." I wave my hand vaguely in the direction of my non-boyfriend and his strained smile as he looks down at the woman clinging to him. "Obviously."

"Your secret's safe with me, Em, but Brett isn't as oblivious as you two think. I'd suggest coming clean soon if it's going to continue." She grabs my shoulders forcing eye contact even though I already feel emotionally naked and vulnerable. "Take a deep breath, square your shoulders, and make sure you feign indifference until we find out what this is about. That's most important. Indifference is far worse to a man's ego than any amount of tears or shouted words. It might not be what it looks like, but if it is, Sienna and I will binge horror flicks and sushi with you until two a.m. once tonight is over. But right now? Muster your confidence."

"Have I mentioned you're too good for my brother?"

"Once or twice, but I don't mind a little stroke to my ego." My laugh comes out as a strangled sob as I watch Ryan get fondled by a stranger. *Why is he letting her touch him like that?*

While I'm watching them, Bri pulls me in close. "Em, I'm so sorry. I just wanted you to be able to come out, let loose and have a little fun. Although now that I'm hearing that something's been going on between you two, it sounds like you've *been* having fun." She winks at me and gives me a little room to get myself together.

I heed her words and step back, rolling my shoulders and plastering a grin on my face. "Okay, let's see what this is all about."

"That's my girl," she says as she grabs my hand, leading me around the column.

Sloan and Brett are facing us, the latter's pupils noticeably dilating when he sees Bri, and I know the whole world disappears for him as she approaches.

I know how you feel, brother.

Before I have a chance to catalogue Ryan's appearance, my

brother's eyes land on me and that familiar look of fury crosses his face.

"What the fuck are you wearing?" he bites. "You think that's going to keep the attention off of you?"

His tone makes Ryan aware of our presence and he turns around to see what has Brett so angry all of a sudden.

I raise my head and finally see the front of Ryan for the first time tonight and I'm pretty sure I'm going into cardiac arrest for how tight my chest feels and how shallow my breathing is.

He's in a heather grey, v-neck t-shirt with a navy-blue blazer over top, dark jeans, and rugged, brown boots.

My breaths are coming much too fast and I can feel my chest heaving, pushing against the ties at the top of my jersey. I left my hair down and now, I wish like hell it was up to allow the heat on the back of my neck to dissipate. I discreetly try to pull it over my shoulder to allow for air flow to my flushed skin.

"Holy shit," Ryan whispers on a breathy exhale that mirrors my own thoughts.

"That better have been *holy shit* as in *we need to cover her up* and not any other kind, *Battle*."

Thankfully, Bri inserts herself knowing she's the only one who can smooth my brother's raised hackles.

"Will you Neanderthals stop dragging your knuckles and beating your chests long enough to tell the lady she looks nice? Honestly, it's like you two were raised in a fucking barn. Your mother would be appalled, drummer boy."

"Oh, she'd be appalled alright. Appalled that her baby is dressed like that in public," he argues even as his hands possessively find Bri's waist.

"Mom took a selfie with us before we left the house so she knows what I'm wearing. It's just *you* that has a problem with it."

"Yeah? And what happens when the cameras start crowding around, Em?" he asks, lowering his voice.

"I'm working through it." He eyes me with a tight jaw and I know he's wondering what's changed.

Everything.

The woman next to Ryan turns her attention to Bri as she grips Ryan's biceps possessively. "I don't appreciate you calling my date a neanderthal."

He brought her as his date? What the fuck, Ry?

"Briana Vorossi, Brett's girlfriend. And just so I'm perfectly clear, I don't give a shit what you appreciate."

"Bri, play nice," Brett chastises as Ryan winces at Bri's harsh introduction. The woman removes her right hand from Ryan's arm and sticks it out for Bri to shake.

"Special Agent Nina Cosgrove," she says calmly, not backing down from Bri's verbal assault. I see Brett nudge Bri in the shoulder forcing her to take the offered hand.

Sloan joins the group before we can learn anything else.

"Still throwing out the 'ol title huh, Cosgrove?" he says, draping a lazy arm across her shoulders.

"A friend of yours?" Bri asks Sloan.

"Something like that. Neen and I go back to the Army. She was an MP that busted me and some buddies for drunk and disorderly conduct and she's clung to me like a leech ever since. Now her uppity ass works for the feds," Sloan says as he looks at her almost lovingly.

"Excuse me?" Nina fires back, a smile on her face. "*Clung to you* is a bit of an exaggeration don't you think, Alexander? It was you who sought me out and asked me to—"

"Let's let the past stay there, shall we?" Sloan interrupts, giving her a pointed look, causing her to grow serious and nod her head.

Something is definitely going on but considering Sloan is

involved, we'll most likely never know what Nina was about to say. Before the awkward silence can drag on too long, Sloan pipes back up.

"Okay, well, that was fun. Bri, you look stunning as always," Sloan greets Bri with a kiss on the cheek, "but I will happily be the first to say Emma Rose, *damn girl*. Where have you been hiding all of this? You look hotter than the sun." He twirls me around and I notice he's lost the joking tone his voice usually carries.

Holy crap. I think Sloan's being serious.

Unfortunately, so does Brett.

"Sloan, I swear to God, I will knock you the fuck out before this night is over."

"Stop it," I tell Brett placing my finger an inch from his face.

"I'm here to have fun, watch hockey, and hang out with your girlfriend. I don't give a shit what the rest of you do," I glance at Ryan to make sure he knows I'm pissed. I'm stuck between trusting him and being pissed that Nina doesn't have to hide her desire. She can just throw it all out there and flirt her ass off ... with *my* man. "I don't want to hear another word out of you, Brett Donovan. I mean it. I deserve to let loose for a night. And," I hitch my shoulders as I square off to my brother wanting to hit him and Ryan both below the belt, "if I want to fuck Sloan in the bathroom tonight, by God, I will. Because I am *not a little girl*."

Immature? Probably. Do I care? Not right now. I didn't think something could hurt any worse than the shit I've been through. Looks like I was wrong.

I turn back to Sloan and kiss his cheek. "Thanks, Sloan. At least *you* know how to make a woman feel good."

Brett shoots warning daggers at Sloan as Sloan holds up his

hands feigning innocence. Finally, Brett rolls his eyes and bites Bri's neck playfully. "You're going to pay for this."

"I'm looking forward to it already, drummer boy." Her smug smile causes him to shake his head and take a chill pill thankfully. "But feed me first, I'm starved. Ems, want anything?"

"A drink would be great. Preferably a strong one."

She squeezes my hand in understanding. "Coming right up. Nina, why don't you join us for a moment?"

Nina looks at Ryan like she's not sure what she should do but her face falls when he nods his head in Bri's direction and says "Go."

Before I can move away and find different conversation partners, I hear Ryan's low, rumbling voice being spoken quietly, directly in my ear. "Are you insinuating the rest of us don't know how to please a woman, Ms. Donovan?"

I don't give him the satisfaction of eye contact as I answer in the same hushed voice, keeping my gaze trained on the empty ice below. "Not at all, Mr. Battle. It looks like your *date* is planning on being plenty satisfied." How I manage to keep my voice from cracking is nothing short of a miracle.

"Em, Brett invited Nina as my date. You know I'd never do that to you."

I turn to face him, wanting to reach out and wrap my arms around him so much but I'm always aware others are watching. I must stare at his waist too long because he throws caution to the wind and pulls me to him.

"Come here. Everyone got a hug hello except me."

"I hate watching her touch you," I whisper, melting into him, my palms landing flat on his back. "I hate that I can't do anything about it. I hate that I can't be here as your date."

"Me too, Em. I tried to tell your brother about us earlier today. The guilt is eating me alive and I just want to get it out there, but he was busy, and then Nina showed up. I tried to text you, but Brett's been watching me like a hawk and—"

"Hey," I reach my arms up, moving them from his back to cup his face as he looks down at me, totally forgetting where we are. The stress in Ryan's voice as he explains himself tears my heart to shreds. "I know. I'm sorry I freaked out. It's okay. We'll figure this out."

"You're not mad?"

"Not at you."

He places his hands over mine before slowly removing them from his face. "I want to kiss you so bad right now."

"Maybe we can bump into each other back by the restrooms," I suggest.

He nods right as Noah and Sienna enter my peripheral vision.

Reaching his arms out, Noah gets to me first even though it's Ryan he's talking to. "If looks could get a girl pregnant, I think she'd be carrying triplets," Noah laughs. "You two forget everyone you know that'll have a problem with this is standing twenty feet behind you?"

"Yeah. Honestly, I did," Ryan says, still holding my gaze.

"Emmie, you look gorgeous. This jersey though ... that has Bri written all over it." Noah has always been mature. Kind of like Ryan, but less sure about himself. I've noticed that ever since finding Sienna, he seems more confident and my heart leaps for joy with how happy I am for them. "Tell me, how was Brett's reaction?"

"Exactly what you'd fucking expect," Ryan bites off.

A look that carries the weight of an entire conversation passes between Ryan and Noah as Nina clears her throat, returning to Ryan's side with a glass of dark liquor, causing Noah to notice her for the first time since arriving. With one arm wrapped around Sienna's waist and his other arm around my shoulders, trapping me in the conversation, Noah looks at Ryan. "Sooner rather than later or it's going to get much worse," he says before kissing me on the side of my head.

Ryan nods as he accepts the liquor from Nina while Noah engages in conversation.

"Nina, we didn't really get a chance to talk at the house. Are you from around here?"

"Transplant. Grew up in the Pacific Northwest."

"Big change going from that to D.C."

Nina laughs but more of a *you have no idea* laugh instead of a *ha ha ha* laugh. "Yeah, a lot of things happened between then and now."

They continue their small talk as we slowly move toward our seats and Ryan waves me into the row in front of him.

"This is exactly why I didn't want to go to the charity event with Trevor. This shit sucks," I pout.

I feel his hand glide across the name on the back of my jersey. "And I don't like seeing someone else's name branded on you," he growls in my ear. "*That* shit sucks."

"Then brand me with yours."

"I plan to, angel. I plan to."

Chapter 22

Ryan

Once the game starts, I'm finally able to get some peace from Nina. She's nice enough but it's impossible to ignore the hard edges of her personality – no doubt, perfect for the military and her current career - when I crave the sweetness, the openness, and the softness of Em.

Em and I are now racing a clock that's got a hydrogen bomb set to detonate at the end of the countdown.

The woman in question is going to be the absolute fucking death of me in that jersey and those goddamn boots. I want to flip her over my knee and spank her ass until it matches the red sequined tornado on the fabric barely covering aforementioned ass for torturing me this way.

Everyone is sitting down in the leather chairs except Sienna and Emma, who are standing at the edge of our box yelling at the referees as the other team's center knocks the Tornadoes' right winger into the boards and smashes his stick across the guy's chest.

"Come on Ref! What game are you watching?" Emma yells

at the top of her lungs. She's doesn't have a competitive bone in her body ... until she watches hockey.

I mentally fist bump the center because the guy he threw is the owner of the name sequined across Em's back. Which is staring me in the face right now.

As is that damn ass.

The zipper on my slacks is about to be the first casualty of the night. My sanity will be the second.

Once the puck was dropped, three servers began making the rounds in the spacious box so we don't have to miss a second of the game. On the row in front of me, Brett takes the end to my left, Bri is next to him, with Emma in the middle of her and Sienna, and Noah on the aisle to my right. In my own row, Nina is to my right between me and Sloan. Behind us are a couple of the record execs and God knows who else.

Instead of our previous waitress, a young waiter comes to our seats this time to see if we need anything. Brett begins to place an order but I don't hear how he finishes his sentence because Emma screams "I love you seventy-eight!" right as a hush falls over the crowd. The announcer catches wind of it and all of a sudden, Emma is on the big screen, turning around so the player's name and number on her back can be seen. She's wiggles her ass before turning back around and blows kisses at the screen. When the cameraman pans to someone else, the audience actually boos.

I'm elated to see her confidence returning. She seems to be transforming back to her original self, that independent, smiley, headstrong woman that always made me laugh. Now knowing what dimmed her light, my heart swells at the thought that perhaps what's going on between us is helping to restore that beautiful beacon.

Em's eyes are a little glassy when she turns around again. Planting her hands on the back of the leather chair in front of me – that one that her ass should be in - and she moves with the beat of the music blaring through the arena. "Do you think he saw me? I was on the screen!" she says excitedly, that luster for life she's always had shining through.

I smile. "Yeah, I do." Dropping my voice and leaning into her further, I add, "Are you trying to tell me I have competition, sweetheart? Because I don't share."

Her pupils dilate and she licks her lips. I feel Nina shift beside me and Em's eyes swing to the woman next to me before she turns back around.

Turning to Nina, I ask if she wants anything from the bar. I've been a terrible date and it's not Nina's fault I'm in this situation. She gives me her request but she huffs an annoyed sigh when I lean forward and tap Emma on the shoulder. Nina's been trying to fold herself around my dick all night but Em has held my attention ever since she walked in.

"I'm going to get a refill. You want anything?"

"I need to use the restroom and some water would probably be good."

I hold out my hand to help her balance in her heels as she climbs the small steps up from the seats. Quickly flashing a glance down the row, I see Brett's attention is on the game but Bri flashes me a discreet double thumbs up, making me smile. It's good to know so many of our friends are on our side.

The restrooms are behind a solid wall so unless someone else comes up here, we're fully hidden.

"We only have a second," I pant against her mouth, sliding my hand around her neck with my thumb resting on her jaw.

"I need more time," she says as her head falls back against the wall while my tongue races along the curve of her neck. Her hands are frantically trying to get under my shirt, pulling and tugging until she gives up and shoves them in my hair, choosing to pull on my roots instead.

God, her wanton need feels good.

"Em, I can't go back out there looking like I just got fucked."

"I can't stop. I'm so tired of having to stay away." She raises my face and brings it to her own, her greedy tongue dancing with mine as I press her into the wall.

Suddenly, a feminine throat clears and Em and I jump apart. Thankfully it's only Sienna. "I thought this might be happening," she says with a smirk. "I just wanted you to know your simultaneous absence is being noticed. I suggest Ryan, you go back out first. I'll stay with Emma and we'll come back in a few."

Em and I share a look of longing so sharp I feel it like the prick of a needle. *We need more time.*

"I'll think of something," I promise her before heading back to my seat, fresh drink in hand.

Toward the end of the third period, a man I recognize as the general manger for the Tornadoes, waltzes into the suite while I'm refilling my scotch. I'll deal with my own hangover in the morning should it come, but I need the buzz to survive the rest of this night.

"Mr. Battle, we're glad to have you here tonight. I trust you've enjoyed yourself?"

"Very much, sir. Thank you."

"There are several fans of yours on the team and they've requested a meet and greet, sort of an exchange of autographs if you will, after the game. Would you all be willing to make that happen?"

Really, I just want to go home, tell Brett about my feelings for Emma, and get my face bashed in as soon as possible. But this is business and the band has certain obligations it has to fulfill.

"Absolutely. We'd be honored."

Everyone is mingling in the suite. Nina's mostly given up on me and is chatting with Sloan. I'm standing in on a conversation with Noah and our record producer when the door to the suite opens and the Tornadoes enter. Out of their hockey uniforms, half are in suits, the other half are in sweats.

The team captain addresses the wardrobe chaos for me when he speaks.

"Thank you guys for meeting with us. We're huge fans. We wanted to put our best foot forward, but a few of us got pretty banged up tonight and getting back into our suits would have been murder."

"No problem, man. Helluva game," Noah answers, stepping forward with an outstretched hand. "Noah Kinkaid." His voice momentarily stuns the captain. People have a hard time with Kink's voice when they realize it's real. No auto-tune sound effects, he *actually* sounds like this when he talks.

"Bro, it's so nice to meet you," one of the defensemen says, stepping forward as he recovers his own voice. And just like that, introductions begin. They're signing jerseys for us, and someone from the label pulled a bunch of our CDs out from somewhere, for us to give to them.

It's a little chaotic but overall, a pretty cool moment for me, until I spot number seventy-eight getting his ego stroked by Emma. Most shockingly, Brett's standing next to them, laughing and gesturing, almost as if he's encouraging their interactions. My teeth slam together and my jaw cramps from clenching so hard.

She points to the guys' side and he lifts up his shirt

revealing a deep bruise from his intimate moment with the boards. The fucker lifts it high enough so that she can see all forty-seven of his abs and his sweatpants might as well be on the floor for as low as they're sitting on his hips. Brett claps the guy on the back and walks away, leaving Emma alone with the NHL superstar.

My teeth grind so loudly as he trails his finger down her sleeve – the one with his fucking name on it - I don't even hear Noah come stand next to me until he speaks.

"How long are you going to let this go on? You think when she goes back to school, it'll be any easier to let her go? You think you won't spend every waking hour texting her, calling her, wondering what the hell she's doing and who she's with? Jesus, man, you're about to break your fucking molars."

"I *know*," I tell Noah. "I was going to talk to Brett earlier but he was busy and she's leaving soon. Now, I just want some time alone with her before I burn our world down."

"Well, I suggest doing it quickly." He nods his head in their direction and when I return my attention to the pair, she's handing him her phone.

I think back to the night she and I shared at Noah's and an idea comes to me.

"Yeah, I hear you. Thanks Kink."

He pats me on the shoulder and turns back to the crowd to talk to more of the players while I pull my phone out of my pants pocket and finally have a chance to send a text to Em.

RYAN 9:07 PM

I need to talk to you. Alone.

I feel my lips spread into an immediate smile when seventy-eight hands back her phone. She plays the game well and doesn't look for me as she types out a response, before handing it back to the hockey player in front of her.

EMMA 9:07 PM

Just tell me when.

RYAN 9:08 PM

Can you go to Jen's? I'll pick you up there.

I've never typed faster in my life. I've completely lost track of what's going on around me. All that matters is her answer. Seventy-Eight gets done typing - what I presume is his number - into her phone, and hands it back once again. I type another message quickly to make sure she got the last one.

RYAN 9:10 PM

Say yes. Please.

She finally looks over at me and I nod my head, ever so slightly. I see her fingers start typing and I wait with baited breath. Finally, my phone buzzes in my hand.

EMMA 9:11 PM

Yes.

I start typing immediately.

RYAN 9:11 PM

> Take the car service that brought you. I'll get Bri back.

> Text me when you get to Jennifer's.

She types one last message before pocketing her phone.

EMMA 9:12 PM

> I didn't want to be obvious or cause a scene so I let him give me his number.

> I don't plan on using it.

When I look back up at her, she's looking at me, worrying her bottom lip between her teeth. I nod my head and mouth *I know*.

Now that she's agreed to let me come pick her up for the night, I need to put the next phase of this not-well-thought-out plan into action: my excuse for why I won't be home until tomorrow.

I had originally thought I'd reserve a hotel room outside the city, until I remembered I just can't do shit like that anymore. That takes coordination because I can't just waltz in there and throw down my ID and a credit card. It would take exactly two minutes before someone in the media caught wind of my presence and we'd be fucked. Nor can I take security with me or have someone call to make the reservation because there will be questions I'm not ready to answer.

I shake a few more hands and take a couple selfies with the players before stepping outside the suite and dialing my dad's cell number.

"Son, twice in three days. I'm starting to think something's wrong." I can tell he's only half joking, giving me an opening to talk if I want to take it.

I don't. Not yet, anyway.

I force a laugh, hoping it sounds real. "No, Dad. Everything's good. We've gotten six songs done on the new album, three to go. Everything's just a little strange with Noah and Sienna packing up. I guess it's got me out of sorts."

"You never did love change," he says, reminiscing.

"Yeah. Anyway, I was calling to see if the cabin was available tonight? I could use a night to clear my head and have some time alone. We have a pretty packed calendar coming up and I'm not sure when the next opportunity to get away will be."

I call from time to time for this exact favor so this isn't totally out of the ordinary. I love the guys, and I'm going to miss living with Kink because he's a permanent fixture in my life, but sometimes, living with three other guys is overwhelming, and after spending day after day in front of the masses, I need a break...even from them. A little solitude goes a long way in this career.

"Of course, son. It's yours anytime you need it. You know the code to get in. Do me a favor and check the water lines while you're there would you? And let me know if I need to bring up a new filter for the fridge?"

"Sure, dad. No problem."

My parents cabin sits alone in the middle of three hundred and sixty acres of hardwoods and pines, completely invisible unless you know where to look. The gravel driveway is over a mile long and you must first pass through three gates and an active cow pasture to get to the start of it. Registered under a bogus LLC, it's my parents' "safe house" if things were to ever get bad.

"And don't forget to turn off your phone while you're there."

"I remember."

That's part of the reason the cabin is perfect. Although it has a landline, and Google maps can locate every-fucking-thing these days, my parents never keep their cell phones on when they're there. Tracking devices totally wig my dad out and he tries his best to keep anything associated with our family away from the cabin.

"Have a good time, Ry. Call me if you need anything. I'm worried about you, son."

"Thanks, Dad." *I plan to have the best night of my life.* "No need to worry, I'm doing okay, just want to take the opportunity while I have it."

"Alright, well, enjoy the cabin. And don't forget to tell me about the filter."

"I will. Thanks, Dad."

I pocket my phone and walk back to the lounge portion of the suite where everyone seems to be waiting for me to take a picture. My bandmates and the Tornadoes are all lined up in two rows.

Sloan and Brett are both looking at me with raised brows as I take my place on the end, in the back row.

"Sorry about that. My dad needs some help with a few last-minute campaign things. Apparently, no one wants to stuff two million envelopes and put address stickers on them. Family makes the best labor." The joke tastes bitter in my mouth. "When we wrap up, I'll drop you guys off at the house, and then I've got to head out.

Em flies back to Harvard in less than twenty-four hours and I won't see her again until Kinky's wedding. This week has gone by too fast and three weeks from now is too fucking long to wait to discuss where this is going.

Pulling into the garage at home, I find it easier than it's been all week to engage in normal conversation.

"Sloan, it's been like three days. When's your next date?" Noah asks as the guys and their women file into the house. Sienna made no arguments when Noah volunteered for her to sit in his lap on the ride back home, everyone – except Nina - opting to ride with me instead of taking the car service the label offered for them.

"I'm actually taking Bri out tomorrow," Sloan responds without missing a beat.

"No way!" Bri shrieks. "Don't you dare drag me into this!"

"Besides, you couldn't handle her even on your best day," Brett fires back.

"Okay, fine. I didn't want to bring it up but ... Emma and I are going out for brunch. That jersey tonight did something to me."

Holy shit, I can't tell if he's joking or not.

"You're walking awfully close to the edge with that one, Sloan," Bri laughs.

"Besides," I chime in in an effort to blend in, "she's *way* too smart to fall into bed with you. Your list of partners is like five miles long."

"Easy," Bri says, "So was Brett's, but people can change when the right person comes along."

"Gag me," Sloan says.

"Actually, that's more Ryan's thing," Noah quips.

I rue the day the guys found that box of shit in my bedroom. Yeah, I have particular tastes, but don't we all? I was unfortunately dubbed the "BDSM King" after that, which is total bullshit. They found silk ties, a small whip, a blindfold, and okay, a few toys that didn't help my case, but I'm not into beating my lovers or withholding their orgasms, or making them crawl to me and shit. I only like the bondage part...and maybe a little pleasurable pain, but I'll be damned if I tell them that.

I push the thought to the back of my mind because if a vision of Emma, naked, knees spread, hands cuffed, with a blindfold on, takes center stage, I'll be sporting a tent so large my whole plan will fall through. Not to mention, after what she's been through, I'll be damned if I bring it up.

"Better not talk about it in front of the ladies or you might find yourselves coming to me for pointers," I joke. I doubt Sienna would be in to that but Bri? Wouldn't surprise me at all.

"Speaking of," the lovable she-devil starts, "do you use that stuff like every time?" She sounds almost nervous as she adds, "I mean, like, do you need it to ... you know ... get off?"

"Bri, darling, is there a particular reason why you're asking Ryan about his sexual preferences and what it takes to make him come?" Brett asks. Unlike if Emma were to ask, Brett doesn't fly off the handle at Bri's question. I can't be certain but I think she's asking out of concern for Em and it's the only reason I offer an answer.

"No, and no. I just enjoy control but it's more important that my partner enjoys herself and feels comfortable," I explain, hoping it's enough for Bri to understand that I would never pressure Em like that.

"Well, as enlightening as this conversation has been, my girlfriend and I are going to bed, so I can remind her whose sexual appetite she *should* be worrying about," Brett says moodily from the living room as he grabs Bri's hand to take her upstairs.

"Just let me know if you want some tips," I shout up the stairs after them. It's so fun poking Brett. So much for talking to him tonight, but I convince myself this is better. A chance for Em and I to talk about us now that she's told me the really heavy stuff. "I'll see you guys tomorrow."

Everyone heads off in different directions. Once I'm in my room with the door shut and locked, I can't help but reach for the box in my closet.

I smooth a hand over the lid, my fingers itching to remove the lid.

Em's never had sex and that won't be changing tonight. I need to go slow. Not only is she a virgin, she's been traumatized in the past. It will be a long while, maybe forever, before I introduce her to this.

I slide the box back into its corner of the closet. *Maybe someday.*

Chapter 23

Emma

The adrenaline coursing through me is causing my hands to shake with every item I place in my bag. I've only had one mildly serious relationship and never any overnights so this is all new to me. Although Henry and I fooled around, I was always ... *happy* isn't the right word ... *relieved* ... when our nights came to an end. Of course, he never knew about what happened, but he was still kind enough to not press for more. Our relationship always felt like my attempt to be "normal" and fit in with the other horny adolescents I knew, but there were never any sparks. Not on my end at least. Half an hour of groping and sloppy kisses were about all I could stomach.

But now there's a whole inferno raging in my veins, the blaze so hot I can feel it in every cell of my body. It's making me restless with the kind of need that has me thinking of sex against walls, blowjobs in cars, and that desire to feel the other person *immediately*.

Once my bag is packed, I take a sponge bath, cleaning all

the essential parts but not wanting to mess up my hair and makeup – except the eyelashes. I have horrible fears of being in the throes of passion and one coming unglued, flapping unattractively as I blink, so I take them off.

As I'm trying to figure out what to wear, I get a text.

RYAN 9:43 PM

Have you left yet?

EMMA 9:43 PM

No, just about.

RYAN 9:44 PM

Dress warmly.

EMMA 9:44 PM

I was hoping you were going to keep me warm?

RYAN 9:44 PM

Em...

Just pack some warm clothes, okay?

EMMA 9:45 PM

Yes, sir.

RYAN 9:46 PM

...

The bubbles disappear.

RYAN 9:48 PM

...

They disappear again. Then finally...

I'm hanging by a thread here, Em.

Twenty minutes later, I pull into Jennifer's apartment complex and text Ryan to let him know I'm ready. While I'm waiting, Jennifer calls.

"Holy shit, this is happening," she says excitedly.

"Finally," I say, returning her excitement.

"How do you feel?" she asks.

"Like I might throw up."

"Okay, well, don't do that. That's not sexy, and you don't want to come across like some amateur."

"But I *am* an amateur. Ryan knows that."

"I can't believe you're finally going to solve the mystery," she says with awe in her voice.

"What mystery?" I'm so nervous I have no freaking clue what she's talking about.

"How big he is."

"How big ... oh ... fuck. What if it doesn't fit? Ryan's *huge!*" I shriek.

"Relax, I'm pretty sure there's never been a case where one didn't fit. Besides, you'd rather have the problem of too much versus too little, am I right?"

"I don't know. I've never had either."

Her giggles in the phone increase my anxiety. It's one thing to fantasize about this in the comfort of my own bed but reality is something else entirely.

"I've gotta go, he's here."

"Have fun!" she sings into the phone. "He's a good guy, Em, and you're one lucky bitch. Think of all the women who dream of getting their hands on their celebrity crush ... especially *that* celebrity crush."

I swallow hard. I can't tell if she's helping or making it worse.

"Bye Jen. I'll call you later."

I hang up before she can say anything else. When Ryan opens the door to my mom's Volvo SUV, his voice is almost a whisper like he's afraid he's going to spook me. "Your bag in the back?"

I nod rapidly, unable to control my movements. Catching it, Ryan places one large, warm hand against my cheek and uses his other to turn my knees so I'm facing him. His thumb brushes across my lower lip.

"Hey, it's just me, Em. We're just going to talk. Don't freak out on me, okay?"

I nod, slower this time, as he drops his hand from my face and grabs my bag from the back seat.

Once I'm in his car, the leather scent and eau de Ryan head straight to my brain almost making me dizzy with how masculine, how powerful, how *rich* it smells.

"Em, you seem unsure. What's on your mind?"

"Where are we going?" It's the first thing that comes to mind and although I trust Ryan implicitly, some details about what awaits me and where it awaits, would do wonders to calm my nerves.

"My family's cabin in Shenandoah National Park. It's about an hour's drive and you'll have to turn your cell phone off before we get there."

"Why?"

"It doubles as a safe house and there can't be any connection to us and it. *You*, are a connection that could tie us to it if someone were to dig deeply enough."

"Oh. Okay. So, a cabin. In the middle of dark woods. With no cell service. And no one knows where I am. Got it." I'm joking, but something in my voice makes Ryan pull over on the shoulder of the on-ramp to the highway, immediately coming to a stop and turning his hazard lights on. When I look at him, really look at him, for the first time on this drive, he steals my breath.

"Em, we don't have to do this," he says gently. "A lot is on the line here so if you're having second thoughts, even if they're small, you need to let me know. I don't want to pressure you or rush this. Your brother is going to find out because I'm going to tell him, but that doesn't mean I'm willing to speed things up and sacrifice your comfort."

I process his words before I answer, begging the really smart part of my brain to kick in. Of course, it would choose now to abandon me, so I just haphazardly throw out the truth like I always do.

"I'm not having second thoughts, Ryan. I'm just a little overwhelmed with the fact that this is happening. With *you*. I've wanted this for so long and I'm not sure what to do now that we're here. I have zero experience, except for like two blow-jobs and letting Henry practice—"

"Em, for the love of God, please don't finish that sentence."

"All I'm saying is, what if I'm not good at it? What if I blow my chance with you because I don't know what I'm doing? It's a lot of pressure, Ry. You haven't exactly been celibate and I won't be able to compete with the models and whoever-the-hell-else you've been banging."

"Sweetheart, I haven't fucked anyone in over a year and even before that, no one has ever evoked the kind of possessive, feral need I have when I'm around you. What I feel for you isn't based on your potential skill level in the bedroom."

I'm not sure if it's the admission itself or hearing the word *fucked* come out of his gorgeous mouth, but my head whips to look at him again. I see his smirk in the lights from the touch screen on his dashboard.

"Oh, I tried," he continues. "On our U.S. tour, I tried like hell to distract myself from waiting impatiently for your phone call or text. But it didn't work. You're all I've thought about since our conversations became a regular thing, so, you aren't going to blow anything." He stops and scrubs a hand down his face as my eyebrows shoot to my hairline and I bite my lip, some of my nerves settling enough to allow my playfulness and a smidge of confidence to return.

"I'm not? That's disappointing," I tease, feeling slightly better.

"My point is, tonight isn't for that, Em. As this conversation would confirm, we have a lot to talk about and we just needed a safe place to do it. There's no expectation of anything physical. And if something does happen, it's going to be the best experience of my life, because it's with you."

"Jesus, Ryan. Where do you come up with this stuff?"

"My heart. Now, are you comfortable with continuing?"

He's serious. He's not making me feel like an immature brat who can't make up her mind. He just wants me to be ready. To be comfortable. And my nerves melt away, leaving me feeling dumb that they even showed up in the first place.

This is *Ryan. My* Ryan.

"I'm ready," I whisper, trying to hide my embarrassment.

He flips his turn signal on and pulls back onto the entrance ramp and grabs my hand.

"Em, this is a big deal. Even without having sex, we're crossing a line we can't come back from. It's okay to be nervous but I will never ask or expect you to do anything you're not fully on board with," he reassures me.

"God, I know. It's just ... how do I explain this? You're ... *you*. You're the poster on my wall," I try to explain, remembering Jennifer's point. "But you're also my safety net. I want all the physical things with you but I'm not sure I'll survive if it doesn't turn out like we hope and I have to give up what we have...what we *had*. The last six months of not speaking to you was misery. I thought a clean break would make things easier, but it didn't."

"You've been around me most of your life, Em. I'm still the same guy that showed up and ate everything in your parent's kitchen when I was fifteen. I'm not going anywhere. You never have to give up what we have. Even if you decide the physical stuff makes the rest of it too messy."

"Ry, you are definitely *not* the same guy who came around at fifteen."

Ryan's always been a big guy, but when he was younger, he had trouble putting on muscle mass, there was no five o'clock shadow, and he sure as hell didn't exude sexual prowess like he does now. "These weren't there," I say, gripping his biceps. "Neither was this." I trace my fingers along his stubbled jaw. "And I'm pretty sure this is rocking far more skill than you had back then too." I lightly dig my palm into his crotch and smile when he hisses a sharp inhale.

Maybe I'm not so bad at this seduction thing after all.

"I suggest not doing that again while I'm driving." His mouth says one thing, but his right hand clamps down on my hand in his lap, holding me against himself. I don't bother holding back my groan when I feel him getting hard beneath my palm.

Suddenly my mouth is watering with the need to taste him.

"Will you teach me?" Slowly, so he doesn't make me move my hand, I start rubbing back and forth.

"Emma, please let me get us to the cabin safely." He's breathing hard and his knuckles are white on the steering wheel.

"I don't think I can wait that long."

"I'm going to come in my pants like an overeager teenager if you don't stop."

I smile because his hand is still on top of mine. "Really? You're that turned on by me?" He uses his hand to wrap my fingers around his shaft through his jeans. He might as well have a steel rod laying against his thigh.

"If you can't tell then we need to stop again and cover some basics."

I squeeze, taking note that it's not just his length that's going to give me a run for my money, but his girth as well.

"Okay, angel, you've really gotta stop because my car is pretty fucking cool but it doesn't drive itself."

When I pull my hand back to my side of the SUV, I can no longer stand the distance so I take my shoes off, tuck my legs under me, and lean over the console.

"Em," he warns.

"Mm hmm?" I hum right next to his ear, letting my breath trail across his neck. I really have no idea what I'm doing, but it feels right and I crave the proximity.

"Sit down," he orders.

"You're so bossy," I whisper. Bracing myself with my left hand on the back of his seat and my right hand on his chest, I trail the tip of my tongue from where his shoulder meets his neck all the way up to just behind his ear, pausing over his birthmark that I love so much.

"You have no idea," he says through gritted teeth. "Fuck, Em. Sit *down*."

"No, thank you," I say defiantly, all my insecurity from earlier gone. It was like once Ryan met me where I was and took the pressure off by assuaging my fears, I was able to relax into the moment, finally having the freedom and confidence to give in to every fantasy and desire I've ever had about the man in front of me.

And that's a *lot* of fantasies and desires.

Chapter 24

Ryan

I can't stop the images playing behind my open eyes as she teases me, licks me, puts her hands on me. Images of her smart mouth being gagged while she's tied to my headboard and I whip her pussy until she's screaming my name. Images of her bent over my bench with her hands cuffed to the rings on the bottom while I pound into her from behind. Knowing I'll have to tread very carefully, considering her past, doesn't slow the torrent of images in my mind.

"*Jesus fucking Christ,*" I spit as I finally take the exit for the cabin. "Emma, we have twenty minutes left. Sit down, turn your phone off, and give me a minute or else I'm not going to be able to get out of the goddamned car when we stop."

She's breathing heavily and when she pulls back, her pupils are still blown out, her cheeks are flushed, and she's chewing on her bottom lip. I'm a fool to have thought I could ever just talk to her.

When I pull up to the gate, I enter the code and feel the weight of the world drop off my shoulders as I pull through and it clangs shut behind us. It may be a false sense of security, but it's comforting nonetheless.

My headlights light up the dirt road in front of us.

"It's kind of spooky out here," Emma observes, finally planting her ass in the passenger seat.

"It's got several security measures in place and a team on standby if needed. It doesn't get much safer than this." I reassure her.

We wind our way up the steep, gravel driveway and I hear her breathy gasp when the house comes into view.

"I thought you said this was a *cabin*," she muses and I feel myself grin.

"Well, *chalet* seemed a little pretentious."

"Ry, if it looks like a duck and quacks like a duck..." she trails off.

"Touché."

I pull into the garage and close the door as I grab her bag and lead her into the mansion in the woods.

There's a fire already in the massive hearth in the living room which is open to the kitchen, a bottle of red wine has been poured into the crystal decanter next to a single glass on the counter with a note.

Enjoy your stay.
Love,
Mom + Dad

I smile and open the fridge, relieved to see eggs, milk, lunch meat, cheese, a fruit assortment, and a pack of steaks. I was so anxious about getting Em up here, I hadn't thought to do any meal planning. It's a detail that often slips my mind since we have a grocery delivery service at home.

When I look up, Em is watching me, a hungry expression on her face. "Are you going to pour that wine or just stare at it?" she asks.

Even knowing she drank champagne all night both at Noah's and the game, the words leave my mouth before I can stop them because here, she's *my* responsibility. "You aren't twenty-one."

She cocks a sassy eyebrow at me, planting a hand on her hip. "So I'm old enough to be impaled by the sword you're wielding, but not old enough for *one* glass of red wine? Seems a bit unfair, don't you think?"

I shake my head and reach for the decanter. "You and that fucking mouth of yours."

I pour the wine and hold the glass out to her as she comes around the island. Then I open the cabinet that houses the scotch and pour two fingers worth of liquid, and finally clink my glass against hers.

"To discussing possibilities," I toast.

"To being impaled by swords," she returns, causing me to choke on the liquid fire now sliding down my windpipe.

I lead her to the couch, feeling the lightest I have in months as I sink into the oversized, buttery leather cushion. Instead of sitting next to me, she climbs on my lap like she's done this a hundred times before.

"Em, we need to talk first."

"You talk," she says, sliding her hands under the sweater I changed into after the game. I couldn't stand the clothes I was in because they all reeked with Nina's perfume. "I want to explore."

"Baby, I can't concentrate when you do that," I admit, sitting my drink on the end table next to us.

"That one," she says, immediately.

"What?"

"Use that one. Call me baby," she clarifies.

I cock an eyebrow, still not following.

"You've called me sweetheart, angel, and now baby. I like the way baby sounds when it leaves your lips the best. It's the most possessive."

"I hadn't realized I'd used them all. I figured you'd like *baby* the least since it insinuates that you're young."

"No. It insinuates that I'm *yours*." I feel my eyes flare with the heat of desire. "Ryan, I've been all over the place tonight. Upset, scared, excited, nervous, peaceful, worried, elated ... you get the picture. But right now, for the first time ever, it's just me and you and all I feel is need and desire. Please don't make me wait any longer."

Her words ignite my soul. I don't want to keep her waiting, but we *need* to talk. I try to distract her by pulling my sweater over my head and planting her hands on my bare torso. It worked at Noah's. Maybe it'll work here, too.

"Fine. You listen while *I* talk." Her hands immediately head south for the button on my jeans. "And keep your hands up here. There's plenty of real estate north of my belt to explore so I know you'll survive until I'm satisfied that we've talked through everything." Putting her hands back on my chest, I warn her one last time. "Yellow, Em."

Her whimper damn near undoes me. She's staring at my pecs like they're the first ones she's ever seen and it does wonders for my ego but does not help this conversation, so I place a finger under her chin and make her look up at me.

"Em, this isn't going to be easy," I start. I see the argument brewing behind her eyes and I hold up a hand. "Hear me out.

This isn't going to be easy because you're going back to school and the band keeps me busy close to a hundred hours a week. If we decide to give this a shot, it may not work out and it won't have anything to do with your brother, who is a whole different issue."

"So, we don't try just because it *might* not work?" she asks defiantly impassioned. I see *and* hear the change as she squares her shoulders ready for a fight.

"That's not what I'm saying. We just need to think through this. There's a lot on the line here. I'll be gone months at a time. I can't ever take you out to the movies or a spontaneous dinner like a normal boyfriend could—"

"I don't want a normal boyfriend," she insists immediately.

"Em, don't be so defensive. Think through this with me or else our night ends here." I know she's young and subject to the reactions of her physical age, but I also know she has the ability to process shit much better than this, so I'm calling her on it and holding her to a higher standard.

She takes a deep breath, nods, and slides off my lap, grabbing her glass of wine from her own end table. I hadn't even noticed when she put it down. She turns to face me and tucks her right leg into her left thigh on the overstuffed couch.

"Okay. I hear you. No normal dates. I can live without them because the reality is I'd much rather chill at home and watch Netflix than be surrounded by a bunch of people in a loud club or bar anyway."

I believe that.

"I'll have to go on tour again and you'll have your own career. You won't be able to come along. That's a lot of nights apart."

She casts her eyes toward the fireplace and brings her stemless wineglass to her lips again. "Yeah, I suppose you're right." She's always been so excited when talking about her future and her plans to practice as an attorney, to learn the legal system, and make a name for herself, but right now, she seems deflated.

"Em, what's wrong?"

"I find my excitement over my chosen career path waning, but that's a conversation for a different day."

"We're here to talk about it all, baby. How long have you felt like this?"

"Since the start of the program, really. I think my expectations were too high. I've spent my whole life building up this path, this career, these goals, and now that they're within arms' reach, I'm just not sure it's what I want anymore."

"What *do* you want?"

"That's just it. I don't know." Her eyes go wide like she said something wrong. "Career wise, I mean. I strived to perform well in school because my parents were dealing with Pen's terrible attitude and acting out. Then Brett moved out and I watched as they saw him make headlines for passing out in another bar. I just wanted to be the one kid that took the burden of worry off of them."

I understand what she means all too well but I stay silent as she continues.

"When Pen died, and Brett spiraled and pulled away, it was up to me to keep moving forward. Honestly, I thought becoming an attorney would be useful if Brett ever found himself in another position like he was with that fan that black-mailed him, so I kept going on the path I'd chosen. But he seems to be doing better, and school isn't all it's cracked up to be. I can do the work but I've lost the joy it used to bring me."

I sigh heavily. "Why am I just now hearing about this?"

"Because we haven't really talked in months."

"You know your parents would support you no matter what, besides, you can't live your life for other people, Em. You have to choose the path that's right for *you*."

She purses her lips. "That's rich coming from you, Ry. All you do is look out for other people."

"Baby, I'm living my dreams."

"All of them?" she asks.

"I'm working on it. Now tell me about yours. If you had no limits or self-imposed expectations, what would you do?"

"I'd paint." She doesn't even hesitate.

"What's stopping you from doing that? You're an amazing artist."

"It's too unpredictable. It's hard to make a living as an artist and make a name for yourself. Maybe I'll paint some on the side after I pass the bar exam."

"We're going to circle back around to that because I have questions, but let's finish discussing us first."

She nods and we continue.

"There will be rumors, and speculation that I'm stepping out. I'd never do that to you, but as you know better than most, people make money off creating drama for celebrities. The media is going to be a problem."

"Yeah, I don't love that," she admits. "But I understand it comes with the territory. I asked Bri how she manages and she said it helps that the world knows Brett belongs to her. They don't have to hide. I think once we don't have to hide either, it'll be better. They seem to respect Bri and Sienna's privacy well enough, unless they're out with Brett and Noah. I'm hoping it'll be the same for me."

"Fair enough. Okay, let's talk about your brother." I'm vaguely aware that I'm moving through topics quickly, eager to get to the part where I kiss her body as the firelight dances over it.

"I hate that you have to ask his permission. You know he'll never give it," she grumbles.

"I'm a grown-ass man, Em. I don't ask for permission

anymore." *No, instead, I just avoid doing things that will hurt others in an effort to the keep the peace.* "But I will talk to him and I expect it's going to go poorly. There's a good chance he'll try to talk you out of this or make you think I'm taking advantage of you. At the very least, our relationship will most likely strain things between all of us."

"If there's anything he could say that would convince me I don't want you, then maybe I shouldn't be here right now. But there isn't. And I am."

Valid point.

She untucks her leg and stands up from the couch, pacing back and forth in front of the fireplace. "Look, I oscillate between emotions. I think that's pretty normal. To your earlier point, this is a big deal. But I had the car ride to think about it. I make no promises that I won't need to revisit some of the topics we've just discussed, and yes, from time to time, I may need reassurance if rumors fly. As new events happen and new timelines form, it's an ongoing process. But for right now and the foreseeable future, you are who I want and although we've chosen a potentially hazardous path, I'm willing to accept the consequences if it means getting to be with you."

I smile at her brilliance. She's argued her point well. I nod, satisfied that she's been informed and warned sufficiently enough. I take a pull of my scotch, and cock a smile as I switch gears, lightening the mood.

"I think we both know what you were thinking about during that car ride, Emma, and it wasn't about how challenging this is going to be."

She meets me head on, grappling for control.

"You're right. I was thinking about hockey players," she taunts back.

"About that ... I'm going to need you to burn that jersey."

She sets her glass on the mantle before coming over to the

couch and placing her hands on my knees, leaning forward into my space. "Happily, but I'm going to need you to take off the rest of your clothes."

"I'll take off my jeans, but my boxers stay in place."

"Oh, come on! *Again?* Why?" She jerks back like I slapped her and I stand, undoing the button on my pants.

"Because we aren't having sex tonight and if I lose those, my mind will be next."

"The fuck you mean, we aren't having sex tonight?"

I love when she gets feisty. I quickly get to work on her nude leggings, sliding them down her silky thighs. God, she has legs a mile long. It takes me a beat to realize she's wearing the black underwear with the laces up the sides that she had on in the picture. The ones I'd asked her to wear.

"Oh, *fuck me.*"

"I'm trying to!" she shrieks, throwing her arms in the air, making me chuckle.

"Baby, you're fucking gorgeous, you know that?" I rasp, slipping her top off and pulling her long, auburn hair over one shoulder. I grab her by the hips and pull her on top of me as I sit back down the couch. There's no hiding my erection and I have to situate her so she's in front of it before it tries to burrow inside her. Her knees are on either side of my hips and just like I knew she would, she fits perfectly. She immediately starts rocking back and forth, her body seeking friction and release.

"You have to talk to me, Ems. Tell me everything."

"Okay, well, I've never dry-humped a guy in my underwear while his dick digs into my ass before," she says bluntly, reminding me how much I love her inability to sugar coat things.

I chuckle. "Good to know. I meant more like is this okay? Too much? Too fast? Does it feel good?"

"It'd feel better if you were inside me."

"How do you know?" I tease while simultaneously pushing down on her hips and moving her back and forth over me.

"Mmm," she hums, closing her eyes and gripping my shoulders, lost to the sensation. "Maybe it wouldn't."

"And the rest of my questions?"

"Everything is good, Ryan. I don't think about what happened to me when I'm with you. The situations are so different. I *want* to be here. I *want* your hands on me. Your smell is different, your voice is different, and I feel safe when I'm with you. I always have. Besides, I was still in therapy processing my grief over Pen when it happened, so I worked through some of the trauma of the assault as well. It's really only triggering when the environment is the same. When people are pressing in all around me, when someone's in my face, when there are cameras." She shudders and her shoulders tremble. "You get the idea."

I do.

"Promise me you'll tell me what you need. Never hide from me. I'm not a particularly gentle lover, but I'll never hurt you." I resume pushing and pulling her across my lap.

"I trust you."

"And you're sure this is okay?"

"*Green*," she says emphatically.

I can only stand rubbing her along my shaft like that for about another twenty seconds and then it's time to move.

"Come with me." I tap her legs indicating I want her to stand.

"Again, I'm *trying to*," she says, frustrated that I'm changing it up. I land a smack on her ass causing her hips to buck as she yells, "*Ow!*" But she stands up, which places her pussy at eye level since I'm still seated. I lean forward to inhale her, talking directly against the fabric hiding her from me.

"*A.* That didn't really hurt and *B.* The growing wet spot on your panties tells me you liked it."

"A little warning next time?" she asks as her cheeks turn pink.

"Color?"

She rolls her eyes. "Still green. Consider this your lifetime *green* signal. If it changes, I'll notify you."

"Fine. Then consider this your lifetime warning that me slapping your ass is going to happen again." I grab her hand and pull her up the stairs to the room I always use when I'm here. Each step is more difficult to take than the last because my cock is so goddamn hard.

When I push the door open, I notice the room is too warm from the hot air rising from the fireplace below. I crack a window and turn the fan on. The lights are next because I like to see my food while I eat it.

"Lay down."

She does as I ask and I follow her onto the bed. She grips my hair and tugs me to her, stopping right before our mouths collide.

"I've always wanted it to be you."

Her lips give way under mine and my tongue tangles with hers for dominance. She's not a timid kisser that's for sure. I break out of her hold and trail kisses down her neck over the lace of her matching bra. Knowing I need to slow down, but unable to, I vow to come back and spend time working her nipples over but if I don't taste her pussy in the next three seconds, I'm a dead man.

I hook my fingers into her panties. "I really like these," I tell her before pulling them off and tossing them on the floor.

"Ohmygod," she says and I feel her tense.

"What's wrong?" I ask, immediately on alert.

"You're about to eat me out, aren't you?" she asks, just throwing it all out there again.

"That's my plan, yes."

"Can I watch?" she asks, catching me off guard while simultaneously reminding me of her limited experience.

I nod. "Grab the pillows behind you and prop yourself up on your elbows." I wait until she's comfortable before burying myself between her legs. I know my stubble is going to cause abrasions on the smooth skin I find here, but the way she's pushing into my face tells me she doesn't mind.

"Oh shit," I hear her say as one of her hands lands on the back of my head, fingers digging into my hair.

Her flavor is unlike anything I've ever had and the sounds bubbling from my throat can't be helped. I slide my hands under her ass to lift her slightly and pull her into me while also trying to keep my pressure on her clit light until she's used to it, alternating between the tip of my tongue and the flat surface.

She's flooding my tastebuds as her desire pours out of her. I feel her back hit the mountain of pillows as her second hand joins her first in my hair, her nails digging into my scalp.

"Ohmygod, Ryan. That feels so good. Why does that feel so good?"

I somehow manage to pull my head away for a split second to answer her rhetorical question, my thumb taking over in the absence of my mouth.

"Because I know what the fuck I'm doing and your pussy was made for me." I return my face between her legs, teasing and tormenting her clit until she comes undone, her hips bucking erratically against my mouth.

Chapter 25

Emma

Holy *fucking shit.* My heart is tripping all over itself as I start to come down from the first non-self-given orgasm I've ever had. I crack an eye open in time to see Ryan lick his lips and start to slide back up my body.

"I could do that forever."

"I could let you forever," I tell him, wiping his chin. "That was the first time someone else ever got me off," I say before I roll my eyes at myself. "Sorry."

"Don't apologize to me, Em. Just be you. If I wanted subtle, demure, and predictable, I wouldn't be here, floating on cloud nine after devouring you."

I smile at him as he shifts and his dick pokes me in the stomach. "My turn," I say, and then because he said to just be myself, I add, "But you'll have to help me. I don't know what you like and I can already tell you I won't be deep-throating you like a porn star. If you're lucky, I *might* be able to get the whole head in."

"Baby, I'm so hard, all you have to do is sneeze in its direction and I'm going to blow my load."

237

"Well, this should be easy then," I tease, letting the blanket of familiarity wrap around me. This is Ryan. The man who has always had my back. The man I always knew I could count on to ease the sting of loneliness caused by my brilliance. The man who has been there for my family in ways no one else ever has.

"Just do what feels right, even if that means stopping," Ryan coaches me.

I move down his hard, defined body, his scent intoxicating me as I go, getting me back on track. I'm shocked to discover I actually *want* to wrap my lips around him. I *want* to feel him let go and fill my mouth. Nothing about this feels like a chore, unlike with Henry, where I didn't hate it, but I also got no personal enjoyment out of it, either. No, I feel my own desire ramping back up at the thought of finally having some part of Ryan Battle inside me.

As soon as he's past my lips, I hum my approval and feel his thighs tense.

"Shit. Em, this won't take long. Maybe you'd better just use your hand first. Hopefully I'll have more control for round two."

I lightly shake my head no and then plunge myself down over him as far as I can go, making myself gag a little.

"*Fuck!*" His hands slap the mattress at his sides.

I like his reaction so much, I do it again, trying to take him in a little farther.

"Holy shit, you aren't the angel I thought you were, are you?"

I answer by letting my hand take over for a minute so I can look up and give him a wicked grin. "The horns hold my halo." I take him back down my throat as far as I can manage, which, admittedly, isn't much but seems to be enough. His precum makes me salivate and I groan around his shaft.

"Em, I'm too fucking close already. This is your last warning."

I hear him, but I don't take my mouth away from him. Eager for him to spill down my throat, I use my left hand to match the rhythm of my mouth while I squeeze a handful of his balls with my right.

"Oh shit ... fuck ... Emma ... I'm ...," he grunts as he comes violently in my mouth, his stomach clenching causing his shoulder blades to lift off the bed.

There is something undeniably hot about bringing a man to orgasm like that.

When I finally pull back, I drape my body over his as he catches his breath, and I smile, feeling satisfied with myself. "Maybe I didn't need your help after all," I say proudly.

"No, I would say you didn't," he agrees.

"Only, that created a problem."

He immediately sits up. "What is it?" he barks, sounding almost angry, which makes me laugh.

"Relax Cujo." I grab his hand and put it between my thighs so he can feel the moisture there. "I just meant the problem is that I'm ready for round two before you are."

"Luckily for you, I'm always in the mood for dessert."

An hour later, I'm wrapped around Ryan in the kitchen while he pulls the fruit out of the fridge for a late-night snack. He's still wearing only his boxers and I have on my panties and a t-shirt from my overnight bag.

"Here, baby. You need to eat something."

I finger the fruit on the plate, keeping my eyes trained on the food as I talk. "I want to go farther."

He stops moving about the kitchen and I can tell he's about to argue.

"I know, you said we weren't having sex tonight, but *please* reconsider that? I'm even more turned on now than I was when we arrived. I want it to be you, Ry. I've always wanted it to be you. I think that's why it hasn't happened for me yet."

He doesn't answer me right away but his stare is intense.

"Baby, I want to so badly, but I need to be able to tell Brett that I've haven't betrayed him in that way, because make no mistake, Em, he will ask."

"Why does he think he has any right to discuss my fucking sex life?"

"Because he loves you and he's concerned for you."

"Well, right now, he's in my way."

Ryan grabs a grape off the counter and feeds it to me. "I want to give you everything you want. Everything you need. But I don't want to have to look my best friend in the eye and tell him we took that step without talking to him first. I've lied to him too many times as it is."

I spin on the barstool so Ryan is between my legs. My fingers dip into his waistband because the smooth skin here is too perfect to not touch.

"So, where does this leave us?" I ask.

"What do you mean?"

"Are we together or not? Even if I can't tell anyone yet, I still need to know what this is. For example, when I get back to school, should I accept Tate's offer for dinner and drinks or no?"

Ryan pulls back to look at me and narrows his eyes. "Who the fuck is Tate?"

"You have to answer my question first," I say, miraculously

keeping a straight face as I tell him the terms before I answer his question.

"No, you should definitely *not* accept that asshole's dinner invitation."

I arch an eyebrow, waiting for him to continue. He still hasn't answered the important question and I can't resist fucking with him just a little. After the emotional night, I feel like I'm returning to my normal self. A version of me that's smart, capable, and in control. A version of me that remembers I'm worthy of being Ryan Battle's girlfriend. A version of me I haven't seen or felt in quite a while.

He places his hands on my thighs, where I sit perched on the stool. I love the way they engulf the widest portion of my leg, making me feel petite and dainty.

"We're a thing, Em. You and me. I don't know what it's going to look like moving forward, but I'm off the market and so are you." He pauses like he's hesitant to say the next part, until finally, with conviction, he says, "You are mine. Now, who. The. Fuck. Is. Tate?"

"She sits next to me in my administrative law class." I give him a sheepish grin.

"Trying to give me a stroke, are you?" he asks, scooping me out of the chair and throwing me over his shoulder as if I were a sack of potatoes. A well-placed smack lands on my ass.

I squeal, wrapping my arms around his waist as he heads for the stairs. "But I'm pretty sure she's in to me! Her last girl-friend was a redhead too."

I thought the explanation would help calm his jealousy, but all it does is earn me another slap on the ass.

"Let me make this clear, Em. I don't care if it's a guy, a girl, or a donkey hitting on you, you belong to me now and I'll threaten anyone or any*thing* that tries to take you away from me."

241

"Hmm, possessive and controlling. You're kind of a walking red flag, you know that, Ry?" I tease when suddenly I'm airborne. My legs flail for a second before I land on the bed, bouncing twice. The change in Ryan is noticeable in both his features and in the air surrounding us.

"You made me call this what it is, Em. You made me say you're mine." His hands are trembling and his shoulders are tense, reminding me of a character I saw once in a movie where their magical power was too much for their human body to handle...this is what it looked like right before they combusted.

"Yeah, I did, and I'm happy we're on the same page about this being a relationship." I say quickly, trying to figure out what's going on. I'm not scared exactly, but the look in his eyes is making me slightly nervous.

"I'm not sure you understand," he says, crawling on the bed toward me.

I fight the urge to scoot back toward the headboard. "Okay, so explain it to me."

"The things I've dreamt of doing to you were kept in check by the physical distance between us and the fact that you *weren't* mine. I had to find an escape hatch for my desire – which, for the last year has only been my hand. Now, we've just established that you *are* mine and only an inch of physical distance separates us. It's like a switch flipped, Em. You're *mine.* And now I want to do things you aren't ready for. I feel like a rubber band being pulled so taut I'm about to snap," he confesses.

He's in my face and we're breathing the same air, trading it back and forth. My brain is addled with lust, and my back arches involuntarily to try and get closer to him.

Nodding my head rapidly in agreement, I whisper, "Okay," knowing I want everything he has to give me. I swallow hard and his eyes follow the movement. "Teach me. Tell me what you want. How you want it. I want to be everything you need, Ryan, just like you've always been for me."

He straddles my thighs and shoves his hand in my hair, kissing me hard. My hands fly to his bare torso and I scrape my nails down his back. He groans in my mouth as his erection pushes against my stomach.

"Ryan, I need you. *Please.* Tell me what you want," I beg again without shame, flexing my hips, almost bucking underneath him. I'm so drunk with emotion I can barely see straight.

He rips my t-shirt over my head and quickly tosses it aside. *How it's managed to stay on this long is a mystery.* He grabs my hands, places them in one of his and pins them over my head as he pushes me down into the mattress. I want to touch him so badly but him calling the shots like this is making me dizzy with lust. A mental note is made that he can, in fact, grip both my wrists in one of his hands.

He sucks on my neck lightly, making my back arch again so my peaked nipples are grazing his chest. His body is so long, he can easily keep a hold on my wrists as his head moves lower and he pulls the sensitive bud into his mouth. I want to put my hands on the back of his head and hold him here but he still has my wrists locked in his grip. I writhe under him, trying to create friction any way I can.

"I knew you'd be sensitive here," he says, his breath floating across my wet flesh. "Fuck, you're perfect." Finally, he lets go of my wrists to grab two handfuls of my breasts as he takes a turn grinding his hips into me before grabbing my wrists again – in his other hand this time – and pinching the nipple he hadn't sucked on.

"Ah!" I cry out, but I'm too turned on for it to really hurt, it's mostly just shocking. Until he replaces his fingers with his teeth and clamps down. "Oh, *shit!*"

He immediately releases his pressure and runs his tongue

over the same spot, turning the pain into a jolt of agonizing pleasure.

"Do that again," I plead between breaths.

I feel him smile against my flesh before he licks, bites down, then licks again.

With his right hand still holding my wrists overhead, and his mouth at work on my nipples, he skates his left hand down my stomach before removing it from my body completely just as he hits the mound of my pubic bone. I'm focused on his movements until his voice claims my attention.

"Is my hand here okay, or no?"

I raise my head off the pillow it's been pushing into for the last five minutes.

"It's all okay, Ryan. Green. I promise. Please don't stop every five seconds and ask my permission. It makes me think about it and I just want to get lost in the moment with you."

He hums and I'm not sure what it means, but he still hasn't returned his hand to my body.

"Feel free to put that back any ti—"

Slap.

My eyes bug out. "Did you just slap my..." I trail off not knowing what to call it. It's not like I use the words *pussy* and *cunt* on the regular. They don't appear in law classes and none of my previous boyfriends were dirty-talkers.

Ryan raises his head to meet my gaze, a sinful smile on his lips. "Say it, baby. Say pussy."

I roll my eyes. "Pussy."

Slap.

"What was that for? I said it!" I squirm against his hold.

"That was for rolling your eyes."

As a natural, knee-jerk reaction, I roll my eyes again.

Slap. Slap.

Two succinct blows land directly over my clit. My panties

are still in place and the thin strip of material makes the sting feel erotic.

I whimper in need.

Ryan releases my wrists, and sits up next to me on the massive bed, his back supported against the headboard. He pulls me on top of him so my back is against his chest, and before I can protest, he gently slides two fingers into my mouth.

"Suck."

I do so without hesitation, latching onto his forearm, thinking about the music these fingers make. The fighting they do. The perfection and strength in their size and shape. As I'm hollowing my cheeks to pull on his fingers, he hooks his ankles around my calves and spreads my legs wider. A picture of him in a jiu jitsu gi holding his opponent captive this same way filters into my mind right before he places light, rapid taps on my clit with his free hand.

I almost choke myself on his fingers as my stomach clenches at the contact, causing me to lurch forward. He presses his left forearm into my chest to pull me back against himself.

"Keep sucking," he commands, his voice sounding foreign with strain.

He removes his forearm and returns his hand to my clit. His slaps intensify in both speed and power until I'm almost sobbing with the need for him to keep his hand there, rubbing with constant pressure to get me off.

Right before my orgasm rips through me, he pulls his fingers out of my mouth, slides out from under me, pulls my panties to the side and buries his face where the fabric just was.

He swipes his tongue from side to side on my swollen clit and my hands involuntarily land on the back of his head again, threading their way into his hair as I unintentionally try to suffocate him with my pussy.

I want to tell him to never stop doing that, but I can't find words. All that's coming out of my mouth is a series of unintelligible grunts as my orgasm consumes my world.

Once I float back to earth, Ryan's hand is clamped firmly on my throbbing sex. The pressure he's applying feels good and I feel his fingers massaging the swollen, sensitive flesh.

"We have another problem," he says seriously.

"What now?"

"I'm not sure how I'm ever supposed to concentrate on anything other than doing that for the rest of my life."

"Jesus, Ryan. You scared me. I thought something was really wrong," I tell him, playfully batting him on the chest.

"Something *is* wrong."

I give him a flat look, waiting for him to explain before I fall into another trap.

"I'm a man who needs to eat often, and you have to fly home tomorrow," he says.

"Just think of it as practice for the next time you leave on tour," I tell him, while placing my hand over the wet spot on his boxers.

"You know, truthfully, I assumed my absence would be harder for you because I've already been tortured on tour with only the sound of your voice to satisfy me, but I'm beginning to believe that assumption was so very wrong." He swipes my hair away from my face. "Now that I know how you taste and what you look like when you come, I'm pretty sure it's going to be me that struggles the most."

"Then we'd better take advantage of the time we have while we have it," I tell him, sliding down his body and pulling his dick out of his boxers.

He reaches down and cups my chin. "You know you don't have to do that every time I do, right? Because I'm going to do that a lot and I can understand if you don't want me painting your throat every sixty seconds."

I pause my movements to look up at him.

"I know you want to protect me, but when it's just me and you, I like it better when you're unhinged. I'll do exactly as much as I want to do, and I promise, nothing about sucking you dry is a chore for me."

Having Ryan to myself tonight along with a few minutes to dissect what the hell is going on and sift through my emotions has set me at ease. I feel all my pieces coming together to make me whole in a way I haven't been until now. Not necessarily like he completes me, but more like he calls forth the parts of myself I like best: my confidence, my intelligence, my strength, my resilience, and those pieces lock into each other allowing me to be the best version of myself.

He allows me to cast aside my fear, anxiety, insecurity, and meekness in favor of the woman I want to be.

I wrap my lips around him and savor his flavor before adding my hand to the mix. It doesn't take long before our roles have reversed and *his* hands are on the back of *my* head and I smile as I feel him encouraging a certain rhythm. I'm all too happy to oblige.

"Emma, I'm—"

I keep my hand pumping but take my mouth away to cut him off.

"Don't warn me, Ryan. Just coat my throat and give me what I've wanted for so long."

"Holy fucking hell, Em."

I smile as his dick pulses in my mouth for the second time tonight, and I drink him down, greedily.

He may like to eat, but my newly-found thirst will give him a run for his money.

Chapter 26

Ryan

The night at the cabin was everything I needed and not nearly enough at the same time. Eventually, we managed to put our clothes on and had more hard conversations, ultimately deciding the best course of action was to wait and tell Brett about our relationship the day after Noah's wedding. It was my beautiful, bright girlfriend who made the suggestion. *Let's give ourselves these next two weeks to get a feel for how this going to be. You were right when you said it might not work out for a reason other than Brett. Let's be sure it will, first.*

Hiding it was much easier when she and I weren't constantly face-to-face as well.

However, the last fourteen days have done nothing but fill me with an increased need to see her again. We're back to talking like we did on tour. She's begun painting a little more but still doesn't have much time. She laughs more frequently, and more easily, and I take every opportunity I can to hear the sound.

Thankfully, between knocking out another song on our

album and completing the collaboration project I was working on, the last two weeks have flown by and I almost get to see her in person again.

Today, I've been incessantly checking the status of Em's flight. When the notification that her plane has landed comes through, I text her right away.

> **RYAN 2:48 PM**
> How was your flight?

> **EMMA 2:49 PM**
> Smooth.

> **RYAN 2:49 PM**
> Your seat mate try anything?

I've never thought myself to be the jealous type, but I'm coming to realize what I've called *being protective* was really *possessive jealousy.* Emma is mine and I'm more than ready for the world to know it.

> **EMMA 2:50 PM**
> No, Edna did not try anything. And even if she had, Ry, I only want you.

> **RYAN 2:50 PM**
> Lucky for Edna ;)

> **EMMA 2:51 PM**
> hahahaha

> I've got to grab my stuff I'll text you when I get to my parents

RYAN 2:52 PM

ok

Later that afternoon, my phone goes off when Em's FaceTime call comes through. The rehearsal dinner is tonight so thankfully everyone is occupied getting ready for that, but because Brett and I's bedrooms are right next to each other, I take the call in my car in the garage.

"Baby," I breathe when the call connects. "Lose the towel."

"So bossy." She wrinkles her nose, but her smile gives her away.

"And yet, we both know you're going to do exactly as I say." She makes a show of untucking the towel and letting it fall. "That's better. Fuck, Em. I can't wait to get my hands on you."

"Just your hands?" she asks, telling me for the thousandth time she's ready to take this step with me.

"Soon, baby. I'm going to burn our world to the ground in two days and then it's happening," I remind her. She offered to be present for the actual conversation with Brett but I feel it's better if I do it alone. I don't want Brett to feel like we're ganging up on him.

"Maybe it won't be that bad," Em says as she brushes light pink powder across her cheeks.

"It's going to be as bad as we think it is, maybe worse, but I'm going to talk to Bri first in hopes she can keep him calm."

She sighs. "This is so ridiculous."

"But necessary," I confirm. "What time are you getting to the restaurant?"

"Sienna told me to be there at six."

"Perfect. I've gotta run. I need to pick Sloan and I's suits up from Jayne and confirm details with security so Noah's mind is at ease. I'll see you soon."

I head inside to see if I can catch Bri before Brett gets out of the shower.

Today's my lucky day when I turn the corner and find her ironing her dress.

"Hey, Bri," I start, suddenly nervous as shit. But then I think of Emma and how long I've wanted this, so I find my balls and dive in.

"Oh hey, Ry."

"I need to talk to you."

She sets the iron down on the counter and gives me her full attention. "Okay?" she says, the last part of the word a higher pitch.

"I, uh, Em and I are officially dating." The words rush out and while the weight drops off my shoulders, it lands straight in my stomach. I rub my hand across the back of my neck in a gesture that gives away my nerves.

Bri leans back against the counter, her fingers curled over the edge by her sides. She has a crooked smile.

"I wondered how long it would be before you came clean," she says.

"Shit. You know?"

"Ry, you've done a total about-face ever since she was home for fall break. You're more present in conversations, you smile more, and even Sloan commented that your creative flow is back."

"Well, fuck. Does Brett know?"

"He was suspicious but he trusts you, Ry, and you told him nothing was going on. You need to come clean."

I pinch the bridge of my nose. "Fuck. Yeah, I know. I plan to tell him Sunday. I just want to get through Kink's wedding without making a scene."

Bri pushes off the counter and grips my forearm. "I'll help

however I can, but you know this isn't going to be good, right? Brett has complicated feelings where his sister is concerned."

I blow out a breath and kiss Bri's cheek. "I know. Thanks, Bri."

Em and I were mostly able to keep our eyes and hands to ourselves during the rehearsal dinner, but it was an extreme exercise in self-control. Especially when Bri and Sienna worked to orchestrate the seating arrangement so Em and I would be next to each other. Now, pulling up outside the aquarium for the actual wedding, I grimace.

There are paparazzi everywhere.

Em's going to hate this and I can't even walk her inside.

Thankfully, as my wedding gift to Noah, I paid for three security teams to patrol inside and outside to ensure nothing ruined their big day. The closer it got, the more the internet started to get crazy. Well, crazier than usual. It was almost like people didn't expect Kink to go through with it, and once it became apparent that he was, a collective effort was launched by obsessed fans to keep he and Sienna from tying the knot.

News articles have appeared citing concerns that without heartbreak and misery, Noah won't be able to write good music. Polls on the internet have begun circulating. *Will they become the shortest celebrity marriage?* People everywhere are throwing in their two cents on my best friends' marriage without even knowing them.

It definitely gives me pause. Emma will have to endure the same bullshit. Then again, Em's been dealing with bullshit most of her life. I park my car around the back of the large, white building, in the parking lot kept private by thick hedgerows and a ten-foot-tall fence. After I make sure my car is locked and I have everything I need, I'm ushered through the side door by security, my tie in hand.

My first thought when security drops me off at Kinky's suite is that it looks just like the hundreds of dressing rooms we've shared over the last two years. A wave of nostalgia blasts through my chest as I finally absorb the fact that Noah and Sienna are getting married and moving out for good.

Pushing the door open, I find my bandmates inside.

"Holy shit, man. I can't believe this is happening," Sloan says as he straightens Noah's tie. "The first one to get married. *Jesus, fuck...*you're about to be *married.*"

Kinky smiles. "Thanks for not adding to my nerves, Sloany," Noah says sarcastically.

"Nerves? What are you nervous about? It isn't like Sienna's gonna leave you at the altar. Hell, she's probably already at the front waiting on you," Brett teases as he looks over at me. "Hey, Ry. Welcome to the party."

"Hey guys. Kink, you got a plan for your getaway when this is over? There's got to be at least a hundred paparazzi out front already."

"Yeah, let's hope it works," he says. We spend the next half hour talking about everything from the actual wedding to the honeymoon – Sienna is going to flip her shit when the jet lands on the small airstrip in Tahiti – to the renovations being done on their house.

Finally, after covering all the topics we can think of, Noah starts pacing. "Are you guys going to get dressed or do you all plan to wear *that,*" he waves his hand in our direction, indicating our jeans and t-shirts, "for my big day?"

The three of us start to unpack the garment bags that were

delivered earlier, and slowly begin talking again, reminiscing about tour and our shows and how far we've come.

"For the next tour, are you and Sienna going to have your own dressing room or are you going to share with us still?" Me, Noah, and Sloan stop moving and look at Brett. His question catches us off guard. Maybe not so much the question as the tone of vulnerability in his voice. "What?" he asks, defensively. "It's a fair question."

"I hadn't really thought about it but I'm sure Si will want her own space to get ready if she's still playing with us. Who knows? Maybe she'll be knocked up by then and I don't want her on stage like that. Too wild and unpredictable."

The look on Brett's face is priceless. It's as if someone just told him where babies come from. I can't help but laugh even though the conversation he and I are going to have tomorrow is sitting in my stomach like a lead weight.

A knock at the door draws our attention and Sidney, the wedding coordinator, informs us the ceremony will start in fifteen minutes. Once she's gone, Noah walks to the black mini fridge in the windowless room and pulls out sparkling cider and four plastic champagne flutes.

"Okay, guys, one last toast as a single man." He starts to fill the glasses. "I'm living out my wildest dreams with you fuckers. This life has had ups and downs, twists and turns we never saw coming, and I suppose Sienna was one of those, but I wouldn't have any of it without you three. Ryan, you're our rock, man. Thank you for always having my back. Sloan, thank you for your humor. Your ability to diffuse any situation is a gift, brother. One I've relied on a lot over the last few years. And Brett, your passion and drive for our music has helped keep my own fire lit. I hope you and Bri are next. I'll miss our routine and our house and...*fuck*." He swipes at his eyes. "I just fucking love you guys and I'm pumped about this next chapter but also,

I'm going to miss the hell out of you. Now drink this nasty ass shit so I can go get married."

We all clink our plastic cups together and down our cider without saying another word.

The three of us leave Noah and go line up with our respective bridesmaids. Brett and Bri are in the front of the line, followed by Kara and I, and then Sloan and Jos. It's good to see these girls again and I'm happy to have a familiar face on my arm as the music starts. When the doors open, the ninety guests stand, and I take in the immaculate room.

I follow Brett and Bri wondering if he's thinking about when it will be his turn. Or maybe it's just me wondering about my own.

Am I getting ahead of myself? Absolutely. But it's hard *not* to think about it when you're in the middle of your best friend's wedding watching your other best friend walk the love of his life down the aisle too. Bri may not be the one in white, but Brett still can't keep his eyes off her. The way his right hand is placed over her own hand as it rests on his forearm is endearing.

He helps her up the steps, lifting the bottom of her crimson gown so she doesn't trip. Only when she's in place, does he kiss her cheek and walk across the steps of the platform to stand behind Noah. I help Kara in place as well but forgo the kiss and take my spot behind Brett, surveying the venue once more as Sloan and Jos get situated.

Behind our platform is a massive fish tank. Like the kind of tank that houses sharks, stingrays, and about fifty other types of gigantic fish and aquatic creatures. It takes up the entire wall like an IMAX screen. There's a crimson runner on the floor and crimson bows on the black chairs. Sienna chose the colors based on the aerial silks used on our tour. It seems that nostalgia for the beginning of things got to everyone because most of the wedding party is crying, including Brett. I've never known him to be so sentimentally emotional.

The lights are dimly lit which makes the tank behind those of us on the platform glow even brighter as stingrays glide through the water as if they were dancing – a fitting tribute to Sienna. Everyone is in attendance. Matt, our tour director, everyone who worked in the crew, all of our families, even Sloan's family is here. Childhood friends of Noah's and family friends of his parents. I spot Nina in the row with Sloan's family and offer a tight smile when her eyes land on mine. I never asked for her number but by the end of that hockey game, I don't think it came as a shock to her. She must be here as Sloan's plus-one.

Sadly, but not surprisingly, the only people not in attendance are Sienna's mom, stepdad, or biological father. Her stepsister is proudly in the front row though.

I can feel Emma's eyes on me and swing my gaze to her right as the doors in the back open again and the first chords of the bridal march begin to play.

Sienna is drop-dead gorgeous in a custom dress made by Jayne, our magician of a wardrobe coordinator who began making dresses for Si when she switched roles on tour and needed something in which she could play the violin since the bodysuits were designed for the silks.

Her copper hair is artfully pinned low to the side behind her left ear, and she's carrying a classic bouquet of blood red roses. Her eyes immediately find Noah and I'm pretty sure if Bri's dad wasn't keeping Sienna on pace with the music, the girl would take off toward Kinky at a full sprint. She loves him so fucking much it makes my throat tight and my eyes water.

The vows are flawless, and the crowd is obviously hypnotized as they listen to Kink talk into the microphone. Before I know it, he and Sienna are sharing their first kiss as husband and wife and the guests erupt with applause.

I lead Kara back out of the large room at the conclusion of the ceremony and wait for the rest of the bridal party so we can take all the pictures. I can already envision these photos adorning Noah and Sienna's walls.

Forty minutes later, the last formal photo is snapped, and I follow the sound of the masses down another sea-creature-lined hallway to the reception area. Just as tastefully decorated as the room where the ceremony was held, I find my name card at the bridal party table and deposit my jacket before heading to the bar that's been set up while Noah and Sienna share their first dance.

"Macallan. Two fingers. Neat."

"Two fingers, huh?" Emma comes to stand next to me at the portable bar. It's the first time I've seen her up close tonight.

"My God, you're beautiful." She's in a tight, black dress with a plunging neck line and small cap sleeves that sit off her shoulders. When she turns her back to me to place her own order – "Just a sparkling water, please" – I notice the back of the dress plunges even farther than the front. It dips so low, there's almost no back there at all.

I can't stop myself from reaching out and placing a hand on her warm, bare skin.

"You want to see me snap, don't you?" I ask, only partly joking.

She takes her water as I take my scotch and lead her to a quiet corner of the room with my hand still pressed to the small of her back.

"I could ask you the same question. It's not right to look better in your tux than the groom, you know."

"I look better than him out of it too," I tease, unable to help myself. It was a mistake though because her pupils dilate and her tongue darts out to wet her lips just the way I like.

"I wouldn't know because I've never seen him without clothes, but I can't imagine anyone looking better naked than you." She pulls her bottom lip between her teeth and it isn't a coy gesture to be seductive, it's more like she's biting her own lip to prevent herself from biting mine.

My lips curve in a smile at her words, and I pull her lip free with my thumb as her eyes close and she leans into me.

Before this conversation – or rather, this public display of lust - can devolve any further, Sloan saunters over to us. "Hello party people. Anyone else starting to get hives from all this matrimony?" Before we can answer, he presses on. "Care to dance, Em?"

"You're just going to swoop in and steal my dance partner?" I ask defensively.

He gives us both the once over. "Doesn't look like you're dancing right now," he says with a smug grin on his face.

"You know, don't you?" I whisper.

"That you and our sweet Emma Donovan here are doing the naked mambo? Anyone with eyes can see it my friend."

Emma's eyes go wide. "Sloan! We are *not* doing the ... *that*."

He turns his attention to her. "Are you telling me you have no desire to sleep with Mr. GQ here? No feelings at all for our beloved bassist?"

Her cheeks flame but she holds his stare. "No. I'm not saying that either," she admits.

"Perfect, then come dance with me before Brett causes a scene at Kink's wedding reception over you two eye-fucking each other in this corner." He holds out his hand and Emma casts a quick look at me.

I throw back my Scotch and nod. "Go."

I mingle while they dance, trying to get all the expected

pleasantries out of the way and keep my eyes off the dance floor. It's just Sloan but I still don't like the way his hand is grazing her skin.

I take a seat at Bill and Holly Donovan's table before heading back to my own.

"Ryan, you look so handsome, honey," Holly fusses as she hugs my waist. I have to fold myself in half to kiss her cheek.

"Thank you, Holly. Bill," I say, acknowledging Brett's dad, and giving him a firm handshake.

"Think it'll ever be Brett out there?" Holly asks, staring wistfully at Brett and Bri on the dance floor.

"If he has two brain cells to rub together, it will be. She's good for him."

"The best. You know, as a parent all you want is for your kids to be happy and loved."

I nod my head, this time staring at Emma and Sloan. Emma looks happy enough but her eyes keep searching the room, and I know she's looking for me.

Brett and Bri make their way off the dance floor and spot me at the Donovan table. Bri plops down next to me while Brett takes the seat next to his dad. Bill and Brett's relationship has been a little strained since Brett told the truth about the night Penelope died, but they're working on it in their own way.

Bri reaches for an untouched water glass on the table. "May I?"

"Of course!" Holly sings.

Brett leans around his dad. "Ry, you look like a dark-haired James Bond in that tux, clutching your Scotch."

"I think he was a vodka drinker. Besides, I'm way scarier than 007," I joke. "And way bigger."

"Speaking of, are you and Em still going to that charity thing for your dad in a couple days?" he asks suddenly changing the topic.

"Oh, what charity thing?" Holly asks, turning her attention back and forth between Brett and I.

I explain about the campaign event that I invited Emma to and Holly has stars in her eyes. "Oh, she'll enjoy that so much!"

I'm not so sure she will, I think to myself. It's less about networking at this point and more about finding time to be together.

Turning to Brett, I answer him. "Yeah, still planning on sending her in with Trevor."

"Look man, I'd rather she go in with you," Brett says quietly, catching me off guard.

"What?"

"I don't really know Trevor. I trust you." This is a big fucking step but damn if it isn't in the wrong direction. When I was keeping my hands to myself, he was suspicious as fuck. Now that I've had my mouth on her pussy, he decides to trust me?

"She can't be with me all night, B. You know the media will go insane. They probably will anyway once they realize who she is."

"Maybe, but that's why she needs to stay close to you. I've given this a lot of thought. Trevor won't have the clout with the media to make them stop if they start harassing her. You do. Plus, you can physically shield her in a way someone smaller than you can't."

"Trevor's only an inch shorter than me and he weighs about thirty more pounds. You know as well as I do, if it's a shield she needs, he'd suffice."

"That's not the point. I can't stop her from going and I trust you to keep her safe."

"Let's talk about this tomorrow."

There's a world of things I need to tell him before he gets comfortable trusting me.

Brett and Bri leave the reception first. As soon as Bri said she was tired, Brett grabbed their shit and hauled her out of there. Ever since he almost lost her, he doesn't take her health lightly. If she's thirsty, she has a drink in her hand within seconds. Same if she's hungry. Tired? He's got her comfortably wrapped up in bed before she can say it twice.

Yeah, they're probably headed for wedded bliss before long despite neither of them wanting anything serious or long term when they started sleeping together.

Once Noah and Sienna give the final goodbye and are whisked away to the private jet, the guests begin filing out slowly. I had to hand it to Kink when he sent six cars out as a diversion for the media. Two black sedans in front of the "wedding car" with blacked out windows, cans on the bumper, and a big ass bow on the grille, and two black sedans in the back. The decoys headed west while Noah and Sienna changed clothes and hopped in the back seat of a rented Tahoe, ducking down. The Tahoe did not have blacked out windows and was driven by Romeo's wife, Tasha. Unrecognizable to the media, they paid the single-passenger vehicle no attention as it drove all the way to the airport.

A few paparazzi remain outside the security perimeter at the front of the aquarium but they aren't harassing anyone, just snapping pictures as the guests leave probably hoping to catch me or Sloan.

Noah's wedding isn't star-studded like one might expect for the wildly famous rockstar. That's not Kinky. His circle is small and unless it's regarding our music, he could do without the fanfare.

A short while later, Sloan leaves with Nina. Whether to fool around or just catch up as old friends, I'm not sure, but they seem more like brother and sister than past or present lovers. Bill and Holly leave, but not before asking if I can give Emma a ride to Jennifer's.

"We don't mind, of course," Holly says. "But our house is in the opposite direction. Jennifer's is on your way.

"I'd be happy to." *More than happy, actually.* I can already taste her lips.

With the chaos of the celebration mostly over, Em and I enjoy just sitting and talking.

It isn't until the cleaning crew has come into the reception hall that we figure it's time to call it a night.

There's only one security team left by this point and the front of the building has cleared out. The paparazzi have either all gotten the shots they wanted or they've given up. Thankful for the privacy of the back parking lot, I guide Emma to my car with my hand flush on her skin again, selfishly marking my territory since Sloan's hand was the last one here. Only, I place my hand lower this time because the creamy skin there is too tantalizing not to touch. By the time we reach my car, my self-control is non-existent and I pin her to the SUV with my body, one hand shoved in her hair, one hand on her hip. Her dress is so tight I can't raise the hem and slip my hand underneath, so I settle for sliding my hand around to cup her ass.

"Ryan," she breathes, rubbing against me, "are you going to make me beg?"

"I do like it when you say please," I mumble against the skin at her neck. I trail my tongue up the column of flesh and smile when I hear her hum.

"*Please.* This is torture. I'm so turned on I can't see straight."

"I like that I do that to you, baby. I like the power."

She trembles beneath my hands and grips the short hair at the back of my head, forcing my eyes to hers. "I want to try so many things. That whole ceremony, I couldn't stop thinking about the way your tie could bind my wrists, leaving me completely at your mercy. I'm tired of waiting. I need you."

"You want to be tied up, do you?" I'm unsure how I can even still speak as strained as my voice is.

"Yes. By you." she answers honestly and unashamed.

"Em, you really were made for me." The grin on my face probably looks as evil as it feels. "I'll tie you up, spank that perfect ass until it's pink, and blindfold you so you can't see the thin strip of leather before it gets whipped across your perfect pussy. We're going to have so much fun learning what that sweet cunt is capable of."

"*Fuck, Ryan.*" She's grinding herself on my thigh, whimpering in my ear. "I keep thinking maybe something is wrong with me since I've never even had regular sex and all I can think about is how dirty and depraved I want it to be with you."

"Emma, there is nothing wrong with you. There never has been anything wrong with you. Just because others travel a different road doesn't mean the one you're on is wrong."

"You always know what to say."

"No. I just know *you.*"

Chapter 27

Emma

"Can we get out of here?" I ask, desperate to be somewhere more private. Anyone who exits the side door of the aquarium is going to know what we're up to, not that there's anyone left, but damn. I'm ready go. *Now.*

"Em, I have to take you to Jennifer's tonight. We have to stick to the plan," Ryan argues sensibly. I know he's right, but then an idea comes to me.

"The back seat."

"What?"

"Get in the backseat, Ryan."

He only stares at me for a moment weighing his options before he yanks the door open, climbs inside and pulls me in after him.

I'm immediately hit with the heavy scent of rain on the horizon. It's intoxicating in a way alcohol isn't even though the scent muddles my brain all the same.

I hike my dress up so I can straddle his lap and spread my knees wide so I sink back down over him, groaning and burying my face in his neck as he grips my thighs pushing and pulling me over his growing erection.

"Fuck, Em. I feel your heat through my pants."

"It's about to be a wet heat," I warn him, running, not walking, toward my orgasm.

"I want it on my tongue."

"Don't think there's enough space." I'm gripping his shoulders and riding him hard when all of a sudden, half of the back of the bench seat tilts forward, tucking into the floorboard behind the front passenger seat. He slides me off of his lap, climbs to the part of the backseat that's now flat, turns his long frame diagonal to give himself the most space possible, and lays down on his back with his knees bent, facing the back of the SUV.

"Straddle my face and grip the the front seat's headrest for leverage."

Thankfully, I'm too turned on to care what I might taste like or smell like after dancing and sweating and having my own arousal dripping out of me all night.

I turn to do as he says but must take too long to get into position because Ryan grips my thighs and pulls me down onto his waiting tongue. I'm not sure he can breathe but he doesn't seem bothered, so I don't mention it.

He pulls my panties to the side and shoves his tongue inside me, rubbing his nose back and forth across my clit.

"Holy shit, Ry. That feels so fucking good."

He hums in agreement and keeps a steady pressure and rhythm. In the heat of a moment like this, it doesn't take long before I'm shattering above him.

"I'm...oh God...yes...*yes...ah!*"

My orgasm rips through me like a tidal wave. The crash and ebb of my release a continuous cycle as he gently licks me through each crest.

Finally, I slump down and slide backwards so he's free to inhale, and I bump against his erection.

"What do I taste like?" My overwhelming curiosity prevents me from being embarrassed that I don't already know and want to find out.

"Like fucking dessert." He grabs the back of my neck and pulls my face down to him, letting me taste myself on his tongue. It's sweeter than I thought it would be with a hint of tanginess, like a pineapple.

"Not bad," I admit. "But I like your flavor better." I leave his lips and push myself backwards until the zipper of his tuxedo pants is right in my face.

As I unbutton his pants and slide his zipper down, his dick jerks violently almost smacking me in the face.

"Sorry," he mutters. "Impatient bastard."

I release him from the confines of his pants and boxers, and run my tongue along his shaft.

I've got the head of his dick at the entrance of my mouth when his cell phone starts ringing.

"Shit," he grumbles, turning the phone screen around for me to see a picture of my brother wearing a gigantic bra over his t-shirt. Must have been one a fan threw on stage. I hold still while he answers. "Hey, B. What's up?"

"Where are you?" I hear Brett ask as Ryan's eyes snap to mine.

"On my way home."

"From the wedding? Wasn't it over like two hours ago?"

"There were a few people who stayed to hang out a bit longer and then your parents asked me to drop Emma off at Jennifer's, so I'm coming from there."

I'm beginning to think Ryan talks too much so in an effort to punish him for oversharing, I slide his dick in my mouth as far as it will go.

He coughs to cover up his obscene groan.

"Ry?" I hear Brett say sharply. "Did you hear me?"

"Uh, no. What?"

"Bri wants a milkshake. Since you're still out, would you mind grabbing one?"

"Oh, uh, yeah, sure, no problem."

I pull hard on his shaft, hallowing out my cheeks.

"Thanks, man. She wants her favorite, orange sherbet with M&Ms."

"You do know that's disgusting, right?" Ryan asks, trying to maintain a normal tone while his dilated pupils watch me bob up and down on his dick.

"Just get it."

"Sure...*fuck*...ing thing." He tries to cover his outburst by repeating himself. "Sure fucking thing."

Ryan hangs up and tosses his phone in the floorboard.

"Oh, you're going to pay for that."

He hasn't even gotten off yet, but he reaches down, grabs me under my arms and pulls me back up toward his chest while simultaneously flipping me over so my back is against his stomach. Then he wraps his legs over mine, pinning my legs wide open, planting his heels on the inside of my knees. We've been in this position before and I already know what's coming.

At least I thought I did, but I'm unprepared for him to grasp my clit between his fingers and pinch lightly, releasing a rush of warm pleasure.

As I'm processing how it feels, he pinches tighter and rolls the bud between his fingertips. My head falls back against his shoulder. If this is me *paying for it*, I'll call Brett back myself just to get in more trouble.

"What if he had figured out what I was up to?"

Ryan tugs lightly on my clit causing my legs to open wider on their own. Is it possible to be tortured with so much pleasure you actually go insane? Because I'm close. My dress is sitting around my waist, the top pushed down and the bottom hiked up. My hands are in my own hair, pulling at the roots as I squirm in Ryan's arms.

I've never known pleasure like this. Hell, I didn't even know you could hold on to a clit like this.

"Do you think it would have taken him long to put two and two together?"

Tug.

"Answer me."

Pinch, roll, tug.

"Do it faster. Please," I beg.

Tug. Tug.

"That's not the answer I was looking for."

He takes his hand away and grabs my own before I can finish the job myself. Frustrated, and so close to the edge, I spill the truth.

"I want to torture you as much as you torture me," I confess. "I don't care if Brett knows. He'll be pissed or he won't. It's my life. Fucking you is *my* choice."

I hear his groan as he releases my hand.

"How I get you off right now is your choice too. You want me to torment this pretty pussy until she explodes?"

"God, yes."

He leans up to bite my neck and renews his hold on the slick part of my anatomy, sending me flying into the orbit of my pleasure.

When I come down, it takes me a minute to get my bearings but as soon as the question pops into my mind, I know I want an answer.

"Where did you learn to do that?"

Even in the self-play I've done to discover what I like, grabbing myself like that would never have occurred to me.

He shrugs. "I watched a lot of porn on tour."

I cock an eyebrow at him in disbelief. Those pinches were too well-placed with just the right amount of pressure for me to believe he learned it all from porn, but I let it go.

He removes his heels from the insides of my knees so I can close my legs and I realize I can still feel his erection digging into my back.

I make a move to alleviate his condition when he grabs my hands and stops me.

"Oh no you don't."

"What? Why?" I ask, genuinely confused and frustrated.

"Because you almost got us caught. That deserves a punishment."

"Isn't that what just happened?"

"You got off. Therefore, it doesn't count."

He's smiling. He may enjoy aspects of BDSM or whatever this is, but it isn't an all or nothing lifestyle for him. I know he can get off without my complete submission and I know he likes a little fight. He's expected to have control in all facets of his life so I guess it makes sense that he'd want it during sex too.

Before I can come up with a different, better way to be punished, he sits up and says, "Tonight's punishment is denying you *my* orgasm."

I narrow my eyes at him. "Doesn't that hurt you more than me?"

"Oh, I'm going to get off. But instead of your mouth or your hands, it's going to be my own hand bringing my release and you're going to have to think about it all night long." He taps my thighs. "Come on, we've got to roll. Apparently, I have a milkshake to pick up."

"I do not like this game, but rest assured, two can play it."

He gives me a wicked grin and shifts so he can climb out of the car via the hatch that opens at the back. After righting myself as best I can, I climb out after him, taking the hand he's offering. The night is chilly and I rub my arms with my hands as I follow him around the side of the SUV to get in the front passenger seat. I'm elated at the moments we just shared but I want more. So much more. I brush my tangled hair back, knowing it's a mess from everything we just did as I let the full force of my "punishment" settle. A pout spreads across my lips. *I want his orgasm.*

Once I reach my door, he catches the look on my face and I instantly see the worry on his.

"Em, what's wrong? Did I hurt you? Did I take it too far?"

"No, Ry. I just wish we could spend tonight together."

"Me too, baby. Tomorrow night, okay?" he holds out his hand for me like I'm Cinderella climbing in the carriage and he shuts my door.

As we pull out of the lot, I can't help but smile.

"This car ride is a lot different than the one we took a few weeks ago," I muse, remembering the night he picked me up from the party, and wondering how time has passed so quickly.

"I'm thankful for that. I don't ever want to go back to a time when I couldn't touch you." He keeps his eyes on the road but places his hand on my thigh like he's trying to reassure himself that I'm still here and he can, in fact, touch me.

When we pull up to Jennifer's apartment, Ryan leans over the center console and kisses me slowly, cocking his head to the left and exploring my mouth from that angle before changing sides and cocking his head to the right, his tongue wrestling mine on an expert level, his lips soft yet commanding.

"I'll call you tomorrow as soon as I get done talking to your brother."

I nod and take a deep breath. "You're all I've ever wanted, Ryan."

"You're everything I shouldn't want, but God help me, I

do." He plants another kiss on my lips before pulling back. "Text me when you get inside Jennifer's apartment. I won't leave until I know you're safe."

ME 12:31 AM

I'm inside. Good luck tomorrow.

RYAN 12:31 AM

Try not to worry. I'll handle it.

Chapter 28

Ryan

I don't lock my bedroom door at the house because none of the guys want to watch me jack off and if they aren't in my room for that show, there's no other reason to be in my space. So, when my bedroom door damn near flies off the hinges and crashes against the wall at seven in the morning, I immediately think the house is on fire.

"What the hell?" I sit up, rubbing sleep from my eyes. I'd only managed to fall asleep a couple hours ago after lying awake, rehearsing my speech for Brett.

Before my eyes are fully open, Brett launches himself at me from the foot of my bed. He lands on my torso and sends a right hook to my face that connects. Blood immediately starts pouring out of a cut on my eye as my head snaps backward.

With his knees planted on either side of my ribs, pinning my arms to my sides, he lands two more blows to my face. Before I can throw him off of me, he quickly shifts and knees me in the fucking solar plexus. I'm not entirely sure he didn't just crack a rib while he was at it too.

He's out for blood and I taste it; both his and mine as the

blood from his knuckles drips into my mouth with each sequential hit. I don't know how many punches he ends up landing before my training finally kicks in and I pull my knees into my chest violently, hitting him in the back, causing him to fly forward.

Once I have him off-balance, I roll out from under him, too angry to hold back and topple him to the floor. I get behind him fast, knowing which position will give me the biggest advantage and wrap my elbow crease around his throat in a rear-naked-choke, squeezing hard. My right thigh is wrapped around his legs to keep him pinned to me. I've given him no route of escape and Brett's size is no match for mine.

"Would you calm the fuck down so I don't break your neck?" I yell at him with bloody teeth as he thrashes in my arms. "What is *wrong* with you?"

The sound of my door smashing into the wall must have woken the rest of the house because it doesn't take long for Bri and Sloan to file into my room.

"What the hell is going—" Bri comes in my room and immediately flies to Brett and starts tugging on my arms. "Ryan! Let him go!" she screams, even though I'm the one with the bashed-in face.

"Are you going to fucking sucker punch me again, you asshole?" I ask Brett whose face is turning purple. He can only grunt.

I release my hold on him and shove him away from me before grabbing a t-shirt and wiping my nose.

He coughs and grips his throat. When he speaks, his voice is hoarse. "I can't *fucking* believe you! I *asked* you *multiple times,* Ryan, and you lied to my goddamn face!"

"Brett, what are you talking about?" I yell, pissed because my fucking face hurts.

"Did you really think no one would catch you, you backstabbing sonofabitch? She's my sister for God's sake, but *no*, you just couldn't resist that virgin pussy, could you? You knew how she felt about you and you couldn't fucking resist."

My hand is flying toward his face before I fully process what I'm doing.

"Do not *ever* talk about your sister as if she's nothing more than what's between her legs." I connect my fist to his cheek and he stumbles backwards, his nose now pouring blood just like mine.

"Will you two *stop it!*" Bri shouts. I know she's yelling but right now she just sounds like a fly buzzing around.

"You shouldn't even *know what's between her legs!* You've known her since she was five fucking years old! You're supposed to be another brother to her!" He shouts, closing the distance between us, ready to take another swing.

"Both of you, stop!" Bri yells over us. "You're stressing me out! Brett, let Ryan talk!"

"Talk?" Brett spits blood from his split lip right on my fucking carpet floor. "They say a picture's worth a thousand words, right? These have done all the talking I need to hear." He pulls his phone out, unlocks the screen and hands it to Bri.

"Anyone care to tell me what the fuck I'm getting my face bashed in for?" I ask the room. What I really mean is *anyone care to tell me how you found out* but I'm not ready to show my hand just yet.

Bri spins the phone around and on it is a picture of me and Emma at my car after the wedding. I've got one hand in her hair and the other planted firmly on her ass as our tongues dance.

I should've fucking known those leeches would still be hiding.

"Goddammit," I mutter. This just went from a complicated - but potentially manageable - conversation to full - on damage control. "Can we do this downstairs? I'd like to have pants on and get some ice before my fucking eyes swell shut."

"I won't be here when you get downstairs."

"Brett, wait," I hear Bri call as she flies out of my room after him.

Sloan's been quiet this entire time just observing. With no joke of his to fill the silence, I feel the need to explain even though he admitted to knowing something was going on.

"We just got together when she came home for fall break," I explain to my curly-headed, bandmate. "She called me to come pick her up from that party and I fucking lost it when she came on to me. I tried to tell her no but then she thought I didn't want her and I just couldn't let her believe that."

"I've known something was up for a while ... you're always on your phone, and when you turned Nina down, I knew there had to be someone else. Granted, at the time, I didn't think it was little Emmie Donovan, but I also don't think you did anything wrong. She's not a little girl anymore. Brett and the rest of the world? I can't guarantee they'll feel the same way." He grabs some sweatpants off the back of my chair and throws them at me. "Cover your dick and let's get some ice."

"I'm wearing boxers," I point out.

He gives my crotch a pointed look. "Yeah, well it looks like between throwing punches and mentioning your love interest, those boxers aren't enough."

I look down and sure as shit I'm sporting an adrenaline-induced hard-on.

Jesus Christ.

When we get to the kitchen, Brett's nowhere to be found and Bri's sitting at the table, her head in her hands. She has bags under her eyes and looks kind of like she did when she got out of the hospital a few months ago.

Sloan wraps an ice pack in a dish towel and hands it to me.

"Sorry about that," Bri says. "I thought maybe he'd throw something or punch a hole in the wall. I didn't expect him to try and a punch a hole through *you*."

"Don't apologize for him," I bark, irritated that Brett can be such a bastard and Bri is always in his corner. "Fuck. I'm sorry, Bri. None of this is your fault." I scan her face and notice she's a little too pale. "Hey, are you okay?" Maybe the stress of the situation set her off or something. I grab a glass and walk to the fridge to pour her some water even though I can only see out of one eye.

"I'm fine. Sit." She kicks at the legs of the chair across from her, pushing it out for me to sit down. Before Sloan can slink back into the living room, she stops him. "You too."

As soon as his ass hits the seat, she drops a bomb on us.

"I'm pregnant."

The ice pack slips from my hand, bounces off the table, and falls to the floor.

"Oh *shit*," Sloan says, his hand coming up to cover his mouth.

"Yeah, that's how we feel too." Bri gives us a tight smile.

"How far along?" Sloan asks, regaining his ability to speak first.

"Eight weeks. We weren't going to tell anyone until we made it through the first trimester." She pulls her foot up onto her chair and wraps her arms around her leg. "That's why Brett's been even more unbearable than usual when it comes to Emma. He keeps imagining people taking advantage of our daughter – and before you ask, no, we don't know what we're having yet, but Brett's terrified. Hell, we both are, but he's going overboard. Between the stuff with Pen being so raw, choosing now to go sober, Noah moving out, and dealing with *this*," she points to her stomach. "Finding out about you and Emma, like *that*, just pushed him over the edge."

"Fuck," I say slowly, trying to process all the major changes in Brett's life, feeling like a selfish asshole for being so wrapped up in my own shit that I missed this.

Bri reaches across the table and grabs my hand. "Ry, stop beating yourself up. You didn't know. And for what it's worth, I'm happy for you and Em. She's been into you for a long time and it sounds like you return those feelings. She deserves to be happy. You both do."

When Bri lets go of my hand, I use it to wipe the trail of blood off my face.

"Can you help me get him back home? I need to talk to him before his thoughts spiral out of control and he makes it worse than it actually is."

"You'd probably have more luck reaching out on your own at this point. Honestly, he doesn't know what to do with me right now. He's hovering worse than he did when I was in the hospital and I'm afraid the stress is going to kill him. To top it all off, we now have to go house hunting because having a newborn in *this* house will really kill the bachelor vibes."

"Bri, you know you guys can stay in this house as long as you want," I reassure her. "Besides, with Noah and Sienna gone, there's an extra room for a nursery."

"That's sweet, Ry, but I think once the shock wears off, this will be good for Brett. It'll give him a chance for a different kind of responsibility. Our kid will have the coolest uncles, but we don't need to all live under the same roof."

"Just know we're here for you guys."

"We know."

I pull my phone out of the pocket of my sweatpants. Ignoring the four unread texts, I fire one off to Brett asking him to come home before pocketing my phone again.

I grab the ice pack from the floor and put it back on my face.

"Does Sienna know?" I ask.

"No. I'll talk to her when they get back."

Sloan huffs out a laugh. "I hope this shit doesn't reach them in paradise. It sucks now, but could you imagine knowing you're coming home to this cluster?"

The thought makes me wince which hurts. Bri stands and disappears before coming back a minute later with six Advil.

"I wasn't sure how much you take so I went with the dosing for an elephant."

"That's about right," I tell her with a half-smile, reaching for the water I poured her and knocking the pills back. "Well Sloan, you're up next. We've all had enough drama to last a few decades."

Sloan shakes his head, curly hair shimmying across his eyes. "No way, man. I got that shit out of the way earlier in life."

"Care to elaborate?" Bri says, planting her elbows on the table after taking her seat.

"Not even a little," Sloan says, no hint of teasing in his voice. He stands from the table and pecks Bri on the cheek. "You let me know if you need anything, momma."

She smiles as she leans into the hand he placed on her cheek. "Thanks, Sloan. No matter what Brett says, you're my favorite."

Sloan laughs. "God, don't let him hear you say that. I don't want my face to look like a raw meat factory like my friend here. Whole 'lotta good those extra training sessions have done you, man."

I flip Sloan the bird. "I was asleep when he jumped me. I had his life in my hands by the time I was coherent enough to realize what was going on."

Sloan smirks as he walks away. "I'll be out back working on new shit. Someone's gotta keep this band afloat."

"I should go too. I need a shower and to figure out my

next move." I slide my chair back, kiss Bri on the opposite cheek and head to my room to find real pants and face the day.

My first stop will be the Donovan house on the off-chance Brett went there. I owe an explanation to Em's parents anyway. I fire up my SUV and call Emma as soon as I'm in the car. My left eye is swollen and purple, but at least I can see out of it. It'll have to do.

"Wow. It's only 8:30. Did you talk to him already?" she says instead of hello.

"Not exactly."

"That doesn't sound promising. What happened?"

"There were reporters in the bushes last night. Long story short, you and I aren't a secret anymore."

"Okay, well," she starts, clearing her throat. I can picture her sitting up straighter, coffee mug in hand, messy bun on her head, preparing to think through this rationally and begin her defense. "That can be good news, right? Just rip the band-aid off. I'm ready for this."

"If only it were that simple. Your brother found the pictures first so he thinks we've been doing this longer than we have *and* he knows I lied to him when he asked me if there was something between us. Technically, we had only shared one kiss at that point and I had no intention of doing it again, but I should've told him then...about both the kiss and the way I feel about you. I'm sorry."

"For what it's worth, I can vouch that you tried to keep us apart," she says, a hint of sadness in her voice. "I'll call Brett."

I swallow and tell her the rest. "Em, the pictures, they make it look bad."

"What do you mean?" Her voice grows quieter and I can tell she's pulled the phone away from her ear to search for them online. I say nothing, letting her come to her own conclusion.

"Oh. *Oh.* Those assholes. *Beautiful Deceit's Bassist working on a Deception of His Own?*" she reads one of the headlines out loud, then another. "*Bassist Ryan Battle Caught with Drummer's Sister: How Young is Too Young?*" Then she reads the first line of one of the articles. "*After issuing a statement of his own, denying any relationship between Ryan Battle (31) and Emma Donovan (20), is Beautiful Deceit's drummer being beautifully deceived by his own bandmate?*" Em groans into the phone. "Okay, so we find a media source to talk to that will set the record straight."

I smile at her bravery. She's so sure about us, she's *willing* to talk to the same media that she despises.

"I need to get your brother on board before we go that far. If he starts running his mouth, this could get way worse."

"Brett can be a total twat, but he wouldn't do that." I can tell by the conviction in her voice, she totally believes it, but with a child on the way and his mindset all fucked up, who can say what he would or wouldn't do if he thought he was protecting Emma.

"I'm on my way to your parents. I at least owe them an explanation."

"Can you swing by for me?" she asks.

"I need to do this alone."

"Are we in this together or not, Ryan? I'm tired of people making choices for me based on what they think is best. I'm not a fucking kid and I refuse to trade one jailer for another."

"Em, that's not—"

"It is and you know it. I'll be ready in ten minutes."

She hangs up the phone before I can respond. *Shit this is moving fast.* I wish Kink was here.

Twenty minutes later I pull into Jennifer's apartment complex and text Em.

She hops in the passenger seat and leans over the console to give me a kiss before coming to an abrupt halt.

"Are you fucking kidding me?" she yells. "That *bastard!* He had *no right* to touch you like this!"

I can't help but grin and melt against her, instantly feeling better that she's with me. That she wants this.

I hadn't realized I had allowed myself to believe the lie those pictures told, that I had somehow coerced her into this even though she made the first move all those months ago.

"It's not as bad as it looks. Plus," I shrug a shoulder, "he gets a pass."

Em doesn't know Bri's pregnant.

The skin under my eye has started to darken, but thankfully my nose isn't broken. Besides, I've suffered far more devastating injuries after catching a couple well-placed elbows in jiu-jitsu. Em gently runs her fingers along my stubbled jaw and I wince. He got me everywhere.

"It kind of makes you look like a badass," she says, but instead of a giggle, her tone is even, telling me she's serious.

"I *am* a badass," I tell her, smiling even as I pretend to be offended.

"Okay, maybe I should've said you look like an MMA fighter," she amends, sucking her bottom lip between her teeth. *She's turned on.*

"You like your man to fight for you, huh?" I tease. "Noted." She has no idea the lengths I'd go to for her.

"That's not what I'm saying," she backtracks. "I don't like to see you hurt."

"This isn't hurt, baby. This is a bruise."

"Will it be painful if I kiss you?"

"It'll be more painful if you don't."

She rolls her eyes playfully. "You just lost all your badassery with that line."

"Damn. And here I thought it was good." I reach over and grab her under her arms, lifting her up and pulling her halfway across the console. She throws her hand out on the driver's side door to support herself even though I can bear her weight without batting a busted, puffy eye.

I pinch her chin between my thumb and index finger and tease her mouth with my tongue. Relaxing, her hands waste no time dipping under the hem of my t-shirt.

"I don't want to hide anymore," she mumbles against my mouth.

"That's good, baby, because it looks like we can't."

We keep making out like horny teenagers, hands groping every inch of skin we can find, until finally the weight of what we have to do distracts me enough to make me pull away. "Em, we need to go talk to your parents and then try to smooth things over with your brother."

"I know," she says, reluctantly letting me go and slipping back into her own seat. "Just promise me we're still spending the next two nights together. It's the only thing that's kept me going, Ryan."

"I promise." I want to add *God, Himself, couldn't keep me away from you tonight,* but then again, He wasn't supposed to be able to sink the Titanic either and we all know how that turned out, so I keep my mouth shut.

When we pull up to Em's parents' house, Holly answers the door with a wide smile ... until she sees my face.

"Why, hello you two ... Ryan, *ohmygod!* Were you mugged? Honey, come in."

Em bristles beside me. "He wasn't mugged, Mom. His face is compliments of your freaking son."

Holly ushers us inside the house. "Brett did this?" she asks on a gasp.

"Yes, but he had a reason. It's why we're here, actually," I tell her, my hand instinctively on Emma's lower back as I follow her inside her parents' house.

"Is Dad here?"

"He just went out. He's helping Eddie Fitzgerald with a leaky sink this morning." Brett's parents had to stop working a couple years ago. People were showing up in the ER just to meet Brett's mom and similarly, they were harassing Brett's dad at work as well. Thanks to Brett, they don't really need the money, but they like to stay busy. "Have a seat, I'll be right back," Holly instructs before she disappears down the hallway.

A minute later, Holly has gloves on and is unwrapping a small plastic package. I stay still but quirk my lacerated eyebrow at her as she approaches me.

"That cut is deep, Ryan. You at least need this steri-strip over the top while it heals."

Holly uses gentle fingers to lay the thin white strip of material across the outer edge of my left eye. I'll take it off as soon as I'm in the car, but Holly has always fussed over me and I understand her need to do it now.

Satisfied with her work, she looks back and forth between Em and I.

"Okay, someone start explaining."

Emma casts her eyes at me and I nod, giving her permission to begin.

"Mom, Ryan and I are dating."

Gotta love a woman who just comes out with it. Even still, the abruptness of the announcement forces a cough from my chest. If this were any other woman, I wouldn't feel the need to explain myself. But this is Emma.

"Holly, I swear nothing happened bef—"

"Oh, honey that's wonderful!" Holly launches herself at Em and pulls her into a hug before holding her arms out to me. "Come here, you!"

Once she releases us from her embrace, Emma sits back and leans into me, my arm snaking around her with the need to be close.

"Thanks, Mom."

I smile at Holly as I lean over to kiss the top of Em's head, remembering words Holly said to me at Kink's wedding. *You know, as a parent all you want is for your kids to be happy and loved.*

"Oh, your father is going to be over the moon!" Holly says, clasping her hands. "I should call him. He'll want to hear this."

"Well, hold on just a second. It gets complicated," Emma says gently.

Holly blows out a sigh and winces. "Your brother." It's not a question.

Emma launches into the story of how she asked for more back in Ireland and I told her no. Then when she called me from the party, it sort of set the ball in motion.

"We were trying to figure things out before mentioning it to Brett but the pictures from Noah's wedding beat us to it and now Brett's M.I.A. and the media has made it look like Ryan coerced me into this *and* insinuated that it's been going on a lot longer than it has."

Holly listens with rapt attention.

"I see. Well, for the record, you know Bill and I don't believe any of that, Ryan. Besides, things like this are never so black and white. We've watched you two interact for years. It's hard to fake the looks you give one another."

Em and I share a look of shock before she smiles wide and I grin back at her like the love-sick fool I am.

While Holly calls Bill, I take the opportunity to shoot Brett another text.

RYAN 9:14 AM

Come on Brett. Talk to me. It isn't what they made it look like. I'm at your parents with Em. Please come talk to us.

BRETT 9:15 AM

Isn't what it looks like? So that isn't your hand on her ass?

At least he answered.

RYAN 9:16 AM

Give me a chance to explain.

And then because I really have nothing to lose, I send another.

Bri told me about the baby.

BRETT 9:20 AM

Shut your fucking mouth. My mom doesn't know.

RYAN 9:21 AM

It's not my news to tell. But it makes sense why you're so upset about me and Em.

BRETT 9:22 AM

You mean how you lied to me about FUCKING my SISTER?

RYAN 9:23 AM

I swear I haven't fucked her.

BRETT 9:23 AM

Yeah, well, forgive me if I don't believe the shit you say anymore.

I back out of our text stream, recognizing a lost cause when I see one. A text from my dad is next at the top. *Call me.*

It's followed by three missed calls from different executives from the record label and six from unknown or blocked numbers. *Reporters.*

What a fucking mess.

Chapter 29

Emma

I knew my mom would be ecstatic when she found out about Ryan and I. Based on the way she's answering my dad's questions, I'm guessing he's thrilled as well.

Now I just have to work on my brother.

Ryan handed me his phone to let me read his text conversation with Brett and I've decided enough is enough.

EMMA 9:31 AM

Call me right now or I swear to God, I'll cut you out of my life forever.

I'm not playing around. He doesn't get to pull this bullshit and I'm done going easy on him because of what he went through with Penelope. He made his choices, and now I'm making mine.

But after several minutes, he still hasn't answered me and his phone goes straight to voicemail.

My mom gives me a sad smile. "He'll come around."

"I'm not so sure."

As we're regrouping to figure out our next move, my phone rings. I don't normally answer unknown numbers, but with Brett potentially on a binger and his location unknown, I feel compelled to take the call.

"Hello?"

"Emma." the voice says, chilling my blood. "It seems you can't stay out of the news recently, and you owe me a story."

"I don't owe you a damn thing and if you contact me again, I'll go to the police." I look up to see Ryan's angry gaze even as the man on the other end of the line continues talking.

"With what dear? My number's untraceable. You don't even know my name. But rest assured, I know yours. I'll get that story one way or another." *Click.*

Looks like I'll be getting a new number... again.

Beside me, Ryan's jaw is clenched and his nostrils flare in anger. The question in his eyes is crystal clear. *Was it him?*

I nod and he stands abruptly, running his fingers through his short hair. I shoot him a warning look because my mom still doesn't know.

"Damn reporters," I huff, willing my voice to stay even. As Ryan collects himself, I notice that there was no adrenaline spike of fear when I heard the voice this time. Only anger. I don't feel the need to run, hide, or shrink away.

"Holly, thank you for your support," Ryan finally says. "I promise to take the best care of Em I can, and if you hear from Brett, could you let him know we'll be home until lunchtime?"

"Of course." Turning to me she asks with a raised brow, "I assume you'll be with Ryan until you go back to school?"

"Yes. We're staying at his family's cabin until Tuesday." I

divulge the details so she doesn't worry. "I won't have my phone on."

"Just send me a message to let me know you two made it to D.C. okay, yeah?"

My mom pulls me in for an embrace and for a brief moment I feel like everything will be alright. Brett will get over it and the world will move on, but before she and I separate, Ryan's phone pings.

I know as soon as he says, "We've gotta go," this day is going to get harder before it gets easier.

When we pull up to the house Ryan shares with my brother, he throws the SUV in park and is barely out of the car when his dad comes outside wearing the expression of a pissed off bull. I climb out of the SUV but hang back, waiting to see how the conversation plays out.

"We need to talk," Senator Battle says, his voice low and matter-of-fact. Although not quite as tall as Ryan, he's still imposing in a tailored, gray three-piece suit. He's tall enough to look Ryan in the eye and has kept himself in shape as he's aged. It's obvious Ryan gets his looks and build from his father.

"I take it you saw the headlines?" Ryan asks, propping an elbow on the hood of his Aston Martin.

"Tell me you didn't."

"Didn't *what?*" Ryan sneers.

"Are you sleeping with her?" he nods his head in my direction as if I can't hear him. *Oh hell no.* I move around the hood of the car to flank Ryan's side, standing up tall. I will not back down to anyone. Not anymore. Not over this. "She's *ten years* younger than you, son."

Ryan blows out a breath. "Eleven. And I'm so tired of this conversation. I'm well aware of how old she is, Dad. And while we're on the subject of age, I'm *thirty-one*, which means who I sleep with is none of your business."

"It sure as hell is if it costs me this election."

Ryan jerks like he's been slapped and narrows his eyes at his father. "We haven't fucking slept together," he grits out, begrudgingly answering his father's question.

"That black eye tells a different story," Senator Battle says coldly.

No, Ryan hasn't claimed the gift I've been begging to give him. He's tried to do the right thing and it doesn't even matter. This situation right here is where the phrase *Do You* was birthed. No matter what you choose to do in life, someone will have a problem with it so you might as well not give a shit about what they think because you'll never please everyone.

"*Damn it*, Ryan. You couldn't have waited until after the election? It's in *four weeks*." The anger and disappointment in his father's voice is the final straw for me to stay quiet and I'm ready to stand up for Ryan when thankfully, he finds his voice to do it himself.

"All I fucking do is take care of everyone else. My entire life, I've never stepped a single toe out of line. I'm *always* aware of what my actions mean for you, our family, the band, *their* families. I keep everyone else in check so they can enjoy the party, enjoy the fame, get the vote, and be envied by the masses, but what that means is that I'm always on edge, always the sober one, always in the background, always biting my tongue, always available and on-call. It's exhausting and the one time... the *one time* I do something for myself, it blows up in my face like this."

"This is the price of fame, son. My phone has been ringing off the hook for interviews since these pictures came out. I go on record in an hour. What am I supposed to say?" he asks, making his voice softer.

I haven't spent much time around the senator but I know Ryan looks up to his dad an awful lot. To hear him berate Ryan and make it clear he values the outcome of the election over his own son's feelings breaks my heart because I know Ryan values his dad's opinion greatly.

Finally finding my way into the heated conversation, I take a stand. "The pictures show Ryan and I together against his car while sharing a kiss, Senator. It isn't like he's holding me against my will."

"Then clearly you haven't seen all the pictures," he snaps at me.

"What?" I ask at the same time Ryan says, "Watch your tone with her."

Senator Battle hands me his phone.

These assholes got a picture of me as I was walking around the side of the car. My head is down and my arms are wrapped around myself. My hair's a mess and although my dress is covering everything, it's still crooked and rumpled. To be honest, it looks like I was just ... assaulted.

"*Fuck,*" Ryan spits, looking over my shoulder even as his hands wind around my waist. "It's like these cocksuckers take a thousand images and then comb through them looking for the one that will do the most damage. She was *cold*, Dad. The wind was blowing and she was upset about us not being able to spend the night together because we hadn't talked to Brett yet. That's why she's hunched over with that look on her face," Ryan explains, although I wish he'd save his breath. We don't owe anyone this explanation. "I'd never hurt her."

"Look, this will most likely die down in a couple days but do you think you could put some distance between you two until after the election?"

I open my mouth to vehemently protest the request, but Ryan beats me to it. "I've kept my distance from Emma to try and protect her, Brett, and the band long enough. I can't help what people choose to believe."

I interrupt, too fired up to stay silent. This is my fight as much as Ryan's, even if his father thinks otherwise.

"Senator Battle, I'm sorry for the distress this has caused you, but I'm not sorry for any moment I've shared with your son. It seems everyone has an opinion about us and quite frankly, we're tired of hearing them all." I use my own hands to wrap Ryan's tighter around myself and smile when he leans down to kiss the top of my head protectively. It's become a habit for him. One I'm all in favor of.

"Forgive me, Emma, but I have to ask. Although I know my son, I also know how alluring the lifestyle can be. Are you certain you feel no pressure to enter into a relationship with him?"

I stand there, my mouth agape, unable to process what his father is insinuating. A man Ryan has respected and trusted his entire life. A man who apparently has more trust and concern for the people he governs than his own child.

"Forgive *me*, Senator, but it sounds like you don't know your son at all. Ryan is the most selfless man I've ever met. For you to insinuate that he somehow conned me into wanting to be with him is not only ignorant on your end, but incredibly disrespectful to my own level of intelligence."

"I think we're done here," Ryan tells his dad without any more lip service to make him feel better for his judgmental attitude. "You should handle the press on your own. Em and I have dealt with enough over the last twenty-four hours."

His father takes a deep breath, pinching the bridge of his nose the way I've seen Ryan do a thousand times, and nods.

Ryan pulls me up the sidewalk behind him. Before shutting the door to the house in his father's face, Ryan says, "We'll be at the cabin until Tuesday morning. See you in D.C."

As we enter the living room, my hands are shaking slightly. Although I anticipated battles in court, I can't say *actually* going toe to toe with a powerful attorney was an experience I'd like to repeat. Somehow, I'd always figured it would be my client under fire, but this conversation just made me realize, as the one representing them, I'll be under attack just as much, if not more.

"Em, you're amazing. Thank you for having my back, baby." Ryan says, nuzzling my neck, causing me to swallow my emotions.

"Aw, look at the lovebirds," Bri says, startling us as she comes into the living room.

"Any word from Brett?" Ryan asks.

She shakes her head. "No. His phone keeps going to voicemail. I'm worried about him but I don't even know where to start looking."

"I've got an idea on a couple of places. I'm going to take a drive. Bri, I think you have some things to share with Em while I'm gone. Just do me a favor and call me if Brett shows up."

I kiss Ryan goodbye as Bri nods and he heads back out the door, leaving the two of us alone.

"What's up?"

"Want me to do your makeup?" she asks, obviously stalling.

"Of course." I always love when Bri does my makeup. She taught me some tricks but it's never the same as when she does it. The girl has a gift. Besides, I can tell whatever she has to say is serious and it'll probably be easier to talk if her hands are busy and her focus is elsewhere.

When we're upstairs in her and Brett's bathroom, I put the lid down on the toilet seat and wait for her to start.

As she's blending my foundation, she whispers, "You're going to be an aunt." It takes me far too long to process what she says and she starts to get nervous. "Em? Say something."

I launch myself – carefully - at Bri and wrap her in a hug,

the stress of the day momentarily forgotten as I pepper her with questions.

"How far along are you? Do you know what you're having? Are you going to find out? Do you have names picked out?"

Laughing, she squeezes me back in a hug. "Slow down, Em." She pushes my shoulders to get me to sit back down so she can go back to work on my makeup. "We found out right before you came home for fall break a few weeks ago. I'm eight weeks along, and honestly, we're still in shock. Neither of us wanted kids."

"Yeah, well, neither of you wanted a long-term relationship either and yet here you are." I pause and think about the time-line in my head. That explains a lot about Brett's behavior when I came home. I allow my gaze to sweep the woman in front of me noticing she looks tired but her eyes are bright with excitement. "You know you guys won't have to do this alone. Do my parents know?"

"No one knows except you, Ryan, and Sloan. We were going to wait until after the first trimester to start telling people but I felt like I should spill the beans to put Brett's behavior in perspective...especially after he punched Ryan in the face." She gives me an apologetic look as if anything us girls say or do could curb the basic instincts of our men. Although Brett's never been much of a fighter, he's still fueled by testosterone. Bri huffs out a laugh. "I'm worried about him. I seem to always be worried about him," she confesses.

"I wish you could have known him before Pen died. He wasn't always so grumpy and uptight. If he can get back to the man he was, he'll make an excellent father ... and husband." I throw the last part in at the end to gauge her reaction but she glosses right over it.

"So much is changing so fast."

I hate that she sounds sad.

"But a lot of it is good. You and I will get to be real sisters one day. Your baby is going to be beautiful and healthy and maybe he or she will help fill the hole Pen left behind in Brett. Things with Ryan and I will calm down and then Brett will realize his best friend also gets to be his brother and they'll continue to make music and everything will fall into place."

"I hope you're right, Em."

So do I. I have no idea where the burst of optimism came from but I hope it stays.

Bri finishes my makeup and we move downstairs to continue talking for two more hours. More about Brett, some about the baby – although I can tell Bri is ready to move on from that subject quickly, and then we spend the rest of the time talking about Ryan and I. It feels so good to just lay it all out there. As the conversation winds down, Bri falls asleep on the couch. I hear growing a human is exhausting.

I drape a blanket over her and curl up in the chair with my phone. Nothing from Brett, but I do have a text from Jennifer.

JENNIFER 9:51 AM

You were gone when I woke up but my news feed has your face on it...again

EMMA 9:51 AM

Yeah, shit's sort of hit the fan.

JENNIFER 9:52 AM

I've already been contacted by two reporters.

EMMA 9:52 AM

Shit, Jen. I'm so sorry!

JENNIFER 9:52 AM

It's all good. I'm having fun fucking with them. My Indian accent is getting pretty good.

EMMA 9:53 AM

Keep up the good work lol. Also, Brett found out before we told him, so that's not great.

JENNIFER 9:53 AM

Ohhhh shiiiiiiit.

EMMA 9:53 AM

Yeah.

JENNIFER 9:54 AM

Well, I'm here if you need me.

EMMA 9:54 AM

You always are, babe. <3

About thirty minutes in to her nap, Bri wakes with a start when the back door opens, and we call out simultaneously.

"Brett?"

"Ryan?"

"Try a third option," Sloan says coming into the living room from the kitchen, making me smile.

"Hey, Sloan," Bri and I say in unison.

"Any word on either of your love interests?"

Bri gives the latest update while I open my phone to send Ryan a text.

"Ry's been gone a couple hours looking for Brett, who still hasn't called or texted me back."

"Well, I hope they don't kill each other. Kink and I can't finish this album on our own," Sloan says, turning back into the kitchen and opening the fridge like the future of his band isn't hanging in the balance.

What is it like to be so carefree, I wonder.

Chapter 30

Ryan

Getting Bri and Emma separated after their visit was not easy. The women had bonded before Em and I were a couple and now that there are so many relationships tying us together, I was a little afraid they were going to invoke some girl code and Emma was going to refuse to come with me tonight, opting instead to stay with Bri until the baby's born.

We still haven't heard from Brett but Juan was kind enough to reach out and let Bri know he was guarding the drummer. I only left with Em because Sloan agreed to watch out for Bri until Brett came back – which would probably happen sooner if I vacated the premises.

After what felt like an eternity, I was able to get Em back to Jennifer's to grab her suitcase so we could disappear into the mountains for a couple of days.

Pulling into the familiar driveway with our cell phones off, I try hard to shed my stress as I mentally check things off my list:

Emma is next to me.

She's my girlfriend.
The world knows.
Brett *knows.*

It's ironic that now that we don't have to hide, hiding is the first thing we do.

And tonight, I'm taking everything Emma offers. I'll be sure to give as good as I get, but knowing what's waiting for me is making it hard to focus on anything else.

She doesn't hesitate this time when I pull into the garage. Instead, she flings her door open, grabs her bag and saunters into the house like she owns the place.

After grabbing my own bag, I meet her in the house and find her in the kitchen, pouring champagne. I had the wherewithal to call the housekeeping service this time and ask them to stock groceries because I don't plan to leave for the next forty hours ... and I now know champagne is her favorite. *Thankfully, I've got a champagne budget for her champagne tastes.*

I slide behind her at the counter, engulfing her in my arms as I plant my chin on the top of her head. She smells like home. Light and fresh with a hint of her airy perfume. "Are you pouring one for me too?"

"You're opting for champagne instead of Scotch?" she asks, surprised.

"I figure tonight's for celebrating."

"And what exactly are we celebrating?"

"We're here together for the next day and a half where I plan to devour you and fulfill every fantasy you've ever had."

I smile when her cheeks flush a beautiful shade of red. She turns in my arms to face me, her butt pressed against the counter that's now behind her. The look in her eyes has my cock hardening. She looks mesmerized and a little scared, like she's waiting to wake up from a dream.

"I know how you feel," I say in response to the look on her face.

"I'm not sure you do," she says softly, reaching up to place her hand over my heart.

"Then tell me," I beg. "Use your words, Em. Tonight, especially, I need all of them."

She licks her lips and lowers her gaze. "Your face is everywhere. Your music is everywhere. I open Google and a headline about the band stares me in the face. People stalk you, and scream for you, and it's mind-blowing that you're standing here with *me*."

"Is it too much?" I ask, knowing how overwhelming the spotlight can be, especially if you're thrust into the middle of it unceremoniously like she was this morning.

"No," she answers emphatically, her fingers digging into my shirt. "It's just, you've always been off-limits and now you're mine and I don't know where to start."

"Luckily, I do."

I keep my eyes on her as I throw the champagne back in one gulp and set my empty glass on the counter. Grabbing her hand, I lead her over to the leather couch we sat on the last time we were here and flip the gas logs on. Housekeeping turned the heat up before our arrival, but there's still a slight chill in the room from the floor to ceiling windows to the left of the couch.

I sink to my knees in front of her and remain almost eye level with her as I skate my hands up her jeans and lick a trail from her collarbone to her ear, keeping my movements slow so she has time to process. I lost my virginity a while ago and don't remember much more than the girl's name. I wasn't an asshole. I just didn't know what I was doing. It wasn't that memorable.

I don't want Em to have that experience. I want her to remember this for the rest of her life.

I suck on the skin at the base of her ear and tease the spot with my tongue, smiling when she arches in to me. Her hands abandon her champagne flute, placing it on the end table next to the couch, and latch on to the back of my head, and shoulders. Before long, she's trying to pull her own clothes off and I still her hands, now tangled in the hem of her shirt.

"Emma," I whisper. "Slow down."

"I can't. I'm burning up. I need you."

"Do you want me to turn the fireplace off?" I ask, concerned.

"I'm burning on the *inside*, Ryan."

I know she is. I can feel the heat radiating from her core through her jeans but that's good. That heat will help keep her loose and relaxed for me.

"Em, you're so fucking beautiful it makes my lungs hurt."

"Ryan, if you won't let me take my own clothes off, then please get us naked. I'm going crazy not being able to feel you."

Having no choice but to honor her request, I grab the bottom of her shirt and start pulling it over her torso. I haven't even gotten it to her chest when I see the straps along her stomach and exhale harshly.

My eyes dart to hers and I see the devious grin on her face.

"You seemed to like it so much in the picture, I thought you'd want to see it in person."

"Have you had this on all day?"

"Yeah."

She's wearing the dark green lingerie that's made out of nothing but straps sewn together. I swear I had planned to go slow. Take my time and be a sweet, gentle lover this first time, but she's making me pull hard against the restraints wrapped around my self-control.

"It's a damn good thing I didn't know. You're playing with fire, Em."

"Maybe I want to get burned," she breathes back.

I rip the shirt over her head, revealing the top of the lingerie. Her breasts are bare except for a thin strip of fabric running between her nipples, teasing me in just the right way. The bottoms of her breasts hang exposed under the strap, calling to me. I grab her waist and tilt my head to the side to run my tongue along the flesh there. She grips the back of my head and holds me to her while she spreads her knees wider, inviting me in. I move closer to the couch on my knees but if my cock so much as brushes the cushion, it's all over.

I scrape my teeth along the underside of her breast and receive a delectable moan as my reward. I slide my palms up her ribcage, my fingers around her sides as I allow my thumbs to graze her nipples through the satin.

"Ryan, how long do you plan to torture me?"

"A while," I tell her honestly. "You wouldn't want me to rush through this and not take my time fully appreciating this outfit, would you?"

"I regret wearing it if it means you're going to drag this out instead of giving me what I want."

"And what is it that you want, Emma?"

"I want you to fuck me. I want your dick so deep inside me I can't think about anything else."

I back up, unbutton her pants, and slip my fingers in the waistband of her black jeans, thankful when she arches her hips so I can slide them down her legs and toss them aside.

"Oh, I will. I'm going to fuck you with my fingers..." I swipe them over the apex of her thighs. "With my tongue..." I bend low to place my mouth between her legs and lick the material. "And finally with my cock." I rub my palm over myself, my hard-on raging in its confines.

"It's going to be hard to use that part considering you still have all your clothes on. *Why* do you still have all your clothes on?"

"Because this is about you."

"If that were true, you'd be naked, allowing me to bask in all your cock's glory."

Hearing her say the word *cock* has me pushing off my knees to stand, pulling my own shirt over my head before quickly removing my pants as well. As I begin sliding my jeans and boxers down my legs, Emma lunges forward, wrapping her hands around my thighs, impaling her face on my dick.

"*Christ*, Em."

My knees threaten to buckle as she slides back and forth, my hands flying to the back of her head.

"This was supposed to be about you, baby."

She pulls back, melts from the couch onto the floor and looks up at me from her knees.

"I'd rather it be about *us*. Besides," she pants, "Ever since the first time I tasted you, I've dreamt about doing this again, so technically, it is about me."

She licks me from the base of my balls to tip of my dick, making me shudder with pleasure. When I look down, I see the strap below her waist that connects to the ones in the front and my sweet, smart, beautiful girl looks like the devil's plaything as she hollows her cheeks, her auburn hair cascading down her back.

"Em, if we're not going to go slow for you, then go slow for *me*."

She hums her discontent and the vibrations around my dick bring me dangerously close to the edge. God, I'm like a fucking fourteen-year-old who just found Pornhub. My balls tighten and I have to gently pull out of Em's warm, wet mouth.

"It's my turn."

"But you haven't come yet," she whines.

"And I'm not going to until you do...at least twice, probably three times."

She narrows her eyes at me like she doesn't believe me.

"Baby, the unfortunate thing about being a man is that I've got like three solid orgasms in me for the night. You, on the other hand, can get off five or six times, which means you're going first...and second...and third."

Her disbelief is written all over her face.

"I know I'm new to certain aspects of this evening, but five or six? That seems a little unrealistic, doesn't it?"

I can't help the cocky smile spreading across my face. "Have you already forgotten the ones I gave you the last time we were here?"

"I will never forget that night as long as I live."

I scoop her off the couch and lay her down on the floor next to the fireplace on the plush, white rug. As I grab a pillow from the couch to place under her head, I use my knee to slide the coffee table back a foot to give us more room and tease her with my words.

"Imagine how much more pleasure I can bring you when my dick is filling you up while I massage your clit," I tell her while working the strappy lingerie from her body. "When I'm pushing into you from underneath, while simultaneously slamming you down onto me, as I control you while you ride me."

Her hand shoots between her legs searching for her own relief as I toss her lingerie onto the couch. I want to make her stop so I can put *my* hand there, but the sight is too beautiful to interrupt. I simply watch her as I stroke my shaft until I see her fingertips start to glisten with her arousal and jump to action.

I wedge my massive frame between her legs. Her pale skin glows in the firelight attracting me like a moth to the flame. Until this moment, I always felt that expression had been over-done but seeing the flames undulate across her flesh, I get it.

Nothing could keep me away.

Not even the pain of death.

My hands find the insides of her thighs and I push them farther apart, wanting access to every inch of her. She opens easily, wantonly writhing on the floor as my tongue takes its first swipe.

"Oh fuck, yes."

I start slow, knowing she needs both pressure and a constant rhythm to get off. I want to torture her a little before giving her release.

She claws at the back of my head, bucking her hips off the ground seeking more friction than what I'm currently giving her.

Pulling away from her, I ask one last time. "It's green until you say otherwise, right?"

She nods as I return my face to her pussy, pushing my middle finger inside her underneath my tongue. I don't meet any resistance thanks to the asshole who stole it from us. I feel myself getting angry and I vow to find him and hurt him. Devastate him. *Ruin him.*

But for right now, if she's not thinking about it, then I don't want too, either.

Rotating my hand, I bend my finger and rub against her anterior wall. She moans and I feel her tighten around my fingers, driving herself farther onto my face. Bracing myself on my left forearm while my right hand gets to work, I instruct her to pinch her own nipples.

"Let me watch them harden under your touch."

She obeys immediately and then cries out. "Lick harder. Please."

I return her obedience, putting my mouth back on her and increasing my pressure on her clit. Hearing her moans and whimpers become more staccato, I pull back, spit on her pussy, and use the fingers of my right hand to swipe my saliva up and down along her slit, coating her well, changing my speed and rhythm.

I smile at her grunt of frustration because I know she was close. Planting my hands on the rug beneath us, I slide my body up hers. It's the first time we've been completely naked and on top of each other like this because I knew I wouldn't be able to control myself before. Now, I have the promise of her tight heaven waiting for me so I give in to the body that's been calling to me for over a year. I pulse my body forward and back, dragging the head of my cock through her pussy without pushing inside.

It's the best kind of torture.

"Please, do it," she begs, almost crying as she grips my ass, tugging me into her.

I keep myself positioned above her, my dick full, as hard and unyielding as steel, as it slides back and forth through her wetness.

"Fuck, you feel so good."

I lean down and pull her pert nipple between my teeth, biting down. Her fingers sink into my flesh everywhere she can reach like she doesn't know where to concentrate her efforts.

Perfect.

I want her to lose her mind with pleasure.

Releasing her nipple, I slide back down her body and give up teasing her, going straight to work for her orgasm. Pushing my fingers inside her and placing my thumb on her clit, I tell her all the dirty things I'm thinking.

"That's it, baby. Give me everything you've got. Ride my fingers. Use me for your pleasure. I can't wait to feel this tight pussy wrapped around my cock, milking me for all I'm worth. Can't wait until I'm buried deep inside you."

She uses her hands to grab my forearm and hold me in place as she bucks against my fingers, grinding her clit against the heel of my hand which has replaced my thumb. As soon as she goes over the edge, I replace my fingers with my face, drinking her in.

My balls are so tight I have to sit up and pull on my shaft a few times to try and alleviate the pressure.

When her breathing evens out, a relaxed smile lights up her face even though her eyes remain closed. "You're really good at that."

"I tend to be good at the things I enjoy."

She pops an eye open and studies me. Seeing my hand still wrapped around my cock, her eyes widen and she licks her lips. Her sweat-soaked hair clings to her cheeks and forehead.

I can't help but brush it back before she rolls over and perches up on all fours giving me a view I've imagined seeing ten thousand times.

"Tell me it's time," she says, looking at me over her shoulder, wiggling her ass right in my face.

"It's time." I'd hoped to get her off a couple more times, but she's making it impossible. If she wants my dick inside her right this second, then that's what she gets.

I stand and hold out my hand, helping her up, pulling her naked body flush against mine but it's still not close enough. I place my hands under her thighs and scoop her up until her legs wrap around my waist. My eager cock nestles himself against her ass and I groan.

Easily taking the stairs two at a time, I move us closer to bliss. She runs her tongue along my neck, pausing to suck on the birthmark there.

"Where are we going?" she whispers.

"The first time my cock enters you isn't going to be on a floor. We're going to the bed where you'll be comfortable and we don't have to worry about hitting the stone edge of the fireplace or the corner of the glass coffee table if we get out of control.

"Just get us there, fast," she urges right as I turn into the room and lay her down.

I can usually control my erections. If not when they happen, then certainly how much they distract me.

But not this one.

Seeing Emma laid out on the bed, naked like an offering on an altar, breathing hard and touching her own scorched flesh has unchained me. I'm no longer in control. I believe she said she preferred me *unhinged*. Well, we're about to find out.

"Ryan, you're shaking."

That's what happens when I can't hold back, I think to myself.

I lean down to capture her mouth with mine, bracing myself on my arms, lining our bodies up. Her thighs open wide, hips arching up to meet mine.

"Em, birth control. Your parents don't want two grandkids at the same time, I'm sure. I have condoms."

"Please, no. I've waited this long to feel you inside me, I don't want anything between us. I've been on the pill since I was seventeen to regulate my periods."

Thank God.

"I'm clean. Do you trust me?"

"Would I be here if I didn't?"

I don't even have to spit in my palm to coat myself because precum is pouring out of me. I can also see she's still wet, and I check in with her one more time.

"If I'm too rough, tell me," I pause, hovering at the gates of heaven. "You might have to yell though. Once I'm inside you, I'll be lost to the need to claim you."

"I trust you, Ryan."

307

"Fuck, I love when you say my name," I growl as I line the head of my cock up to her entrance, breathing hard.

I swear I try to go slow, but the way she tightens around me has me ready to *fuck*, all thoughts of *making love* gone out the window. The primal need to pump her full of my release stronger than any emotion I've ever felt.

I drive into her, wrapping my hands around the slats of the headboard, my biceps flexing as I try to channel some of my energy into the frame of the bed in an effort to protect her. My hips flex and suddenly, I'm seated in her as deeply as I can get, my balls flush against her skin. Without thinking - un*able* to think - I pull my hips back and push into her again.

She whimpers beneath me, clutching my forearms.

"Fuck. Em, are you okay?" My strained desire makes my voice sound foreign, even to myself.

She nods but doesn't speak which brings me back to the moment, concerned that it was too much, too fast.

"Does it hurt?"

"It's just...a lot."

I hold still for a second, knowing if I start moving, it's going to be worse.

"Fuck you take me so well," I praise her as she acclimates to the invasion.

The expression on her face is pain mixed with pleasure and I swear I blackout for a second. Her eyes are open, head raised slightly off the pillow, trying to watch where we're joined. I grab her hand and place her index finger on one side of my shaft and the rest of her fingers on the other side, laying her palm against herself so she can feel me when I start sliding in and out of her.

"*Fuck*," I grit out through the torture of holding still.

"Did I hurt *you*?" she asks alarmed.

"No, baby. I'm about to fucking blow, and I want you there

with me. It's hard to keep my cock in check when it's burrowing inside you."

She wiggles her hips a little forcing me to still her immediately. The look on her face is diabolical.

"You like the power you hold here, don't you?" I ask her.

"Mmhmm," she hums breathlessly, beginning to relax around me.

I flex my hips and push into her further making her gasp, smiling as I reclaim control. I slide out a couple inches and slowly push back in, working harder than I ever have to keep my orgasm in check. It's almost useless when she moans beneath me.

Without any prompting on my part, she reaches overhead and grasps the slats of the wooden headboard between my own hands. An image of her cuffed to those same boards with a blindfold on blasts through my head.

"Em," I rasp. "I need to fuck you."

"What are you waiting for?"

I sit up, hooking her knees under my elbows and hold her open for both our pleasure before slamming into her. Her groans spur me on and I roll my hips, grinding into her before going back to creating piston-like movements.

"I can't hold back," I say, rocking into her.

"You don't have to."

I release her left leg and use my right thumb to brush rhythmic strokes against her clit as I push my hips forward, filling her up, my cock trying to find his way into her soul.

Chapter 31

Emma

I 've heard horror stories about people's first-times. I've also read some pretty unrealistic tales of the milestone as well. After spending the night at the cabin with Ryan after the hockey game, I knew he could deliver on his shit-talk, but I still hadn't expected sex to be quite so...mind-blowing. I could *feel* him spilling inside me. As I contracted around him, I felt his dick jerk and the ensuing warmth told me he was painting my insides.

Holy shit. I just lost my virginity to Ryan Battle.

I lay my head back against the pillows, instinctively reaching for him. He emptied himself and then rolled next to me so he didn't crush me as we recovered.

My hand connects with his sweaty chest and I roll to my side, propped up on my elbow to look at his gorgeous face.

"You're staring," he says with a smile even though his eyes are closed.

"You might as well get used to it."

He opens his eyes and pulls me on top of him.

"How do you feel?"

I do a quick body check followed by a mental status check and grin. "Like I'm hoping your recovery period is short."

"I might need a minute. I don't think I've ever come so hard in my life," he says, brushing my hair off my face again.

With our naked chests touching, I can feel his racing heartbeat.

"I'm glad it was you." I pepper his chest with kisses and can't help but feel my desire begin rebuilding. With my knees on either side of his hips, I start rubbing myself back and forth.

"Me too. I have an idea," he says, gently sliding me off him and slipping off the bed.

"Where are you going?"

"To grab something from my bag, I'll be right back."

I'm so wound up even after my orgasms that I lay back on the bed and touch myself until Ryan comes back in the room carrying what looks like a shoebox. By the time he's standing in the doorway, I've worked myself into quite a frenzy.

"Oh fuck, baby. Keep doing that."

He sets the box on the end of the bed and stays standing at the footboard. His stance is wide, one hand around the back of his neck, one hand tugging his shaft, while I trace small circles over my clit. I should probably be self-conscious since no one's ever watched me do this before, but the look in his eyes tells me he really likes what he sees which boosts my confidence.

"Look how swollen that pretty pussy still is." I don't think he realizes he's begun to get hard again. "She's begging to be worshipped, baby."

I rub harder, the look in his eyes and the movement of his hand, driving me closer to the edge.

"Do you want to get off like that or do you want me to do it?" he asks roughly.

"You. Always you."

"Okay, then take your hand away."

He reaches for the box and pulls out two red silk ties and a matching blindfold.

"Do you want to try these?" he asks, holding all the items up.

I nod. I'll try anything with him.

He looks down at the semi he's sporting. "This may be my fastest turn-around time ever," he chuckles. "Spin around and face the headboard on your hands and knees."

I do as I'm told, eager to have him inside me again.

"Good. Can you drop onto your forearms but leave your ass in the air?"

I shoot him a look of trepidation.

"I'm not fucking you in the ass tonight, Em. We've got a long way to go before we're there. I just want you to be comfortable when I secure your hands to the headboard."

"Oh." I'm actually not sure if I'm disappointed or relieved as I drop to my forearms and lace my fingers around one of the wooden slats, my ass in the air like he told me.

"Fuck, baby. I'm already hard again," he says as he begins to weave the red silk tie around my wrists.

"That's the point, remember?" I say, mustering all the sass I can manage.

Slap.

I jerk forward as his palm connects with my ass. I grin even though he can't see me. I like this game.

"That mouth is going to get you in trouble, Em," he warns as he pulls tightly on the restraints satisfied when they don't give.

"I bet your cock can get me into more." I've never had the chance to let this version of myself free, but I like it a lot.

Satisfied with his handy work, he moves behind me on the bed and uses his knees to nudge mine wider. "Tell me if you're uncomfortable, okay?"

"I'm so horny, you could be pulling my fingernails off with pliers and I'm not sure I'd notice. Are you always going to talk this much or will you eventually—"

Slap.

That one was on my pussy and it wasn't from his hand. I try to sit up and look behind me, but the ties around my wrists prevent me from doing so.

"What was that?"

"Did it hurt?"

"Yes." I immediately retract my statement. "Well, not really. I just wasn't expecting it."

A small, black leather-tasseled whip enters my vision.

Oh.

"Fuck, you look so hot like this, Em." I feel the bed shift as he leans forward and bites my ass cheek. The quick flash of sharp pain dulls when he runs his tongue over my skin.

I need to feel him inside me again. I think perhaps I'll need it every day for the rest of my life.

I tug on the restraints losing my vision as Ryan slides the blindfold over my eyes. I'm already facing away from him and can't see his face so the blindfold seems like overkill but before I can ask him about it, he answers my question.

"If I take away your sight, your other senses will heighten from trying to figure out your surroundings. For example, your sense of touch," he pauses his words as he runs the tassels from my clit, through my slit, and between my ass cheeks before popping me lightly on the ass with it, "will be heightened."

I whimper and push back toward him as much as I can.

Suddenly, I hear a low whirring sound and my sex clenches.

A second later, I feel the vibrator.

"Holy shit." Unable to help myself, I push my ass up

further like a cat in heat. "I think I might die if you don't touch me."

"We can't have that now, can we?" His voice is low and full of seduction as I feel the head of his dick spread me wide. The vibrator is still whirring somewhere nearby but is no longer against my aching flesh.

He plants his left hand on my left hip and I feel his right hand below us, guiding himself in.

"Em, you have to relax or I'll never fit in this position."

I'm trying, but I'm so turned on, I don't know how to relax those muscles. After another minute, I hear him spit right before his wet fingers dip inside me. I can feel his hand rotate and his fingers spread creating an insane amount of pressure and need in me.

"Oh, *fuck*, Ryan."

"Keep breathing, baby."

His left hand leaves my hip, presumably to assist in helping him enter the recently stretched space.

"That's it," he purrs.

"*Jesus Christ,* you're *huge.*"

"Keep stroking my ego like that and see what it gets you," he says darkly before removing his fingers and sliding his cock in further, ever so slowly, stealing my breath.

"Don't hold back on me. I can take it," I force out through gritted teeth. It feels so good but it also feels like he's about to rip me in half.

"I'm holding back for *me,* baby. Eventually, I'll last more than two minutes inside you, but that probably won't happen tonight so I'm trying to take my time."

The deeper he gets, the better it feels and finally, I relax enough to fuck myself on his dick.

"Oh shit, Em. That's so hot, you pumping my cock like that."

He's picking up his pace.

"I think you're fucking my tonsils from the bottom. Is it possible to rupture a lung like this?"

"If you're coherent enough to talk, I'm not doing something right."

Without warning, he pulls out, flips me over, winding the ties even tighter on my wrist so they're biting into my skin.

There's a brief pause in the action making me excitedly anxious for what's coming next. I can't see him but I feel his large hands clasp around my ankles in a vice grip before holding them out to the sides and driving into me for all he's worth. I feel my tits bouncing as he plows into me, and when his balls are flush against my skin, I cry out in pleasure, twisting and bucking.

"I don't hear you talking now, angel," he says smugly.

"Uh huh."

I'm not sure if I'm agreeing or arguing or singing or praying. All I know is I'm about to fly over the edge of my third orgasm of the night and we've only been here two hours.

Hiding in the mountains is my new favorite pastime. After my latest orgasm, I'm ravenously hungry and Ryan's stomach gives away the fact that he's starving too.

"I think we need to eat," I point out, trailing my fingers over the contours of Ryan's chest, still slightly in a state of shock.

"I agree." He begins to move between my legs when I grab his face, laughing.

"We need to eat *food*, Ryan."

"If you insist," he pouts, but before he gets off the bed, he braces on his hands and knees hovering over me. "Thank you," he whispers before placing a gentle kiss to my lips. It almost feels like a goodbye kiss and it has me on edge.

I catch his wrists before he pulls away from my face.

"Thank you for what?" I ask.

"For entrusting me with that."

"Is that all? You seem so contemplative and remorseful, like you regret everything we just did."

"Is that *all*?" he repeats, sounding almost mad. "I know a lot of people view virginity as something to get rid of quickly, but it's a big fucking deal, Em. You don't get that back."

"I know, Ry. Why are you so mad at me? Until thirty seconds ago, it was the best experience of my life thanks to you."

He sits up with me still straddling his lap. "Shit, Em. I'm sorry. I'm not mad at you, and I certainly don't regret what we just did." He drops his gaze but I pull a play out of his book and raise his chin so he looks at me.

"Use your words, Ryan."

I see his face relax and his grin returns as I throw his words back at him.

"Smartass. I'm mad at myself because I can't give mine to you ... and I wish I could."

My heart simultaneously melts and implodes.

"I'd rather be your last than your first," I say and immediately regret it. It sounds like I just asked him to marry me and while I'm all in favor, we've been officially dating less than a month. As I'm panicking over how he's going to respond, he shifts his hips to get comfortable and the motion distracts me.

"Em, I have every intention of holding you to that." Before I can react or question him further about any other *intentions*, he slips off the bed and reaches in his bag before pulling on his sweatpants.

Goddamn sweatpants.

"You were right, I need to feed you before we get naked again." He pulls a royal blue t-shirt over his head obstructing my view of the most ripped, solid torso I've ever seen.

"Or we could just skip that part and I can try a liquid diet?" I suggest, fighting my smile as Ryan's pupils dilate. "I'm thinking I was wrong about the whole food thing." I crawl to the edge of the bed and palm him through his sweatpants.

"You're going to be the death of me, woman."

Chapter 32

Ryan

I keep expecting a call from my dad cancelling our invitation to the charity event, or at the very least, reneging his agreement for Emma to come along, but when my dad calls me on the landline at the house, the opposite happens.

"My team has advised that we face this head on. No hiding, we put it all out there. The event will give our family the chance to show a united front for your relationship as well as provide support for the campaign. Two birds. One stone."

"Yeah, Dad. We'll be there as planned."

"I'm sorry my reaction was less than supportive, Ryan. I blame it on the stress but the reality is there was no excuse to talk to you or Emma that way, much less, question your character."

To say I was shocked when my dad was so blatantly rude to Emma, and so questioning of me, would be an understatement. His apology now helps heal the cut he inflicted, but more importantly, it makes me realize that instead of me being there for people in a way that allows them to *forfeit* personal responsibility, perhaps I need to work on supporting my friends and family in a way that makes them *embrace* it. This means allowing them to suffer the consequences of their actions.

My current feud with Brett is forcing me to put my money where my mouth is.

"Apology accepted." Perhaps I let my dad off the hook too easily, but I'm also learning stress can cause people to do shitty things and honestly, there's enough strife in my life right now.

"See you tomorrow, son."

It's only been twenty-four hours since Em and I arrived and I wish we could stay forever. We'll head to D.C. tomorrow afternoon and I already dread having to share Em with the public.

The reality of having to leave the cabin so soon weighs on me.

Em and I finally detached ourselves from each other long enough to get some work done. Her papers, books, and laptop are spread out on the dining room table. She's drinking earl grey tea and I've set out a plate of fruit and cheese for her because she won't stop until she's meticulously dotted every *i* and crossed every *t*.

I should let her work, but I'm growing more and more selfish where she's concerned.

"Em?"

"Yeah?" she says, looking up from her laptop. She looks tired, like the screen and the material on it deplete her instead of filling her up.

"Can you let me know when you reach a good stopping point?"

Her mouth curls in a grin. "Insatiable, aren't you?"

"Yes. But I have a surprise for you that is not sex-related." I tell her, laughing.

She puts her pen down and closes her laptop. "Okay, I'm at a good stopping point."

I don't really believe her, but I'm excited to give her the present so I don't argue.

"Okay, close your eyes."

As she's sitting at the table with her eyes shut, I grab the easel and pack of canvases out of the closet. This place always stirs my creativity and I thought it might do the same for Em as well. I hastily reach back in to grab the small set of paints I had housekeeping pick up in addition to the groceries.

When it's all set up, I smile.

"Okay, open your eyes."

She surveys the scene and slowly walks over to the easel by the window.

"This is my favorite brand of paint. And brushes," she says, picking a brush up from the tray and caressing it, lovingly.

"I know."

"What's all this for?"

"I want you to know I support you. Whatever path you choose to take, just make sure you take it for *you*. If this is where your passion lies, this is what you should do."

She wraps her arms around me, immediately diving under my shirt, her hands pressing against my back.

"Thank you."

I see her glance at the canvas and I know she's eager to get started.

"You're welcome. I'll refill your tea. You paint."

She doesn't waste any time. Emma's always beautiful but when she's zoned in, mixing colors and swirling them together, it's hard not to get a little jealous. It's like she's making love to the canvas. I imagine it's similar to the feeling I have every time I hold my bass.

While she had been working on school assignments, I used

my laptop to listen to our recent songs and create new bass lines.

Too antsy to work any longer myself, and not wanting to interrupt Em's concentration, I head to the bedroom to change. There's a small home gym in the basement and I could use the outlet. Em's got her headphones on so I scribble out a note to let her know I'm going downstairs and leave it on the plate of food she has yet to touch.

After completing a short workout with the available dumb-bells and pull-up bar, I switch to my second favorite cardio workout: the heavy bag. My dad had one hung for me a while back. With sweat dripping down my bare torso, I sit on the bench and begin to tape my knuckles with the white athletic tape kept in one of the built-in lockers. I strap the shin pads on and work on some ingrained combinations I use as a warm up.

With my music playing, I don't hear the basement door open or Em's footfalls on the hardwood stairs a while later. I hear nothing at all but the sound of my gloves and shin-pads smacking the bag until she says my name with such desire, all my senses would have to fail me at once in order to misunder-stand her need.

My eyes catching hers is the only invitation she needs as she makes her way to me across the room. I strip the gloves off, using my teeth to loosen the Velcro and catch her in my arms as her tongue licks the sweat from my skin.

"I take it the painting went well?" I ask through heavy breaths.

"Very." She gives me a wide smile. "I also happen to listen to Beautiful Deceit while I paint, and the bass lines in *Virtuous* and *Vindictive* really turn me on. I figured it was a shame to keep painting when the man who's as sinfully delicious as the music he creates was somewhere in this house without me trying to tear his clothes off," she says between kisses, licks, and sucks. "Not to mention, this whole shirtless and sweaty thing really works for you."

My arousal feeds off of hers and hers is currently sky-high. I pull her with me toward the locker where the tape is stashed. Grabbing what I need, I push her against the lockers and begin to tape her wrists together in front of her.

"Anytime you want out of this, just clasp your fingers together, raise your arms overhead and pull down, throwing your elbows out to the sides. The force will rip the tape, got it?"

She nods her understanding.

Once I have her wrists bound, I place her arms over the post on the six-foot tall rack that organizes the weights, her back to me. I relieve her of her pants and thong and kick her feet wide. Without prompting, she bends forward, placing her ass in the air. I spit in my palm and coat myself before I line up, slowing nudging inside her.

She groans and allows the weight of her upper body to hang by the tape, her hands limp as she fucks herself on my cock for the second time today.

"So greedy," I tell her, squeezing handfuls of her ass, letting her set the pace.

"Only for you."

Desperation has never sounded sweeter.

"Which part of me, Emma?"

"All of them."

I know she's wet based on how easily I'm sliding in and out of her and now I want a taste. Slipping out of her, I pull her arms off the post. "Get on your knees."

She does so without hesitation and I lay on the ground behind her, face up.

"What are you doing?"

"Deciding which part of me to give you." I inch toward her on my back, pushing myself along on my shoulder blades until my head is passing under her. I stop when my mouth is directly beneath her pussy. "Sit down, Em."

She hesitates long enough that I grab her by the waist and pull her on top my face. I'm sure she's still swollen from our previous encounters so I'm not as rough as I want to be, but neither am I gentle. She fights me at first, but I lick her through her sensitivity until she's grinding into me, chasing her release.

I can't form words but hopefully she gets the picture from all my hummed pleasure. She leans forward and grinds herself onto my face.

"Oh my God, Ryan. Oh fuck. Yes...*yes*."

She shatters on my tongue and I'm damn near ready to lose it as I slide back out from under her. I slip my shorts off, leaving me completely naked, before asking if she wants to keep the tape on.

Without blinking, Emma holds her hands at eye level, clasps her fingers, and throws her elbows out to the sides just like I told her. As soon as the tape loses it hold on her, she rips her shirt over her head and jumps on me, wrapping her legs around my waist.

"No. I want to touch you this time," she finally answers.

Her nails bite my shoulders as I use my body to press her back against the wall.

Can I fuck her here? *Absolutely.*

Will we get off? *Hell yes.*

Is it my favorite? *Not by a long shot.*

But what kind of man would I be if I never properly fucked her against a wall? So here I am, leaning my body weight into her as I grip her thighs and lower her onto myself.

As I bounce her on my cock, trying to go slow so I don't hurt her, I feel the heels of her feet dig into my ass. She speeds up, wanting more, but she cries out in frustration like she's close but she can't get there. Meanwhile, I'm wound so tightly I'm about to spray paint her *and* the wall behind her.

"Slow down, baby. I can support you just fine so there's no need to rush. Lock your ankles behind me, and roll your hips so your clit grinds against my pubic bone," I instruct her.

"Oh. Oh yeah, that's better," she breathes, taking my advice. I readjust my grip to gain handfuls of her ass to help with the motion. "Ryan—"

"Fuck, Em. I hope that means you're close because I'm coming baby." I can't hold back. I feel like a selfish jackass until I feel her clench around me as I'm emptying inside her.

She yells my name a second time and tightens around me with her face buried in my neck as she rides the waves of her orgasm. Once the last spasm subsides, she unlocks her ankles and I set her down on wobbly legs. She picks up her discarded t-shirt before she bursts into laughter.

"That laughter is damaging to a man's ego, you know."

"Ryan, trust me when I say *nothing* should damage your ego ... besides, I'm laughing because I didn't realize what I'd thrown on today."

She holds it up so I can see the image.

Brett's face stares back at me.

Half his face is in shadow even though you can still see the outline. His drumsticks are in a "V" behind his head. The words above him say *Victory over Virtue* and have a whole new meaning than they did before.

"We're burning that shirt."

Emma just laughs harder and holds it out for me.

"Be my guest."

I wait for her to get all the other articles of her clothing in place and then grab my shirt from the pool table and toss it at her. "Here. Put this one on."

She takes it obediently and I smile when I see her hold it to her nose and inhale. As we head for the stairs, her gaze bores into the side of my head. When I finally turn to look at her, she's chewing on her bottom lip.

"What's wrong, angel?"

She smiles and shakes her head. "Nothing."

I stop moving and grab her hand to still her next to me.

"Don't hide from me, Em."

She swallows and says, "I'm dreading going back to school. I knew this would be hard but I'm not ready to be apart from you again."

I know what she means. It's one thing to talk about the time apart and think you understand and are prepared for it, and something else entirely when the time comes to separate with no plan in place for the next time you'll see each other.

I crowd her space and cup her chin, forcing her head back in order to look up at me.

"We'll figure it out. I know it's only been one night but I can't fathom not having you in my bed." I brush her hair back from her face and lean forward to kiss her. "Let's not think about it now. We still have tonight. Let's get dinner and then relax in the hot tub. I know you have to be sore and I think the heat will help."

"Always watching out for everyone else. What do *you* need, Ryan?"

"To know you're safe, and happy, and healthy."

She rolls her eyes. "I'm serious."

"So am I." I kiss her knuckles and pull her up the stairs toward the kitchen.

When we reach the top of the stairs, I can see her painting as soon as I come into the kitchen.

"Holy shit, Em. What's that?"

Her face breaks into a prideful smile. "Do you like it?"

"Em, that's fucking incredible. That's...that's... our next

album cover!" I can't keep my own excitement hidden over the image before me.

"What? Really?"

"Can we use that?" I ask, walking closer to see it better.

"Um, yeah, of course you can if you really think the guys will like it."

In the center of the canvas is a burning lotus flower opening to display an ouroboros, giving this painting two symbols of transformation, rebirth, and new beginnings.

The next day comes too soon and before we know it, it's time to leave. We'll check into the hotel and get ready there and I'm already planning on getting Em naked as soon as the door locks behind us.

As we hit the road, I feel the weight of the world begin to bear down on us again and when I turn my cellphone back on, I have to silence the four hundred and fifty-seven text alerts.

It seems mine, Sloan's, and Brett's phones have all been ringing off the hook. The band email is inundated with interview requests, and people must love a good scandal because our Spotify numbers are up as well, as if our listeners will find answers to the gossip in our music.

I called my father first just to check in and was told our agent from the label has been on the phone with my dad's office coordinating security and dealing with what my dad has called a "PR nightmare". Apparently, his opposition has really gone overboard with trying to prove that Em and I were together while she was underage.

"Don't look at the press, Ryan. We'll combat this soon

enough, but they've managed to get their hands on pictures from years ago: trips you took with the Donovans when Emma was a little girl, her face as she watches you on stage when she's seventeen, a hug you guys shared at what appears to be a birthday party. My guess is they were pulled from people's social media."

"This is such bullshit."

"I know you're angry. So am I, but for now, don't return their calls or lash out. Let my PR team handle it."

"Yeah, okay." I take a deep breath but it does nothing to curb my anger.

When my dad and I get off the phone, I look down to notice my gas tank is low. I'd rather fill it up out here in the middle of nowhere before needing to do it at a packed station just outside D.C. My bodyguard will meet us there, but for now, we're on our own.

While I wait for the tank to fill up, I update the guys on what's going on. I keep Brett in the loop because he deserves to know more than anyone.

RYAN 11:16 AM

Bad news: the guy running against my father is really trying to use Em and I as ammunition. Dad's team is working hard to get this under control.

Good news: Em is painting again and I think she just painted our new album cover.

Picture Message

SLOAN 11:19 AM

That's sick. Let's use it.

RYAN 11:20 AM

Any word from Brett?

BRETT 11:20 AM

I'm home, but Bri and I will be out by the time you get back.

RYAN 11:21 AM

Come on, B. There's no need to move out.

BRETT 11:21 AM

I can't live with you.

RYAN 11:22 AM

Look, the media will all get bored once they realize we're in a stable, committed relationship. Just give it a second. You know how things go.

I need you to talk to me.

BRETT 11:23 AM

This kind of attention was exactly what I didn't want for Em.

RYAN 11:23 AM

She told me. Everything. I'll keep her safe. You know I will.

SLOAN 11:24 AM

God, what else can there be?

BRETT 11:24 AM

Butt out Sloan. I don't want you involved.

SLOAN 11:25 AM

No, what you don't want is for Ryan's King-Kong-sized cock to taint your sister.

RYAN 11:26 AM

Not helping, Alexander.

NOAH 11:26 AM

What the actual fuck am I missing?

SLOAN 11:27 AM

KINKY!!!!

BRETT 11:27 AM

What are you doing on your phone Kink?

NOAH 11:28 AM

We were taking a selfie and it started going off. REPEATEDLY. I thought someone died.

SLOAN 11:28 AM

Ryan almost did.

RYAN 11:28 AM

That's a bit of an exaggeration.

SLOAN 11:29 AM

Okay, well Brett almost did. And that's NOT an exaggeration. His face was purple for a while.

NOAH 11:30 AM

What the fuck is going on?

BRETT 11:30 AM

We'll fill you in when you get back. Go bang your wife.

SLOAN 11:31 AM

Don't tell him what to do. I miss him. Brett, go bang your baby mama.

NOAH 11:31 AM

WHAT THE FUCK?

BRETT?

BRETT 11:32 AM

Jesus, fuck, man. You're on your honeymoon, we'll talk when you get back.

SLOAN 11:32 AM

Bri's pregnant.

Ryan's banging Emma.

Brett bashed Ry's face in.

The tabloids caught wind of Ry and Em and shit's hit the fan.

Now you're all caught up.

NOAH 11:33 AM

I can't leave you three alone ever again. Wait, how'd Brett get punches in on Ry?

BRETT 11:33 AM

Go. Fuck. Your. Wife.

SLOAN 11:34 AM

Ryan was asleep.

NOAH 11:34 AM

Ry?

RYAN 11:35 AM

We're handling it. See you when you get back.

Chapter 33

Emma

Everything finally feels right as we make our way into D.C. Ryan's by my side and since the new objective for the night is to set the record straight about he and I, we don't have to stay in separate hotel suites which is a relief.

The trip into D.C. takes just over an hour and my hands don't leave him the entire ride.

When we arrive, we're directed to the gated, underground parking garage of the hotel.

Unsurprisingly, there are already hundreds of people surrounding the building as we slip down into the guarded lot. Before the SUV is even in park, our doors are flanked by security.

"Is it always like this?" I ask, thinking back to the crowd outside of the hockey arena.

"If someone tells them where any of us will be, yes."

I try to let that process. After tonight, I'll be followed, photographed, and harassed just as much as Sienna and Bri. People will try to get to me in order to get to Ryan.

It's all becoming real in this moment.

331

Sensing my slight turmoil, Ryan locks the car doors before security can yank them open, and turns to face me.

"If this makes you uncomfortable, we'll bail on the whole thing. We can go back to the cabin or I can drive you back to your apartment in Boston myself."

"No. We can't. This is what it means to be with you and I will do whatever it takes to be with you. Besides, I'll just shift my perception of what's normal. *This*," I wave my hand around indicating the twelve body guards outside my door, "is my new normal."

"Are you scared?" he asks, searching my eyes for the answer.

"No." I place my own hand over his reassuringly. "Maybe a little overwhelmed, but not scared."

"If at any point tonight, you've had enough, just tell me and we'll go back to the room, okay?"

"We need to be here for your father," I remind him.

"My father's agenda is secondary to your comfort tonight. Understood?"

I nod, too emotional to speak.

"Good. Let's get this over with."

As soon as Ryan opens his car door, there is a flurry of activity. Two men immediately try to usher him away from the car as someone pulls my door open, reaching inside to grab my arm."

I look up in time to see Ryan break through the group of guards, immediately grabbing the man who has his hand around my forearm, and putting him in a headlock.

"Unhand her before I snap your fucking neck."

The man immediately opens his hand, dramatically splaying his fingers to show he's released me. Ryan removes his forearm from the man's throat and turns around to face the group of burly men. Standing between me and them.

"Let me make myself very clear. I don't know how you handle my parents, but you will *not* lay a single hand on me or my girlfriend."

"My apologies," the man who grabbed me says, not sounding sorry at all. "But we really need to get you two inside quickly. Your father has concerns about Ms. Donovan's safety."

This is news to me.

"What concerns?" Yeah, I knew tonight would be hard but I didn't think I would be in any actual danger.

"We'll discuss this inside. Let's go," the barrel-chested man says to me with more than a hint of attitude in his voice.

Ryan grabs him by the collar of his shirt and plants his face so close to the man's it looks like he might kiss him. "Learn some fucking manners before you speak to her again. None of this bullshit is her fault. Are we clear?"

He swings his eyes to me and says through gritted teeth, "Crystal. Can we *please* go inside?"

Ryan lets the man go and places his large hand on the small of my back. I feel him behind me creating a shield against the men who are supposed to be protecting us.

We're ushered directly to an elevator that requires a code to before it'll begin its ascent. One of the guards flashes a key card and presses the button labeled PH, which I'm assuming stands for penthouse.

The burliest body guard looks at Ryan. "We were notified that a couple of uninvited guests have made attempts to get inside the ballroom already, disguised as servers. They were detained and claim they're fans of Beautiful Deceit and only wanted a chance to meet you, but it didn't take long for our men to discover they're registered with the opposing party."

"And you think if they were truly here for me, they would only vote for my father?" Ryan asks, skeptically.

"Of course not. But I also don't think it's a coincidence that they chose *this* event to try and meet you."

Ryan narrows his eyes but says nothing more, only nodding as he places his hands on my shoulders, pulling me back into himself.

When the doors open on the top floor, everyone exits and a man I've seen before makes his way to Ryan.

"Ryan, I want this in your ear at all times tonight." He hands Ryan a small black ear wig. Ryan takes it without arguing and makes introductions.

"Em, you remember Tim?"

"Ms. Donovan, it's a pleasure to see you again." Tim's certainly more polite than the men we encountered downstairs, but he's all business right now.

"I asked Tim to come tonight because he's the only one I trust to watch over you. If we get separated for any reason, he will stick to you like glue. You do everything he tells you to the second he tells you to do it."

"Ryan, you're kind of freaking me out," I admit.

"Political functions always carry a certain security risk simply because people get so heated over candidates and campaigns, but people are far more interested in this one because of those pictures."

I reach up to trace his black eye.

"I'm sure they'll have something to say about this too."

"Hair and makeup will be here an hour before the event starts," he says, leaning closer to my mouth.

Tim coughs lightly into his hand, causing Ryan to release me.

"This floor is private. Only accessible with this keycard." He holds up a piece of rectangular plastic with the hotel's emblem on it.

Tonight was supposed to be a way to make connections and

spend time with Ryan afterwards figuring out what the hell it is we're doing. Those damn pictures changed the course of everything. It'll be up to me to show the media, and one reporter in particular, that I'm not some cowering, coerced, damaged, little girl anymore.

And I'm certainly not someone they can bully, harass, and break down. *Or assault.*

People want answers? It's time I give them some.

Squaring my shoulders, I turn to Ryan. My boyfriend, my rock, my anchor.

"I'd like a shower and a glass of champagne. Tim, if that's all, will you excuse us?"

"Certainly."

Ryan claps Tim on the shoulder.

"Thank you," he says and then swipes his own card at the door and pushes it open from behind me, allowing me inside first.

The room is beautiful. Modern and muted. I've never seen a hotel room like this in my life. The walls are a light grey with sheer white curtains pulled closed. Behind them, the blackout curtains hang to the sides. An open air-vent above causes the curtains to flutter as if there were an actual breeze from an open window. Although the building isn't that tall, a thousand lights are below us as the city comes alive at sundown. Our living room is in the corner of the suite and offers not one, but two walls of windows. I can see the long reflection pool between Lincoln and the National Monument. It's breathtaking.

As I'm surveying the landmarks below, Ryan appears at my back holding a glass of cold, crisp champagne. He presents the drink to my left and snakes his right arm around my waist.

"Do you want me to fuck you against these windows while you watch all the people down below?" he murmurs.

"Mm hm." I nuzzle into him, pressing my ass against his thighs as I take a sip from the crystal glass.

With both of his hands now free, he skates them up and down my sides.

"Do you want me to eat that sweet pussy the second we get back up to this room?"

I flash him a grin over my shoulder. "Why wait?" Suddenly, his brows pinch together and I can feel his tension rising. "What is it?"

"I always thought Brett was so overprotective, wanting to keep you in a cage. But with all those people downstairs, and the way security grabbed you, I'm realizing I'm no better than he is, Em. I want to lock you away and keep you all to myself."

I spin around in his arms so we're face to face – chin-to-chest, but it's the best I can do.

"The difference is I like it when you want to protect me." I cup him through his jeans and smile when he moans. "Let's take this champagne into the shower and find a way to relieve this tension, shall we?"

I smile when his hooded eyes find mine. "Lead the way." He swipes the bottle off the counter and follows me into the large en-suite.

I'm briefly afraid I won't be able to get him off with so much anxiety trying to rob him of his pleasure, but it appears *my* pleasure is an aphrodisiac he can't ignore. As soon as we're in the gigantic shower, he tips the bottle of champagne upside down, letting it run over my breasts and down my stomach before he drops to his knees on the tile floor and licks the expensive liquid off my skin. By the time he stands back up, he's hard as a rock.

"You know that bottle's like $300, right?" I ask, placing my hands on his wet chest, unable to tear my eyes from his flawless skin.

"You want a better one?" he asks.

I shake my head at him. "No. I want to drink this one, not waste it."

"Who said I was wasting it?"

"Half of that champagne went down the drain," I argue.

"But the half that made it in my mouth was worth far more than $300. Let me show you."

He tips the bottle up, taking a long pull before leaning down. Using his thumb to open my mouth, I feel the champagne fizz as it moves from his mouth into mine, the excess running down my chin.

"Mmm, maybe you're right."

I drop to my knees with my hands on his thighs. As soon as I put my mouth on him, he leans forward and braces himself by planting his hands on the glass shower wall.

A devious plan comes to mind. I don't know if he'll like it, but it's worth a shot so he has something to think about during the stress of tonight's event.

I grin to myself as I start to work him over.

Yes, Ryan makes me the version of myself I've always wanted to be. Even with the stress of everything going on, I'm painting again, I'm laughing more, I'm *not* tainted or broken and I'm so relieved to discover I can give as good as I get.

When I hear him groan and feel his hand in my wet hair, a peace washes over me like I've never known.

Chapter 34

Ryan

Perhaps it makes me a selfish bastard. Somewhere in my brain, I know I should be making sure she's ready to face the masses downstairs, or at the very least, *I* should be wringing pleasure from *her*. But when Emma puts her hands and mouth on me, I'm powerless to tell her no.

Seeing her on her knees for me makes me so fucking weak.

She's gagging herself on my cock on purpose after seeing my response the first time it happened and my balls are aching and heavy. They've turned into a fucking cum factory working overtime as if I needed any increase in production.

"Em," I warn. I know she doesn't mind swallowing, but that doesn't mean I can't offer her a heads up.

She pulls on me harder, adjusting her position and bringing her other hand up to cup my balls.

"Oh shit, Em."

Just as I'm about to spill over the edge, her mouth leaves me, causing me to open my eyes and look down. She's now pumping my cock with both hands, the tip of my dick aimed right at her face.

"Em, move o—"

Before I can finish my sentence, streams of hot cum shoot across her face and chest. Her eyes are closed and her mouth is open.

Holy shit. She did that on purpose.

The realization sends another wave of pleasure through me, coating her skin even more.

"Fuck, Emma." I can't tear my eyes away. Some people would find the act degrading but the way I see it, there aren't many acts I can think of that demonstrate such trust. She *wants* to be mine. She *wants* to be claimed by me. And fuck if it isn't hot.

My heart swells as my dick finally calms down.

She licks her lips before placing her face under the spray from the shower. "Did you like that?"

"I've never seen anything so sexy in my life." Did I ever, in my wildest dreams, imagine she would willingly use me like that to mark herself as mine? Hell no. "I know I've said it before, but I'm convinced you were made just for me, Em."

"I'm glad you finally realize that," she sasses back, quickly cocking an eyebrow at me.

She wants to play?

Excellent. It's my turn anyway.

I stay silent as I quickly wash her body while she washes her hair. As soon as I'm satisfied that we're clean enough, I shut off the water and prepare to make her dirty all over again.

As we're recovering from the last thirty minutes, a knock sounds on door and I hear Tim's voice.

"Mr. Battle, hair and makeup are here."

"Shit. Thanks, Tim!" I yell, hopping out of bed. I hand one of the plush hotel robes to Emma and pull my boxers on before walking toward the door.

"You'd better be planning to put more clothes on before you open that door... *Mr. Battle*," Em says, crossing her arms.

I love that she's possessive.

"Baby, the man on the other side of that door is no threat," I reassure her.

"Man?"

My smile widens as I open the door for Freddie and all his bags. As soon as he's over the threshold, the immaculately dressed man pulls me in for a hug and kisses my cheek before smacking me on the ass. He's the only man outside of my band-mates that could perform that act without losing his hand.

"I see I've got my work cut out for me," he says, taking in my busted eye. "Yet somehow, you still get sexier every time I see you." He holds me at arm's length and looks me over before swinging his attention to Em. "And *you* must be the reason all my hopes of getting Ryan to bat for the other team have gone up in smoke."

I laugh as I introduce the two.

"Em, this is Freddie. He's been doing my family's wardrobe and makeup for functions like this since I was about twenty-years old. Freddie, this is Emma, my girlfriend."

He plants a kiss on each of her cheeks and then turns back to grab his bags and begins to set up in the bathroom.

"You two are creating quite the scandal it seems. I just left your father's suite." Turning to Emma he says, "the man adores you, by the way. It's just unfortunate that some people can be so closed-minded. If the senator seems hesitant, it's only because he's fearful for the election. Don't take it personally, Bunny."

Em smiles and seems to relax around Freddie which makes me happy. This is a part of my life she's never seen before.

"Have a seat," he instructs her. "I like to be entertained while I work so as I start on this hair, which people would murder their best friend for, mind you, you can start by telling me if our beloved bassist, here, is as well-proportioned as I hope he is."

Em's eyes go wide before she lets out a bark of laughter.

"Freddie, behave."

"Oh, you're still here? Be a doll and go pour some drinks, would you? You know I do my best work with a bit of a buzz," he winks.

I roll my eyes and kiss Em on the cheek. "You can trust him, but don't tell him anything."

Their soft chatter sets me at ease. Choosing to stay in this mindset, I avoid my phone and scroll through the hotel T.V. channels instead, until I hear the bathroom door slide open an hour later.

"I'm ready for you to come tell me how amazing I am," Freddie says from the bathroom.

Rolling off the bed, still in just my boxers, I stop at the doorway.

Amazing isn't the right word. Emma's natural beauty has nothing to do with Freddie, but his knowledge of hair, makeup, and fashion is certainly unparalleled.

"Your silence is insulting," he chides when I take too long to answer.

"I..." I start but quickly stop, truly at a loss for words. Trying again, I open my mouth and hope the right thing comes out. "In all the sunsets I've seen, in all the places I've been, whether it was reflecting off turquoise waters or snow-covered peaks, I have never seen beauty that compares to you in this moment."

I'm vaguely aware of Freddie clapping his hands. "That's better."

Emma's makeup is done to perfection. Light and naturally highlighting her skin tones. The contouring done on her cheekbones accentuates the liner and mascara around her almond-shaped emerald eyes, making them appear exotic. Her lips are dark, the shade deeper than crimson. She looks professional, not overdone, mature but not like she's trying to prove a point.

In a word, she looks *perfect*.

Freddie's chosen a long, royal blue, silk dress with thin, spaghetti straps. The neckline is enticing but appropriate and just under the hollow of her throat hangs a necklace I've seen her wear before. It's a sapphire that matches the color of her dress.

"You excel at your craft," I tell Freddie, my eyes on Em. "But it helps when your canvas already had a masterpiece on it." I finger the necklace as I talk, remembering I saw her wearing it in Ireland.

"Okay, now I'm swooning." He grabs me by the biceps. "Come on, big boy. You're next."

"How'd you know it would match?" I ask Emma, ignoring Freddie.

"I didn't. I just always have it with me when I travel."

"A gift from your parents?" I ask, knowing there has to be something special about this necklace for her to keep it so close. She's not a flashy-jewelry kind of woman.

Demurely, she shakes her head.

"From your ex-boyfriend?" I ask, through my clenched jaw.

"No, Ryan. I wear it for *you*."

"Me?"

"Sapphire is September's birthstone."

I'm overcome with emotion as I pull her to me, ready to crash my lips to hers when Freddie's arm lands between us.

"Oh no, you don't. We don't have time for me to redo this look and I think we can all agree it's better if she doesn't enter that ballroom looking freshly fucked. You'll have to wait."

I take a painful step back from Emma and she sails past me out the bathroom door, a giggle on her painted lips.

As I sit my ass in the chair, Freddie grows serious. "She's a beautiful girl, and she seems good for you. I hope it works out."

"It'll work out. I want it and she wants it. Everyone else can go to hell."

Freddie does an incredible job covering up my bruised face without making me look like I'm caked in foundation. He's chosen a black tux with black shirt and royal blue tie to match Em's dress.

When she and I are side by side, we look damn good.

"I don't know how I'm supposed to keep my hands off you," she whispers.

"You don't have to."

She smiles and loops her arm through mine, instantly transporting me back to Noah's wedding. The way I watched Brett protectively place his hand over Bri's as it rested on his forearm when he led her down the aisle. I copy the move now, ensuring that Em feels comfortable and safe.

"Shall we go set the record straight?" I ask.

Her confident smile makes my heart falter.

"Let's go."

We say goodbye to Freddie and pick Tim up as we head to the elevator, going over the plan for the night.

"A select few from the press are allowed inside. After all, these events are about getting my father's name out there, and showcasing some of the work he's involved in. It shouldn't be more than ten or twelve, but just assume every face you make and every word you say will be recorded," I tell her.

"Got it."

There's a light sheen of perspiration breaking out on her forehead, and her hand has a slight tremble to it.

"Em," I turn to face her, taking in how her chest is rising and falling rapidly. "Em, deep, slow breaths, baby. I won't leave your side. I'll do all the talking. Just keep a hold of me, okay?"

All too soon, the elevator hits the ground floor and we're led down a couple of narrow, back hallways before we enter the ballroom.

The first thought I have is *money.*

No expense was spared. An event this close to election day requires that you pull all the stops. The top campaign supporters are here, along with other potential donors for future campaigns. The leaders of the charity are all present as well. Seeing as it's for wounded soldiers, several of them are in their military dress uniforms. Of course, I feel this money would have been better spent on the soldiers themselves, maybe putting on a family day, or a concert, but that isn't how it works. Part of my father's political agenda is providing financial assistance as well as health insurance that includes extensive mental health benefits for Maryland's recently discharged soldiers and their families. Partnering with this organization is a smart strategic move and unfortunately, in order to provide assistance in the way he wants, he first needs to spend money on those who control his ability to implement the programs.

The food tables display racks of lamb, lobster tails, fresh oysters on the half shell, and wagyu steaks. The sides are no less intimidating in the quality of their ingredients or cooking methods. Beside me, I feel Emma taking it all in. She was at the hockey game and Kink's wedding, so she's no stranger to the extravagance, but this is on a different level.

We haven't even stepped three feet inside the ballroom when one of the reporters gets wind of our arrival. All it takes is one click of a camera before they're circling us like sharks scenting blood in the water.

But I'll be damned if it's my blood or Em's blood they get.

I feel Em's hand grip my forearm through my jacket and place my hand over hers again. *I've got you.*

Keeping a small smile on my face, I wait for one of reporters to begin firing off a question before I open my mouth. I make eye contact with a woman close to the front and I see her press a button on her phone.

As soon as the woman takes the bait, I interrupt her. The rude gesture done purposefully as a way to communicate who's in charge.

Me.

Because I have something they want; valuable information is the currency right now. And right now, my information is worth everything, and if they want it, then they'll play by my rules.

"Mr. Battle, can you—"

"Let me begin by thanking you all for being here tonight. This evening means a great deal to my father and our family as he seeks his eighth reelection to office. I understand my relationship with Ms. Donovan has caused a stir and we would hate to be a distraction from the importance of tonight's event. So, in the interest of placing our undivided attention where it belongs, once my family arrives, we'll take ten minutes to address your concerns and then we ask you to move on and focus on the gala and on the programs being promoted tonight."

With that, I take Em's clammy hand in mine and lead her away from the cameras. I hear Tim's voice in my ear.

"You're going to have to let her talk, you know. Otherwise, they're going to think you gave her a gag order."

"I pay you to keep us safe, not manage our PR," I bite back.

Nothing about Tim is soft, so I know I didn't offend him. His response confirms it.

"Just want you to know what it looks like. You also pay me to read a room, right? Give her some space to breathe."

I ignore him as we head to the table reserved for my family near the stage. Somewhere in the back of my mind, I know Tim's right. I don't like it, but he's right. If I don't let Em spread her wings, this whole night will have been pointless.

Looking around the room, I catch sight of my father and mother walking in, my two brothers behind them. Trevor is a welcome sight and unsurprisingly, Carey looks like my next punching bag. But that's only because I know how fucking slimy he is under his three thousand dollar suit and perfectly coiffed hair he paid for with our father's money.

I hug my mother first. She's always been quiet. Polished and refined, but almost meek in her demeanor. My mother hasn't had an opinion of her own the entire time I've known her. My father is so confident and knowledgeable but none of that confidence transfers to my mother. I shake my father's hand before turning to my brothers. I clap Trevor's hand and pull him in to pat him on the back. Knowing we're being watched, I reluctantly give the same greeting to Carey, before reintroducing my brothers to Emma.

She's perfect in her poise and speech. It looks like they're friends greeting each other after a long time apart, not meeting for only the fourth or fifth time. My mother takes Emma's hands in her own and kisses her cheeks in greeting before trying to whisk her away to the table, both women wanting to shy away from the limelight. Emma casts a nervous glance at me over her shoulder so I step in, grabbing her hand.

"Before you ladies get too comfortable, I promised ten minutes to the media so we could enjoy the rest of our evening in peace without Em and I being a distraction."

My dad nods, making me assume he's on board with the plan to get this over with. We walk to the back of the room where the reporters are fidgeting with their equipment, waiting for the main event to begin. I feel Em dragging her feet slightly but she's still making forward progress.

I kiss the side of her head and lean down to whisper, "If at any point this becomes too much, I want you to tap on my forearm like I taught you at the gym. That will let me know you're done and it's time to go, okay?"

She nods and then turns to face the crowd before us.

"You all have ten minutes. Please conduct yourselves in an orderly and respectful manner or you won't be getting any information tonight," my dad says evenly, moving to stand on Emma's other side. He pulls my mom in front of him, next to Emma to send a message in all the pictures they're taking.

This woman is as important as the senator's wife. Not a fling. We are family.

I've never been so grateful for my dad as I am right now. If he hadn't already apologized with words, this act would suffice to smooth things over.

The reporters immediately start in on Emma as I suspected they would. I clench my jaw and close my fingers in a fist behind her back. My other hand rests on her hip, ready to pull her behind me the second they fuck up. I want to answer for her. Jump in front of her so they don't even get to lay eyes on her, but I know she has to do this herself.

"Ms. Donovan, could you tell us what happened the night those pictures were taken of you and Mr. Battle by the car?"

And just like that, the camera flashes start, microphones are thrust in Emma's face, and she's addressing the world.

Chapter 35

Emma

The lights from the cameras momentarily daze me. I swallow hard, desperately praying I don't lose the champagne I consumed before coming down here. I know Ryan's behind me but in this moment, all I can see are the expectant eyes staring back at me.

Come on, brain. Work! Don't make Ryan or his dad look bad. Show the world you belong here. You can do this.

"Ms. Donovan?" the reporter repeats herself.

I feel Ryan give my back a light tap.

I can do this, I repeat to myself before raising my head and plastering a smile on my face.

"I don't think it would be appropriate nor should it be expected of me to divulge any details about a consensual, intimate moment between my boyfriend and I. After all, I wouldn't expect you to share your private moments with the world. What makes you think the world should be privy to mine?"

I feel Ryan's laugh along my left arm that's pressed against his abdomen.

"Next?" I ask sweetly.

A man toward the back of the pack speaks up. "If you won't elaborate, you leave people to draw their own conclusions and I must say, those conclusions don't look great, especially with some of the photos we've seen. You never know what else could surface."

Slowly, I find my groove. This isn't so bad. With the support of Ryan and his family, I'm able to remain calm and not allow the reporters to goad me.

I turn to the man who spoke.

"I appreciate your opinion Mr..." I trail off, waiting for the reporter to fill in the blank.

"Graham."

"Well, Mr. Graham, that sounds an awful lot like an implied threat, also known as coercion. So, I'd be careful with your statements moving forward. Thanks to your hostile nature, I'm not inclined to satisfy your need for answers. Next?"

I give a genuine smile this time as my law classes finally come in handy for something.

"Emma, what *are* you willing to share about your relationship?" another reporter asks.

I answer her honestly because I appreciate that she left me room to breathe with her question.

"Three weeks ago, Ryan and I decided to pursue a romantic relationship. Like any relationship, we found a mutual attraction to each other that was heightened by a history of friendship. Yes, my family has known Ryan for a while but rest assured, our physical attraction to each other is recent." I turn to look over my shoulder at Ryan's father, I give him a tight smile in warning, knowing he'll recognize my next words. "For anyone to insinuate that I've been taken advantage of like a child incapable of making her own decisions is not only ignorant, but incredibly disrespectful to my own level of intelligence which I'm sure you all know by now is much higher than most in this room."

Several of the reporters' mouths drop after being openly insulted.

Ryan's dad covers a laugh with a cough, and addresses the crowd. "Are there any other questions we can address before turning our attention to tonight's events?"

"How does your brother feel about this union?" another woman in the front asks, her voice too breathy for my liking. Although her question is directed at me, her eyes are raking over Ryan. "Didn't he issue a statement saying none of the band members, and I quote, *would dare lay a finger* on his sister?"

"We're working through that. We chose to wait and tell my brother until we were sure our feelings and intentions were long-term. As you can imagine, it will take some getting used to for my brother and we didn't want to cause unnecessary stress if we decided things weren't going to work out. Unfortunately, the pictures told him before we could."

"Is there any concern that the band will divide over this?" she follows up.

"No," Ryan's deep voice answers beside me. "And that's all we'll be answering for now. Thank you."

With his back to the dispersing crowd, he says, "I'm so fucking proud of you."

I grin up at him. "Thanks. I'm proud of myself."

Senator and Mrs. Battle move on to make the rounds as more guests enter the ballroom, leaving Ry and I alone with Trevor and Carey.

"Emma, that was great. Before the heavy stuff, did you see that reporter's face when you told her off? I thought she was going to piss herself," Trevor laughs, grabbing a glass of amber colored liquid from a passing server. I appreciate his attempt to diffuse the tension. He reminds me of Sloan.

"I must say, I figured my brother would end up with someone smoking hot because girls love guys in bands, especially when they have money, but I didn't think he'd pick one smarter than himself," Carey says with a laugh.

Feeling carefree after proving to myself that I have the strength to live my life on my terms, I lean in to whisper to Carey.

"Hey Carey?"

"Yeah, gorgeous?"

"Your douchebag is showing. You might want to cover that up." Trevor and Ryan throw their heads back in laughter as their brother's face turns red in embarrassment and I continue, still close to his face. "Do not *ever* suggest I'm with Ryan for his fame or money again."

Carey storms off as Ry, Trevor and I take our seats.

It's wonderful to be able to relax a little. Ryan's hand stays possessively over the back of my chair as he sips his scotch, lost in conversation with Trevor. The best part is not having to hide.

People are watching Ryan's every move. Men and women alike discreetly slow down as they pass our table obviously hoping for some sign of acknowledgement from Ryan. A few people saunter directly to our table. They're so practiced in the art of deception it's impossible to tell if their congratulations are sincere but my heart rate has slowed down enough to allow me to interact normally, almost enjoying myself. I think Bri was right. It's easier now that we don't have to hide. Although things are not yet resolved with Brett, I've overcome so many hurdles recently and this is a huge, positive step for Ryan and I.

Halfway through the meal, I pat Ryan on the thigh.

"I'll be right back, I need to use the restroom."

"I'll go with you." He moves to push his chair back but I stop him.

"I'm doing okay. It feels good to not be so afraid and intimidated. Besides, this was a good reintroduction to the media. They seem to have a pretty short leash thanks to the crowd in attendance."

Ryan's jaw is tight. I know he doesn't want me out of his sight. Finally, he nods at me.

"Fine, but take Tim."

His gruff words cause me to chuckle. "Ry, if anyone is going to escort me to the bathroom, I'd rather it be you versus him. Give me five minutes."

"I'll give you four," he says.

I lean down to brush a quick kiss across his lips and make my way to the edge of the room.

I heave a sigh once I'm in the hallway, pressing my back against the wall, briefly closing my eyes and taking a deep breath. I'm proud of myself for the way I handled the media. It sets the stage moving forward, that much like Noah and Sienna, the public won't be privy to Ryan and I's lives.

Lost in thoughts about the future and trying to figure out how to reach Brett, I don't notice the arm reaching out for me until it's too late and I'm pulled against a body and dragged through a door.

That smell.

"I think it's time you give me that story."

That voice.

His hand clamps down on my mouth, making it so my scream is muffled and certainly not audible through the heavy door he just dragged me through. My assailant runs a hand from my knee to my thigh as I thrash against his hold. The man isn't in shape, but he's big.

"I've dreamt of that sweet, tight cunt every day since I last touched it. So we're going to make a deal. You either give me a groundbreaking story about your boyfriend, the band, or the senator ... and I'm talking a career-making story, or I'm going to finish what I started two years ago."

Unadulterated rage fills my body as he keeps talking. I quickly survey my surroundings and notice we're in one of the ground floor guest rooms right off the hallway to the ballroom where the event is being held.

Dragging me back toward the bed, he whispers, "You didn't think I'd miss this opportunity to get my interview, did you? Thought I wouldn't show up? No, I was just biding my time."

My heart is beating so hard, it's almost making me dizzy and I need to regain control before I pass out and this man does far worse to me than the last time.

I speak against his hand, trying to get him to remove it. Even though my words are unintelligible, he can tell I'm trying to speak and not scream, so he lightens his pressure enough for my lips to move.

"I'll answer your damn questions."

"I want more than that now. You know this dress really looks good on you." He trails a finger across my collarbone, making my skin crawl.

I have to get out of here.

He reaches behind him for something, loosening his hold around my waist and I seize the chance to rip free of his grasp. I yank the door open but he's immediately behind me and throws his palm against it, slamming it closed again.

When I turn to face him, he brandishes a roll of duct tape, and I think I'm going to be sick.

"You see, I've been waiting a long time for my big breakout story. It was supposed to be you. I was supposed to have an exclusive article. As the world was getting hot on the drummer of Beautiful Deceit and his tragic past, *I* was going to release an interview with the person who shared a face with his dead sister and offer insight and a point-of-view no one else could give. But no, you wouldn't even give me five minutes. So now, you're going to give me a whole lot more than that."

My mind races, trying to remember something Ryan taught me at the gym but most of those moves are impossible in this dress.

Unless I gain control.

I'm done being terrorized. I'm done meeting the expectations of others, including this asshole, who's name I still don't know, but I know he expects me to be just as fragile and weak as I was during our first encounter.

I stop fighting him, and turn to face him once again, my back against the door. I take deep breaths like Ryan always tells me to.

"You really don't have to do this. I'll give you the story. Any story. I'll tell you all about my sister's drug problem." The one she didn't have, but I need to sell this like my life depends on it, because it just quite might.

His eyes move to my heaving chest, before dropping lower and his eyes flare.

"We'll get there."

He tears a strip of tape and places it over my mouth before pushing me to stand next to the bed.

Stay calm, Emma.

I want to scream, but that didn't help last time and it won't help this time either. I'm not the victim I was back then.

I don't fight back when he unzips my dress and it falls to the floor. I don't cry. I don't scream through the tape. I begin to fight when he grabs at my hands, trying to bind them with the tape. Getting frustrated when he can't grab them both at the same time, he smacks me so hard across the face, it causes me to land on my back on the bed. He immediately crawls on top of me, his legs straddling my waist as he winds the duct tape around my wrists.

Chapter 36

Ryan

Something's wrong.

It's been six minutes and Emma isn't back. I hear murmurs as Tim and I exit the ballroom not giving two fucks that my father's speech is going on.

"I should never have let her out of my sight."

"Relax, she probably just needed a break from the pressure of that room. It's suffocating," Tim says rationally, trying to keep me calm.

"You're wrong. She knows I don't like it when she's away from me. She wouldn't make me wait like this. She knows I'll worry. Something's happened."

I race down the hallway calling her name, reminding me of the night I picked her up from that party. The night my whole life changed and Emma Donovan became mine.

Mine to love.

Mine to cherish.

Mine to protect.

Fuck, how did I let this happen?

I call her name several more times with no answer.

"I'm going to bang on every fucking door in this hotel. Go to the front desk, get their security footage and make sure no one took her out of this building."

Tim turns to leave and I start making a scene that rivals all scenes.

"EMMA!" I bellow, my voice echoing through the halls.

It doesn't take long before someone from my father's security team rushes up to me asking what's going on and if I could keep it down.

"No and no. Until I find Emma, you can tell the senator that I don't care what consequences my actions have for his campaign."

"EMMA!" I yell again, my fist pounding on the next door like a madman.

Chapter 37

Emma

Now in nothing but my bra and panties, with my wrists secured and the duct tape across my mouth, my assailant seems content to take his time perusing my body beneath him. He stretches his own, soft, large body out along mine. I try to stay calm as I wait for his false sense of security to kick in. He's seemingly unaware that I have no intention of allowing him to get any further than this.

I adjust myself by rolling slightly to my side and bringing my knee up.

He thinks I'm opening for him and encourages my knees wider.

Perfect.

Right before I make my move, I hear Ryan calling my name. My assailant looks down at me and grins.

"Looks like he's noticed your absence. Better make this quick."

My time has come.

I raise my arms over my head, which he mistakes as a sign of offering, before quickly bringing my arms back down, forcing my elbows out to the sides. My smile of violent fury spreads across my face as the duct tape tears.

I throw my right arm out to the side, sending the heavy metal lamp clattering to the floor, hoping the sound is loud enough to attract Ryan to the correct room.

The man on top of me moves to catch my wrists again and I remember watching Dillon and Ryan struggle on the mat. Ryan's words ringing loud and clear. *Don't get too focused on controlling the arms when the power and control is in the legs.*

I give up my right wrist to occupy my assailant as I throw my hips out to the side.

He chuckles. "Now this is what I wanted. You like a fight?"

Using his hold on my right wrist as leverage, I push my upper body away from him and throw my left leg across his chest. The move brings the apex of my thighs dangerously close to his face and when he raises his head, I tilt sideways and slide my right leg behind his neck, clamping down like an alligator's jaw. At the same time, I pull my right wrist toward me, causing his arm to come along. Once it's straight, I buck my hips forward as hard as I can, satisfied when I feel the joint pop.

The man lets out a howl. "*Fuck! You bitch!*"

Right. I'm the bitch because I wouldn't let you rape me.

Suddenly, there's pounding on the door and Ryan's pissed off voice is on the other side.

"Emma!"

I pull the tape off my mouth and answer. "Ryan!"

I hear his shoulder or his boot kick at the door, but of course it doesn't budge. A second later, an electronic beep is followed by a click and the door opens. I've pressed myself against the wall while the guy on the bed moans and clutches his arm which is hanging at a strange angle.

Before anyone else can enter the room – and I see a large group of people gathering just across the threshold, Ryan pockets the keycard and kicks the door shut. He tears his tuxedo jacket off and wraps it around my shoulders, kissing my head. Looking in my eyes he asks if I'm okay. As soon as I nod, he turns to the man whimpering on the bed.

"That's him, isn't it?"

Knowing I'm probably sealing the man's fate, and not caring at all, I nod right before Ryan launches himself at the writhing figure.

The man holds up his good hand – as if that will stop the wall of muscled flesh from flying at him.

Ryan drags the man off the bed and sends a punch straight to his eye. The man's head snaps against the floor.

"What's your name?" he growls.

When the man shakes his head like he isn't going to answer, Ryan plows his fist into the man's nose.

"Name. Now. Or I'll make sure every joint in your fucking body matches your elbow." To prove his point, Ryan twists the dislocated joint, causing the man to yell out in pain.

I'm vaguely aware of more beating on the door but I make no move to answer it. A sick part of me wants to watch this man suffer.

"Larry," he chokes out. Ryan captures the man's other arm and begins applying pressure. He wants the man's whole name. Finally, Larry obliges. "Larry Whitsef." Finally, after two years, I have a name to go with the hideous face.

Ryan's straddling the man's torso on the floor, one hand around his neck, his other fist repeatedly knocking into the man's face. There's blood everywhere and I think I just saw a tooth land on the carpet. Another electronic beep alerts me that the door's just been opened again and I don't hear it latch shut this time. I can't tear my eyes away from the gruesome scene in front of me. Hell, I'm vaguely aware of camera flashes, although this time they don't faze me.

"You sick sonofabitch! You'll be lucky to be alive by the time I'm done with you!" An officer tries to pull Ryan off the man but Ryan easily shrugs out of his grip and throws the police officer backwards. The motion spurs me to action. I can't let Ryan kill Larry. Ry and I only just got to each other, I can't lose him now.

I push off the wall on wobbly legs.

"Ryan. Ry!" I touch his shoulder but he just keeps pounding Larry's face, lost to the moment. Larry's now unconscious on the floor beneath him. "Baby! Look at me!" I kneel next to Ryan and his unfocused eyes are swimming with hatred. "Ry, I'm okay. Please don't kill him. I can't lose you."

His eyes swim into focus as he abandons the man on the floor and grabs me in his arms, pulling me onto his lap while people tend to the heap of flesh in front of us. Tugging the edges of his jacket tighter around me, he attempts to speak several times but always ends up closing his mouth, unable to choose what he wants to say.

This time, he needs *me* to anchor *him*, and I'm ready for it. I cup his face in my hands like he's done to me so many times before.

"Ry. I'm here. I'm okay. Take deep breaths with me."

When I finally get him calmed down enough to talk, his eyes flare to my cheek where I can already feel the bruise forming. "Did he hit you?"

"I'm fine," I say, avoiding the question, not wanting him to finish the job he started. "He didn't hurt me. Thanks to you, I was able to protect myself."

"You shouldn't have had to protect yourself. I should never have let you out of my sight."

"We aren't playing the blame game, Ry. This is no one's fault but his." I nod to the bloodied man paramedics are loading onto a stretcher. "Besides, we already know I'll spend a lot of time out of your sight. As soon as the new album drops, Bri said you guys are heading back out on the road."

He studies me for a minute. "I don't want to think about that right now."

I nod in agreement as we stand.

"Do you want to put your dress back on?" he asks, noticing I'm still wearing just his jacket.

"No." Ry's jacket hangs almost to my knees and I feel comforted here. A sound draws our attention and we turn to face an officer who's just come into the room to take our statements. As Ryan's talking, the paramedics wheel the stretcher out of the room and that's when it hits me.

"He's been keeping tabs on me for *two years*." My body wracks with a shudder at the realization.

The officer asks me more questions about the first attack and by the time I've rehashed it all, I need a shower and a stiff drink, but my evening is far from over.

The media is trying to give us space, despite catching what they could on camera and I feel for them. They've been betrayed by one of their own. Larry Whitsef has further damaged the relationship between those in the public eye and those whose job it is to document it. No, I don't owe these people anything, but if Ryan and I stay together, I'll be dealing with them a lot more and this isn't how I want to begin this new chapter of my life, so thirty minutes later, dressed in fresh clothes, hair still wet from my shower, and only a light layer of makeup in place, I return to the spotlight once again.

This time, Ryan's parents and brothers are in the crowd with the rest of the attendees instead of next to us. Apparently, Ryan's departure and subsequent shouting caused such a ruckus, they shut the entire event down. Obviously, it didn't get any better after they found him ... and me.

I clear my throat and focus on the faces staring back at me.

With their cameras ready, I feel that familiar sweat build at the base of my neck, but I plow ahead.

"Two years ago, I was sexually assaulted by a reporter who felt I didn't give enough detail to make his story worthwhile." Perhaps I should tell my parents first, but I'm done sacrificing myself for what's best for everyone else. It's my turn, and telling this story now is what's best for *me*. "Attempting to capitalize on my brother's recent fame and the tragic death of my twin sister, his desire for a story robbed me of my peace of mind, my joy, my sense of safety and security. Not to mention, it impaired several of my relationships."

I hear gasps from the audience and feel Ryan's hands land on my shoulders in support. Everyone stays quiet, displaying a level of respect as if they *finally* see me, see *us*, as humans and not their next promotion.

"Ever since then, I've avoided the spotlight and kept my distance from the media. Tonight, however, that same man attacked me a second time. Thankfully, after recently finding out about the first incident, Ryan has given me the knowledge and the confidence to protect myself, and I was out of harm's way by the time he found me." Really feeling the fire behind this soapbox, and hoping I can make a point that may somehow also protect Ryan, the band, Ryan's family, and others in the spotlight, I gain momentum.

"You all have a responsibility to report *facts*. To report *news*. It's pathetic and demeaning to use your power and narrative talent for speculation and gossip. I don't believe every reporter is a predator like Larry Whitsef, but neither do I believe there are healthy boundaries in place. It's because of the media that there is currently a rift between my brother and I. The damage caused by the pictures that were taken without Ryan and I's consent has caused a lot of stress for our families, and I think it's safe to say, my family has been through enough.

I understand, as the girlfriend of a highly sought after rockstar, you and I will meet again, but my hope is that as you continue in your line of work, you report with honor and integrity, always aware that there are real people on the other side of your lens, who suffer real consequences due to your actions. Ryan and I ask for privacy as we and I grow in our relationship, and heal with our families."

After a brief moment of silence, Ryan's dad stands from his front row seat against the stage he was speaking on earlier, and addresses the small group, bringing the interview to an end.

"I would like to reiterate that Ms. Donovan and my son have our family's full support and we happily stand by them. I trust Emma has made her point. That will be all the questions we'll be answering tonight. Thank you."

Senator Battle then turns his attention to me. He places a hand on the back of my head and pulls me into his chest the way my own father sometimes does. "Emma, I'm so sorry. I had no idea you'd been through all of that. I am so very impressed with how you've conducted yourself tonight." Stepping back, he shakes Ryan's hand. "It takes a strong woman to handle the lifestyle you've chosen, son. Looks like you've found one."

In my head, I muse how facing the things we fear the most is often the only thing that sets us free.

Chapter 38

Ryan

I closed the door to the penthouse wanting nothing more than to shut the entire fucking world out. My phone's been ringing nonstop. I got reamed out by our label. Sloan sent a message of support – without a joke this time. Holly called, left a voice mail, and sent a text – I answered that one because she deserves answers and Emma was too tired to give them. The officer dealing with the beating I gave Whitsef called. And my parents called, even though they're right across the hall. But the one person I'd hoped to hear from hasn't checked-in.

I asked Em if she wanted to go back to her parents', back to the cabin, back to school or somewhere new, like Paris. Hell, I'd take her anywhere she wanted to go to get away from here. She answered that she just wanted to curl up next to me in bed, so that's where we are. She's asleep with her head on my chest while I mindlessly scroll through channels, avoiding the news because the story has broken already and footage of me beating that man to a pulp is everywhere. Tim and one of the local police officers are camping outside our room tonight just in case Em's words stirred up more trouble.

The paramedics took a look at my hand and are pretty sure I have a boxer's fracture, unsurprisingly. It hurts like hell now, in this Velcro splint they forced on me, but in the moment, I could have kept pounding that guy forever.

Every twenty seconds, I lean down and inhale the woman in my arms, elated that I'm her safe place.

A knock on the door makes Em stir, but not wake, and whoever's on the other side better count their blessings she's still asleep. Confused, because no one should be able to get up here, I slide my sweatpants on and pad out into the living room. Peering through the peephole, my shoulders relaxing before I open the door.

"Your sister's asleep. I'd appreciate if you'd keep your voice down so it stays that way."

Brett looks at me and nods once, rubbing the back of his neck, his discomfort clear, before stepping inside. He looks like hell with his hair all knotted and down around his shoulders. His shirt looks like he hasn't washed it in days and his skin is sallow.

"I can't believe that fucker tried again," he says, staring to pace like the Donovans do.

"He won't be trying anything for a long, *long* time. And if he does, I can guarantee he won't get anywhere near Em." I turn and close the door so it softly clicks instead of slams, and then move to the couch. "One doesn't easily forget the pain of a dislocated elbow."

The diagnosis must jar Brett's memory because his eyes go wide.

"Holy shit. It was you, wasn't it? You're the reason that douche from prom couldn't finish his senior year of football."

I say nothing but nod once as I sink down onto the microfiber couch.

"Thank you for finding her and taking care of him...them... *all* of them. Jesus, it's like she's a creep magnet." He winces when he sees my expression. "Sorry, not how I meant that."

"She handled him herself, honestly. The guy was already incapacitated when I got there. Since I was the first one through the door, people just assume I pulled him off her, but she held her own. I just flipped my fucking shit when I saw him."

"What? Em did it? How?"

I shrug. "Said she remembered some stuff I taught her at the gym."

"When did you take her to the gym?"

"The day after she told me about the first assault. I want to protect her as much as you do, but we're gone a lot. She needed to know how to do it herself.'"

He blows out a breath. "Why didn't I think of that?"

"Because you have a lot going on. We all do. But Em makes all the other shit in my life manageable. As long as she's okay, I can deal with the rest."

"How long have you felt this way?" he asks, keeping is eyes on the floor.

"Almost two years, but I swear to you, man, none of this started until she came home for fall break."

"Yeah, I believe you. It's just..." he trails off, still trying to wrap his head around this reality.

"Look, B, I don't want to lose what you and I have. You're my best friend. And I definitely don't want to fuck anything up with the band. So, please don't make me choose, because I'll choose her."

"It's that serious? You'd give up the fucking band for her?"

Frustrated, I spread my hands wide before letting them fall

in my lap. "I'd give up my fucking life for her. You really think, after all this, I'd what? Risk our friendship for a booty call? The fact that you think I'd even *use* Emma like that, fucking pisses me off, Brett. Do you know me at *all*?"

Brett finally plops down in the arm chair and drops his head into his hands. "Yes. No. *Fuck!*" he shrieks. "I don't know. This is just weird, man. It's *Emma.*"

"I know. But I don't see Emma like you do. I don't see her as my sister. She's *not* my sister."

"I'd fucking hope not. *Shit*," he growls. "I can't even keep my fucking sisters safe without losing my mind. How the fuck am I supposed to manage a kid? Christ, Ry, what if I have a daughter? I'm going to spend her childhood in the fucking psych ward."

A laugh escapes my throat despite the somber mood. "You're going to be a great dad, Brett. And you're not alone. We're all going to help you guys raise this kid. Hell, it's already got more people in its corner than most others I know."

He looks up at me, the strain in his features easing slightly. "You honestly believe that, don't you?"

"Of course I do. Kids just need to be loved and supported. Parents try to overcomplicate things, you know? Sure, he or she may not have a traditional upbringing because of who you are and what you do, but BBQs? Ball in the front yard? Open skate on weekends? Jam sessions in the studio? Your kid's gonna have it all."

"It sounds kind of nice when you put it like that," Brett admits.

"We're family, Brett. We'll be actual uncles to each other's kids. How many best friends get that opportunity?"

"Oh God," he says dramatically.

"What now?"

"I know how babies are made," he says, confusing me.

"No shit, Sherlock. What's your point?"

"If Em gets pregnant..." he shakes his head unable to finish which causes me to laugh quietly. Taking advantage of the lightness of the moment, and also wanting to pester him because that's what best friends do, I respond with full-force.

"Brett. I'm sleeping with your sister. I have seen her naked and if you weren't here right now, I'd still be curled around her."

"Oh my God, stop," he says, holding up his hands. Like any good best friend, I keep going.

"I plan to make her the mother of my children as soon as she says she's ready," I add, wagging my eyebrows suggestively.

He covers his ears with his hands. "Fuck you!" I'd have stopped if I thought he was really pissed, but he's laughing and the sound warms my heart. *We're going to be okay.*

"Brett?" Emma's voice makes me whip my head to the side.

"I told you to keep it down," I growl at my bandmate, growing serious.

"My bad." He flashes a grimace at me before looking at his sister. "Hey, Emmie. I, uh, saw the news and just got in the car and started driving. Are you okay?"

"I'm glad you're here," she says, moving to the chair and hugging her brother. "I'm fine. Tired, but fine." She bites her lip and jumps right in with both feet. "Look, I didn't keep this from you to hurt you. You know that, right?" she asks.

"Uh, yeah. I'm working on getting there."

"I heard you laughing. That's a good sign," Em tells her brother.

He nods slowly. "Are you sure you're up for this? You've kind of, uh, had a long night. We can talk about it later, but for what it's worth, I'm really fucking proud of you for standing up to them and saying what you needed to say," Brett says.

"Thank you. It felt good. And yes, I'm up for this. I'd rather just get it all out in the open." Emma comes to join me on the couch. She doesn't drape her body across me like I wish she would, but she curls into my side, wanting my arm around her. "I'll be even more fine, when you two are good," she says, her finger drifting back and forth between Brett and I before placing it on my bare chest.

So, we start at the beginning and hash it out. We talk about *everything*. Finally, when we've damn near talked ourselves into a coma, Brett comes around.

"I knew she was going to end up with someone at some point. All things considered, I guess I'm glad it's you," Brett says, finally able to process the lengths I'd go to for his sister. "But let me be clear," he continues, pointing at Em. "You're not spending the night," Brett says. "I'd fucking die if I heard you two through the walls." I laugh when Emma gives her brother an incredulous look. "I changed your diapers, Emma Rose, it'd be weird."

"I thought you were moving out?" I ask.

"It seems my girlfriend has separation anxiety and with our baby on the way, she wants to be close to Sienna. We bought two acres off her and Noah and are going to build. So it looks like we've got a little more time in the house."

"Hey man, that's great. Congratulations." I'm really happy for them but my heart is heavy that he's moving on and our band will be divided with me and Sloan still sharing the house and Noah and Brett moving on with their families forty-five minutes away.

Chapter 39

Emma

The following morning, Ryan wakes me up by placing a room service breakfast tray across my lap. He holds on with his left hand and balances it on the black splint of his right hand. His shirtless frame has me ready to forgo the food on my plate altogether but he shakes his head.

"Don't even think about it."

The smell of the coffee hits my nose at that exact moment and it's the only reason I don't argue.

He leaves the room but comes back a minute later with his own coffee his phone.

"Em, I have some really great news."

"That's good. We could use some great news," I tease. Even though things with my brother went well last night, he's not just suddenly comfortable with Ryan and I's relationship, but he isn't as angry, he isn't leaving the band, and he's talking to us, so overall, big wins.

"I talked to the art director at the label. They love your painting for the cover and want to use it."

My eyes go wide with excitement. Although the band gets

a lot of say in their music, art, and merchandise, they don't get all of it.

"That's awesome! I can't wait to see it as the actual CD cover."

Ryan smiles wide. "There's more. They showed it to another musician at the label and she wants something, not similar in design, but similar in style. She really loved the style of your art."

"I'd love to work with her. How do I contact her?"

"The label asked if I could pass along your number, but I wanted to check with you first. You know, I was thinking ... this could be your thing."

"Designing album covers?" I ask, just to make sure I'm on the same page.

"Not just album covers but, I don't know, call it something like *band art*. You know? Design paintings based on popular songs. They could be turned into posters and shit. Obviously Beautiful Deceit will be your first customer."

I set the tray on the table next to the bed so I can move easier.

"I love that idea so much but it requires me to piggyback off your fame, and I really don't want to do that."

Making my own way is important to me, especially now. It's not so much that I care what others think anymore, it's just my own morality at play.

Ryan scoots closer to me on the bed.

"Em, you are not piggybacking off our fame. You're using your connections just like you would for your law internships."

I grimace at the mention of my internships. After the debacle last night, I lost even more fire for my choice in profession. The stress, the heartache, the drama, the lies. It's an environment that only promotes my intelligence, not my overall wellbeing.

"I guess," I finally relent, seeing his point. He chews on his lip and drops his eyes. Is Ryan *nervous?* I'm not sure I've ever seen this expression on his face. "Ry, what's wrong?"

He keeps his head down, but angles his chocolate eyes up to look at me through dark lashes.

"Talk fast because I'm 2.4 seconds away from mauling you on this bed," I warn, kicking the covers off my legs so I'm prepared to pounce.

"I was thinking. What if you give up law school?" I feel my eyebrows shoot to my hairline. "Just think about it," he continues quickly. "You can break into the art world with the album covers, build a brand for yourself. We can turn Brett or Noah's old room into an art studio until we get our own place." He's gaining speed as he's talking and I'm unsure if he realizes his smile's growing too. "Stay with me. Let me help you get your business going."

"Are you suggesting you'll be my sugar daddy?" I'm trying to be serious, but this is a lot to process and I'm resorting to Sloan's method of deflection.

"Em, be serious. You once told me if you could do anything, you'd paint. I saw the way you got pulled in when it was just you and that canvas in the mountains. That's where your heart is. That's what you should spend your time doing."

"I love the idea, but my parents..." I trail off.

"Your parents just want you to be happy." Before I can make another argument, he cuts me off. "And I know it's not about money, but I make enough to support us both until your career takes off. Let me do this for you. *With* you."

I'm hesitant.

"This is a huge step, Ry. We haven't been together that long. What if I agree and then it all goes to hell? I'll be out my spot at school, living with my parents, trying to jumpstart an art career with no formal art education. That's terrifying."

"More terrifying than what you did last night?" he asks.

I think about it for a second. "Different, but equal."

"Do you really think this thing between us will fizzle out that quickly?"

"I don't think it will ever fizzle out on my end."

"I feel the same way, baby. Em, I'm in love with you and now that I've finally got you, I'm not giving you up. We have to stop letting the expectations of others dictate our choices."

I can't deny that he's right. I also can't deny that what he's suggesting is what I want more than anything in the world.

"Say it again," I tell him.

"I love you, Emma."

"I love you too, Ryan. I always have."

"So, what do you say?"

"Okay," I whisper, nodding my head, slowly giving in to the massive, life changing turn I'm about to take.

He smiles brightly. "Let's go home, baby."

When we pull up to my parents' house, my mom and dad are both home. They pull me into a hug first before tackling Ryan, making me laugh.

"Thank you," my mom chokes out through tears, clutching the man beside me. "Thank you for protecting her."

We all move deeper into the house and I let my mom ask her questions.

"How could you keep this from us, Em?"

"You guys were dealing with enough. I didn't want to add any stress."

"You're our daughter, Emmie. It might be stressful, but

we're always on your side," my dad says, his own emotions making his Irish accent thicker.

"I know. I'm sorry."

Ryan fills the silence and looks at me, encouraging me to continue. "There's something else Emma would like to tell you."

Mom claps a hand over her mouth. "You're not pregnant too, are you? We'd be happy for you of course but with school —"

"No, mom. I'm not pregnant."

She sags back in her chair. "Oh, thank goodness."

"I'm dropping out of law school."

She sits back up, elbows on the table. "What? Why?"

I explain my feelings over the last couple of months, how my passion diminished, I didn't feel like I fit in with any of the other students, and finally landing on the fact that I just don't want that chaos in my life.

"I've asked Emma to move in with me once Brett and Bri have moved out," Ryan chimes in. "I fully plan on getting our own place at some point, but there's a lot of change, and I don't want to leave Sloan alone quite yet."

I nudge Ryan in the side playfully. "So much for living for ourselves," I tease, under my breath.

"I can't completely change my nature," he smiles back, kissing my temple.

The truth is, I love that about Ryan, and I never want him to change.

"What will you be pursing instead?" My father asks from across the kitchen table.

"Art."

We finish updating my parents on all the new plans and at the end my mom pulls me in close. "We just want you to be safe, healthy, and happy, Em. I believe Ryan is all those things for you and that you are those things for him, but in the future, let your dad and I be the parents. Let us help shoulder your burdens alongside you."

I nod, tears welling in my eyes.

"I will, Mom. I love you."

"I love you too, honey."

Next on the list, I call Jen to fill her in while Ryan texts Brett to give him a heads up we're coming over.

And my last act of the morning is to email my professors and the admissions department at Harvard. At one time in my life, I would have offered explanations and platitudes, afraid of offending the powers that be. Now, I type a short email. The details of the decision aren't their business.

To Whom It May Concern,

I want to thank you all for the incredible opportunity I was given with my acceptance to your law program. After enduring recent events, I've decided a career in law is no longer in my future. Consider this my notice of resignation from the program.

Sincerely,

Emma Donovan

It feels really fucking good to hit send.

We may not be able to change our DNA or those basic traits that make us *us*. Ryan and I may always sit in the watch-tower looking out for others and doing what's needed to achieve the greater good for our friends and families, but we can at least pull the yolk together. Two oxen plowing the field. Beasts of Burden who've learned how to both embrace the role and set boundaries.

Epilogue

Ryan

The past six months have been the best of my life. Emma and I broke the no-sleepover rule eight days after we came back from D.C. I thought it would cause another fight, but Brett wasn't too pissed once Emma told him she doesn't sleep well without me anymore.

Besides, Bri's enjoyed having another girl in the house since Noah and Sienna are officially moved into their new place. Brett and Bri found out they're having a boy, much to Brett's relief. He's having a hard time keeping his excitement hidden and I'm happy for him. The builders are putting the finishing touches in place on their house, and the final walk-through is in a couple days which will get them moved in just before Riddik is born.

Our new album is done and we're playing our first concert with the new songs tonight. We always play our first show of a new tour in Richmond. It's our biggest fan base because it's our home town, and because of that, we also get the most feedback on what they like and what they don't.

Tonight, Em's in the audience along with everyone's families. Knowing she's here and she's *mine* makes this the most excited I've ever been to play a show.

"You still want to do the thing?" Noah asks as we make our way toward the stage.

"Hell yeah, I do." I know I'm grinning like an idiot, but I can't help it.

"What thing?" Brett asks.

"It's a surprise." I wink at my best friend and bark out my laughter when I see his face.

"I never want to hear those words again."

I smile. *You and me, both.*

Noah and Sloan join in the laughter as the lights dim in the arena and the crowd reaches a deafening roar.

"Well boys, I think we've still got it," I yell over our fans.

Sienna starts to play the violin in the dark and a hush falls over the crowd as we make our way on stage to our instruments and get ready to roll.

There aren't too many hiccups but I ended up having to improvise during one new song, and Noah had to make up the words in another because he forgot the chorus.

Shit happens. These songs are still new to us.

Right before we take an intermission, Noah sets me up.

"Thank you all for being here tonight." The crowd cheers. "Before we take a quick break, Ryan would like to say something," He waves me over to his mic stand.

"This is the first show I've played since Emma Donovan became my girlfriend. We've been through hell and back in a short amount of time, and I'd happily go there again if needed. She may be our drummer's little sister, but she's also going to be my wife!"

I watch as the screen pans to Em who's holding up her ring for the camera and blowing me kisses right as I catch a drumstick in the back.

I turn around, expecting to see Brett glaring at me from behind his drums, but he's already on me, pulling me in for a hug, much to the enjoyment of the fans.

As the birth of his son gets closer, Brett's emotions have been running rampant and I see the tears in his eyes when he pulls back. To get himself in check, he rubs his knuckles across my scalp and slaps the side of my head before pulling me back in again, wrapping an arm across the back of my shoulders.

"I couldn't pick anyone better for her. Welcome to the family, officially, *brother*."

Will I ever stop worrying about and taking care of my friends and family?

Of course not.

It's just my nature, but it doesn't mean I have to let their expectations totally consume me, either.

However, when I glance at Sloan, who has yet to give a reaction to my news, I'm instantly worried. He's staring at something in the crowd and he looks ready to commit murder. His chest is heaving and he's pale despite sweating from head to toe.

Thankfully, our short intermission is now but before I can check in on him, he flies down the steps and disappears down the hallway, leading back stage.

The three of us follow behind him, ready to have his back for whatever is haunting him in this moment.

He's talking to one of the security guards and we only hear the end of the conversation.

"...and bring him back here."

The guard nods and rushes off.

"Sloan?" I ask hesitantly. Our guitarist whirls around with bloodlust in his eyes, glaring at Noah, Brett, and I. "Whatever it is, we've got you, man."

"Just give me a second alone, okay?" He sounds almost panicked.

"Yeah, sure. We'll just be down the hall."

The three of us move around the corner but stay within earshot. No way are any of us prepared to give him the privacy he asked for. Not while he's acting so cagey.

A couple minutes later, we hear Sloan.

"What the *fuck* are you doing here?" I'm not sure I've ever heard Sloan so pissed. It's the first time I hear the solider in him come out. To be honest, it's kind of scary.

"I..." the male voice starts but before he can utter another word, we hear the unmistakable dull thud of a fist connecting to a face.

When we race around the corner, Sloan's conversation partner is on his knees rubbing his jaw as Sloan pulls back and lands a roundhouse kick to the side of the man's head, knocking him unconscious.

Looks like it's Sloan's turn for a little drama, after all.

Acknowledgments

Writing a book takes a village. Even as an indie author, I couldn't make this book the best it could be without an entire team of people. My extreme gratitude goes to my pa, Amanda Eastling. I probably wouldn't sell a single book if it weren't for her tireless efforts of pushing my book, helping to manage my street team, my Facebook page, and generally keeping me on track with what needs to be done next.

My beta readers, Emilie, Tonya, Xeny, Bella, and Julia. Your feedback is invaluable. Thank you for reading this story in its ugliest form and helping me make it shine.

Of course a huge thank you to my cover designer, Tessa Harris. I give you absolutely zero direction and yet you produce the most amazing results. I feel so fortunate to have had you for this journey and can't imagine these guys being painted by anyone else.

Lastly, to my family who deals with my mental absence for days at a time while I live in make believe worlds with make believe people. Thank you for understanding that they're real to me.

About the Author

Jillian lives in North Carolina with her incredibly supportive husband and three awesome stepkids. After over ten years in the healthcare industry, it was time to pursue a new passion. An avid reader her whole life, she sat down one night and let the words begin to flow. Four hours and ten thousand words later, a love of writing was discovered. She writes spicy, binge-able reads that encourage self-discovery and come with all the angst and excitement of a new relationship. When she isn't reading or writing, you can either find her in her vegetable garden, at CrossFit™, or on a plane headed toward her next adventure.

facebook.com/wraysromancereaders

instagram.com/jillian_wray_author

Made in the USA
Las Vegas, NV
26 July 2024

93002353R00225